"ONE OF THE BEST NOVELS
OF [THE YEAR]...
Giles Blunt has a tremendous talent."
—**Tony Hillerman**, *New York Times* bestselling
author of *Hunting Badger*

"Forty Words for Sorrow is brilliant...
This book has it all—unforgettable
characters, beautiful language, throat-
constricting suspense."
—**Jonathan Kellerman**, *New York Times*
bestselling author of *Flesh and Blood*

"An exciting crime story."
—*Library Journal*

"Intensel___vid."
—**Lee Child**, ___ bestselling

___orbing."
___ooklist

Forty Words for Sorrow

Nominated for the
Arthur Ellis Award: Best Novel

"The highest praise a writer can give another is to say that he wishes he had written his book. I wish I had written *Forty Words for Sorrow*. Giles Blunt has a tremendous talent."

—Tony Hillerman,
author of *Hunting Badger* and *Seldom Disappointed*

"Giles Blunt writes with uncommon grace, style, and compassion, and he plots like a demon."

—Jonathan Kellerman, author of *Flesh and Blood*

"Riveting ... relentless ... distinguished by a smooth, literary style, several smartly defined complex characters, and chillingly described northern Canada." —*Los Angeles Times*

"Finely crafted ... realistic ... intelligent ... Blunt masterfully unfolds the tale, set amid a Canadian winter, using uncanny detail of police work to involve the reader. His ear for dialogue pulls you into the action. ... This is a tale of how police really do go about their business of catching criminals, complete with mistakes, missed chances, and red herrings ... a fine piece of writing ... Blunt has come up with a thinking person's thriller, one that deserves attention." —*The Denver Post*

"A taut and enthralling tale that is as dark as the Canadian winter setting is cold. Humane, intelligent, and gripping, *Forty Words for Sorrow* is a haunting journey into the human heart in all its complexities."

—Val McDermid, author of *A Place of Execution*

"Blunt's atmospheric thriller ... effectively permeates the reader's consciousness ... vivid ... chilling ... intelligent."

—*Publishers Weekly*

"Absorbing ... The police procedural aspects of the story become great and entrancing stuff ... dazzling."—*The Toronto Star*

"Excellent." —*The San Jose Mercury News*

continued ...

"This is the book I've been waiting for through twenty years of reviewing crime fiction. The first great Canadian crime novel . . . Blunt has done for Canada's north what James Lee Burke did for Cajun Louisiana."
—Margaret Cannon, *The Toronto Globe and Mail*

"*Forty Words for Sorrow* is a smart, superbly written novel which tests a likable, fallible pair of investigators with some intriguing ethical questions as they use their considerable skills to solve a set of monstrous and disturbing crimes."
—Thomas Perry, author of *Death Benefits*

"Intensely vivid characters, terrible crimes, and a brutal deep-frozen landscape all prove beyond a reasonable doubt that cold nurtures good and evil as readily as heat. . . and that Giles Blunt is a really tremendous crime novelist."
—Lee Child, author of *Echo Burning*

"Blunt's handling of procedure (involving both local and regional police and the Royal Canadian Mounted Police) is masterful, and his treatment of character is especially intriguing, as he shows us believable protagonists, caught up in the confusion of their own lives yet called to respond to an overarching menace. . . . A completely absorbing series debut."
—*Booklist*

"An exciting crime story, the book is also a novel of place (the chilly isolation of a rural community is vividly portrayed) and a meditation on sorrow. . . . Strongly recommended."
—*Library Journal*

"Polished, at times poetic . . . [Blunt] is a helluva storyteller."
—*Kirkus Reviews*

"Giles Blunt takes you out of your world and drops you into someplace you've never been before. *Forty Words for Sorrow* will stick to you; it's complex, suspenseful, and acutely atmospheric." —George P. Pelecanos, author of *Hell to Pay*

"A highly professional tour de force: excellently plotted, with fleshed-out characters and a well-portrayed, interesting setting." —*The London Evening Standard*

"This atmospheric account . . . is extraordinary for its psychology and tension. The market abounds with serial-killer thrillers, which are mostly written by writers who people their lurid worlds with cardboard cut-outs, and a book like this shows them up for what they are. Giles Blunt manages to inhabit the minds of killer, victim and investigator alike, a feat that very few writers can manage. It moves his work to a different level." —*The London Independent*

"A superior Canadian police procedural with an evocative sense of place: The frozen lakes and forests are as integral to the plot as the flawed detective . . . an impressive achievement." —*The London Guardian*

"Chilling . . . *Forty Words for Sorrow* satisfies right down to the marrow." —*Quill & Quire*

"A gem." —Mel Chabrow

FORTY words for SORROW

GILES BLUNT

BERKLEY BOOKS, NEW YORK

If you purchased this book without a cover, you should be aware that
this book is stolen property. It was reported as "unsold and destroyed"
to the publisher, and neither the author nor the publisher has received
any payment for this "stripped book."

This is a work of fiction. Names, characters, places, and incidents either
are the product of the author's imagination or are used fictitiously,
and any resemblance to actual persons, living or dead,
business establishments, events, or locales is entirely coincidental.

FORTY WORDS FOR SORROW

A Berkley Book / published by arrangement with
the author

PRINTING HISTORY
Marion Wood hardcover edition / June 2001
Berkley mass-market edition / March 2002

All rights reserved.
Copyright © 2001 by Giles Blunt.
Text designed by Julie Rogers.
Cover design by Lesley Worrell.

This book, or parts thereof,
may not be reproduced in any form without permission.
For information address: The Berkley Publishing Group,
a division of Penguin Putnam Inc.,
375 Hudson Street, New York, New York 10014.

Visit our website at
www.penguinputnam.com

ISBN: 0-425-18516-8

BERKLEY®
Berkley Books are published by the Berkley Publishing Group,
a division of Penguin Putnam Inc.,
375 Hudson Street, New York, New York 10014.
BERKLEY and the "B" design
are trademarks belonging to Penguin Putnam Inc.

PRINTED IN THE UNITED STATES OF AMERICA

10 9 8 7 6 5 4 3 2 1

ACKNOWLEDGMENTS

The following people all read earlier versions of *Forty Words* and made numerous suggestions for cuts and improvements or helped in other ways: Bill Booth; Anne Collins, my editor at Random House of Canada; my wife, Janna Eggebeen; my agent, Helen Heller; Linda Sandler; Staff Sgt. Rick Sapinski of the North Bay Police Department; and my editor at Penguin Putnam, Marian Wood. I am grateful to them all.

My thanks are also due to the Writers Room in New York, where much of this book was written.

IN MEMORIAM

Philip L. Blunt
(1916–2000)

1

IT gets dark early in Algonquin Bay. Take a drive up Airport Hill at four o'clock on a February afternoon, and when you come back half an hour later the streets of the city will glitter below you in the dark like so many runways. The forty-sixth parallel may not be all that far north; you can be much farther north and still be in the United States, and even London, England, is a few degrees closer to the North Pole. But this is Ontario, Canada, we're talking about, and Algonquin Bay in February is the very definition of winter: Algonquin Bay is snowbound, Algonquin Bay is quiet, Algonquin Bay is very, very cold.

John Cardinal was driving home from the airport where he had just watched his daughter, Kelly, board a plane bound for the United States by way of Toronto. The car still smelled of her—or at least of the scent that had lately become her trademark: Rhapsody or Ecstasy or some such. To Cardinal, wife gone and now daughter gone, it smelled of loneliness.

It was many degrees below zero outside; winter squeezed the car in its grip. The windows of the Camry were frosted up on both sides, and Cardinal had to keep scraping them with an ineffective plastic blade. He went south down Airport Hill, made a left onto the bypass, another left onto Trout Lake Road, and then he was heading north again toward home.

Home, if you could call it that with both Catherine and Kelly gone, was a tiny wooden house on Madonna Road, smallest among a crescent of cottages set like a brooch along the north shore of Trout Lake. Cardinal's house was fully winterized, or so the real estate agent had told them, but "winterized" had turned out to be a relative term. Kelly claimed you could store ice cream in her bedroom.

His drive was hidden by four-foot-high snowbanks, so Cardinal didn't see the car blocking his way until he almost rear-ended it. It was one of the unmarkeds from work, great pale clouds of exhaust blasting out from behind. Cardinal reversed and parked across the road. Lise Delorme, the Algonquin Bay Police Department's entire Office of Special Investigations, got out of the unmarked and waded through the exhaust toward him.

The department, despite "great strides toward employment equity," as the bureaucrats liked to phrase it, was still a bastion of male chauvinism, and the general consensus around the place was that Lise Delorme was too—well, too something for her job. You're at work, you're trying to think, you don't need the distraction. Not that Delorme looked like a movie star; she didn't. But there was something about the way she looked at you, McLeod liked to say—and for once McLeod was right. Delorme had a disturbing tendency to hold your gaze just a little too long, just a split second too long with those earnest brown eyes. Well, it was as if she'd slipped her hand inside your shirt.

In short, Delorme was a terrible thing to do to a married man. And Cardinal had other reasons to fear her.

"I was about to give up," she said. Her French-Canadian accent was unpredictable: One hardly noticed it most of the time, but then final consonants would disappear and sentences would sprout double subjects. "I tried to phone you but there was no answer, and your machine, it's not working."

"I switched it off," Cardinal said. "What the hell are you doing here, anyway?"

"Dyson told me to come get you. They've found a body."

"Got nothing to do with me. I don't work homicides, remember?" Cardinal was trying to be merely factual, but even he could hear the bitterness in his voice. "You mind letting me through, Sergeant?" The "Sergeant" was just to nettle her. Two detectives of equal rank would normally address each other by name, except in the presence of the public or around junior officers.

Delorme was standing between her car and the snowbank. She stepped aside so Cardinal could get to his garage door.

"Well Dyson, I think he wants you back."

"I don't care. You mind backing out now so I can plug my car in? I mean, if that's okay with Dyson. Why's he sending you, anyway? Since when are you working homicides?"

"You must have heard I quit Special."

"No, I heard you *wanted* to quit Special."

"It's official, now. Dyson says you'll show me the ropes."

"No, thanks. I'm not interested. Who's working Special?"

"He's not here yet. Some guy from Toronto."

"Fine," Cardinal said. "Doesn't make the slightest difference. You gonna get lost, now? It's cold, I'm tired, and I'd kind of like to eat my supper."

"They think it could be Katie Pine." Delorme scanned his face while Cardinal took this in. Those solemn brown eyes watching his reaction.

Cardinal looked away, staring out into the blackness that was Trout Lake. In the distance, the headlights of two snowmobiles moved in tandem across the dark. Katie Pine. Thirteen years old. Missing since September 12, he would never forget that date. Katie Pine, a good student, a math whiz from the Chippewa Reserve, a girl whom he had never met, whom he had wanted more than anything to find.

The phone began to ring inside the house, and Delorme looked at her watch. "That's Dyson. He only gave me one hour."

Cardinal went inside. He didn't invite Delorme. He picked up the phone on the fourth ring and heard Detective Sergeant Don Dyson going on at him in his chilly quack of a voice as if they had been separated in the middle of an argument and were only now, three months later, resuming it. In a way, that was true.

"Let's not waste time going over old ground," Dyson said. "You want me to apologize, I apologize. There. Done. We got a body out on the Manitou Islands, and McLeod is tied up in court. Up to his ears in Corriveau. Case is yours."

Cardinal felt the old anger burning its way into his veins. I may be a bad cop, he told himself, but not for the reasons Dyson thinks. "You took me off homicide, remember? I was strictly robbery and burglary material, in your book."

"I changed your case assignments. It's what a detective sergeant does, remember? Ancient history, Cardinal. Water under the bridge. We'll talk about it after you see the body."

"'She's a runaway,' you said. 'Katie Pine is not a homicide, she's a runaway. Got a history of it.'"

"Cardinal, you're back on homicide, all right? It's your investigation. Your whole stinking show. Not that it has to be Katie Pine, of course. Even you, Detective Has-to-Be-Right, might want to keep an open mind about identifying bodies you haven't seen. But if you want to play I told you so, Cardinal, you just come into my office tomorrow morning, eight o'clock. Best thing about my job is I don't have to go out at night, and these calls always come at night."

"It's my show as of this moment—if I go."

"That's not my decision, Cardinal, and you know it. Lake Nipissing falls under the jurisdiction of our esteemed brothers and sisters in the Ontario Provincial Police. But even if it's the OPP's catch, they're going to want us in on it. If it is Katie Pine or Billy LaBelle, they were both snatched from the city—*our* city—assuming they *were* both snatched. It's our case either way. '*If* I go,' he says."

"I'd rather stick with burglaries, unless it's my show as of this moment."

"Have the coroner toss a coin," Dyson snapped, and hung up.

Cardinal yelled to Delorme, who had stepped in out of the cold and was standing diffidently just inside the kitchen door. "Which one of the Manitous are we on?"

"Windigo. The one with the mineshaft."

"So we drive, right? Will the ice take a truck?"

"You kidding? This time of year, that ice would take a freight train." Delorme jerked a mittened thumb in the direction of Lake Nipissing. "Make sure you dress warm," she said. "That lake wind, it's cold as hell."

FROM the government dock to the Manitou Islands seven miles west, a plowed strip lay like a pale blue ribbon across the lake; shoreline motels had scraped it clear as an inducement to ice fishers, a prime source of revenue in winter months. It was quite safe to drive cars and even trucks in February, but it was not wise to travel more than ten or fifteen miles an hour. The four vehicles whose headlights lit the flurries of snow in bright cubist veils were moving in slow motion.

Cardinal and Delorme drove in silence in the lead car. Delorme now and again reached across to scrape at the windshield on Cardinal's side. The frost peeled off in strips that fell in curls and melted on the dash and on their laps.

"It's like we're landing on the moon." Her voice was barely audible above the grinding of gears and the hiss of the heater. All around them the snow fell away in shades that ranged from bone white to charcoal gray and even—in the dips and scallops of the snowbanks—deep mauve.

Cardinal glanced in the rearview at the procession behind them: the coroner's car, and behind that the headlights of the ident van, and then the truck.

A few more minutes and Windigo Island rose up jagged and fierce in the headlights. It was tiny, not more than three hundred square meters, and the thin margin of beach, Cardinal remembered from his summer sailing, was rocky. The wooden structure of the mine's shafthead loomed out of the pines like a conning tower. The moon cast razor sharp shadows that leapt and shuddered as they approached.

One by one, the vehicles arrived and parked in a line, their collective lights forming a wide white rampart. Beyond that, blackness.

Cardinal and the others gathered on the ice like a lunar landing party, clumsy in their calf-high boots, their plump down coats. They shifted from foot to foot, tense with cold.

They were eight, including Cardinal and Delorme: Dr. Barnhouse, the coroner; Arsenault and Collingwood, the scene men; Larry Burke and Ken Szelagy, patrol constables in blue parkas; and last to arrive in yet another unmarked, Jerry Commanda from OPP. The OPP was responsible for highway patrol and provided all police services for any townships that lacked their own police force. The lakes and Indian reservations were also their responsibility, but with Jerry you didn't worry about jurisdictional disputes.

All eight now formed into a gap-toothed circle, casting long shadows in the headlights.

Barnhouse spoke first. "Shouldn't you be wearing a bell around your neck?" This by way of greeting Cardinal. "I heard you were a leper."

"In remission," Cardinal said.

Barnhouse was a pugnacious little bulldog of a man, built like a wrestler with a broad back and a low center of gravity and perhaps in compensation cherished a lofty self-regard.

Cardinal jerked his head toward the tall gaunt man on the outside of the circle. "You know Jerry Commanda?"

"Know him? I'm sick of him," Barnhouse bellowed. "Used to be with the city, Mr. Commanda, until you decided to go native again."

"I'm OPP now," Jerry said quietly. "Dead body in the middle of the lake, I think you'll want to arrange for an autopsy, won't you, Doc?"

"I don't need you to tell me my job. Where's the fine flatfoot who discovered the thing?"

Ken Szelagy stepped forward. "We didn't discover it. Couple of kids found it round four o'clock. Me and Larry Burke here got the call. Soon as we saw, we made a perimeter and called it in. McLeod was in court so we called D. S. Dyson and I guess he called in Detective Cardinal here."

"The talented Mister Cardinal," Barnhouse murmured ambiguously, then added: "Let's proceed with flashlights for the moment. Don't want to disturb things setting up lights and so on."

He started toward the rocks. Cardinal was going to speak, but Jerry Commanda voiced the thought for him. "Let's keep it single file, guys."

"I'm not a guy," Delorme noted tartly from the depths of her hood.

"Yeah, well," Jerry said. "Kinda hard to tell the difference right now."

Barnhouse gestured for Burke and Szelagy to lead the way, and for the next few minutes their boots squeaked on the hardpack. Blades of cold raked Cardinal's face. Beyond the rocks, a distant string of lights glittered along the edge of the lake, the Chippewa Reserve, Jerry Commanda's territory.

Szelagy and Burke waited for the others at the chain-link fence surrounding the shafthead.

Delorme nudged Cardinal with a padded elbow. She was pointing to a small object about four feet from the gate.

Cardinal said, "You guys touch that lock?"

Szelagy said, "It was like that. Figured we better leave it."

Burke said, "Kids claim the lock was already broken."

Delorme pulled a Baggie out of her pocket, but Arsenault, a scene man and like all scene men ever-prepared, produced a small paper bag from somewhere and held it out to her. "Use paper. Anything wet'll deteriorate in plastic."

Cardinal was glad it had happened early and that someone else had stopped her. Delorme was a good investigator; she'd had to be in Special. She'd put a former mayor and several council members in prison with painstaking work she'd done entirely on her own, but it didn't involve any scene work. She would watch from now on, and Cardinal wanted it that way.

One after another, they ducked under the scene tape and followed Burke and Szelagy around to the side of the shafthead. Szelagy pointed to the loosened boards. "Careful going in, there's a two-foot drop and then it's sheer ice all the way."

Inside the shafthead, the flashlight beams formed a shifting pool of light at their feet. Gaps in the boards made the wind moan like a stage effect.

"Jesus," Delorme said quietly. She and the others had all seen traffic fatalities, the occasional suicide, and numerous drownings—none of which had prepared them for this. They were shivering, but an intense stillness settled over the group as if they were praying; no doubt some of them were. Cardinal's own mind seemed to flee the sight before him—into the past with the image of Katie Pine, smiling in her school photograph, and into the future with what he would have to tell her mother.

Dr. Barnhouse began in a formal voice: "We are looking at the frozen remains of an adolescent—Damn." He rapped sharply at the microcassette in his gloved paw. "Always acts up in the cold." He cleared his throat and began again in a less declamatory manner. "We're looking at the remains of an adolescent human—decay and animal activity preclude positive determination of sex at this time. Torso is unclothed, lower part of the body is clothed in denim jeans, right arm is missing, as is the left foot. Facial features are obliterated by animal activity, mandible is missing. Christ," he said. "Just a child."

Cardinal thought he heard a tremor in Barnhouse's voice; he would not have trusted his own. It wasn't just the deterioration—all of them had seen worse: victims of hunting accidents, drowning victims—it was that the remains were preserved in a perfect rectangle of ice perhaps eight inches thick. Eyeless sockets stared up through the ice into the pitch dark over their heads. One of the eyes had been pulled away and lay frozen above the shoulder; the other was missing entirely.

"Hair is detached from the skull—black, shoulder length—and pelvis shows anterior striations which may indicate a female—it's not possible to say without further examination, precluded at this time by the body's being fixed in a block of ice formed by conditions peculiar to the site."

Jerry Commanda swung his light up to the rough boards

overhead and back down to the depressed concrete platform below them. "Roof leaks big time. You can see the ice through it."

Others swung their lights up and looked at the stripes of ice between the boards. Shadows leapt and darted in the eyeless sockets.

"Those three warm days in December when everything melted," Jerry went on. "The body probably covers a drain, and when the ice melted, the place filled up with water. Temperature dropped again and froze it right there."

"It's like she's preserved in amber," Delorme said.

Barnhouse resumed. "No clothing on or near the remains, except for jeans of blue denim that—I already said that, didn't I? Yes, I'm sure I did. Gross destruction of tissue in the abdominal region, all of the viscera and most major organs missing, whether due to perimortem trauma or postmortem animal activity impossible to say. Portions of lung are visible, upper lobes on both sides."

"Katie Pine," Cardinal said. He hadn't meant to say it aloud. He knew it would provoke a reaction, and it came at full volume.

"I hope you're not telling me you recognize that poor girl from her high-school yearbook. Until such time as the upper jaw may be matched with dental records, any identification is out of the question."

"Thank you, Doctor," Cardinal said quietly.

"There's no call for sarcasm, Detective. Remission or no, I'm not putting up with sarcasm." Barnhouse turned his baleful eye once more upon the object at their feet. "Extremities, those that remain, are nearly skeletonized, but I believe that's a healed greenstick fracture in the radius of the left forearm." He stepped back from the edge of the depression and folded his arms belligerently in front of his chest. "Gentlemen—and lady—I'm going to remove myself from this investigation, which will clearly require the services of the Forensic Center. As Lake Nipissing falls under the jurisdiction of the Ontario Provincial Police, I'm

officially turning the investigation over to you, Mister
Commanda."

Jerry said, "If this is Katie Pine, here, the investigation
belongs to the city."

"But surely Katie Pine is one of yours? From the reserve?"

"She was abducted from the fairground by Memorial
Gardens. That makes it a city case—has been since she disappeared. Cardinal's case."

"Nevertheless," Barnhouse insisted, "pending positive
identification, I'm turning it over to you."

"Fine, Doctor," Jerry said. "John, you can run it. I know
it's Katie."

"You can't possibly know. Look at the thing. " Barnhouse pointed with his recorder. "Except for the clothes, it
barely looks human."

Cardinal said softly, "Katie Pine fractured the radius in
her left arm when she was learning to skateboard."

FIVE of them were scrunched in the ident van. Barnhouse
had gone, and the two uniforms were waiting in the stake
truck. Cardinal practically had to shout over the roar of the
heater. "We're going to need rope: As of now, the whole island is our perimeter. There was no blood and no sign of
struggle in the shafthead, so this is probably not the murder
scene, only a dump site. Even so, I don't want any curious
snowmobilers zipping through the evidence, so let's get it
good and secure."

Delorme handed him the cell phone. "I've got Forensic.
Len Weisman."

"Len, we've got a body here frozen solid in a block of
ice. Adolescent, probable murder. If we cut the block of ice
and ship it to you entire in a refrigerated truck, can you
handle something like that?"

"No problem. We've got a couple of variable coolers that
go well below freezing. We can thaw it out at a controlled
rate and preserve any hair and fibers for you that way." Surreal to hear a Toronto voice in this lunar landscape.

"Great, Len. We'll call with an ETA when we're ready to roll." Cardinal handed the phone back to Delorme. "Arsenault, you're the scene expert. How do we get her out of there?"

"We can cut her out in a cube easy enough. Problem will be separating the cube from the concrete underneath."

"Get a guy from the city to cut it, they cut concrete all the time. And you can clear your calendars, everybody. We're going to have to cull the snow."

"But she was killed months ago," Delorme said. "The snow won't tell us anything."

"We can't be sure of that. Anybody have a good contact at Armed Forces?"

Collingwood raised a hand.

"Tell them we need a huge tent. Something the size of a circus tent that'll cover the whole island—last thing we need is any more snow on the scene. Also a couple of their biggest heaters. Ones they use to heat their hangars. We'll melt the snow and see everything that's underneath."

Collingwood nodded. He was sitting closest to the heater, and his glove was steaming.

SECURING a perimeter and arranging a twenty-four-hour watch on the island took longer than anyone expected; everything about police work takes longer than expected. In the end, Cardinal did not get home until one o'clock in the morning, too keyed up to sleep. He sat himself in the living room with two fingers of Black Velvet straight up and made notes about what he would have to do the next day. The house was so cold, even the rye couldn't warm him.

Kelly would be back in the States by now.

At the airport, Cardinal had watched his daughter heave a suitcase onto the baggage scale, and before she could even lift the next one, a young man in line behind her had picked it up and placed it on the scale for her. Well, Kelly was pretty—Cardinal had the usual father's prejudice about his daughter's looks, and he believed any objective person would find his daughter as lovely as he did. But having a pretty face, Cardinal knew, was like being wealthy or famous; people were always offering to do things for you. "You don't have to hang around, Daddy," she had said as they descended the stairs to the waiting area. "I'm sure you have better things to do."

Cardinal hadn't had anything better to do.

Algonquin Bay's airport was designed to handle about eighty travelers at a time, but it rarely had that many. A tiny coffee shop, boxes for *The Algonquin Lode* and the Toronto papers, and that was about it. They sat down, and Cardinal bought the *Toronto Star,* offering his daughter a section, which she declined. It made him feel as if he shouldn't read, either. What was the point of staying if he was just going to read the paper? "You're all set for your connections, then?" he asked. "You have enough time to change terminals?"

"Tons. I have an hour and a half in Toronto."

"That's not too much. Not by the time you get through U.S. customs."

"They always put me straight through. Really, Daddy, I should go into smuggling."

"You told me you got stopped last time. Almost missed your connection."

"That was a fluke. The customs officer was a mean old battle-ax who wanted to give me a hard time."

Cardinal could picture it. In some ways, Kelly was becoming the kind of young woman who annoyed him—too smart, too educated, too damn confident.

"I don't know why they can't have a flight directly from Toronto to New Haven."

"It's not exactly the center of the universe, sweetheart."

"No, it only has one of the best colleges in the world."

And it cost a damn fortune. When Kelly had finished her BFA at York, her painting instructor had encouraged her to apply to Yale's graduate program. Kelly had never dreamed she would be accepted, even when she put together a portfolio and hauled it down to New Haven. It had occurred to Cardinal to deny her, but not for long. It's *the* art school, Daddy. All the big-name painters went there. You may as well study accounting if you don't go to Yale. Cardinal had wondered if that could possibly be true. To him, Yale meant indolent snobs in tennis outfits; it meant George Bush. But painting?

He had asked around. Quite true, he had been assured by those who would know. If one wanted to be visible in the international art scene, which really meant the U.S. art scene, an MFA from Yale was the way to go.

"Really, Daddy, why don't you go home? You don't have to stay."

"It's okay. I want to stay."

The boy who had helped with Kelly's luggage had now taken up a seat facing them. If Cardinal left, the kid would be sitting next to his daughter like a shot. I'm a possessive bastard, he accused himself, nursing these miniature panics over the women in my life. He was the same way about his wife, Catherine.

"It was good of you to come home, Kelly. Especially in the middle of term. I think it really made a difference to your mom."

"Do you? Pretty hard to tell, she seems so out of it these days."

"I could tell."

"Poor Mom. Poor you. I don't know how you stand it, Daddy. I mean, I'm away most of the time, but you have to live with it."

"Well, that's what you do. Better or worse, sickness and health. You know how it goes. "

"A lot of people don't live by that stuff anymore. I know you do, of course. But Mom really scares me sometimes. It must be so hard for you."

"It's a lot harder for her, Kelly."

They sat in silence. The boy pulled out a Stephen King novel, Cardinal pretended to read the *Star,* and Kelly stared out at the empty tarmac where thin flurries of snow swirled in the ground lights. Cardinal began to hope the flight would be canceled, that his daughter would have to stay home another day or two. But Kelly had lost any affection for Algonquin Bay. How can you stand this dinky little backwater? she'd said to him more than once. Cardinal had felt the same at her age, but then ten years on the Toronto police force had convinced him that the dinky little backwater where he grew up had its virtues.

The plane finally arrived, a propeller-driven Dash 8 that seated thirty. In fifteen minutes it would be gassed up and ready to take off.

"You have enough cash? What if you get stuck in Toronto?"

"You worry too much, Daddy."

She hugged him, and then he watched her wheel her carry-on through security (which consisted of two uniformed women not much older than she was) and head for the door. Cardinal moved to the window and watched her cross through the blowing snow. The boy was right behind her, damn him. But outside, brushing the snow from the windshield with his glove, Cardinal had condemned himself for being a jealous twerp, a smothering parent who couldn't let his child grow up. Cardinal was a Catholic—a lapsed Catholic—and like all Catholics lapsed or devout, he retained an almost gleeful ability to accuse himself of sin, though not necessarily the sin he had actually committed.

Now, the whiskey sat half-finished on the coffee table. Cardinal had drifted off. He rose stiffly from his chair and went to bed. In the darkness, images came: headlights on the lake, the body fixed in ice, Delorme's face. But then he thought of Catherine. Although his wife's circumstances were at this moment anything but happy, he forced himself to imagine her laughing. Yes, they would go away somewhere together, somewhere far from police work and their private sorrows, and they would laugh.

DON (short for Adonis) Dyson was a youthful fifty, trim and wiry as a gymnast, with a gymnast's agile movements and sudden graceful gestures, but as the detectives under his command never tired of pointing out, he was no Adonis. The only thing Detective Sergeant Don Dyson had in common with the carved Adonises found in museums was a heart as cold as marble. No one knew if he had been born that way or if fifteen years as a Toronto homicide detective had added frost to an already chilly disposition. The man hadn't a single friend—on the force or off—and those who had met Mrs. Dyson claimed that she made her husband seem drippingly sentimental.

D. S. Dyson was fussy, declamatory, bald, and calculating. He had long fingers, spatulate at the tips, of which he was inordinately vain. When he handled his letter opener or toyed with a box of paper clips, those fingers took on a dangly, spidery aspect. His bald head, trimmed with a geometrically exact circle of hair at the sides and back, was a perfect orb. Jerry Commanda loathed him, but Jerry was intolerant of authority in general, a trait Cardinal put down to his Native heritage. Delorme insisted she could use Dyson's head for a mirror to pluck her eyebrows—not that she did pluck her eyebrows.

That same mirrory dome was tilted toward Cardinal, who was seated in a chair placed at an exact forty-five-degree angle to Dyson's desk. No doubt the detective sergeant had read somewhere that this angle was good leadership psychology. He was an exact man with exact reasons for everything he did. A honey-glazed doughnut was parked on the corner of his desk, waiting for the clock to strike exactly 10:30—not a minute earlier, not a minute later—when he would consume it along with the thermos of decaffeinated coffee parked beside it.

At this moment, Dyson held his letter opener suspended

between his outstretched palms, as if he were measuring his desk with it. When he spoke, he appeared to be addressing himself to the blade. "I never said you were wrong, you know. I never said that little girl wasn't murdered. Not in so many words."

"No, sir. I know you didn't." Cardinal had a tendency, when irritated by authority, to become extremely polite. He fought that tendency now. "You only put me back on burglary as a spiritual exercise."

"Do you remember what kind of expenses you were running up? This was and is the age of cutbacks. We can't pretend we're the Mounties; we can't afford it. You allocated all your investigative resources to this one case."

"Three cases."

"Not three, maybe two." Dyson numbered them on his flat fingers. "Katie Pine, I grant you. Billy LaBelle, maybe. Margaret Fogle, not at all."

"D. S., with all respect, she didn't turn into a toad. She didn't vaporize."

Again the fingers, the manicure displayed to advantage, as Dyson counted the reasons why Margaret Fogle could not be dead. "She was seventeen—far older and more streetwise than the other two. She was from Toronto, not local. She had a history of running away. For God's sake, the girl went around telling everyone who would listen that nobody—*nobody*—would find her this time. And she had a boyfriend to hell and gone, Vancouver or some damn place."

"Calgary. She never got there." And she was last seen alive in our fair city, you bald blockhead. Please, God, just make him give me McLeod and let me get on with it.

"Why are you resisting me on this, Cardinal? We live in the biggest country in the world—now that the Soviet Union has kindly dismantled itself—and three separate train lines run up and across this billion-hectare skating rink. All three of those lines intersect on our little shore. We have an airport and a bus station, and anyone going anywhere across this gigantic bloody country has to pass through our neighborhood. We get more bloody runaways than we know what to do with. Runaways, not murders. You were spending department resources on phantoms."

"Should I go? I thought I was back on homicide," said Cardinal mildly.

"You are. I didn't mean to go over old ground, no point in it, but Katie Pine, Cardinal." Here, he aimed a flat finger at Cardinal. "With Katie Pine there was no evidence of murder, not a shred, not at the time. I mean, except for the fact that she was a child—obviously something was *wrong*—there was just no evidence of murder."

"No courtroom evidence, maybe."

"You were coming to me with disproportionate man-power, disproportionate office resources, and overtime that was completely unjustifiable. The overtime alone was stratospheric. I wasn't the only one who thought so—the chief backed me totally on this one."

"D. S., Algonquin Bay is not that big. A missing child, you get a million leads, everyone wanting to help. Some-one pulls a knife in the movies, you have to check it out. Someone sees a young hitchhiker, you have to check it out. Everyone in town thinks they've seen Katie Pine some-where: She's at the beach, she's at the hospital under an-other name, she was in a canoe in Algonquin Park. Every one of those leads had to be followed up."

"So you told me at the time."

"None of it was unjustified. That's got to be obvious by now."

"It was not obvious then. No one saw Katie Pine with a stranger. No one saw her get into a car. One minute she's at the fair, the next minute she was gone."

"I know. The ground opened."

"The ground opened and swallowed her up, and you chose to believe—without evidence—that she was mur-dered. Time has proved you right; it could just as easily have proved you wrong. The one incontestable fact was that she was g-o-n-e gone. A genuine mystery."

Well, yes, Cardinal thought, Katie Pine's disappearance

had been a mystery. Sorry—I had a fantasy that policemen were occasionally called upon to *solve* mysteries, even in Algonquin Bay. Of course the girl was Native, and we all know how irresponsible *those* people can be.

"Let's face it," Dyson said, inserting his letter opener precisely into a small scabbard and laying it neatly beside a ruler. "The girl was Indian, too. I like Indians, I really do, there's a calmness about them that's practically supernatural. They tend to be good-natured and they're extraordinarily fond of children, and I'd be the first to say Jerry Commanda was a first-rate officer, but there's no point pretending they're just like you and me."

"God, no," said Cardinal, and meant it. "Different people entirely."

"Relations scattered to hell and gone. That girl could have been anywhere from Mattawa to Sault Sainte Marie. There was no reason to be searching boarded-up mineshafts in the middle of the bloody lake."

There had been every reason, but Cardinal didn't phrase it like that; he didn't have to. The point was nestled inside a more important one. "The thing about the Windigo mineshaft is that we *did* search it. We searched it the week Katie Pine disappeared. Four days after, to be exact."

"You're telling me she may have been kept stashed away somewhere before she was killed. Held prisoner somewhere."

"Exactly." Cardinal suppressed the urge to say more; Dyson was warming up, and it was in his interest to let him. The letter opener emerged once again from its scabbard; an errant paper clip was speared, hoisted, and transferred to a brass holder.

"Then again," Dyson continued, "she could have been killed right away. The killer could have kept the body somewhere else before moving it to a safer place."

"It's possible. Forensic may be able to help us with place—we're shipping the remains to Toronto as soon as the mother's been informed—but this is shaping up to be a long investigation. I'm going to need McLeod."

"Can't have him. He's in court with Corriveau. You can have Delorme."

"I need McLeod. Delorme has no experience."

"You're just prejudiced because she's a woman, because she's French, and because, unlike you, she's spent most of her life in Algonquin Bay. You may have put in ten years in Toronto, but you're not going to tell me her six years as Special Investigator amounts to no experience."

"I'm not putting her down. She did a fine job on the mayor. She did a fine job on the school-board scam. Keep her on the white-collar stuff, the sensitive stuff. I mean, who's going to look after Special?"

"What do you care about Special? Let me worry about Special. Delorme is a fine investigator."

"She has no experience at homicide. She came close to ruining an important piece of evidence last night."

"I don't believe it. What the hell are you talking about?"

Cardinal told him about the Baggie. It sounded thin, even to him. But he wanted McLeod. McLeod knew how to hustle, how to keep a case in play.

There was a silence as Dyson stared at the wall just behind Cardinal. He was utterly still. Cardinal watched the snow flurries that swirled past the window. Later, he couldn't be sure if what Dyson said next had just popped into his boss's head or if it was a planned surprise: "You aren't worried that Delorme is investigating you, are you?"

"No, sir."

"Good. Then I suggest you brush up on your French."

IN the 1940s, nickel was discovered on Windigo Island and was mined there, on and off, for twelve years. The mine was never very productive, employing at its peak a mere forty workers, and its location in the middle of the lake made transport a problem. More than one truck had plunged through the ice, and there was talk that the mine was cursed by the tormented spirit for which it was named. A lot of Algonquin Bay investors lost their money in the venture, which closed forever when more accessible lodes were discovered in Sudbury, a city eighty miles away.

The shaft was five hundred feet deep and continued laterally for another two thousand, and the Criminal Investigation Division heaved a collective sigh of relief when it was established that only the shafthead and not the shaft itself had been disturbed.

By the time Cardinal and Delorme arrived at the island, it wasn't nearly as cold as it had been the previous night, not much below freezing. In the distance, snowmobiles buzzed among the fishing huts. Sparse snowflakes drifted down from a soiled pillow of cloud. The work of freeing the body was almost complete. "Ended up we didn't have to saw right through," Arsenault told them. Despite the below-freezing temperature, there were beads of sweat on his face. "Vibrations did the trick for us. Whole block came away in one piece. Moving it's going to be a little work, though. Can't put a crane in here without destroying the scene. Just gonna have to pull it over to the truck on a sled. Figure the runners'll do less damage than a toboggan."

"Good thinking. Where'd you get the truck?" A green five-ton with black rectangles covering its markings was backing up to the shafthead. Dr. Barnhouse had reminded them in no uncertain terms that, no matter how badly they might want a refrigerated vehicle, the use of a food distribution truck for transporting a dead body would be against every health regulation known to man.

"Kastner Chemical. They use it to transport nitrogen. Was their idea to black out the markings. They wanted it to look more respectful. I thought that was pretty classy."

"It was classy. Remind me to send them a thank-you."

"Hey, John! John!"

Roger Gwynn was waving at him from behind a roped-off area. The amorphous shape beside him, face masked by a Nikon, would be Nick Stoltz. Cardinal raised a gloved hand in return. He was not really on a first-name basis with the *Algonquin Lode* reporter, even though they had been more or less contemporaries in high school. Gwynn was trying to get the jump on the competition, exaggerating his connections. Being a cop in your hometown had its advantages, but sometimes Cardinal felt a pang of nostalgia for the relative anonymity of Toronto. There was a small camera crew jockeying for position around Stoltz and behind them a diminutive figure in a pink parka, its hood trimmed fetchingly with white fur. That would have to be Grace Legault from the six o'clock news. Algonquin Bay didn't have its own station; it got its local news from Sudbury. Cardinal had noted the CFCD van parked on the ice beside the police truck.

"Come on, John! Give me three seconds! I need a quote!"

Cardinal took Delorme with him and introduced her. "I know Ms. Delorme," Gwynn said. "We met when she was incarcerating His Worship. What can you tell me about this business?"

"Adolescent dead several months. That's it."

"Oh, thanks. Great copy that'll make. What are the chances it's that girl from the reserve?"

"I'm not going to speculate until we hear back from Forensic in Toronto."

"Billy LaBelle?"

"I'm not going to speculate."

"Come on. You gotta give me something. I'm freezing my ass off here." Gwynn was a slack, pudgy man—graceless in manner, lazy in outlook, an *Algonquin Lode* lifer. Cardinal's diagnosis: Ambition Deficit Disorder. "Is it a homicide at least? Can you tell me that?"

Cardinal gestured to the Sudbury team. "You wanna get in here, Miss Legault? Don't want to say all this twice."

He gave them both the basic facts, no mention of murder or Katie Pine, and finished with assurances that when he knew more, they would know more. As a show of goodwill, he handed Grace Legault his card. He didn't catch any flicker of gratitude in her skeptical, newscaster's eyes.

"Detective Cardinal," she said, as he turned away. "Do

you happen to know the legend of the Windigo? What kind of creature it is."

"Yeah, I do," he said. "A mythical one." He sighed inwardly. She's going to have a field day with that. Grace Legault was a different animal than Gwynn. No ambition deficit there.

"You finished here?" he asked Collingwood when he and Delorme were once more in the shafthead.

"Five rolls of stills. Arsenault says to keep running the video, though."

"Arsenault's right."

Straps of webbing had already been slung under the ice. Now, a block and tackle that were hooked up to a Honda generator were swung into position. One for the scrapbook, Cardinal thought, as the entire block was hoisted three feet above its resting place like a translucent coffin, the wasted and torn human figure trapped inside.

Delorme murmured, "You think we should cover it with something?"

"The best thing we can do for this girl," Cardinal said evenly, "is to make absolutely sure that everything Forensic finds inside that ice was there before we came on the scene."

"Okay," Delorme said. "Dumb idea, right?"

"Dumb idea."

"Sorry." A snowflake landed on her eyebrow and melted there. "It was just, seeing her like that—"

"Forget it."

Collingwood was videotaping the suspended block of ice, stepping from side to side. He looked up from his Sony and said exactly one word: "Leaf."

Arsenault peered into the ice block. "A maple leaf, looks like. A piece of one, anyway."

The forests of the near north are mostly pine, poplar, and birch. "Anybody do any sailing round here?"

Arsenault said, "Me and the wife were out here for a picnic last August or so. We can do a quick survey to make sure, but if I remember right, this whole little island was jack pine and spruce. Lots of birch."

"That's what I think, too," Cardinal said, "which would tend to confirm the murder happened somewhere else."

Delorme called Forensic on the cell phone to let them know they could expect the body in approximately four hours. Then they moved the remains, ice and all, down the snowy slope of the beach and into the waiting truck.

Remains, Cardinal thought. The word was not adequate.

5

SERGEANT Lise Delorme had been clearing the decks of Special Investigations for some time, a couple of months to be exact. There were no major cases pending, but she had thousands of little details to clear up. Final notes to make. Dispositions to update. Files to archive. She wanted everything to be shipshape for her replacement, who was due to arrive at the end of the month. But the entire morning had gone by and all she'd managed to do was clear sensitive material off her hard drive.

Delorme couldn't wait to get going on the Pine case, even if she was in the completely weird position of having to investigate her partner. So far, it looked like Cardinal was going to keep her at arm's length, and she couldn't really blame him for that. She wouldn't have trusted anyone right out of Special, either.

A phone call in the middle of the night, that's how it had started. She had thought at first it was Paul, a former boyfriend who got drunk every six months and called her at two in the morning, weepy and sentimental. It was Dyson. "Conference at the chief's house in half an hour. His house, not his office. Get dressed and wait. Horseman'll pick you up. Don't want certain parties seeing your car outside his place."

"What's going on?" Her words were slurry with sleep.

"You'll know soon enough. I've got a ticket waiting for you."

"Tell me it's for Florida. Someplace warm."

"It's your ticket out of Special."

Delorme got dressed in three minutes flat, then sat on the edge of the sofa, nerves singing. She'd spent six years working Special, and in all that time she had never once had a midnight summons, nor ever seen the inside of the chief's house. Ticket out of Special?

"No point asking me anything," the young Mountie told

her before she'd even opened her mouth, "I'm just the delivery girl." A nice touch, Delorme thought, to send a woman.

Delorme had grown up revering the Mounties. The scarlet uniform, those *horses,* well, they went straight to a little girl's heart. She had a vivid memory of the first time she saw them perform the Musical Ride in Ottawa, the sheer beauty of such equestrian precision. And then in high school, the glorious history, the great trek west. The Northwest Mounted Police, as they were then known, had ridden thousands of miles to ward off the kind of violence that was plaguing the westward expansion of the United States. They had negotiated treaties with the aboriginals, sent American raiders hightailing it back to Montana or whatever barbaric pit they had crawled out of, and established the rule of law before settlers had even had a chance to think about breaking it. The RCMP had become an icon of upstanding law enforcement around the world, a travel agent's dream.

Delorme had bought the image wholesale; that's what images are for, after all. When, sometime in her late teens, she had seen a photograph of a *woman* in that red serge uniform, Delorme had seriously considered sending away for an application.

But reality kept breaking through the image, and reality was not nearly as pretty. One officer sells secrets to Moscow, another is arrested for smuggling drugs, still another for tossing his wife off the balcony of a high-rise. And then there was the whole Security Service fiasco. The RCMP Security Service, before it had been dismantled in disgrace, had made the CIA look like geniuses.

She glanced at the fresh-faced creature in the car beside her, wearing a shapeless down coat, blond hair pulled back in a neat French braid. She had stopped for the traffic light at Edgewater and Trout Lake Road, and the streetlights silvered the down on her cheek. Even in that pale wash, Delorme could see herself ten years ago. This girl, too, had bought the straight-arrow image and was determined to make it stick. Well, good for her, Delorme figured. Cowboys armed with brutality and incompetence may have betrayed those true-North ideals, but that didn't make a young recruit dumb for clinging to them. Delorme spurred her on silently: Go get 'em.

They pulled up in front of an impressive A-frame on Edgewater. It looked like something out of the Swiss Alps.

"Don't ring the buzzer, just walk right in. Doesn't want to wake the kids."

Delorme showed her ID to a Mountie at the side door. "Downstairs," he said.

Delorme walked through the basement amid smells of Tide and Downy, then past a huge furnace into a large room of red brick and dark pine that had the leathery, smoky look of a men's club. Fake Tudor beams crisscrossed stucco walls that were hung with hunting prints and marine art. A feeble fire flickered in the fireplace. Above this, a moose head contemplated the head of R. J. Kendall, chief of the Algonquin Bay Police Department.

Kendall had an open, congenial manner and a big laugh that he used all the time, often accented with a backslap. He laughed too much, was Delorme's opinion; it made him seem nervous, which perhaps he was, but she had also seen that genial manner vanish in an instant. When angered, which was thankfully not often, R. J. Kendall was a shouter and a curser. The whole department had heard him tear up one side of Adonis Dyson and down the other for undermanning the winter fur carnival, with the result that it had become a noisy, rowdy affair that made the front page of the *Lode* for all the wrong reasons.

And yet Dyson still spoke highly of Kendall, as did most people who carried shrapnel wounds from one of his explosions. Once his anger was over, it was really over, and he usually made a gesture or two to soothe ruffled feathers. In Dyson's case, he'd gone out of his way—on TV—to give him credit for downturns in robberies and assaults. It was far more than his predecessor would have done, and Dyson noticed.

Dyson himself was in one of the red leather armchairs talking to someone Delorme couldn't see. He waved a languid hand in her direction, as if midnight meetings were routine with him.

The chief jumped up to shake Delorme's hand. He must have been in his late fifties, but he affected a boyish air, the way some powerful men do. "Sergeant Delorme. Thanks for getting here so fast. And on such short notice. Can I get you a drink? Off-hours, I think we can afford to relax a little."

"No thank you, sir. This time of night, it would just knock me out."

"We'll get right down to it, then. Someone I want you to meet. Corporal Malcolm Musgrave, RCMP."

Watching Corporal Malcolm Musgrave emerge from the red leather chair was like watching a mountain emerge from the plains. He had his back to Delorme, so the granite block of head emerged first, pale hair trimmed to no more than a sandy bristle. Then the escarpment of shoulders, vast cliff-face of chest as he turned toward her, and finally the rock formation of his handshake, dry and cool as shale. "Heard about you," he said to Delorme. "Nice job on the mayor."

"I've heard about you, too," Delorme told him, and Dyson shot her a dark glance. Musgrave had killed two men in the line of duty. Both times there had been hearings about the use of excessive force, and both times he had got off. Delorme thought: We *really* get our man.

"Corporal Musgrave is with the Sudbury detachment. He's their number two man in Commercial Crime."

Delorme knew that, of course. The RCMP no longer maintained a local detachment, so Algonquin Bay fell within Sudbury's jurisdiction. As federal police, the RCMP worked any crimes of national import—drugs at a national level, counterfeiting, commercial crime. Now and again, the Algonquin Bay police would work with them on major drug busts, but, as far as Delorme knew, Musgrave himself never put in an appearance.

"Corporal Musgrave has a little bedtime story for us," the chief said. "You won't like it."

"Have you heard of Kyle Corbett?" Musgrave's eyes were the palest blue Delorme had ever seen, almost transparent. It was like being scrutinized by a husky.

Yes, she had heard of Kyle Corbett. Everyone had heard of Kyle Corbett. "Big drug dealer, no? Doesn't he control everything north of Toronto?"

"Obviously Special Investigations keeps you off the street. Kyle Corbett cleaned up his act at least three years ago when he discovered counterfeiting. You're surprised. You thought when Ottawa changed to colored bills we stumped the counterfeiters, right? Bad guys all moved on to those oh-so-boring and oh-so-easy-to-copy American bills. You're absolutely right, they did. Then a small thing came along called a color copier. And another little item called a scanner. And now every Tom, Dick, and Harry's going into the office on Saturday morning and printing himself a batch of phony twenties. Major headache for the Treasury. And you know what? I couldn't care less." Those arctic eyes sizing her up.

Delorme shrugged. "It's not costing the taxpayer enough?"

"Good," Musgrave said, as if she were his pupil. "Bogus Canadian currency costs businesses and individuals some five million dollars a year. Chicken feed. And, like I say, it's mostly weekend counterfeiters."

"So why the fuss about Corbett? If you don't care about phony money . . ."

"Kyle Corbett is not counterfeiting money. Kyle Corbett is counterfeiting credit cards. Suddenly we're not talking five million dollars. Suddenly we're talking a hundred million. And that's not Bob's All-Nite Esso getting hit. Or Ethel's Kountry Kitchen. We're talking major banks, and believe me, when Bank of Montreal and Toronto Dominion get upset, we hear about it loud and clear. Which is why our guys and your guys—not to mention the OPP's guys—have been working a JFO for the past three years, trying to take Corbett down."

Dyson leaned forward, apparently worried at being left out of the conversation. "Joint Forces Operation. November 1997."

"November 1997. JFO includes our guys, Jerry Commanda with OPP, and your guys McLeod and Cardinal. We have solid information that Corbett's happy band of brothers has a stamping machine, five thousand blanks, and a very expensive supply of holograms at his club out behind Airport Road. But when the forces of righteousness swoop down, Corbett and Co. are doing nothing more exciting than playing pool and drinking Molsons."

The chief was now thrashing at the fire with a poker, sending sparks flying. "Tell her Episode Two."

"August 1998. Solid intelligence puts Corbett and his merry men in West Ferris with Perfect Circle. You've never heard of Perfect Circle so don't pretend you have. Perfect Circle runs the biggest counterfeiting operation in Hong Kong. They have reciprocity with Corbett. In other words, they exchange stolen account numbers for use overseas. You buy a new Honda in Toronto with an American Express card out of Kowloon, and before anyone's the wiser, you've driven it to hell and gone. And vice versa. Perfect Circle, as their name suggests, also manufacture dead-perfect holograms. They're Asian, right? High tech is in their blood.

"Meanwhile, our two Horsemen have gone their separate ways: one's quit to go into the private sector, the other's doing fifteen-to-life for killing his wife."

"Right. The high-rise guy."

"If you'd met his wife you'd know why. Your Detective McLeod gets wired to the Corriveau murders, and the OPP has Jerry Commanda sequestered in Ottawa on some no-doubt crucially important training course."

"There's no need to malign ongoing officer education," the chief put in. "Your point is, Detective Cardinal turns out to be the single unit of law-enforcement continuity on Kyle Corbett."

"Exactly. Drum roll, please."

Kendall turned to Dyson. "Didn't you tell me there were rumors about Cardinal when he worked in Toronto?"

"We did our homework, Chief. There was nothing substantial."

Musgrave didn't even slow down. "Age of globalization. Perfect Circle are doing the grand tour from Hong Kong to B.C. to strengthen their linkage in Vancouver. Solid information says they're headed for Toronto, stopping off for a courtesy call in Algonquin Bay. According to this information, Corbett and the Yellow Peril have a meet set for the Pine Crest Hotel—the Pine Crest! It's like they're the ladies' auxiliary or something. Perfect Circle guys arrive on time. Appointed hour rolls around, JFO stakes out the hotel. No, we did not do the Musical Ride. And no, we were not in full-dress uniform. This was a strictly old-clothes operation. Guess what happens?"

Delorme didn't say anything. Corporal Musgrave was enjoying his pedagogical act; it wouldn't do to interrupt the flow.

"Nothing happens. No Corbett. No Perfect Circle. No meeting. Once more, the combined forces of the RCMP, the OPP, and the Algonquin Bay Police Department have come up empty. Dumb flatfoots. So stupid. Can't get anything right."

The chief was standing by the fireplace, poker in hand, his face in shadow. It was rare to spend more than ten minutes with R. J. and not hear that preposterous laugh of his, but hearing Musgrave's Horseman's Tale had clearly depressed him. He said in a subdued voice, "It gets worse."

It did indeed get worse. Another piece of solid information. Another date and time. The single change: This time, Jerry Commanda was back playing left wing for the OPP. Another raid. Another zero. "This time," Musgrave added, "Corbett files suit for harassment."

"I remember that," Delorme said. "I thought that was pretty funny."

Dyson glared at her.

Musgrave shifted in his chair. It was like watching a continent change shape. "You've got the facts. I'll let you draw your own conclusions. You have any questions?"

"Just one," Delorme said. "What exactly do you mean by 'solid'?"

That was the only time the chief had laughed that night. Nobody else cracked a smile.

Now, two months later, Delorme was feeding the shredder in her Special Investigations office and hoping without much optimism that her new partner would come to trust her. As she carried a wastebasket full of shreds to the incinerator, she saw Cardinal putting on his coat. "You need me to do anything?" she asked him.

"Nope. We got a positive ID back on the dental records. I'm just going out to tell Dorothy Pine."

"You sure you don't want me to come?"

"No, thanks. I'll see you later."

Terrific, Delorme muttered to herself as she dumped the trash. He doesn't even know I'm running a check on him and still he doesn't want me for a partner. Great start.

6

To reach Chippewa Reserve, you follow Main Street west past the railroad tracks and make a left just past the St. Joseph's mother house, formerly a Catholic girls' school and now a home for retired nuns, at the junction with Highway 17. There are no signs to Chippewa Reserve, no gates; the Ojibwa have suffered so much at the hand of the white man that to lock the door against him now would be pointless.

The most remarkable thing about entering the reserve, Cardinal often thought, is that you don't know you're on the reserve. One of his very first girlfriends had lived up here, and even then he hadn't registered its status as a separate enclave. The pre-fab bungalows, the slightly battered cars parked in the drives, the mutts chasing each other over the snowbanks, these could belong to any lower middle-class neighborhood in Canada. Of course the jurisdiction changed—law enforcement here was in the hands of the OPP—but you couldn't see that. The only visible difference from any other part of Algonquin Bay was, well, the place was full of Indians, a people who for the most part moved through Canadian society—or rather, alongside it—as silent and invisible as ghosts.

A shadow nation, Cardinal thought. We don't even know they're there. He had stopped a hundred yards past the turnoff, and now, since the day was sunny and a seasonable minus ten, he was walking with Jerry Commanda along the side of the road toward a perfectly white bungalow.

When not encased in a down parka, Jerry was extremely thin, almost frail-looking, a deceptive morphology because he also happened to be a four-time provincial kickboxing champion. You never saw what Jerry did exactly, but the most recalcitrant villain, in the course of a disagreement with him, would suddenly turn up horizontal and in a highly vocal mood of compliance.

Cardinal had never been partnered with him, but McLeod had, and McLeod claimed that, had they lived two hundred years earlier, he would have probably turned on his ancestors and happily fought the white man at Jerry's side. The detectives had held a big party for Jerry when he left, a party he did not attend, being no lover of sentiment or fuss. When he moved to OPP, he could have taken an assignment at any of the townships the provincial force covered, but he had asked to work exclusively on reserves. He got the same pay as the municipal police, except—a point on which he was as infuriatingly verbose as his race is said to be silent—he was exempt from income tax.

Last night, Jerry had irritated him by pretending he hadn't been aware of Cardinal's exile from homicide. Jerry's sense of humor tended to be opaque. And he had a disarming habit, perhaps ingrained in him from countless hours of tripping up suspects under interrogation, of changing topics suddenly. He did so now, by asking about Catherine.

Catherine was fine, Cardinal told him, in a tone that suggested they move on to something else.

"What about Delorme," Jerry asked. "How're you getting along with Delorme? She can be kind of prickly."

Cardinal told him Delorme was fine, too.

"She has a nice shape, I always thought."

Cardinal, though it made him uncomfortable, thought so, too. It was no problem having an attractive woman working in Special—with a separate office, separate cases. It was another to have her for a partner.

"Lise is a good woman," Jerry said. "Good investigator, too. Took guts to nail the mayor the way she did. I would have chickened out. I knew she'd get tired of that white-collar stuff, though." He waved to an old man walking a dog across the street. "Of course, she could be investigating you."

"Thanks, Jerry. That's just what I wanted to hear."

"Got our new streetlights working," Jerry said, pointing. "Now we can see how homey it's getting around here."

"New paint jobs, too, I notice."

Jerry nodded. "My summer project. Any kid I caught drinking had to paint an entire house. Made them all white because it's more painful. You ever try to paint a house white in the summer?"

"No."

"Hurts your eyes like a bastard. The kids hate me now but I don't care."

They didn't hate him, of course. Three dark-eyed boys carrying skates and hockey sticks had been following them since Jerry came out of his house. One of them threw a snowball that hit Cardinal in the arm. He packed some snow together in gloveless hands and hurled one back, way off the mark. Must have been ten years since he'd thrown anything other than a tantrum. A skirmish ensued, Jerry taking a couple of missiles indifferently in his skinny chest.

"Ten to one the little guy is your relative," Cardinal said. "Little smart-ass there."

"He's my nephew. Handsome like his uncle, too." Jerry Commanda, all hundred and forty pounds of him, was indeed handsome.

The boys were chattering in Ojibwa, of which Cardinal, no linguist, understood not a word. "What are they saying?"

"They're saying he walks like a cop but he throws like a girl. Maybe he's a faggot."

"How sweet."

"My nephew says, 'He's probably going to arrest Jerry for stealing that fucking paint.'" Jerry continued translating in his monotone. "'That's the cop that was here last fall—the asshole that couldn't find Katie Pine.'"

"Jerry, you missed your calling. You should have been a diplomat." Later, it occurred to him that Jerry might not have been translating at all; it would have been like him.

They walked around a shiny new pickup, approaching the Pine house now.

"I know Dorothy Pine pretty well. You want me to come with you?"

Cardinal shook his head. "Maybe you could stop in later, though."

"Okay, I'll do that. What kind of person kills a little girl, John?"

"They're rare, thank God. That's why we'll catch him. He'll be different from other people." Cardinal wished he was as certain of this as he sounded.

ASKING Dorothy Pine last September for the name of her daughter's dentist—so he could get her chart—had been the hardest thing Cardinal had ever had to do. Dorothy Pine's face, the heavy features scarred by a ferocious, burnt-out case of acne, had expressed no trace of grief: He was white, he was the law, why should she?

Until then, her only experience of the police had been their sporadic arrests of her husband, a gentle soul who used to beat her without mercy when drunk. He had gone to Toronto to find work shortly after Katie's tenth birthday and had found instead the business end of a switchblade in a Spadina Road flophouse.

Cardinal's finger shook a little as he rang the doorbell.

Dorothy Pine, a tiny woman who barely cleared his waist, opened the door and looked up at him and knew instantly why he had come—she had no other children, there could be only one reason.

"Okay," she said, when he told her Katie's body had been found. Just the one word, "Okay," and she started to shut the door. Case closed. Her only child was dead. Cops—let alone white cops—could be of no assistance here.

"Mrs. Pine, I wonder if you'd let me in for a few minutes. I've been off the case for a couple of months and I need to refresh my memory."

"What for? You found her now."

"Well, yes, but now we want to catch whoever killed her."

He had the feeling that, had he not mentioned it, the thought of tracking down the man who killed her daughter would never have entered Dorothy Pine's head. All that mattered was the fact of her death. She gave a slight shrug, humoring him, and he stepped past her into the house.

The smell of bacon clung to the hallway. Although it was nearly noon, the living room curtains were still drawn. Electric heaters had dried the air and killed the plants that hung withered on a shelf. The place was dark as a mausoleum. Death had entered this house five months ago; it had never left.

Dorothy Pine sat down on a circular footstool in front of the television where Wile E. Coyote was noisily chasing the Roadrunner. Her arms hung down between her knees, and tears plopped in miniature splashes onto the linoleum floor.

All those weeks Cardinal had tried to find the little girl, through the hundreds of interviews of classmates, friends, and teachers, through the thousands of phone calls, the thousands of fliers, he had hoped that Dorothy Pine would come to trust him. She never did. For the first two weeks she telephoned daily, not only identifying herself every time but explaining why she was calling. "I was just wondering if you found my daughter, Katharine Pine," as if Cardinal might have forgotten to look. Then she'd stopped calling altogether.

Cardinal took Katie's high-school photograph out of his pocket, the photograph they'd used to print all those fliers that had asked of bus stations and emergency wards, of shopping malls and gas stations, Have You Seen This Girl? Now the killer had answered, oh yes he had seen this girl all right, and Cardinal slipped the photograph on top of the television.

"Do you mind if I look at her room again?"

A shake of the dark head, a shudder in the shoulders. Another tiny splash on the linoleum floor. Husband murdered, and now her daughter, too. Eskimos, it is said, have forty different words for snow. Never mind about snow, Cardinal mused, what people really need is forty words for sorrow. *Grief. Heartbreak. Desolation.* There were not enough, not for this childless mother in her empty house.

Cardinal went down a short hallway to a bedroom. The door was open, and a yellow bear with one glass eye frowned at him from the windowsill. Under the bear's threadbare paws lay a woven rug with a horse pattern. Dorothy Pine sold these rugs at the Hudson Bay store on Lakeshore. The store charged a hundred and twenty bucks, but he doubted if Dorothy Pine saw much of it. Outside, a chainsaw was ripping into wood, and somewhere a crow was cawing.

There was a toy bench under the windowsill. Cardinal opened it with his foot and saw that it still contained Katie's books. *Black Beauty,* Nancy Drew, stories his own daughter had enjoyed as a girl. Why do we think they're so different from us? He opened the chest of drawers—the socks and underwear neatly folded.

There was a little box of costume jewelry that played a tune when opened. It contained an assortment of rings and earrings and a couple of bracelets—one leather, one beaded. Katie had been wearing a charm bracelet the day she disappeared, Cardinal remembered. Stuck in the dresser mirror, a series of four photographs taken by a machine of Katie and her best friend making hideous faces.

Cardinal regretted leaving Delorme at the squad room to chase after Forensic. She might have seen something in Katie's room that he was missing, something only a female would notice.

Gathering dust at the bottom of the closet were several pairs of shoes, including a patent leather pair with straps— Mary Janes? Cardinal had bought a pair for Kelly when she was seven or eight. Katie Pine's had been bought at the Salvation Army, apparently; the price was still chalked on the sole. There were no running shoes; Katie had taken her Nikes to school the day she disappeared, carrying them in her knapsack.

Pinned to the back of the closet door was a picture of the high-school band. Cardinal didn't recall Katie being in the band. She was a math whiz. She had represented Algonquin

Bay in a provincial math contest and had come in second. The plaque was on the wall to prove it.

He called out to Dorothy Pine. A moment later, she came in, red-eyed, clutching a shredded Kleenex. "Mrs. Pine, that's not Katie in the front row of that picture, is it? The girl with the dark hair?"

"That's Sue Couchie. Katie used to fool around on my accordion sometimes, but she wasn't in no band. Sue and her was best friends."

"I remember, now. I interviewed her at the school. Said practically all they did was watch MuchMusic. Videotaped their favorite songs."

"Sue can sing pretty good. Katie kind of wanted to be like her."

"Did Katie ever take music lessons?"

"No. She sure wanted to be in that band, though."

They were looking at a picture of her hopes, of a future that would now remain forever imaginary.

7

WHEN he left the reserve, Cardinal made a left and headed north toward the Ontario Hospital. Advances in medication coupled with government cutbacks had emptied out whole wings of the psychiatric facility. Its morgue did double duty as the coroner's workshop. But Cardinal wasn't there to see Barnhouse.

"She's doing a lot better today," the ward nurse told him. "She's starting to sleep at night, and she's been taking her meds, so it's probably just a matter of time till she levels out—that's my opinion, anyway. Dr. Singleton will be doing rounds in about an hour if you want to talk to him."

"No, that's all right. Where is she?"

"In the sunroom. Just go through the double doors, and it's—"

"Thanks. I know where it is."

Cardinal expected to find her still adrift in her oversize terry dressing gown, but instead, Catherine Cardinal was wearing the jeans and red sweater he had packed for her. She was hunched in a chair by the window, chin in hand, staring out at the snowscape, the stand of birches at the edge of the grounds.

"Hi, sweetheart. I was up at the reserve. Thought I'd stop in on the way back."

She didn't look at him. When she was ill, eye contact was agony for her. "I don't suppose you've come to get me out of here."

"Not just yet, hon. We'll have to talk to the doctor about that." As he got closer, he could see that the outline of her lipstick was uncertain, and her eyeliner was thicker on one eye than the other. Catherine Cardinal was a sweet, pretty woman when she was well: sparrow-colored hair, big gentle eyes, and a completely silent giggle that Cardinal loved to provoke. *I don't make her laugh enough*, he often thought. *I should bring more joy into this woman's life.*

But by the time she had begun this nosedive, he had been working burglaries and was in a bad mood himself most of the time. Some help.

"You're looking pretty good, Catherine. I don't think you'll be in here too long this time."

Her right hand never stopped moving, her index finger drawing tiny circles over and over again on the arm of the couch. "I know I'm a witch to live with. I would have killed me by now, but—" She broke off, still staring out the window. "But that doesn't mean my ideas are insane. It's not as if I'm . . . Fuck. I've lost my train of thought."

The swear word, like the obsessive circling movement of her hand, was a bad sign; Catherine didn't swear when she was well.

"So pathetic," she said bitterly. "Can't even finish a sentence." The medication did that to her, broke her thoughts into small pieces. Perhaps that was why it worked, eventually; it short-circuited the chains of association, the obsessive ideas. Nevertheless, Cardinal could feel the hot jet of anger gushing inside his wife, blotting everything out like an artery opened in water. Both of her hands were making the obsessive circles, now.

"Kelly's doing well," he said brightly. "Sounds practically in love with her painting teacher. She enjoyed her visit."

Catherine looked at the floor, shaking her head slowly. Not accepting any positive remarks, thank you.

"You'll feel better soon," Cardinal said gently. "I just wanted to see you. It was a spur of the moment thing. I thought we could have a chat. I don't want to upset you."

He could see Catherine's thoughts growing heavier. Her head sank lower. One hand now covered her eyes like a visor.

"Cath, honey, listen. You will feel better. I know it feels like you won't just now. It feels like nothing will ever be right again, but we've got through this before and we'll get through it again."

People think of depression as sadness, and in its milder

manifestations perhaps it is, but there could be little comparison between a tearful parting, say, or a sense of loss, and these massive, devastating attacks Catherine suffered. "It's as if I am invaded," she had told him. "It rolls into me like black clouds of gas. All hope is annihilated. All joy is slaughtered." *All joy is slaughtered.* He would never forget her saying that.

"Take it easy," he said, now. "Catherine? Please, hon. Take it slow, now." He put a hand on her knee and received not the slightest flicker of response. Her thoughts, he knew, were a turmoil of self-loathing. She had told him as much: "Suddenly," she said, "I can't breathe. All the air is sucked out of the room, and I'm being crushed. And the worst thing is knowing what a misery I am to live with. I'm fastened to you like a stone, dragging you down and down and down. You must hate me. I hate me."

But she said nothing, now. Just remained motionless, with her neck bent forward at a painful angle.

Three months before, Catherine had been bright and cheerful, her normal self. But gradually, as it often did in winter, her cheerfulness had ballooned into mania. She began to speak of traveling to Ottawa. It became her sole topic of conversation. Suddenly, it was vital she see the prime minister, she must talk sense into Parliament, she must tell the politicians what had to be done to save the country, save Quebec. Nothing could jog her from this obsession. It would start every morning at breakfast; it was the last thing she said at night. Cardinal thought he would go mad himself. Then Catherine's ideas had taken on an interplanetary cast. She began to talk of NASA, of the early explorers, the colonization of space. She stayed awake for three nights running, writing obsessively in a journal. When the phone bill arrived, it listed three hundred dollars' worth of calls to Ottawa and Houston.

Finally, on the fourth day, she had spiraled to earth like a plane with a dead engine. She remained in bed for a week with the blinds pulled down. At three o'clock one morning, Cardinal awoke when she called his name. He found her in the bathroom, sitting on the edge of the tub. The cabinet was open, the rows of pills (none of them in themselves particularly lethal) waiting. "I think I'd better go to the hospital," was all she had said. At the time, Cardinal had thought it a good sign; she had never before asked for help.

Now, Cardinal sat next to his wife in the overheated sun-room, humbled by the magnitude of her desolation. He tried for a while longer to get her to speak, but she stayed silent. He hugged her, and it was like hugging wood. Her hair gave off a slight animal odor.

A nurse came, bearing a single pill and a paper cup of juice. When Catherine would not respond to her coaxing, the nurse left and returned with a syringe. Five minutes later, Catherine was asleep in her husband's arms.

The early days are always bad, Cardinal told himself in the elevator. In a few days the drugs will soothe her nerves enough so that the relentless self-loathing will lose its power. When that happens she will be—what?—sad and ashamed, he supposed. She'll feel exhausted and drained and sad and ashamed, but at least she'll be living in this world. Catherine was his California—she was his sunlight and wine and blue ocean—but a strain of madness ran through her like a fault line, and Cardinal lived in fear that one day it would topple their life beyond all hope of recovery.

8

IT wasn't until Sunday that Cardinal got the opportunity to review background material. He spent the entire afternoon at home with a stack of files labeled PINE, LABELLE, and FOGLE.

In a city of fifty-eight thousand, one missing child is a major event, two is an out-and-out sensation. Never mind Chief R. J. or the board of commissioners, never mind the *Algonquin Lode* or the TV news, it was the entire town that wouldn't let you rest. Back in the fall, Cardinal could not so much as shop for groceries without being peppered with questions and advice about Katie Pine and Billy LaBelle. Everyone had an idea, everyone had a suggestion.

Of course, this had its bright side: There was no lack of volunteers. In the LaBelle case, the local Boy Scouts had spent an entire week treading step by step through the woods beyond the airport. But there were drawbacks, too. The station phones never stopped ringing and the small force had been overwhelmed with false leads—all of which had to be followed up sooner or later. The files filled up with stacks of supplementary reports—*sups,* as they were not very affectionately called: follow-ups on tips that led like a thousand false maps to dead ends.

Now, Cardinal sat with his feet to the fireplace and a fresh pot of decaf on the stove, weeding through the files, trying to winnow the stack of data into facts: From these solid facts, newly regarded, he hoped to extract one solid idea, one fragment of a theory, because so far he had none.

Armed Forces had graciously lent them a tent big enough to cover Windigo Island and two heaters formerly used to heat hangars for the local squadron of F-18s. Down on their knees like archaeologists, Cardinal and the others had culled the snow foot by square foot. That took most of the day, and then, turning up the heaters bit by bit, they had slowly melted the snow and examined the sodden carpet of pine needles and sand and rock that lay beneath. Beer cans, cigarette butts, fishing tackle, bits of plastic—they were buried in trash, none of it tied to the crime.

The lock had yielded no fingerprint.

This, then, was Cardinal's first sad fact: Their painstaking search had rendered not a single lead.

KATIE Pine had disappeared on September 12. She had attended school that day, leaving just after the final bell with two friends. There was the initial report—a phone call from Dorothy Pine—and then there were the sups: Cardinal's interview with Sue Couchie, McLeod's interview with the other girl. The three girls had gone to the traveling fair that was set up outside Memorial Gardens. Cardinal set this among the solid facts.

The girls didn't stay long. The last they'd seen of Katie she'd been throwing balls at some bowling pin targets, hoping to win a huge stuffed panda she'd liked the look of. It was almost as big as Katie, who was thirteen but looked eleven, tops.

Sue and the other girl had gone to a dark little tent to have their fortune told by Madame Rosa. When they came back to the ball-throwing attraction, Katie was gone. They looked around for her, couldn't find her, and decided she must have left without them. This was around six o'clock.

There was Cardinal's interview with the young man who operated the ball-throwing game. No, she didn't win the bear, and he hadn't noticed anyone with her, hadn't seen her leave. No one saw her leave. The ground, as Dyson said, had opened up.

Thousands of interviews, thousands of fliers later, Cardinal had learned nothing more about her disappearance. She had run away twice previously, to relatives in Mattawa. But her father's drunken rages had driven her to it, and when he was dead, her running stopped. Dyson had not wanted to hear it.

Cardinal got up and put a dressing gown on over his clothes, stirred the fire in the woodstove, and sat down again. It was only five, but it was already dark and he had to switch on the reading lamp. The metal chain was cold to the touch.

He opened the LaBelle file. William Alexander LaBelle: twelve years old, four foot-eight, eighty pounds—a very little kid. The address in Cedargrove was upper middle-class. Catholic background, parochial school. Parents and relatives ruled out as possible suspects. History of running, though only once in Billy's case. Never mind, it was enough for Dyson. "Look. Billy LaBelle is the third son in a family of high achievers. He's not doing as well as his football-star brothers, all right? He's not getting the grades of his high-wattage sisters. He's twelve and his self-esteem is in the basement. Billy LaBelle opted out, okay? The kid took a walk."

Where the boy had taken a walk *to* was a matter of less certainty. Billy had disappeared on October 14, one month after Katie Pine, plucked from the Algonquin Mall where he had been hanging out with friends. Sup reports included interviews with teachers and the three boys who had been with him at the mall. One minute he's playing Mortal Kombat in Radio Shack (sup reports of interviews with the salesman and cashier), the next minute he says he's going to catch the bus home. He's the only one of the four friends who lives in Cedargrove, so he leaves by himself. No one ever sees him again. Billy LaBelle, age twelve, steps out of the Algonquin Mall and into the case files.

Dyson had given Cardinal free rein for a few weeks after Billy's disappearance, and then the walls had closed in: no proof of murder, a history of running, other cases deserved priority. Cardinal resisted, certain that both kids had been killed, probably by the same person. Dyson on Billy La-Belle: "Christ, man. Look at his problems. He's got noth-ing going for him. My guess is he offed himself somewhere and he'll turn up in the spring floating in the French River."

But why were there no previous attempts? Why no obvious depression? Dyson had cupped his ear, feigning deafness.

Cardinal tossed the LaBelle file aside. He poured himself another cup of decaf and put another log into the woodstove. Sparks shot up like smithereens.

He opened the Fogle case, which contained little more than the top sheet—the facts from the initial report—courtesy of the Toronto police. I should have seen how things would go, Cardinal reflected, and perhaps he had. Dyson had been right: He had spent a lot of money, a lot of manpower. What else were you supposed to do when children vanished into thin air?

Margaret Fogle—at seventeen not really a child—had been the straw that broke Dyson's back. A seventeen-year-old runaway from Toronto? Not high priority, thank you very much. Last seen in Algonquin Bay by her aunt. McLeod's sup report with characteristic misspellings (*where* for *were*, "her parents where separated") was in the file. The girl's stated destination: Calgary, Alberta. "Which leaves half a continent and several hundred police forces responsible for finding her," Dyson had pointed out. "You hear me, Cardinal? You are not the country's sole policeman. Let the Horsemen earn their keep for a change."

All right, give him Margaret Fogle. With her out of the equation, it seemed even clearer there was a killer at work.

"Why do you keep saying that?" Dyson had fumed, not conversational anymore, not avuncular. "Molesters? Perverts? They go for boys, they go for girls, but they almost never—never—go for both."

"Laurence Knapschaefer went for both."

"Laurence Knapschaefer. I knew you'd say Laurence Knapschaefer. Too far out for me, Cardinal."

Laurence Knapschaefer had murdered five kids in Toronto ten years previously. Three boys, two girls. One girl got away, which was how they finally got him.

"The exception that proves the rule, that's what Laurence Knapschaefer is. There are no bodies, therefore this is not homicide. You don't have one scrap of evidence that it is."

"But even that could be taken as evidence for murder."

"What could?"

"The lack of evidence. It only bolsters my theory." He had seen in Dyson's cold blue gaze the doors slam shut, the bolts shoot home. But he couldn't leave it alone, couldn't shut up. "A runaway is seen—by bus passengers, ticket takers, hostel workers, drug dealers. A runaway is noticed. That's how we find them. A runaway leaves clues: a note, extra clothes or money missing, warnings to friends. But a murdered child—a murdered child leaves nothing: no warning, no note, nothing. Katie Pine and Billy LaBelle left nothing."

"Sorry, Cardinal. Your reasoning is out of *Alice in Wonderland.*"

Next morning, Cardinal had ordered a grid search—his third in six weeks—that had come up empty. That afternoon, Dyson yanked him off Pine and LaBelle. Off homicide altogether for the foreseeable future. "Bring in Arthur Wood. He's robbing the citizenry blind."

"I don't believe this. Two missing children, and you're putting me on burglaries?"

"I can't afford you, Cardinal. This is not Toronto. If you miss the big time so much, why don't you go back there? In the meantime, you can bring me the head of Arthur Wood."

The Fogle file landed on top of the others.

Cardinal warmed up a tourtière he'd thawed out earlier. Catherine had wheedled the recipe out of a French-Canadian friend, but McLeod had tried it once and claimed they'd stolen it from his mother. It was the sage that gave them away.

He ate in front of the television, watching the news from Sudbury. The discovery of a body on Windigo Island was the lead. Grace Legault had pulled back her hood to do her stand-up on the island, snowflakes winking out like stars on the lion's mane of chestnut hair. She looked a lot taller on television.

"According to Ojibwa legend," she began, "the Windigo is the spirit of a hunter who went out in winter and got lost in the icy woods, where he was forced to live off human flesh. It's easy to believe such a legend when you set foot on this desolate island, where yesterday afternoon the body of an unidentified adolescent was discovered by a couple of snowmobilers."

Thanks, Grace, Cardinal said to himself. We'll be having the "Windigo killer" next, or even "The Windigo." Going to be a circus.

The report cut to file footage of the OPP dragging Lake Nipissing in the fall, while Legault speculated on whether the body might be that of Billy LaBelle or Katie Pine. Then they cut to Cardinal on the island acting cool and official, telling them let's wait and see. I'm a conceited prick, he thought. I see too many movies.

Cardinal wished he could phone Catherine, but she didn't always respond well to such calls, and she rarely called him from the hospital. I feel too embarrassed and ashamed, she told him, and it all but undid Cardinal to think that she could feel that way. Yet somewhere within that welter of feelings, he was aware of a lurking anger that she could abandon him like this. He knew it was not her fault, and he tried never to blame his wife, but Cardinal was not a natural loner, and there were times when he resented being left on his own for months at a time. Then he would blame himself for being selfish.

He wrote a short note to Kelly, enclosing a check for five hundred dollars. With both her and Catherine gone, the house seemed way too big, he wrote, then screwed up the note and tossed it in the wastebasket. He scrawled, *I know you can use this,* and sealed the envelope. Daughters like their fathers to be invulnerable, and Kelly always squirmed at the least expression of feeling on his part. How strange, that someone he loved so much would never know the truth about him, never know how he had come by the money that paid for her education. How strange and how sad.

He thought about missing persons, missing kids. Dyson was right: If you crossed the country, you went through Algonquin Bay, and it was bound to get more than its fair share of runaways. Cardinal had made a separate file of top sheets from other jurisdictions: cases from Ottawa, the Maritimes, even Vancouver, that had come in over the fax within the past year.

He called the duty sergeant, horse-faced, good-hearted Mary Flower, to dig up some statistics. It wasn't her job, but he knew Flower had a minor crush on him and she would do it. She called him back just as he was getting undressed to take a shower. Naked and goosebumped, he gripped the phone in the crook of his neck and struggled back into the sleeves of his bathrobe.

"Last ten years you said?" Mary had a piercing nasal whine of a voice that could peel paint. "You ready?"

For the next few minutes he was scribbling numbers onto a pad. Then he hung up and called Delorme; it took her a long time to answer. "Hey, Delorme," he said when she finally picked up. "Delorme, you awake?"

"I'm awake, John." A lie. Fully awake, she wouldn't have used his first name.

"Guess how many missing persons—adolescents—we had year before last."

"Including ones from out of town? I don't know. Seven? Eight?"

"Twelve. An even dozen. And the year before that we had ten. Year before that, eight. Year before that, ten. Year before that, ten again. You getting my drift?"

"Ten a year, give or take."

"Give or take exactly two. Ten each year."

Delorme's voice was suddenly clearer, sharper. "But you called to tell me about this past year, right?"

"This past year, the number of missing adolescents— again, including those from out of town—came to fourteen."

Delorme gave a low whistle.

"Here's how I see it. A guy kills a kid, Katie Pine, and discovers he's got a thing for it. It's the biggest thrill of his life. He grabs another kid, Billy LaBelle, and does it again. He's on a roll, but by this time the entire city is looking for missing children. He gets smart, he starts going after older kids. Kids from out of town. He knows there won't be the same uproar over a seventeen-year-old, an eighteen-year-old."

"Especially if they're from out of town."

"You should see. The open cases are from all over the map. Three from Toronto, but the rest are from hell and gone."

"You have the files at home? I'll come right over."

"No, no, we can meet in the squad room."

There was the briefest of pauses. "Jesus Christ, Cardinal. You think I'm still working Special? You think I'm investigating you? Tell me the truth."

"Oh, it's nothing like that," he said sweetly, thinking, God, I'm a good liar. "It's just, I'm a married man, Lise, and you're so all-out attractive, I don't trust myself with you."

There was a long pause. Then Delorme hung up.

9

THEY had the files spread out over three desks and were getting on the nerves of Ian McLeod, a red-haired, knobby, over-muscled cop with a well-nursed persecution complex. He was trying desperately to catch up on the backlog caused by the Corriveau case—a double murder at a hunting lodge. A good investigator, yes, but even on his best days, McLeod was a bad-tempered, foul-mouthed hard-ass; Corriveau had made him just about unbearable. "Can you guys maybe keep it down a little? Like not shout down the entire fucking building?"

"So sensitive these days," Cardinal said. "Have you been taking one of those New Male workshops?"

"I'm trying to catch up on anything that isn't Corriveau, okay? Some normal stuff. Believe it or not I had another fucking life before the Corriveau Brothers decided to murder their no-good stinking father-in-law and his no-good stinking partner. I *still* have another life—I just don't remember what it is right now, owing to the fact that I wake and sleep in this pathetic little butthole of a police station."

Cardinal tuned him out. "None of these cases has been cleared," he said to Delorme. "Let's divide the stack in two and run them down as fast as we can. Pretend they just landed on our desk. I mean, it doesn't look like anything was done."

"I heard that," McLeod yelled across the room. "I don't need my so-called brothers—oh, excuse me—my so-called brothers- and *sisters*-in-arms second-guessing me. You try chasing after runaway teenagers when His Majesty Judge Lucien 'N'-for-Numbnuts Thibeault has taken over your life. It's like he considers himself personally responsible for the legal rights of Corriveau Le Prick Incorporated."

"Nobody was talking about you, McLeod. You're getting paranoid in your old age."

"Detective John 'The Undead' Cardinal tells me not to

be paranoid. That's when I *really* get paranoid. Meanwhile Judge Lucien 'A'-for-asshole Thibeault visits me in my dreams howling about chains of evidence and fruit of the goddam tainted tree. Fucking frogs all stick together."

"Watch your mouth, McLeod." Delorme wasn't that big, but she had a glare that could freeze your blood.

"I'll say what I want, thank you very much. My mother was as French as you—except, unlike you, she wasn't a closet separatist."

"Oh, boy."

"Leave it alone," Cardinal said to Delorme. "You don't want to talk politics with him."

"All I said was the Quebecois have some legitimate grievances. What the hell is he talking about?"

"Can we not get into it, please?"

While McLeod muttered to himself over his sups, Cardinal and Delorme cleared three cases in under an hour: a simple matter of matching initial reports with follow-up faxes announcing that the subject was no longer missing. They organized the remaining cases in descending priority: Two of the reports had been posted nationally, meaning there was no particular reason to think the subjects—one from Newfoundland, one from Prince Edward Island—had ever set foot in Algonquin Bay.

"This one looks interesting." Delorme held up a fax-photo. "She's eighteen but looks thirteen. Only five feet tall and ninety pounds. She was actually seen at the bus station."

"Hang onto it," Cardinal said, as he answered the phone. "Criminal Investigations, Cardinal speaking."

"Len Weisman—yes, I'm in the morgue on a Sunday night—why? Because a certain detective of the female persuasion was making my life a living hell. Does she realize Toronto is an actual city? Does she know how many cases we get? Does she have any idea what kind of pressures we have?"

"The victim was thirteen, Len. She was a *child.*"

"And that's the *only* reason I'm talking to you. Just tell

your junior next time she waits in line like everybody else. Did Chemistry section call you?"

"Nope. All we got is Odontology, and we got that the other day."

"Well, Chemistry should have something for you—they kept her long enough."

"What can you give us, Len?"

"Wasn't a lot to work with—you saw the body—so I'll cut to the chase. One finding on the limbs: The one wrist and one ankle both showed ligature marks, so she was tied up somewhere—Chemistry may have more for you on that. Star attraction? We had one eyeball and fragments of upper lobes of the lungs. Both places, Dr. Gant found signs of petechial hemorrhage. Wouldn't have left a trace if she hadn't been frozen. Never would've seen it."

"You're saying she was strangled?"

"Strangled? No, Dr. Gant doesn't say strangled. Not much neck left, you know—so no ligature marks there and no available hyoid bone. Call the doc if you want, but strangled, no, I don't think we can go out on that particular limb. One way or another, though, this little girl suffocated."

"Any other findings?"

"Talk to Setevic in Chemistry. His report says one fiber: red, trilobal. No blood, no hair—except the girl's."

"Nothing else about the fiber?"

"Talk to Setevic. Oh, there's a note here—they found a bracelet of some kind in her jeans pocket."

"Day she disappeared, Katie was wearing a charm bracelet."

"Right. Says here it's a charm bracelet. You'll get it with the rest of the stuff. Is Detective Delorme there with you?"

"Yes."

"I've never met this woman, but I'm guessing she's good-looking. Sex appeal in the red zone?"

"Yeah, you could say that." Delorme just then was squinting at a fax, creases of concentration between her brows. Cardinal tried and failed not to find it appealing. "You want a phone number or something, Len?"

"Do I ever not. Her attitude is like someone used to getting her way, that's all. In fact, put her on right now. Let me talk to her."

Cardinal handed the phone to Delorme. She closed her eyes and listened. Gradually, the skin over her cheekbones colored—it was like watching the mercury rise in a thermometer. A moment later she placed the receiver gently on the hook. She said, "Okay. That's fine. So some men they don't react well to pressure."

McLeod yelled from across the room, "I heard that, Delorme."

10

THE turnout for Katie Pine's funeral was larger than anyone had expected. Five hundred people showed up at St.
Boniface, a tiny red-brick church on Sumner Street, to pray
over the small, closed coffin. The media were out in force.
Delorme recognized Roger Gwynn and Nick Stoltz from
the *Lode,* Nick Stoltz had got her into hot water as a
teenager by snapping a picture of her and her boyfriend ro-
mantically entwined on a bench in what was then Teachers
College Park. To him and most readers of the *Lode,* it was
simply a picture of autumn splendor, but to Delorme's parents it meant that their daughter had not, after all, spent the
evening with her friends at the sodality. She had been
grounded for two weeks—a punishment that gave her
boyfriend's wandering heart time to conceive an affection
for Delorme's rival. Ever since, photographers had been
assigned a place in Delorme's personal inferno only
slightly cooler than that reserved for rapists.

There was the Sudbury newswoman, with a female camera operator, Delorme noticed, and a three-hundred-pound
sound man. She had seen a CBC van out front, and two
pews up, she recognized a reporter from *The Globe & Mail*
who had done a piece on Delorme after she had put Algonquin Bay's three-term mayor in prison. It's not every day a
child is found murdered on a desolate island in a frozen
lake, but Delorme hadn't figured it for national news.

The *Globe* reporter trained his famished, newshound's
eye on Dorothy Pine, slow with grief, being led up the
front steps. The reporter moved forward, but Jerry Commanda somehow managed to interpose his frame between
him and the grieving mother, and when the aisle cleared,
the reporter had subsided into his pew, apparently nursing
a sudden abdominal spasm.

The police were here not only to pay their respects to a
murdered little girl but also on the off-chance the killer

might show up at the funeral. Delorme was in the last pew, a good vantage point from which to see any lurkers. Cardinal was standing at the front well off to one side, looking somber in his black suit and—Delorme had to admit—handsome in a battered kind of way. Bruise-colored rings under his eyes lent a soulful cast to his appearance that a romantic—and Delorme did not for one minute consider herself a romantic—might find very compelling. Fiercely loyal to his wife, Cardinal, if what Delorme heard was true, despite her bouts with mental illness. It was mentioned only infrequently in the squad room, and then in hushed tones.

As a ticket out of Special Investigations, working a homicide with the subject of her own investigation was not what Delorme would have chosen. Not a way to make friends or influence people, but then that isn't why you go into Special Investigations in the first place.

John Cardinal seemed as uncorrupt as any cop Delorme had ever met; it was hard to give much weight to Musgrave's worries about him. Before the funeral began, he'd chatted amiably with the old priest, whom Delorme pegged as a not-too-secret drinker. She hadn't thought of Cardinal as a churchgoer; she'd never seen him in St. Vincent's, but then he'd hardly be likely to attend the French church.

The truth was, she didn't know him well. The nature of her job kept her aloof from the rest of the force. And one thing you learn in Special: Everyone has a story, and it's never the story you expect. So she put the RCMP–Kyle Corbett business and the Toronto rumors into one compartment of her mind, and concentrated on watching those citizens of Algonquin Bay who thought it worthwhile to attend the funeral of a murdered girl.

Arsenault and Collingwood were outside, videotaping mourners and license plates—a purely speculative endeavor, since they had neither a suspect nor a license plate at this point.

Suppose the killer shows, Delorme wondered. Suppose

he were to sit down right next to me, instead of this white-haired lady in the parrot-green suit. How would I recognize him? By smell? Fangs and a long tail? Hooves? Delorme was not very experienced with murderers, but she understood that expecting a killer to look different from Cardinal or the mayor or the boy next door was complete fantasy. He could be the heavyset man in the Maple Leafs jersey—what kind of slob wears a hockey sweater to a funeral? Or he could be the Indian in the overalls that said Algonquin Plumbing on the back—why wasn't he with the group surrounding Mrs. Pine? She recognized at least three former high-school classmates; the killer might be one of them. She remembered pictures from the books on serial killers—Berkowitz, Bundy, Dahmer—unremarkable men, all. No, no. Katie Pine's killer would *be* different, but he wouldn't necessarily *look* different.

You should be making me do more, Delorme thought to herself, as she looked at Cardinal. You should be on my back night and day, getting me to chase down even the slenderest threads. We should be making Forensic's life a misery till they cough up everything they've got.

Instead, Cardinal had somehow got Dyson to hand her the lowest-priority stuff in his In box—his bloody burglaries and robberies. A knight move? Keep her too busy to run her check on him? Then again, it could be just business as usual at The Great Hall of Chauvinists. Lucky for them I happen to be proud of my work in Special. I'm single and I'm still young—young enough, anyway—and I can devote every waking hour to an investigation if I want. What else do I have? she might have added on a darker day. What a thrill it had been to close in on the mayor, to nail his corrupt little friends. And Delorme had done all that herself. But Dyson and Cardinal and McLeod and the rest, sometimes she cursed their anglophone heads, the bunch of them.

"Have to pay your dues, Delorme," Dyson had quacked at her this morning. She was tempted to grab the honey-glazed doughnut off his desk and wolf it down, just to see the expression on his face. "Everybody pays their dues. You don't come onto the squad and go straight to the top; it doesn't work that way."

"I've only been six years in Special. That counts for nothing, I suppose. I don't want to work his damn robberies, his break-and-enters."

"Everybody works robbery. You will, too, because A—" and here he started counting off on those weird flat fingers of his, which always drove Delorme crazy. "Cardinal is heading up a major murder case and does not have time to handle anything else; B: because you are his junior on the squad; and C: because Cardinal bloody well *asked* me to put you on them. End of mystery, end of discussion. Look, you need an excuse to get away from him anyway, right? Get a little distance? You can hardly investigate the guy when you're sharing an unmarked all day. In fact, you could do worse than to check out his house—should the opportunity present itself."

"I can't search his place without a warrant."

"Of course not. I merely point out that you're partners. You will spend a lot of time together. If you should find yourself in his house—well, use your imagination. Not, I hasten to add, that I think he's guilty."

"I can't run a check when I'm clearing old cases. When am I supposed to look at the Corbett files?"

"I have been known to approve overtime, you know. I'm not the Scrooge people like McLeod and Cardinal make me out to be."

"With respect, D. S., why are we pursuing this now? The Pine case, surely it outweighs all this."

"Kyle Corbett is not just a former drug dealer and current counterfeiter. He's a stone-cold killer, as the world will know, if we ever catch the bastard. If someone's been tipping him off, that is not a petty crime. It's corruption, it's aiding and abetting a murderer, and I want the guilty party off my team—if he is in fact on my team—and in jail where he belongs."

"Me, I think we should both be down in Toronto chasing Forensics."

"Forensics can do their job without our breath condensing on their necks. By the way, there's a stack of burglaries in that backlog that I expect you to clear by the end of the week. We all know who's doing them, it's just a matter of nailing the little creep."

Snow flurries were ticking at the windowpane behind him, and the window reflected as a perfect white rhomboid on Dyson's polished head. Oh, she wanted to smack him.

Now, a pretty Indian soloist finished her rendition of "Abide With Me," and the priest stepped into the pulpit. He spoke for a few moments about the promise that was Katie Pine's life. He spoke warmly of her intelligence and her sense of humor, and the sobbing in the front rows intensified. If it were not for his slight hesitation every time he said Katie's name, Delorme might have thought he had actually known the girl. Holy water was sprinkled on the coffin. Incense was burned. The 23rd Psalm was sung. And then the coffin was trundled to the back of the church, hoisted awkwardly by four pallbearers into a waiting hearse, and driven away to the cemetery where all that remained of Katie Pine would be transformed into smoke and ash.

LATER that afternoon, Delorme carried a box of personal stuff out of her old office and dumped it on her new desk, back-to-back with Cardinal's. She stared down at his things without a trace of guilt. Squad room desks were one right next to another; anything left out was on public display. McLeod's desk was a landfill of overstuffed manila folders, a junkyard of evidence envelopes, affidavits, sup reports: geysers of paper shooting from accordion files.

Beside it, Cardinal's desk was by contrast a field lying fallow. The metal desktops were made to resemble, not at all convincingly, fine oak. Most of Cardinal's with its swirls of faux grain lay exposed to the open air. Pinned to the corkboard above it was a copy of Dyson's latest memo. (The new Beretta automatics: every officer expected to become a shining example with the new weapon by end of

February, and let's show the opposition what's what in the annual contest, which the Mounties, damn them, always won. Dyson did not think this could be blamed on budgetary imbalances.)

There was a picture of Cardinal's daughter, a pretty girl with her father's confident smile, and beside this, a parking ticket. Delorme leaned over without touching anything to read the address on the parking ticket: 465 Fleming Street, right downtown, it could mean anything.

The Rolodex was open to Dorothy Pine's number. Delorme flipped it back to A, and for the next twenty minutes made her way through to F, not looking for anything definite. It was full of hastily scrawled names that meant nothing to her, along with the numbers of various lawyers, probation officers, and social workers that any cop would have on hand. There was Kyle Corbett, but you'd expect that. It listed three different addresses and several phone numbers, which Delorme copied into her notebook.

There was a noise from out front, and Delorme turned back to face her own desk. Low voices, laughter, a slamming locker. Delorme lifted the handset on Cardinal's phone and hit the automatic redial button. While waiting for it to pick up, she stared at a snapshot pinned next to Dyson's memo. It was a felon, obviously—a huge man with a flat head made flatter by a brush cut. He was leaning back, apparently at ease, on a car, his weight seriously depressing the vehicle's springs. Cops often kept pictures of their favorite collars, men who had shot them, that kind of thing.

Delorme's reflections were interrupted by a voice she recognized. "Office of Forensic Medicine."

"Oh, sorry. Wrong number."

Cardinal's top drawer was open, hardly the habit of a guilty man—on the other hand, possibly the calculated gesture of a man who was very guilty indeed.

The door banged open and a voice called out, "Well, well. Imagine my surprise to find the office of Special Investigations taking her own private inventory."

"Give me a break, McLeod. I work here now, remember?"

"On Sundays, too, apparently." McLeod was carrying a big cardboard box labeled CANADIAN TIRE. He eyed her suspiciously over the top through red-rimmed lids. "Thought I was the only dedicated bastard in this place."

"You are. I was just moving some of my stuff over," said Delorme.

"Fine. Welcome. Make yourself at home." McLeod slammed the box down on his desk. Something inside it clanked. "Just stay away from my desk."

11

CARDINAL called Vlatko Setevic in Forensic's Micro section. They had taken hair and fiber from Katie Pine's thawed-out body.

"Quite a few fibers we found. Indoor/outdoor stuff. The kind they use in cars or basements. Fibers are red, trilobal."

"Can you narrow it down to makes? Ford? Chrysler?"

"No chance. It's very common, except for the color."

"Tell me about the hair."

"Exactly one hair we found—other than the girl's own. Three inches long. Brown. Probably Caucasian."

Delorme looked disgusted when Cardinal told her the results. "It's no use for anything," she said, "unless we get another body."

Cardinal spent the next two days on the phone, chasing down the out-of-town cases: calls to originating police departments, calls to parents or others who made the initial complaints. Delorme helped out, when she wasn't following up on old robberies. They cleared five more cases. That left two that looked like they might have finished up in Algonquin Bay: a St. John's girl who had been seen in the local bus station and a sixteen-year-old boy from Mississauga, near Toronto.

Todd Curry had been reported missing in December. The notice was just the standard fax sent to all police departments in such cases; the photo was not high-definition. One thing caught Cardinal's eye: The kid's size was listed as five-four, ninety-five pounds. To a killer with a taste for runts, Todd Curry might look like prime prey.

Cardinal called the Peel Regional Police and established that none of the boy's parents or friends had heard from him in the past two months. Missing Persons gave him the name of a relative in Sudbury, Clark Curry.

"Mr. Curry, this is John Cardinal, Algonquin Police."

"I imagine you're calling about Todd."

"What makes you say that, sir?"

"The only time I hear from the police is when Todd is in trouble. Look, I'm just his uncle, I've done all I can. I can't take him back this time."

"We haven't found him. We're still trying to track him down."

"A Mississauga boy is being sought by the Algonquin Bay police? He's really turning into a federal case."

"Has Todd contacted you since December? December twentieth, to be exact?"

"No. He was missing all through Christmas—his parents were frantic, as you can imagine. He called me from Huntsville—this was the day he took off—called from Huntsville and says he's on the train, can he stay with me. I told him he could, but he never arrived, and I haven't heard anything since. You have to understand, this is one messed-up kid."

"In what way, sir? Drugs?"

"Todd got his first sniff of glue when he was ten and hasn't been the same since. Some kids can mess with drugs; other kids, they get one whiff and it becomes their *vocation.* Todd's one joy in life is getting high—if you can call that joy. Mind you, Dave and Edna say he's gone completely clean, but I doubt it. I doubt it very much."

"Will you do me a favor, sir? Will you call me if you do hear from Todd?" He gave Curry the number and hung up.

Cardinal hadn't taken a train in years, although he never passed by the station without remembering the long trip out west he and Catherine had taken on their honeymoon. They had spent practically the entire trip sequestered in their narrow, rocking bed. Cardinal checked with the CNR and learned that Huntsville was still the second-to-last stop on the Northlander before Algonquin Bay. There was no way to tell if Todd got off in South River or Algonquin Bay or not. He could have stayed in Huntsville, he could've continued north to Temagami or even Hearst.

Cardinal took a run over to the Crisis Center, at the corner of Station and Sumner. Algonquin Bay had no youth hostel, and sometimes runaway kids ended up in the center, which was just two blocks from the train station. The place was meant for domestic emergencies—mostly battered wives, but it was run by a lanky ex-priest named Ned Fellowes, and Fellowes had been known to take in the occasional stray if he had room.

Like most of the houses in the center of town, Algonquin Bay's Crisis Center was a two-story, red-brick affair with a roof of gray shingle, steeply pitched to slow the buildup of snow. Some workmen repairing the roof of the verandah had covered the front of the house with scaffolding. Cardinal could hear them cursing in French overhead as he rang the bell—*tabarnac, ostie*—taking their swear words from the Church, unlike the Anglos, who wield the usual sexual lexicon. We swear by what we're afraid of, Cardinal mused, but it was not a thought he wanted to dwell on.

"Yes, I remember him. That's not a good likeness, though." Ned Fellowes handed the faxphoto back to Cardinal. "Stayed with us for one night, I think, around Christmastime."

"Can you tell me exactly what night that was?"

Fellowes led him into a small front office in what used to be a living room; a fireplace of painted brick was filled with psychology texts and social-work periodicals. Fellowes consulted a large maroon ledger, running his finger down lists of names. "Todd Curry. Stayed the night of December twentieth, a Friday. Left Saturday. I remember I was surprised, because he had asked to stay till the Monday. But he came in Saturday lunchtime and said he'd found a cool place to stay—an abandoned house on Main West."

"Main West. There's a wreck of a place where St. Claire's used to be. Is that the one? By the Castle Hotel?"

"I wouldn't know. He certainly didn't leave a forwarding address. Just wolfed down a couple of sandwiches and left."

THERE was only one empty house on Main West. It was not in the downtown area, but a couple of blocks beyond it, where the street turned residential. St. Claire's convent had been torn down five years before, exposing a brick wall with the faint outlines of a sign exhorting one to drink Northern Ale—a product of a local brewery out of business for at least three decades. After the convent, other houses had fallen one by one, making way for Country Style's ever-expanding parking lot. Surrounded by overgrown weeds and stumps of long-dead trees, the house leaned in its corner lot like one last rotten tooth waiting to be pulled.

It made sense, Cardinal considered, as he drove down Macpherson toward the lake: The place was just a block from D'Anunzio's—a teen hangout—and a stone's throw from the high school; a young drifter couldn't ask for a better address. A slight humming sensation started up in Cardinal's bloodstream.

The Castle Hotel came up on his right, and then he parked in front of a jagged, tumbledown fence tangled in shrubbery. He went to the front gate and looked through bare overhanging boughs at the place where the house used to be. He could see clear across the block to D'Anunzio's over on Algonquin Avenue.

The acrid smell of burnt wood was strong, even though the ruins were covered with snow. They had been bulldozed off to one side in a heap. Cardinal stood with hands on hips like a man assessing the damage. A charred two-by-four pierced the thin coverlet of snow, pointing a black, accusing finger at the clouds.

12

DELORME wondered if Cardinal was making any headway. It was irritating as hell to go back to this small stuff when there was a killer out there. Wasting half the morning with paperwork on Arthur "Woody" Wood, Delorme came to realize how badly she wanted to nail Katie Pine's killer. Perhaps only a woman could want to punish a child killer as badly. Delorme was thirty-three and had spent many hours fantasizing about having a child, even if she had to raise it herself. The idea that someone could snuff out a young life put her in a rage that she could barely control.

But was she allowed to go out and work on tracking down this sick, this disgusting, this grossly evil *thing*? No. She got to interview Arthur "Woody" Wood, the poster boy for petty crime. Delorme had been following him along Oak Street in an unmarked car. After he sped up to make the light, she had pulled him over for "burning an amber," only to see a vintage MacIntosh all-tube amplifier on the seat beside him. She had read the description to him from her notebook there on the street, right down to the serial number.

"Okay," Woody said now, as she led him out of the cells. "Suppose by some freak of nature you get me for one little case. I can't exactly see that putting me away for life, can you, Officer Delorme? You're French, I guess. They tried to teach me French all the way through grade school, but I don't know, it never stuck. Miss Bissonette—man, was she a Nazi. Are you married, by the way?"

Delorme ignored it all. "I hope you haven't sold the rest of your haul, Woody. Because in addition to going to Kingston for ten years, you might have to make restitution, and then where will you be? It would be a nice gesture if you gave the stuff back. It might go easier for you."

Engaging criminals are a rarity, and when one comes along, police tend to be overly grateful. Arthur "Woody"

Wood was a hopelessly amiable young man. He had un-
fashionably long sideburns that gave him the look of a
fifties rockabilly singer. He had a bounce in his walk and a
rangy slouch to his shoulders that put people at their
ease—especially women, as Delorme was finding out. She
was right now having an argument with her own body: *No,*
you will *not* react this way to the physical attractions of
this silly little thief. I won't allow it.

As she led him toward the interview room, Woody
yelled a greeting to Sergeant Flower, with whom he proceeded to carry on a lively conversation. Sergeant Flower
only stopped gabbing when she registered Delorme's high-
intensity scowl. Then Woody had to say hi to Larry Burke,
just coming in. Burke had apprehended him six years before with a car radio in his fist—*installing* it, Woody had
claimed.

"Woody, listen to me," Delorme said in the interview
room.

Someone had left *The Toronto Star* on one of the chairs,
and Woody snatched it up. "The Leafs, man. I can't believe
this team. It's like they have this appetite for self-destruc-
tion. This *craving.* So unhealthy."

"Woody, listen to me." Delorme took the paper with its
two-column headline: NO LEADS ON THE WINDIGO KILLER.
"That bunch of burglaries down Water Road is giving me
hives, okay? I've got you cold for the Willow Drive job,
but I know you did the others, too. So why don't you save
us both a lot of time and energy—confess to one, we'll
maybe forget the others."

"Now, hold on."

"Confess to one, that's all I'm saying. And I'll see what
I can do. I know you did the others, too."

"Hold your horses, there, Officer Delorme. You don't
know I did them." Woody's grin was beatific; it held no
trace of guile or suspicion or malign intent. Honest men
should have such grins. "You're indulging in exaggeration,
plain and simple. If you *suspect* me of some old burglary,
well, I can understand that—I have been known to keep

company with objects not my own, after all. But *suspect* is not *know.* You could drive a Mack truck between *suspect* and *know.*"

"There's another count, Woody. Suppose somebody actually saw you? Then what? Suppose somebody actually saw a blue ChevyVan pulling away from the Nipissing Motor Court?" The proprietor of the motel hadn't in fact got a decent look at him, but he had seen someone driving off in a van just like Woody's. Three thousand dollars' worth of TVs missing. No jewelry.

"Well, if the guy saw me, I guess you'd put me in a lineup. Ms. Delorme, you're single, aren't you?"

"Suppose they saw your van, Woody? Suppose we have a license plate?"

"Well, if they give you the license plate, I guess you better hang me for that one. You look single to me. You have the air of a single person. Officer Delorme, you ought to get married. I don't know how I'd get through life without Martha and Truckie. Family? Children? Why, it halves the sorrows of life and doubles the pleasures. It's the single most important thing there is. And police work involves a lot of pressures."

"Try and pay attention, Woody. A blue ChevyVan was seen driving away from the job on Water Road. You say you were home, but other witnesses say your van was not parked in your driveway. Add that to the one who saw your van at the scene, and what do you come up with? Ten years."

"How can you even say that to me? Eyewitnesses are notoriously unreliable. Hell, you know as well as I do, nobody ever sees me. I like to go about my work undisturbed. God's sake, ma'am, I didn't get into this business to meet people."

Sergeant Flower knocked on the door. "His wife's here. She paid his bail."

"I'm going to nail you for the whole bunch, Woody. You can make a plea, now, or you can make me catch you. But I'm going to nail you for the whole bunch."

"If I wanted to *meet* people, I'd be a mugger."

* * *

ONE ability Delorme prided herself on was a knack for putting anything that wasn't immediately essential out of her mind. When, later that afternoon, she drove along the winding south branch of Peninsula Road, Arthur Wood had left her thoughts entirely, and she was once more in the murky waters of Corporal Musgrave's suspicions.

The road got narrower and narrower, until tree branches heavy with snow scratched at the roof of the car. The white woods reminded her of a sleigh ride long ago. Thirteen-year-old Ray Duroc and she had lain among the heap of juvenile bodies and kissed with closed mouths until her lips were bruised. Last she heard, Ray was living on the other side of the world—Australia or New Zealand or some damn place—where the trees were green instead of white and the sun actually put out some heat.

She noted the names on the mailboxes, then took a sharp left, and then she was almost past the driveway before she saw it. There was no name nailed to the tree. She parked the car on the side of the road and went down the driveway on foot. There was a big brown Mercedes at the end of the drive. Delorme didn't even want to think what it had cost.

After Corporal Musgrave, former senior constable Joe Burnside was pure oxygen. Joe Burnside was blonde, six-foot-four in his socks—where does the RCMP find this species? Delorme wondered—and happy as a clam. "You're working Special? I know you. You're the one that bagged Mayor Wells! Come in! Come in!"

Delorme shed her boots and joined him in the kitchen, where he poured her a steaming cup of coffee. She revised her estimate: six-foot-six if he's an inch.

"Man, you gotta get out of police work and into the money," he was telling her ten minutes later. They were sitting in overstuffed armchairs that faced a blinding white view of Four Mile Bay. "With your background? Your achievements? You're perfect! Look at me—eight years a corporal in the Commercial Crimes Unit and now I've got

my own business—me! Joe Burnside! Trust me, I'm the
last guy I would have thought could do it, and I'm telling
you I'm turning offers away. There's more work than we
can handle. And you know where it's not going? It's not
going to the RCMP. Excuse me a second." He crossed to a
couch where a bony old collie was curled up asleep. He
bent down close to its head and yelled, loud enough for it
to hurt Delorme's ears: "Get offa there, you lazy-ass good-
for-nothing mutt!"

The dog opened a glassy eye and regarded him calmly.

"Deaf as a post," he muttered, and pulled the dog from
the couch by its collar, leading it like a pony to the fireplace, where it lay down once more and returned immediately to its canine dreams. "Everybody says I should put
him down. Well, people that don't have dogs say put him
down. They don't cost you a dime for fifteen years, then
the minute they get sick, people say kill 'em. Sorry, you
want to talk business. Puts me off, though. People have no
loyalty. How long you been doing white-collar?"

"Six years."

"You see what's happening? With cutbacks? I don't
know about you guys, but I'll tell you the Mounties are
just toothless. Toothless. They're taking everybody off
white-collar and putting them on the street, you know
why? Because street work is visible and white-collar isn't.
People like to see their tax dollars at work. And with the
Mounties going out of business, that means someone's
gotta take up the slack. Good ol' private enterprise.
Which—I'm happy to say—is me. A two-month investigation on copyright infringement? Piracy? Forty thousand
bucks. And Corporate America is happy to pay it—it's
mostly U.S. companies that hire us—and the great thing
about Americans, they don't trust you unless you ask for a
lot of money."

He's born-again, Delorme thought. He should be a
preacher. But all she said was, "Kyle Corbett."

"Ohhh," Burnside groaned theatrically. "Don't remind
me. Kyle Corbett. That one really hurt."

"You had the background sewn up. You had solid stuff. It was you and Jerry Commanda all the way."

"We had a source. Good source, too. Guy named Nicky Bell worked with Corbett for years, but happened to be facing an unrelated charge on computer porn that Corbett didn't know about."

"And he gave you a time and a place."

"*A* time? *A* place? No, no, no, Nicky Bell was the best singer since Gordy Lightfoot. He gave us *months* of stuff. Me and Jerry picked that bird clean. But the big windup was gonna be at the Crystal Disco out behind Airport Road, and for that we needed one of your guys. We got John Cardinal—smart guy, but always depressed it seemed to me."

"What happened then?"

The affable manner disappeared. Burnside's face—formerly as bright and wide open as Four Mile Bay—suddenly darkened. It was like an eclipse. "You know what happened," he said. "Or you wouldn't be here."

"You hit the club. You came up empty."

"Bingo."

"What went wrong?"

"Nothing. That's just the point, isn't it? Everything went right. Everything went exactly according to plan. It was like watching the insides of a Swiss watch. Except for the ending. Corbett was tipped off. You know it, and I know it. But if you're expecting me to say who I think did it, you're barking up the wrong tree. There's no proof of anything."

"What did your source tell you?"

"Nicky? If you think anybody's ever going to see Nicky Bell again, you're in the wrong line of work. Wife confirmed there was a suitcase missing from his house, some clothes were gone, but I think that's just cover. I think Kyle Corbett fed him to the fishes."

The dog was back on the couch, but Burnside didn't seem to notice.

As Delorme was putting her boots on, he looked her up and down. She got a lot of that, but for once she didn't think it was sexual. "You're working that Windigo thing, too, aren't you? Well, I know you are."

"Yeah, I am. I'm moving out of Special."

"Windigo's an ugly case."

"Uh-huh."

"A real ugly case, Ms. Delorme. But investigating your own partner, well, there's a lot of cops—Mounties, OPP, you name it—a *hell* of a lot of cops would say investigating your own partner's a lot uglier."

"Thanks for the coffee. I needed warming up." Delorme did up the snaps of her coat, put on her gloves. "But I never said who I was investigating."

13

D'ANUNZIO'S was still a magnet for teenagers, just as it had been when Cardinal was growing up. Part fruit store, part soda fountain, at first glance D'Anunzio's had always been an unlikely hangout. But Joe D'Anunzio, with the manners of a monk and the girth of an opera star, numbered everyone who came into his store among his friends. He looked after his soda fountain with the expertise of an old-time bartender and treated his young patrons like his old ones, letting them linger for hours in the wooden booths at the back over their Cokes and chips and chocolate bars. As kids, Cardinal and the other altar boys had always trooped over from the cathedral after Mass, and later, when they had grown out of their surplices and soutanes, they would come to D'Anunzio's instead of Mass—substituting Rothmans and Player's for the frankincense, ice-cream floats and Aero bars for the bread and wine.

Cardinal sipped his coffee and watched the kid playing the video game.

In Cardinal's day it had been a pinball machine. A pinball was more physical, less hypothetical, and for your nickel you got lots of bells and rattles. Under the ministrations of the youth at the controls, its replacement uttered an irritating series of beeps and boops.

"When did that house burn down, Joe?"

"Over on Main there?" Joe served cherry Cokes to two blond girls who had their hair cut identically: buzzed on one side, long on the other. Both sported nostril studs, which looked to Cardinal like chrome zits. In his day the girls had worn their hair long and parted in the middle, giving them—at least to Cardinal's nostalgic eye—a gentle, soulful look. Why did these girls scar themselves with fashion?

Joe came back the length of the counter to the cash register. "November, I think it was. Early November. Must've been five or six fire trucks out there."

"You sure it wasn't later? After New Year's?"

"Definitely not. It was before my hernia operation, and that was November tenth." Joe swung his girth around and poured more coffee into Cardinal's cup. "How could you miss a fire like that?"

Two missing kids. And November was when Catherine had started to drift. Cardinal had had other things on his mind.

He took his coffee to the other end of the counter near the front window. On the west side of the square, a funeral was coming out of the cathedral, four men in black suits bearing a coffin on their shoulders. They had to be freezing with no overcoats on. Across the square in the empty lot stood a man wearing a green and gold parka with matching toque. He was writing notes of some kind, his breath ragged plumes lit by the sun.

Cardinal left the soda fountain and dodged through the traffic on Algonquin. The man was filling in a form on a clipboard. Cardinal introduced himself.

"Tom Cooper. Cooper Construction. Just certifying our lack of progress with the demolition guys. They were supposed to clear the entire mess away by Tuesday. It's now Friday. It's hard to find professionals in this town. I mean real professionals."

"Mr. Cooper, I imagine a contractor keeps an eye out for lots like this. You wouldn't happen to know of any other vacant houses on Main West?"

"Nope. Not on Main West. Got one over on MacPherson. Another one out on Trout Lake. But in town here they don't stay empty long."

"It's just I heard there was an empty place on Main West. Empty in December, anyway. Some teenagers were hanging out there, possibly a drug thing. You hear about anywhere like that?" Cardinal could hear the hush in his voice. Such a frail thread, this lead, the slightest weight might snap it.

Cooper pressed the clipboard under one elbow and squinted west up the street, as if an empty house might appear there. "Nothing on Main that I know of. Oh, but maybe you're thinking of Timothy." He swung back around, seeming to pivot on his heels. "It's not really a Main Street address, but it's on the corner."

"The corner of Timothy and Main? By the railroad tracks?"

Cooper nodded. "That's it. No way teenagers were hanging out there, though. Place is sealed tight as a drum. It's been in probate court for over two years. Contentious family's what I heard."

"Mr. Cooper, thank you. You've been very helpful."

"This wouldn't be in reference to that wretched Windigo thing, would it?"

Cooper, like everyone else in Algonquin Bay, was keeping abreast of the case. Any suspects? Was it strictly a local thing? Any chance of the Mounties coming in on it? You couldn't blame people for being curious. Cardinal had to listen to a theory involving a satanic cult before he could get free.

He drove the half-dozen blocks to Timothy Street, taking it slow over the ridge of the railroad tracks. The northern line was mostly freights taking oil up to Cochrane and Timmins. The hoot of its whistle as it crossed Timothy woke Cardinal every night when he was a kid. A lonely sound but somehow comforting, like the cry of a loon.

The house was an old Victorian place with a wraparound verandah. The red brick above the boarded-up windows was blackened with years of railway soot, so that the building looked not just blind but black-eyed. Massive icicles were fixed to the roof corners like gargoyles. The yard, which was large by Algonquin Bay standards, was surrounded by a high hedge.

Cardinal got out of the car and stood on the snow where the front path should have been. Except for the faint hieroglyphics of bird tracks, there was not a single footprint.

The stairs to the verandah were filled in with hardpack

snow. Gripping the rail, Cardinal stomped his way up and examined the front door, also boarded over. The public trustee's seal was intact. The lock had not been tampered with. He checked the boarded-up windows, and then did the same around the side of the house.

The crossing bell started to clang, and as he checked the side door a train clattered by, a long one.

Anyone breaking into this house would be likely to go through the back: There was nothing there but the high hedge and the railroad tracks. And thieves liked basement windows. Trouble was, the basement windows were buried below the snow. Using the heel of his boot, Cardinal dug a trench along the back wall of the house.

"Damn." He'd scraped the back of his leg on the thick crust of ice. About four feet from the corner he found the top of a window. After clearing away the crust, he pulled the rest of the snow away with his hands.

"Gotcha," he said quietly.

THE Provincial Court in Algonquin Bay is on McGinty Street. It's a modern, plain-brick building with no pretensions; it might be a school or a clinic. Perhaps in compensation for its plainness, the sign that announces it as Provincial Court, District of Nipissing, is the size of a highway billboard.

The receptionist told him Justice Paul Gagnon was in traffic court until lunch, and lunch was booked for a meeting.

"See if he'll squeeze me in, will you. It's for the Katie Pine case." Cardinal knew Gagnon would never grant him a search warrant to pursue some runaway Mississauga youth who was now over the age of sixteen. He filled out the necessary form, and while he was waiting for court to get out he called in to headquarters. Delorme was out on the Woody case and was not expected back for at least another hour. Cardinal felt a twinge of guilt for leaving her out of this; she'd been upset about handling his backlog.

Justice Gagnon was a small man with very small feet and a toupee that was two shades lighter than his hair. He was a few years younger than Cardinal, a completely political animal whose robe drowned him as if he were a child. His voice was a reedy pipe.

"Sounds pretty feeble, Detective." Gagnon hung his robe on a coathook and put on a camel-hair sports coat. "You *think* the person who killed Katie Pine and abducted Billy LaBelle may have stayed in the Cowart house? And you base this on information received secondhand from Ned Fellowes at the Crisis Center. Information that doesn't even relate directly to the killer but to another missing person—this Todd Curry." Gagnon checked his tie in the mirror.

"The house was broken into, Your Worship. I'm sure the parties contesting the will would want that investigated anyway. But if I go through them it's going to take a long time and upset people who are already upset about the will."

Gagnon's skeptical eye fixed him in the mirror. "For all you know, it may be one of the family who broke in. Maybe to haul off some contested stick of furniture. Family heirloom. Who knows?"

"The window is only about ten inches high, maybe two and a half feet wide."

"Jewelry, then. Grampa's pocket watch. My point, Detective, is that you have no substantive reason to suspect a killer was there."

"It's the only place I have reason to suspect the killer set foot, other than the shafthead on Windigo Island. He likes deserted buildings maybe. The Curry kid was last seen alive saying he was going to stay in an abandoned house on Main Street."

Gagnon sat down behind a desk that dwarfed him and examined the form. "Detective, this address is on Timothy."

"It's at the corner of Main. It looks like it's on Main. The Curry kid was from out of town. He probably thought it was Main Street."

Justice Gagnon looked at his watch. "I've got to run. I have a lunch with Bob Greene." Bob Greene was the local member of parliament, a voluble fool of the back benches.

"Just sign the warrant, Your Worship, I'll be out of your hair. We have zero leads on Billy LaBelle, and as for Katie Pine, this is it. This is all we've got." Katie Pine was the magic number—Katie Pine and Billy LaBelle were a combination that would slip the tumblers in Gagnon's tiny heart. Cardinal could hear the mechanism turning over: Famous case equals opportunity. Opportunity seized equals advancement. Personal advancement equals justice.

The J.P. furrowed his toy brow, timing his resistance like a modestly talented actor. "If there were people living in this house, no way would I sign this. No way would I let you disrupt a sovereign household on grounds this tenuous."

"Believe me, Your Worship, I know how tenuous this is. I wish I had something ironclad to give you, but unfortunately the killer decided not to leave his name and address next to Katie Pine's body."

"That's not a high moral tone, I hope. You're not lecturing me, are you?"

"God, no. If I wanted to lecture J.P.s I'd have been a politician."

Justice Gagnon vanished into his overcoat as if into a fog, then reemerged decisively from cuffs and collar. He snatched up the Bible from his desk and shoved it at Cardinal. "Do you swear the contents in the application are true, so help you God?"

FIVE minutes later, Cardinal was back at the Cowart place, scooping snow away in handfuls from in front of the basement window. His knees were numb as wood. The snow was stratified into alternate layers of powder and ice. Cardinal went back to the car and retrieved a shovel from the trunk.

There were crowbar marks at both ends of the two-by-four that held the plywood in place, and the nails were loose. The two-by-four came away easily, then the plywood. There was no pane of glass behind it.

Cardinal removed his down coat, and the frigid air sucked the breath out of him. He dropped to his knees and crawled backward into the opening, lowering himself inside. Snow got under his shirt and into his pants, melting against his skin. He could feel a platform, possibly a table, under his foot. Whoever had broken in had probably put it there to ease his exit.

Cardinal pulled his coat inside after him, fought with the zipper, then stood there on the table flapping his arms and exclaiming at the cold. The few foot-candles of light that squeezed through the window did little to ease the darkness.

He climbed down from the table—a laundry table, he could now see—and switched on his flashlight. It was a heavy-duty instrument that took six D-cells and on occasion had doubled as a billy club; the glass was cracked and the tube dented. It swept a white beam like a cape over the silent furnace, the washer and dryer, a tool bench he immediately envied. There was a drop saw he'd seen going at Canadian Tire for close to five hundred.

Even in the cold, he could smell the stone and dust, the raw old wood, the laundry smells from the washer and dryer. He opened a door, breaking old spiderwebs with his flashlight, and found shelves of preserves: peaches, prunes, even a gallon of red peppers that looked like fresh hearts.

The stairs were new, unfinished, and open. The flashlight beam revealed no obvious footprints, but Cardinal kept to the edges and took the stairs two at a time to preserve any marks he might have missed.

The door opened to the kitchen. Cardinal stood for a moment to take in the feel of the house. Cold and dark, it exuded despair. Cardinal held in check the excitement of the chase, the sense of something about to happen. He had long ago learned to distrust such feelings; they were almost always wrong. Evidence of intruders did not mean a killer had been here, or even the errant Todd Curry.

The kitchen looked untouched. A thin layer of dust covered every surface. A narrow flight of stairs was tucked in the corner with a cupboard underneath. Cardinal lifted the latch with the toe of his boot, revealing neat rows of canned food. On the wall above the cupboard, a calendar from a local sporting goods store showed a man fishing in a plaid hunter's jacket with a little boy laughing beside him. A sudden memory of Kelly, a summer vacation, a cottage: her little girl's excitement at catching the fish, her squeamishness at baiting the hook. How his daughter's brassy hair had flashed against the deep blue sky. The calendar showed July, two years ago, the month the owner had died.

In the plastic garbage pail he found nothing but a crushed doughnut carton from Tim Hortons.

The dining room was furnished with heavy old furniture, and Cardinal, no expert in such matters, had no idea if it was antique or reproduction. The painting on the wall looked old and vaguely famous, but Cardinal was no art critic, either. Kelly had been appalled one day to discover he had no idea who the Group of Seven were, stars of Canadian art history apparently. The glass doors of a cabinet displayed pretty glassware, neatly arranged. Cardinal opened a cupboard and found bottles of Armagnac and Seagram's V.O. The chair at the head of the table was the only one with arms, and the fabric was a good deal more worn than the others. Had the old man continued to eat at the place of honor long after his family had dispersed? Had he sat here, imagining his wife and children around him?

Cardinal's flashlight beam found a pair of sliding doors, presumably leading to the living room, but they were frozen shut. He returned to the kitchen and took the back stairs to the second floor.

Upstairs, the bedrooms showed no sign of disturbance. He lingered briefly in the master bedroom, the last one to be occupied. There was a small television on an antique dresser, which would have been easy to steal.

The bathroom cabinet contained antihistamines, laxatives, Fixodent, and a gigantic bottle of Frosst 222s.

Cardinal went down the main stairway into the front den. An old piano took up most of the space. A pair of elaborate silver candelabra stood on top, surrounded by photographs of the Cowart family. A closer examination of the piano lid showed that the candelabra had been moved, the hexagonal bases had left their outlines in the dust, and the candle stubs looked fairly recent. So some-one had sat at the piano by candlelight. Possibly Todd Curry. The lid of the keyboard was smudged with hand-prints. Cardinal shuddered; his bones ached from the cold.

The living room looked like a stage set: two armchairs, plant stand with dead plant, circular rug in front of brick fireplace. The fireplace had been used. The ashes of a log fire lay in the grate, covered with a white dusting of snow. Yes, you would need a fire—no heat, no electricity. Any-one planning to stay here in December would have made a fire right away. A fire would have lit the room up. Wouldn't they be afraid someone would see the smoke? A normal person would be, but I'm not looking for a normal person, Cardinal told himself; I'm looking for a runaway drug user and a child killer, and God knows what else.

Cardinal swung his flashlight past a mantelpiece, past a large television. Above the couch hung a dark old painting, a man in black, a Spaniard, judging by the pointy little beard. His cape was a flowing black velvet with unusual markings.

Beneath this, the couch looked as if someone had up-ended a gallon of paint over the back. The design in the fabric was completely obliterated. Then Cardinal leaned closer and saw that it was not paint but blood. Blood in large quantities. He shone his flashlight on the wall and saw now that what he had taken to be a wallpaper pattern was in fact droplets of blood—droplets flung upward, as if from someone swinging a heavy instrument. There was blood on the painting, too, he now saw. Those marks on the Spaniard's cloak.

He stood in front of the couch, sweeping the flashlight slowly from one end to the other. One of the cushions was bare, the cover having been removed. A burglar could have used the seat cover to carry booty outside, but what did the killer use it for? He didn't bother to steal those silver candelabra, Cardinal thought, or the tiny television upstairs. He doesn't do this for money.

Cardinal was shivering with cold—at least he thought it was the cold—and tried to figure out where they would have put the body. They hadn't taken it outside, he was reasonably sure, and the upstairs had looked untouched. He went down to the basement, wishing fervently he had more light.

He stopped before a flimsy-looking door under the stairs. In older houses you often found coal chutes under the stairs, although nobody burned coal anymore. There were drag marks in the dust.

Cardinal put the flashlight down on the floor. The beam cast his hunchbacked shadow up and down the wall as he bent to open the half door. It came back with a scrape and a clatter. He knew what would be in there. Even though he could not smell it, he knew what would be there. The cold had killed his sense of smell. He wanted to see it, then get the hell out of there and come back with a team. He picked up the flashlight and ducked into the tiny space.

Polyethylene sheeting had opened up around the body, giving it an unwrapped look, like something precious in a black gift box. The body itself, perfectly preserved by the cold, was curled up in an almost fetal position. The head was wrapped in a bundle stiffened with cold and black with blood. But Cardinal recognized the fabric; it was the seat cover from the couch upstairs. Why had he covered the head? The trousers, raveled about the shins, were black denim, the shoes were black Converse high-tops. Cardinal knew the particulars by heart: *Caucasian male, last seen wearing . . .*

Cardinal was aware of the nausea lurking in his belly but he ignored it. Forms passed through his mind, calls he had to make: the coroner, Delorme, the lawyers for the estate, the Crown Attorney. But even as these things flashed in his mind he was taking in the physical details: the cheap watch around the thin wrist, the shriveled and tormented genitals. Cardinal's heart went out to the parents, who would have to be informed, who would be clinging to the hope that their son was alive. Whether or not there was an afterlife, a dead person moved to a place beyond pain and shame and insult. So why did he now feel the same instinct he had criticized in Delorme—to cover the boy up?

CARDINAL was taking a break outside, grateful for the cold and the snow that kept the crowd of onlookers down to a manageable size. Between the coroner, the ident boys, and the body-removal service, the basement was so full of people and equipment it was impossible to move around. It was dark now, and the front yard was lit up like the CN Tower; there were cars all down the block.

A slight edginess was building inside him. He had done excellent work—no high-tech flash, but he had done good work, and had he been a better man, he told himself, and a better cop, he would have been enjoying the moment of satisfaction. He missed the honest cop he had been years ago, wished yet again he could undo the thing he had done, if only because it was spoiling this moment. If Delorme was investigating him, if she looked back far enough, she might find something. It was not likely, but it was possible; it could happen anytime. Just let me finish this case, he prayed to the God he sometimes believed in, just let me finish off the man who did this to Todd Curry.

A pack of media people pressed against the crime-scene tape surrounding the yard. This time it was not just Gwynn and Stoltz from the *Lode*. Not just Sudbury TV. The Toronto papers were here. The CBC again. CTV. Is it the Windigo? they all wanted to know. Cardinal had nothing to say beyond the bare particulars, until next of kin had been informed. The whir of motor drives was loud.

"Miss Legault? Can we talk a sec?" He steered her a little away from the pack.

"The Windigo," he said. "You must be proud of that one. Way they all picked up on it."

"Oh, come on. Windigo Island? It was only a matter of time."

"You came up with it, though. Don't sell yourself short."

"Two murders and it's only February. About twice what you'd normally get in an entire year, right?"

"Not really."

"Murders of this *type*. Obviously we're not talking about domestics. Look, what are the chances of a real interview? Off the record, no cameras." Those cool newscaster's eyes taking a reading on him. Cardinal thought of a cat watching a mouse.

"Believe it or not, things are going to be pretty hectic around here. I don't know if—"

"Believe it or not, TV news doesn't try to be stupid."

"Oh, no. I would never accuse you of trying."

Miss Legault pressed on. "So give me a break. Educate me."

She was looking earnest now, and Cardinal had a soft spot for earnest people. Catherine was earnest. So was he, probably. "If you call Katie Pine's killer the Windigo," he said, "you're only likely to get the guy's motor running."

"Is that a refusal?"

Cardinal pointed to the house. "Excuse me. Duty calls."

Body Removal—two men who worked for the local funeral homes when they weren't working for the coroner—came out of the house with the body bag and placed it in the back of the hearse. The younger of the two looked pretty shaky; he blinked in the glare like a mole.

Delorme came out a moment later. "So kind of you to call me in on this, *partner*. Such a colleague. Such a believer in teamwork."

"I called. You were out."

"If I was a man, you would have waited for me. If we're not going to work together, maybe I should go back to Special. You can explain to Dyson."

"You say that as if you left Special."

She looked him up and down, her eyes sweeping over him like searchlights. "You sound like McLeod, you know? If you're going to be paranoid, I can't stop you. But me, I'm not going to get dragged into it." She watched the hearse drive away. "They go straight to Toronto?"

Cardinal nodded.

"Arthur *maudit* Wood, I could kill that little bastard."

"You ready to drive to Toronto?"

"Tonight? You mean to Forensic?" Excitement changed her voice instantly. She sounded like a girl.

"Next plane isn't till morning, and I don't want to wait." Cardinal nodded toward the dark square that was Dr. Barnhouse. The coroner could be heard halfway down the block berating someone for some perceived outrage. "I'll get the scoop from Barnhouse and pick you up in half an hour. We'll pass the hearse before Gravenhurst. I want to be there when Forensic opens up that little gift."

14

MURDER is a rare event in Canada. So rare that most of the country's ten provinces are allocated only one forensic unit, usually in the province's biggest city. It's a thrifty approach—convenient, too, if you happen to be investigating a murder in Toronto or Montreal. Cardinal and Delorme had to drive over two hundred miles, a good part of it behind a convoy of lumber trucks. At the coroner's building on Grenville Street, a Sikh in a blue uniform with a white turban buzzed down to the morgue to announce their arrival.

Len Weisman met them in the hall and led them into a cramped office. He was a small, compact man, with a thatch of black wiry hair. He wore spectacles with dark, fashionable frames, a white lab coat, and—incongruously, given the medical surroundings of white tile and linoleum—leather sandals.

Before he became director of the morgue, Weisman had put in ten years as a homicide investigator. His police badge and sergeant stripes were mounted in a frame on the wall behind his desk. Surrounding this were framed citations and a photograph of Weisman shaking hands with the mayor of Toronto.

"Sit, sit," he said in a friendly way. "Make yourselves at home."

At home in a morgue, Cardinal said to himself, and wondered if Delorme was thinking the same thing. She was certainly more subdued than usual. They had passed a dead woman in the hall—barely out of her teens and parked on a gurney beside the elevators like a shopping cart. The body bag was open to her throat, and her pale face with its penumbra of yellow hair had emerged from the white plastic as if from a cocoon. Her hair was beautiful, somewhere between saffron and gold; just hours earlier she would have been brushing it avidly, with a pretty woman's mixture of pride and self-criticism.

"Coffee, anyone? Tea?" Weisman gave the impression of bounding everywhere—reaching for a door halfway across the room, lunging to open a drawer, plucking a file from a desk. "Or there's a Coke machine in the lunchroom. Sprite? Pepsi?"

Cardinal and Delorme declined.

Weisman snatched up his phone before it could escape. "I'll just check if our pathologist is ready. Patient just arrived twenty minutes ago."

Cardinal had forgotten that they called them patients in this place, as if the silent occupants of those plastic bags and metal drawers might recover.

There was a knock on the door and the pathologist came in. She was a tall woman in her thirties, with wide shoulders and prominent cheekbones that gave her face a sculpted look.

"Dr. Gant, these are Detectives Cardinal and Delorme from Algonquin Bay. Dr. Gant is our pathologist this morning. You can go with her now if you like."

They followed her to the morgue. The dead girl had been moved, and now the white tiles and linoleum might have been any clinic, anywhere. The morgue had not the slightest smell of death, just a faint chemical odor. They crossed through the main autopsy room and into a side room reserved for "stinkers." Dr. Gant handed them both surgical masks, and they put them on. When the photographer was ready, Gant put on surgical gloves and unzipped the bag. Delorme gagged.

"It's filthy," Dr. Gant observed quietly. "Where'd you find him, a coal cellar?"

"Exactly right. Coal cellar in an old sealed house. Guess he's starting to thaw out."

"All right, let's get him X-rayed first. Radiography's next door."

She declined their inexpert assistance with the trolley, wheeling the "patient" next door to radiography, where a machine with a huge steel U attached stood ready. This was run by a scruffy man in check shirt and blue jeans that revealed the cleft of his buttocks every time he bent over.

"That sack. It was wrapped around his head just like that?"

"It's a seat cushion cover, Doctor. I'm not sure why the killer covered his head like that. Remorse doesn't seem likely. And I don't think he's squeamish, either."

"Let's get someone from Chemistry here before we disturb that too much. Start with the torso, Brian."

She spoke quietly into a telephone mounted on the wall. Her voice was collegial but firm; a man would have to be either extremely busy or extremely stupid not to do her bidding.

"Aren't you going to take the plastic sheeting off first?" Delorme asked.

Dr. Gant shook her head. "We X-ray them fully clothed. That way we pick up any bullet or blade fragments that might be lodged in the clothing." She nodded toward the table. "Trousers pulled down around the ankles indicate probable sexual activity just prior to the attack."

The technician readied the machine and closed the door. Then he flipped a switch, and a faint mosquito-sized whine filled the room. The bones of the feet materialized on the fluorescent screen. The beam traveled up the body, but Dr. Gant remained silent until the rib cage appeared on the screen. "Obviously massive trauma, there: fractures to the seventh, fifth, and third ribs. No foreign objects so far."

"The dark blur," Delorme said, pointing to a round dark spot on the screen. "It's not a bullet, is it?"

"Probably a medal or a crucifix."

The image changed, and the bones of an arm began to appear. "Examining extremities, now," Dr. Gant noted. She pointed to a long white line that broke in two like a highway breached by earthquake. "Defensive wounds to the left forearm, fractures of the ulna and wrist bones. Right forearm shows similar injury to the ulna. Collarbone is snapped right through."

The head was still sheathed in its bloody cover, but now the shattered sphere of the skull appeared on the X-ray screen. "Well," Dr. Gant said softly. "Multiple trauma there, obviously." She spoke into an intercom. "We're getting some kind of white line down the middle, Brian. Can you adjust it at all?"

"The image is fine, Doctor. You've got something in there."

Dr. Gant moved closer to the screen. "It could be an ice pick. Possibly a screwdriver blade. It must have been driven down into the top of the skull and then the handle broke off."

Several facial bones had been broken. Dr. Gant summarized these quickly, all of them blunt-force trauma possibly caused by a hammer.

The machine was switched off and the high thin whine faded, leaving a ghost of itself in the room.

A sadness hung in the air. They were looking at a small person who had tried unsuccessfully to ward off terrible, killing blows. And the death had taken time. However bleak Todd Curry's sixteen years may have been, however dissolute and unavailing, he hadn't deserved to die like that.

Vlatko Setevic from Chemistry joined them. "Cops of the Great White North," he said. "You ever get any victims that aren't frozen?"

Setevic unrolled white paper from a reel at the end of the table. Carefully, they lifted the body, still in its wrappings, and placed it on the sheet.

"Okay," Setevic said. "Let's get the cover loosened around the head. Then I'll take the cover off and place it on this table behind me. I have to do this gently. It's going to take time."

Setevic worked delicately at this task, while Dr. Gant and an assistant removed the plastic sheeting, blackened with soot and blood, from the torso. Another assistant took photographs. The plastic was tied with thin cord of the type used in venetian blinds. The inside of the sheeting was covered with a thick cracked paste of old blood. The camera flash went on and off like a strobe.

The body remained perfectly still, curled up.

"I've taken some hair and fiber from the outside of the seat cover," Setevic said. "I'll look at them next door."

Delorme took one glance at the face and turned away.

Dr. Gant moved around the body but did not touch it. "Left parietal region shows blunt-force trauma, a depressed fracture caused by a heavy instrument, possibly the side of a hammer. Right anterior parietal shows a circular depression about an inch in diameter, possibly caused by a hammer, hard to say. Tissue is partially peeled away from the left cheekbone, also probably by blunt force."

"Frenzy?" Cardinal asked. "Looks like overkill to me."

"Definitely a frenzy, judging by the ferocity of the attack. But there are aspects of control here, too, if I'm not mistaken. The wounds are fairly symmetrical, notice. Both cheekbones, both sides of the jaw, both temples. I don't think that symmetry is accidental. And then there's this." She pointed to the top of the head. "You've got a hole in the occipital crown approximately ten millimeters in diameter, a puncture wound, judging by the puckering at the edges. That'll be the blade we saw on the fluoroscope. You don't drive a screwdriver into someone's head in a frenzy."

"True."

"Any one of these injuries could be the cause of death, but we won't know for sure until we do a full autopsy, and we can't do that until he thaws out."

"Great," said Cardinal. "How long will that take?"

"At least twenty-four hours."

"I hope you're kidding me, Dr. Gant."

"Not at all. How long does it take to thaw out a twenty-pound turkey?"

"I don't know. Four or five hours."

"And this patient was in a surrounding temperature of what, minus forty? The inner organs are going to take at least twenty-four hours to thaw, possibly longer."

"There's something in here." Delorme was standing to one side, peering into the body bag.

Cardinal came over and looked into the bag, too. He put on a surgical glove and reached into the bag with both hands like an obstetrician. Moving slowly and holding it gingerly by the corners, he extricated the object—cracked, bloodstained, and covered with soot.

"An audiocassette," Delorme said. "It must have stuck to his clothes and it fell off when he started to thaw out."

"Well, don't get too excited. It's probably blank," Cardinal said, and dropped it into a paper evidence bag. "Let's just hope it has prints on it."

15

"I wanted to ask Dr. Gant what a nice girl like her was doing in a place like the morgue, but I thought she'd take it funny."

"Of course she would," said Delorme. "So would I."

"Young woman like that, she should be an internist—a cardiologist, maybe. Why's she want to spend her life working with corpses?"

"Same as you, Cardinal—fighting the bad guys. I don't see the mystery, me."

They were in the Forensic Sciences Center, just behind the coroner's building. They'd had the audiocassette dusted for prints, and now they were taking the elevator to Chemistry.

Setevic was bent over a microscope. He didn't even look up. "One hair, aside from the victim's. Three inches long, medium brown, Caucasian, probably male."

"And the fiber?"

"Red. Trilobal."

"That's our boy," said Cardinal.

"You don't know that."

"The likelihood of two separate killers—both with red carpet, no less—in a place the size of Algonquin Bay? Nonexistent."

Delorme stepped in. "Todd Curry spent some time in the same place as Katie Pine—for sure, you can say that much. The same car, right?"

Setevic smiled, shook his head. "You won't nail him with this. It's widely used in basements, patios—you name it—not just here, but in the States, too. I told you that when we found one on the Pine girl. Give me some credit here, okay? Assume I'm not stupid. You got something else for me? What's in the bag?"

"We need to hear what's on this." Cardinal handed him the evidence bag.

Setevic peered inside. "You already dusted it?"

"Lifted one partial next door. Computer's chewing it over, but we're not optimistic. You happen to have a tape player handy?"

"Not a good one."

"Doesn't matter. We just need to know if there's anything on here."

Setevic took them to a cramped office he shared with two other chemists. There were scientific journals stacked on every available surface. "Sorry about the mess. We only use the place for writing reports and making the odd phone call."

He reached into a drawer and pulled out a grimy little Aiwa. He pressed a button, and a middle-aged woman's voice was dictating a biology report. *Sample showed proliferation of white cells, indicating advanced state of . . .* The voice went woozy, then stopped.

"Mandy!" Setevic called toward the door. "Mandy! Do we have any double-A batteries?"

An assistant came in and handed him a package of four batteries. She watched him struggle to open the back of the machine, then held out a perfectly manicured hand. He handed it over and, expertly, she removed the housing, took out the old batteries and reloaded. She pressed a button, and the biology report resumed at the proper speed.

"I thank you. The forces of law and order thank you."

When Mandy closed the door behind her, he jerked his head toward it and, eyebrows raised, asked Delorme, "So, how you think I'm doing?"

"She hates you."

"I know. Call it my Slavic charm." He slipped in the audiotape and pressed the button. "Any idea what's on here?"

"None. Most likely *Aerosmith Unplugged*."

The tape started.

A series of clicks. Someone blows into the microphone and taps on it, testing it.

Delorme and Cardinal looked at each other, then immediately away. Mustn't get too excited, Cardinal told himself. It could be anything, anyone. It could be totally unrelated. He realized he was holding his breath.

More clicks, the rustle of cloth. Then a man's voice, angry, far from the microphone, says something indistinct.

A girl, impossibly close, her voice quivering: "I have to go. I have to be somewhere by eight o'clock. They'll kill me if I don't show up."

Heavy footsteps. Music starts up in the background—the end of a rock song. Barely audible: ". . . or you'll make me very angry."

"I can't. I want to go now."

Man's voice, now too distant to record properly: "[Unintelligible] . . . snapshots."

"Why do I have to wear this? I can't breathe."

"[garbled]. . . sooner you'll be on your way."

"I'm not taking my clothes off."

Heavy footsteps approach the microphone. Several slaps, loud as pistol shots. Screams. Then sobs. Then muffled sobs.

"Bastard," Cardinal said quietly.

Delorme was looking out the window, as if the apartment building across Grenville Street were of intense interest.

Background music switches to the Rolling Stones.

A series of distant clicks.

"That could be the camera, maybe," Delorme observed, still at the window.

The girl: "Please let me go now. I promise I won't tell anyone. Take your pictures and let me go. I swear to God I'll never tell anyone."

". . . repeat myself . . ."

"You're not listening! I have to be somewhere. I have band practice. It's really important! We have a concert in Ottawa and if I don't show up they'll call the police! There'll be all kinds of trouble! I'm trying to help you!"

[Inaudible.]

"Where? I live on the reserve. Chippewa. But my father's a policeman. He's with the OPP. I'm just warning you. He's gonna go crazy."

[Inaudible.]
"No. I don't want to do that. I won't."
Footsteps approach. Fierce sounds of rustling cloth. Then the girl, barely coherent, "Please! Please! Please! I have to be at practice before eight o'clock. If I don't—" Ripping sound, possibly duct tape. Her voice is a muffled whimper.
Clicks continue.
Music changes to a familiar female vocalist.
Muffled sobs.
More clicks.
More clicks.
A rustling sound.
A man coughs, close to the microphone.
More rustling sounds.
Ninety seconds of silence.
A final click as the recorder is switched off.

The rest of side one was blank. So was side two. They listened to the entire half hour of tape hiss to make sure, Cardinal, Delorme, and Setevic in utter silence. It was a long time before anyone spoke. Cardinal's voice sounded terribly loud, even to himself. "You got anybody in Documents who can tell us more about this?"

"Uh, no," Setevic said, still stunned.

"Because we just listened to the murder of a young girl, and I want to know everything there is to know about this tape. Don't you have anyone in Documents?"

"Documents? Documents people are strictly paper and handwriting. Bunco stuff. But I'll—" Setevic coughed. Cleared his throat. He was a big man, looked like a man who could take care of himself, too, was Cardinal's assessment. But he was still having a hard time with what they'd heard. "I'll give you a phone number," he said at last. "There's a guy the OPP likes to use."

THE new headquarters of the Canadian Broadcasting Corporation on Front Street had cost a scandalous amount to build, and Cardinal could see why. The atrium, bathed in a wash of soft light from the skylight eight floors up, was like an indoor park, profuse with trees. Marble gleamed underfoot. His tax dollars at work.

Cardinal and Delorme followed a luminous receptionist to the elevator. Thin pale men glided across the corridors. The receptionist led them past a series of studios to the end of a hallway. She opened a crimson door, and they entered a dimly lit recording studio.

A man in a houndstooth jacket was parked in front of a bank of electronic controls, a pair of headphones clamped over his head. A yellow bow tie sat primly at his neck. His crisp white shirt looked as if it had just been unwrapped. Cardinal had never seen anyone so neat.

The receptionist announced them loudly, "Your police friends, Brian."

"Thank you. Have a seat. Be right with you." He did not raise his voice the way most people do when wearing headphones.

Cardinal and Delorme sat down behind him on high-backed swivel chairs.

"Oohh," Delorme said, caressing the chair. "We're in the wrong job."

The studio smelled strongly of new carpet—even the walls were carpeted—and the atmosphere had a pleasant hush.

For the next five minutes they watched the technician's pale hands flutter gently over the controls—now nudging a slide up, now tweaking a dial. Lights and graphs blinked along the length of the console. The man's face, with its serious, abstracted expression, was reflected in the glass above the console, hovering over them like a disembodied intelligence.

Over the speakers an interview droned on and on, two gravel-voiced men jawing about federalism. Delorme rolled her eyes and made a spinning gesture of tedium with her index finger. Finally the interview came to an end, and the man removed his headphones and spun around, hand extended into space. "Brian Fortier," he said. He had a "radio" voice, deep and resonant. His hand waited in the air independently of him, and Cardinal saw that he was blind.

He shook the man's hand, introducing himself and Delorme.

Fortier jerked a thumb toward the tapes. "Cleaning up some archival material for rebroadcast. That was John Diefenbaker and Norman DePoe. Don't make them like that anymore."

"That was Diefenbaker? He turned my hometown into a nuclear arsenal when I was a kid."

"You're from Algonquin Bay, then."

Delorme said, "You're from up North, too, you?"

"No, no—Ottawa Valley boy." He said a few sentences to Delorme in French, which Cardinal did not exactly follow, but he saw Delorme instantly relax. Fortier said something that made her laugh like a girl. All Canadians study French into high school, and Cardinal had struggled with it right up to grade twelve. But there had been little call for French in Toronto, and by the time Cardinal had moved back to Algonquin Bay, he'd forgotten most of it. Have to take that extension class at Northern U., he told himself for the fortieth time, I'm such a lazy bastard.

"OPP says you have a tape for me?"

Cardinal took the tape out of the envelope. "The content does not leave this room, Mr. Fortier. Are you comfortable with that?"

"Investigation in Progress. I know the drill."

"And I'll have to ask you to wear these latex gloves while you handle it. The tape was found in a—"

A pale hand flew up to cut him off. "Don't tell me anything—I'll be more use to you if I hear it fresh. Give me the gloves."

He put on the gloves, and they watched his sheathed fingers palpate the cassette, turning it this way and that, stopping to feel and think like small independent animals. "Safety holes are covered up. Whatever's on here, someone didn't want it recorded over. Cassettes are all virtually identical from the outside. What make is this?"

"Denon. Thirty minutes. Chromium dioxide. We know it's a common type, available pretty much anywhere."

"Well, you wouldn't find it in the smallest towns, maybe, but certainly in a place as big as Algonquin Bay. It's not a cheap product. It'll run you five times the cost of the bottom end, maybe more."

"Would you classify it as a professional product?"

"A professional sound recordist—recording engineer, anybody with a passion for quality—would not use a cassette; you want a faster tape speed and the flexibility of more tracks—depending on the job of course. It's up there: Ampex, Denon, sure. But as I say, you can get it anywhere."

Delorme said, "He could have stolen it. Shoplifted it, no?"

"Retailers tend to keep these behind the counter—or at least near the register." Fortier's thin face wagged from side to side for a moment, as if he were sniffing for a lost aroma.

"What," Cardinal said. "You're not happy."

"Second thoughts. I said a professional wouldn't use a cassette. I meant a sound-recording professional. But musicians use them all the time. If I were putting a demo song on tape, for example, I'd use a high-quality cassette like this. There are so-called portable studios made for cassettes—Tascam, Fostex—the sound isn't clean, but with pop music, clean is often beside the point, right?"

"What about stand-up comics, people like that who want to audition?"

"Stand-ups send video. They want you to see how they look on stage. But radio announcers send cassettes to us all the time. Sure, someone like that."

Fortier opened a cassette slot on the console and popped in the tape. Delorme and Cardinal sat watching his back as they listened to the tape from beginning to end once more. The sound was much clearer on the professional equipment, and like an image being focused ever sharper, it became clearer still as Fortier adjusted various dials and knobs. The leather of his chair creaked beneath him as he leaned this way or that, his hands hovering over the console like hummingbirds.

"Some physical deterioration there. Obviously wasn't stored in optimum conditions."

"To put it mildly."

Under Fortier's ministrations, the tape hiss all but vanished. Within moments, Katie Pine's voice sounded as if she were in the room with them. Her terror in such proximity, her attempts to talk her way out, the fictitious cop father—Cardinal fought an urge to cry out. Fortier cocked his head like a spaniel, identifying sounds as they came up. "Girl's voice: twelve or thirteen years old. That accent, she's got to be an Indian."

"That's correct. What about the male?"

Fortier hit a pause button. "He's too far from the mike to place with any certainty—definitely not French, or even francophone. Ottawa Valley's out, too. Southern Ontario, though, that's possible. He doesn't have those terribly round vowels you get up North. Not a lot to work with there, I'm afraid. He's just too far from the mike."

When the tape was done, Fortier spoke quickly as if afraid he might forget something if he stopped to breathe. "First thing: This was made on a pretty good machine with a pretty good microphone."

"Begins to sound like a professional again."

Fortier shook his head impatiently. "No way. Placement of the microphone is grabbing a lot of air. Lot of noise. A professional gets as close to the source as possible."

"Can you tell us anything about the place?"

"Let me put it through again. I had it set to bring up the voices. Let me set it for the background." He lowered some of the sliders on the console and raised others. His index finger sat poised over the play button. "Just for the record, Detective: Those are the ugliest sounds I've ever heard."

"I'd be worried if you didn't think so."

Almost immediately, Fortier hit the pause button. "Something I can hear that maybe you can't: This is a

small room, quite bare. Hardwood floor. I can hear the re-
verberation off his heels. Hardwood floor . . . leather
soles—big heels, possibly cowboy boots."

Even Katie's voice sounded thin and far away, now. But
the footsteps, the rustling of cloth, the slaps—these
pressed themselves into the dark studio.

"Not much traffic outside. One car, one truck in the entire, what, fifteen minutes? You're not near a highway. It's
an old house—you can hear the glass rattle in the window
when the truck goes by."

"I can't," said Delorme.

"I can. Blind as a bat and hearing to match. He's taking
photographs now." He hit the pause button. "Random
thought for you: Do a soundprint of the shutter and winding mechanism. Then you can record other camera models
until you get a match."

Delorme looked at Cardinal. "It's a good idea," she said.

Fortier was still focused on what they'd heard. "I'm no
camera buff, for obvious reasons, but the technology on
that camera is old—no servo motor, no auto advance, and
you can hear the click is mechanical, not electronic. Puts
the technology—at the latest—somewhere in the mid-sev-
enties. The shutter is slow, which tells me he's in a low-
light situation, arguing again for nighttime, right?"

"Good thoughts, Mr. Fortier. Keep 'em coming."

He restarted the tape. "I'm out on a limb here, but I think
you've got an upstairs situation. The car and the truck
sound like they're coming from below, slightly."

"Can you really tell that?"

"Listening for the internal combustion engine is one of
the first things a blind person learns to do."

"What about the music? We know the approximate date.
If we can find out which radio station played those songs in
that order, we'll know what day and time Katie was
killed."

"Uh, sorry to disappoint you, Officer Delorme, but I
don't think that music was coming from a radio."

"But it was by all different performers."

"Yes, I can name them: Pearl Jam, the Rolling Stones, and Anne Murray. I'm sure you know the Stones album, and I can tell you the others, if you like. But two things: First, it's an odd selection of music. The first two selections might be played together on the air, but it would be very peculiar to follow the Rolling Stones with Anne Murray. I doubt if any broadcaster would do that. And, second: There was too long between cuts for that to be a radio station. No radio station—even up North—is going to give you that much dead air."

"But there's no sound of records being changed. He walks over, hits a switch, and the music comes on."

"My guess—well, it's more than a guess—is that it's a home recording."

"He might have borrowed the record, you mean. From a library?"

"It's a CD. Even through two tape players, I can hear that electronic sheen they have—a sort of brassy veneer over everything. Not to mention the lack of tics and pops. Yes, lots of people borrow music from the library and tape it. Drives the copyright folks mad."

"But if he's already using the tape recorder to record what's going on . . ."

"Right. He would have to have two tape recorders."

16

THE Sundial restaurant just outside Orillia on Highway 400 is as circular as its name suggests. The dining room is bright and cheerful, surrounded with high curved windows, and the waitresses are friendly. Cardinal always stopped here on his way home from Toronto.

Delorme came back from the ladies' room, threading her way through the pink vinyl banquettes. She had a distracted look on her face, and when she sat down, she muttered something about getting back on the road before the snow turned into a real blizzard.

"Can't go yet," Cardinal said. "I just ordered the coconut cream pie."

"In that case, I'll have more coffee."

"Personal tradition of mine: stop at the Sundial, have the coconut cream pie. It's the only place I ever eat it."

Delorme nodded vaguely, staring out the window. In a mood, apparently. Cardinal debated whether to ask her about it. Instead, he studied the paper place mat decorated with Canadian prime ministers.

The waitress brought the pie and coffee, and Cardinal pulled out his notes. "I'm not convinced the radio stations are as dead an end as Fortier thought. Anyway, it's not like we've got twenty stations."

"I'll check out the library, if you want."

"You sound a little depressed."

Delorme shrugged. "When we first heard the tape I thought for sure we'd nail this guy quick—tomorrow, the end of the week, soon. I mean, how often do you actually have a murder on tape? But we take it to an expert and what do we come up with? Nothing."

"You're jumping the gun, Delorme. Fortier may come up with something more by the time he's finished his digital enhancement. If he can bring up the killer's voice . . ."

"But he said he couldn't do that."

"Well, there's still the camera angle to follow up."

"I admit I got excited about that in the studio. It sounds so scientific: soundprints. But think about it. Even if we can say for sure that it's the sound of a 1976 Nikon or whatever, how's that going to help? Might be different if it sounded like something manufactured last year—might actually lead to a sales slip, a credit card. But an old camera? An old camera could have gone through ten different owners by now."

"God, you are depressed."

Delorme was half-turned in the banquette, looking out at the tiny flakes of snow that had been drifting down steadily since Toronto. A Pop Shoppe truck was pulling out of the parking lot, wipers flapping. After a few moments she said, "When I was a little girl, I used to think this place looked more like a spaceship than a sundial."

"I thought so, too. I still think so."

In the space where the truck had been, a father was helping his tiny daughter with the zipper of her parka. She was wearing a bright green toque with a bobble that hung down to her waist. Their breath joined together in a mist, and Cardinal became aware of the cupboard in his heart where fear and regret were locked away. A crimson thread of fear ran through a father's love for his daughter, he reflected. That's why we're so protective.

"You have a kid at university, don't you?" Delorme's train of thought seemed also to be traveling in the direction of daughters.

"That's right. Her name's Kelly."

"What year's she in?"

"Second-year grad school. Fine arts. Straight A's, too," he couldn't help adding.

"You could have stopped in to see her. We had plenty of time."

"Kelly's not in Toronto. She's studying in the States." As you very well know, Detective Delorme, despite the innocent act. Run your Special Investigation on me, if you must, but don't expect me to help.

"Why'd she go to the States? Is that where your wife's from?"

"Kelly's mother is American. But that's not why Kelly went there. Yale's about the best art school on the continent."

"Such a famous university. And I don't even know where it is." It was just possible Delorme wasn't faking. Cardinal couldn't be sure.

"New Haven. Connecticut."

"I don't know where that is, either. New Haven, I mean."

"It's right on the coast. Ugly place." Go ahead, Delorme, ask me how I can afford it. Ask me where I got the money.

But Delorme just wagged her head in wonder. "Yale. That's great. What did you say she was studying?"

"Fine art. Kelly's always wanted to be a painter. She's very talented."

"Smart girl, sounds like. Doesn't want to be a cop."

"Smart girl."

As they headed north through the snowstorm, the atmosphere in the car was tense. One of the wipers squealed every time it crossed the windshield so that Cardinal wanted to rip it out. He turned on the radio and listened to exactly one verse of Joni Mitchell singing "Both Sides Now" and switched it off again. As they approached Gravenhurst, the first rocks of the Precambrian Shield reared up on either side of the highway. Cardinal usually felt he was truly heading home when he reached that first rock cut, but now he just felt smothered.

At Forensic that morning, Cardinal had telephoned Dyson to bring him up to date. Before he could say anything, the detective sergeant broke in: "I have two words for you, Cardinal."

"Which two?"

"Margaret Fogle."

"What about her?"

"I am holding in my hand—hot off the press, so to speak—a fax from Vancouver P.D. Turns out Miss Fogle is not, as some may have thought, a victim of murder in our fair city. Turns out Miss Fogle is alive and well and having a baby in Vancouver." The glee in Dyson's voice came over the phone line loud and clear.

"Well, that's good," Cardinal said. "Alive is definitely good."

"Don't feel too bad, Cardinal. We all make mistakes."

Cardinal had let that pass, but Dyson had still managed to sour his day.

As they drove by Bracebridge, where the turnoffs were little more than vague outlines in the whirling snow, Delorme brought up the music angle again, and as they tossed theories back and forth, they both began to cheer up. Cardinal became aware that Delorme's good opinion mattered to him. Must be something to do with those sharp features, those serious eyes. There couldn't be any other reason; they didn't know each other well enough.

Okay, Cardinal thought as he opened an inner debate with himself, you have the distinct sensation that your partner is investigating you. What's the best way to handle this unpleasant state of affairs without coming off too badly? He decided he would do whatever he could to help her. Without being too obvious, he would give her every opportunity to get on with it—let her have a go at his locker, his desk (if she hadn't already). Hell, he would let her have a go at his house. Yale was the most damaging thing against him, and she already knew about that. There was little chance of her finding anything else, not at this point.

Once they were past Huntsville, Cardinal began to feel he was really on home territory again. It was always good to work with the folks in Toronto; he liked the snappy professionalism down there. But he liked the North: He liked the cleanliness, the rocky hills and forests, and the deep clarity of the skies. Most of all he liked the sense of working for the place that had formed him, the sense of protecting the place that had protected him as a kid. Toronto provided a wider variety of career opportunities, not to mention more money, but it could never have been home.

Home. Suddenly Cardinal wished Catherine was here beside him. He never knew when it would hit, this ache.

Hours would go by when he thought of nothing but the case he was working; then he would notice a pressure building in his chest, a hurt and a hunger. He wished Catherine was with him—even Catherine mad, even Catherine with delusions.

It was getting darker now, and the snow was flapping around the car like lace curtains.

THE snow was still coming down the next day as Cardinal and Delorme sat in Dyson's office while he read to them from the RCMP's profile of the killer. How the detective sergeant had got Ottawa headquarters to respond so quickly was a mystery to Cardinal. The fax wires must have been humming. And now—this was so like Dyson it verged on self-parody—he was making fun of the document he had gone to so much trouble to secure.

"*Analysis of site photographs is hampered by the fact that only one is the site of a murder. The island mineshaft is a dump site only.* Oh, really. That's wonderful." Dyson addressed himself to the report he was holding. "Tell me something else I don't know."

He didn't look up. Just flipped through a couple of pages, breezing his way through a paragraph here, a paragraph there. "*Differing causes of death . . . asphyxiation . . . blunt trauma . . .* Blah and blah and again blah. *Boy attacked while seated . . . facing attacker, indicating knew attacker and to some degree trusted . . .* Well, we know all this."

Cardinal said, "What I don't understand is why you tapped the RCMP profilers so soon. I would have waited till we had more to give them."

"And when might that be?"

"You should have kept me informed. We all know the Horsemen can destroy a case faster than you can say Musical Ride. I mean, look at Kyle Corbett, for God's sake. I don't even want to speculate how they screwed that one up. But their profilers are a different story, and Grace Legault—who we may as well call Miss General Public—called me last night and wanted to know when we'd be calling them in. I told her we had no need to call in RCMP profilers, OPP profilers, or any other damn profilers and now I'm going to look like an idiot."

"Look, it was the chief's idea and it was a good one. You should be thanking him. Haven't you ever heard of a pre-emptive strike? This'll keep the media off our backs with this call-in-the-feds crap. And it gets us points with our brothers and sisters in red, always a good thing."

"But there's nothing here Toronto Forensic can't handle—"

Dyson didn't wait to hear the further thoughts of John Cardinal. He plowed on, *"Girl taken from crowded place . . . no visible struggle . . . again indicating degree of familiarity . . ."*

"Children, even teenagers will trust anyone if they're approached the right way," Delorme said. "Remember we had that molester a few years ago who would pretend to be from the hospital and tell them their mother was in Emergency."

"I'm just amazed that they call this a service." Dyson tapped the report.

"One dump site and thirty seconds with some photographs," Cardinal said. "No profiler's going to come up with much under those circumstances."

"Suddenly you're in love with the Horsemen? How many murder scenes has this so-called profiler worked, that's what I want to know."

"That's Joanna Prokop. She profiled Laurence Knapschaefer right down to the type of car he drove. She's got more brains than the entire O division put together."

Dyson flipped to the last page and glared at the summary he found there. *"Nature of both sites indicates loner . . . Knowledge of mineshaft indicates local resident . . . Ah, here we are: This killer shows characteristics of both the organized and disorganized type. He's not afraid to face intended victims head-on. Has requisite social skills—surface ones—to entice a young person into dangerous circumstances. The abandoned house, the mineshaft, the tape recording, all indicate careful planning. Careful planning suggests attacker probably holds a steady job. May be an obsessive cleaner or neat freak, a list-maker. May hold a job that requires a high degree of organization.* Todd Curry didn't look very neat to me, but no doubt we have different housekeeping standards than the Horsemen. Or Horseladies, sorry.

"On the other hand," he read on, *"evidence of frenzy in the Curry murder indicates explosive personality.... Killer will be someone who is missing more and more days of work, getting more and more out of control.* Really, what they expect us to do with this I can't imagine. According to this, you're looking for Jekyll and Hyde. Which is all very well if he happens to be in Hyde mode. But how do you know him when he's Jekyll?"

"Not by sitting in here all day." Cardinal got up and left.

Delorme would have followed, but Dyson stopped her. "Hold on a second. Was it my imagination or was he a little too touchy?"

Delorme could not miss the change in tone. They weren't talking about Pine–Curry, now. "I think he's just pissed off that you didn't keep him informed."

"Yeah. You're probably right. How's he doing in your own . . ."

"Fine. Nothing so far."

"Finances?"

"Nothing back, yet. The banks don't like to part with information. But my impression, I don't think—"

"I don't want your impressions, Delorme, and neither does the chief. We all have the impression that Sergeant John Cardinal is a first-class detective. We all have the impression that he's straight as an arrow. So, thank you, but I don't need any more impressions. What I need is a few solid facts—and not just rumors—that will explain to me how Kyle Corbett can slip through our fingers three separate times. Cardinal wants to lay it off on Corporal Musgrave and his merry men. Fine. But how does an Algonquin Bay cop afford a house on Madonna Road? And how does an Algonquin Bay cop send a daughter to

Yale? Do you have any idea what the tuition is at Yale?"

"About twenty-five thousand Canadian dollars. I already checked."

"That includes residence fees?"

"No, sir. That's just tuition. Food, lodging, books and supplies—all that brings it to about forty-eight thousand a year Canadian."

"Jesus."

17

A Gray Coach bus turned the corner with a roar and pulled into the station, twirling capes of snow in its wake.

Passengers disembarked stiffly, some exchanging hugs with waiting relatives, others making straight for the pay phones, still others rushing toward the taxi stand. A small knot of people gathered around the belly of the bus from which the driver began to deliver luggage like a litter of puppies. Diesel fumes billowed around their feet.

The driver pulled out a guitar in a hardshell case and handed it to a thin youth shivering in a thin parka. He had long hair that he had to keep flicking out of his eyes. His eyes were round, his eyebrows high and arched, as if life were taking him by surprise. He hefted an enormous knapsack onto his back, picked up his guitar, and went inside to the bank of luggage lockers; it took two to stow his stuff. Then, holding his thin parka together at the throat, he went out to the taxi stand. He bent over and talked to a driver, then with one last flick of his hair, got in.

The cab was the last one at the stand. There was only one other car in the bus station parking lot—a gray Pinto near the entrance. All the Toronto passengers had cleared out by now, but as the taxi pulled out of the lot, the gray Pinto—motor running, windows fogged—remained by the DO NOT BLOCK ENTRANCE sign, patiently throbbing.

The cab drove exactly four blocks downtown, made a left, and let the boy out in front of Alma's Restaurant. He made his way through the snowdrifts like a high-wire artist, placing one foot carefully in front of the other. Snow melted in his shoes; his boots were in the knapsack back at the station.

He was the restaurant's only customer. On a small TV screen behind the counter, Chicago was playing the Canadiens. The bearded bear who took his order scarcely took his eyes off the game. When he brought the food, cheers and organ notes cascaded from the TV. "Damn," the bear muttered. "That better not be Chicago."

"I was gonna go out for a beer or something," the kid said. "Can you tell me where young people hang out around here?"

"How young? My age?"

"Mine."

"Try the St. Charles." The bear waved a paw like a traffic cop. "Make a right on Algonquin. Go two blocks till you reach Main. It'll be across the street."

"Thanks."

The restaurant was about what you'd expect a cabdriver to recommend: vinyl banquettes, Formica tables, plastic plants everywhere, and, despite the name, no Alma in sight. The boy sat at the counter looking out at the silent street. The red neon of the diner's sign turned the falling snow bright pink. Chances of finding any excitement were looking slim. Nevertheless, when the kid had finished his hamburger, he headed out to find the St. Charles.

ELDERLY inhabitants of Algonquin Bay may remember the days when the St. Charles was one of the city's better hotels. For decades, its location at the elbow of Algonquin and Main drew visitors who wanted to be right downtown, as well as tourists looking for easy access to Lake Nipissing, just two blocks south. The train station was less than five minutes away on foot, so for passengers arriving from Quebec City or Montreal, it would be the first building of any size they'd see. The St. Charles in that earlier incarnation prided itself on pleasing both tourist and businessman with charm, convenience, and first-class service.

Unfortunately, that day had come and gone. When the St. Charles could not compete with the cut rates charged by such self-service enterprises as the Castle Inn or the Birches Motel, it converted its upper stories into small, oddly shaped apartments that now housed mostly transients and ne'er-do-wells. All that remained of the former hotel was the bar downstairs, the St. Charles Saloon, which retained nothing of its original elegance and was now the establishment where the young of Algonquin Bay learned to drink. The management wasn't overly strict about checking driver's licenses, and they served beer in enormous pitchers.

The kid, whose name was Keith London, was standing at the bar, smoking and looking around in the slightly anxious way of a stranger. The St. Charles Saloon was essentially a warehouse divided by two long tables where boisterous parties of young folk were making an enormous amount of noise. Along the walls, smaller groups of drinkers perched around tiny, disklike tables. Carved above a door beside the bar a sign, the remnant of an earlier era, said LADIES AND ESCORTS ONLY. A multicolored jukebox was blasting out Bryan Adams. Above it all hung the murky cumulus of a hundred cigarettes.

Keith London finished one beer and debated whether he should have another; that hamburger had been the only food he'd eaten since Orillia. The crowd looked as if it had passed the point where a newcomer might be welcomed. To his left a couple was discussing in harsh terms other people not present. To his right, a man stared in autistic wonder at the hockey game swirling across a silent TV screen. Keith's adventurous spirit began to wilt.

He ordered another Sleeman. If nothing interesting happened before he finished it, he'd head over to the motel the cabdriver had pointed out.

He was only about halfway through his beer when a man in a knee-length leather coat left the jukebox and came over to the bar. He shouldered his way between Keith and the couple next to him. The coat was like something you'd hide a shotgun under.

"Boring joint," he said, tipping the muzzle of his Labatt's toward the crowd.

"I don't know. They look like they're having a good time." Keith nodded toward the middle of the room from where gusts of laughter kept blowing.

"Idiots always have a good time." The man upended his

beer, pressing it to his lips like a trumpet, and drained half at one go.

Keith turned away a little, feigning a sudden interest in the jukebox.

"Hockey. If you took hockey away, this country would shrivel up and die."

"It's a decent game," Keith said. "I'm not a fanatic about it, though."

"Why do Canadians do it doggy-style?" The man didn't look at Keith as he spoke.

"I don't know."

"So they can both watch the hockey game."

Keith left the bar and went into the men's room. When he was at the urinal he heard the door swing open behind him and then the creak of leather. There were several urinals available, but the man bellied up to the adjacent one. Keith washed his hands quickly and headed back to the bar; he still had more than half a beer left.

The man came back a moment later. He kept his leather-clad back to the crowd this time, and Keith had the feeling the man was staring at the back of his head in the bartender's mirror. "I think I've got stomach cancer," he said. "Something not right in there."

"That's rough," Keith said. He knew he should feel sympathy for the guy but somehow he didn't.

The music changed to some ancient Neil Young song. The man pounded the bar in time to the music, hard enough to rattle his ashtray. "I know what we could do," he said, suddenly gripping Keith's bicep. "We could go to the beach."

"Uh-uh. It must be twenty degrees out there."

"Twenty degrees, big deal. Beach is great in winter. We could buy a six-pack."

"No, thanks. I'd rather stay where it's warm."

"I was kidding," the guy said, but the grip on Keith's arm intensified. "Could take a drive out to Callander, though. Car's got a CD player. What kind of music do you like?"

"Lots of kinds."

A woman materialized out of the haze and asked Keith if she could bum a smoke. The man instantly let go of Keith's arm and turned his back. It was as if a spell had been broken.

Keith offered the woman his Player's Lights. He would never have paid her the slightest attention if she hadn't spoken to him. She was pudgy around the edges, with almost no chest. And there was something off-putting about her face. The skin was stiff and shiny from some skin disorder. It was more like a mask than a face.

"My boyfriend and I were just saying you looked interesting. Are you from out of town?"

"It's that obvious?"

"We thought you looked interesting. Come and have a beer with us. We're dying of boredom."

Now, never mind how someone looks, Keith said to himself. This is just the kind of thing you always want to happen and never does: friendly people taking an interest. He regretted his inner critique of her appearance.

The woman led him past the jukebox to a small table in the corner where a guy who looked maybe thirty was peeling the label from his Molson bottle, frowning as if it were the most important project in the world. He looked up as they approached, asking before they even sat down, "So, was I right? Is he from Toronto?"

"You two are amazing," Keith said. "I just got into town an hour ago. From Toronto."

"Well, it's not that amazing, really," the woman said, watching her boyfriend pour beer into their three glasses. "You look far too cool to be from around this dump."

Keith shrugged. "Place doesn't seem so bad. Guy at the bar was a little strange."

"Yeah, we noticed," the man said quietly. "Figured someone should come to your rescue."

"Hey! You've got cigarettes!"

The woman said, "It was the only way I could think of to introduce myself. I'm terrible at talking to strangers." Her boyfriend was lighting an Export "A" and offering the pack with a flick of the wrist. He was not quite handsome. Dark hair swept back from his brow and sat up in oily spikes along the crown of his head, as if he had just matured from a punk rock phase. And his skin was so pale that blue veins showed below his eyes and at the temples. It was the ferretlike cast to the eyes that spoiled his face a little, but he had a huddled attitude, an intense way of moving—now leaning forward to pour beer, now offering a cigarette— that captured Keith's imagination. It seemed to say he had far more important things to do at any moment, but just now he would pour you a beer or offer you a smoke. It was very compelling, and Keith wondered what he was doing with this woman with the fiberglass face.

"I guess I forgive you," Keith said cheerfully. He took a sip of beer. "My name's Keith, by the way."

"I'm Edie. He's Eric."

"Eric and Edie. Awesome."

Keith became chatty over the second pitcher of beer. It was a weakness he was aware of in himself but could not stop. "Such a Chatty Cathy," his girlfriend teased him sometimes. He was telling Eric and Edie he had just completed high school and was taking a year off, before university, to travel the country. He had already been to the East Coast and was now headed in a leisurely way toward Vancouver. Then he got on to politics and the economy. He delivered his opinions about Quebec; now he was going on about the bloody Maritimes. God, I'm a motor-mouth, he thought. Somebody stop me.

"Newfoundland," he heard himself saying. "Man, what a disaster area. Half the province is out of work because we ate all the fish. Can you imagine? There's no goddam cod left! If it wasn't for oil, the entire island would be on unemployment." He flicked his hair for emphasis. "Entire island."

The couple didn't seem to tire of him at all. Edie kept her face in the shadows, probably to hide that weird skin, but she fired off question after question. And Eric spoke up every now and then, asking this or that, and off Keith would go with another opinion, another report. It was like being interviewed.

"What brings you to Algonquin Bay, Keith?" Edie asked. "Do you know anybody here? Do you have relatives?"

"Naw, my family's all from Toronto. Toronto from way back. Real old-school Anglican, you know?"

Edie nodded, although Keith had the sense that she didn't really understand. She kept bringing a hand to her face or pulling her hair over her cheek like a curtain.

"I didn't really have any reason to stop here," he told them, "except a friend of mine passed through Algonquin Bay a couple of years ago and said he had a really good time."

"Didn't he give you some names of people to stay with? You're not staying at a hotel, are you?"

"Thought I might head over to the Birches after. Cab-driver said it's pretty decent for the price."

They asked him more questions. About Toronto, the crime, all the films being shot down there. Who were the hot bands? Where were the hot clubs? How could he stand the crowds, the pace, those subways? Pitchers of beer appeared. Packs of cigarettes. It was exactly the kind of convivial scene Keith loved, the kind of thing that made travel such a kick, the three of them really hitting it off. All the time, Edie seemed to hang off Eric's every word, and Keith began to see what it was he saw in her: adoration.

"We've been thinking of visiting Toronto," Edie said at one point. "But it's so expensive. It's outrageous what hotels charge down there."

"Stay with me," Keith said. "I expect to be back there by August at the latest. You could come and stay at my place. I could show you the big city. Man, we could have a time."

"It's awfully kind of you . . ."

"Consider it done. Give me something to write on. I'll write down my address."

Eric, who had been practically motionless all this time,

pulled a small pad from his pocket and handed him a mechanical pencil.

While Keith was writing down his address, phone number, e-mail, and everything else he could think of, Edie and Eric conferred in whispers. He tore off the square of paper and handed it to Eric, who studied it closely before slipping it into his pocket. Then Edie said decisively, "We've got an extra room, Keith. Why don't you come and stay with us?"

"Oh, hey, I wasn't angling for a free room."

"No, no. We realize that."

"It's so nice of you, I don't know what to say. I don't want to impose. Are you sure it's all right? You're not just being polite?"

"We're not polite," Eric said, staring into his beer. "We're never polite."

Edie said, "It's easy to get into a rut up here, Keith. It would be interesting for us to have you. You'd be doing us a favor. It's just so interesting to hear your views about the country."

"Fascinating," Eric agreed. "Refreshing, even."

"You seem to have a special insight into people, Keith. Maybe because you've traveled so much. Or were you born that way?"

"Not born that way," Keith said, and raised a professorial finger. Oh, boy, listen to that Molson talk. He gassed on, couldn't help himself, about what an ignoramus he used to be—saying how it wasn't travel so much, but his experience with girlfriends, with teachers, with his high-school buddies, that was where he had learned so much about himself. Experience. And when you learn about yourself, he explained, you learn about everyone.

Eric suddenly leaned forward. It was a dramatic gesture after his stillness. "You have an artistic look about you," he said. "I'm thinking you're an artist of some kind."

"Pretty close, Eric. I'm a musician—not professional, yet, but I'm not bad."

"Musician. Of course. And I bet you play guitar, too."

Keith paused with his glass in midair; he set it slowly back down on the table, as if it were an object of extreme fragility. "How could you know I play guitar?"

Eric poured more beer into Keith's glass. "Your fingernails. They're long on your right hand, short on your left."

"Jesus, Edie. You're married to Sherlock Holmes, here." Were they married? He couldn't remember if they'd told him they were married.

"It so happens I've got some recording equipment," Eric said quietly. "If you're as talented as I think you are, we could make a tape. Nothing elaborate. Just a four-track cassette."

"Four tracks? Four tracks would be awesome. I've never done that."

"We can put you and the guitar on two tracks. Mix them down to one, and it would leave three for keyboard, bass, drums, whatever you want."

"Fantastic. Have you done a lot of recording?"

"Some. I'm not a pro."

"Well, me neither. But I'd love to do that. You're not just making a joke, are you?"

"Joke?" Eric leaned back against his chair. "I don't make jokes."

"He's very serious about it," Edie said. "He's got two machines. The cassette thing and a reel-to-reel outfit. When Eric makes a recording, it's really something special."

18

"IF you want them to die slowly, shoot them in the stomach. Put one low down in the belly. Takes them hours to die that way. And they die in agony. They'll put on a real show."

Edie gripped the Luger the way he had showed her, one hand bracing the other, feet apart, poised in a slight crouch. *I feel like a little kid playing cops and robbers. But when the gun goes off there's nothing like it.*

"Save your belly shot for special occasions, Edie. For now, just imagine he's coming over that hill at you. He doesn't want to talk, he doesn't want to arrest you. He has only one objective: your death. Your job? Stop the bastard cold. It's your right and duty to make the bastard dead."

His hands showing me the way to squeeze the trigger. Long bones rippling under the skin.

"A head shot is always first choice, got that, Edie?"

"A head shot is always first choice."

"You always try for a head shot, unless you're more than twenty yards away. Then you go for the chest. Chest is second choice. Repeat."

"The chest is second choice. Head is first choice. Second choice is chest."

"Good. And you always empty the magazine. Don't fire one off and hang around waiting to see how it turns out. You empty your load. BOOM! BOOM! BOOM!"

I jumped a mile when he did that. I cried out, but he didn't hear, so intense he gets, when he's teaching me things. His spiky hair seems to bristle on his head. His eyes go absolutely black.

"Edie girl, you give them everything you've got. Bullet-proof vest? Doesn't matter. Three of these will drop him flat—temporarily at least—giving you time to effect your escape."

"My arms are killing me." *He ignores me. He's a ma-*

*rine. He's a taskmaster. He's a born teacher. I'm his born
student. I'm weak, but he makes me strong.*

"Take a breath, Edie. You take a deep breath and hold it,
just before you squeeze one off. On your own time."

When Edie took too long, Eric said it again. "On your
own time," then added with irritation, "you'd be stone cold
fucking *dead* by now."

Edie squeezed the trigger, and the bang was louder than
she expected, it always was. "It's got such a kick," she said.
"It's making my arms tingle."

"Don't close your eyes, Edie. You'll never hit anything
that way." Eric tromped away through the snow to examine
the target. He came back wearing what Edie called his slab
face, his stone face. "Beginner's luck. One through the
heart."

"I killed him?"

"Purely by accident. He'd have shot your fucking head
off an hour ago, you're so slow. Take it again. Go for the
chest. And for Christ's bloody sake keep your eyes open."

She took a while getting ready, and he repeated his earlier observation. "Of course, if you want them to die
slowly, you shoot them in the stomach. You ever see a
worm on a hook?"

"A long time ago. When I was little."

"That's how they squirm. Unhhhh!" Eric grabbed his
stomach and fell to his knees, flopped onto his back and
writhed horribly, making retching sounds. "That's what
they do," he said from down on the snow. "Wriggle in pure
agony for hours. Pure agony."

"I'm sure you've seen it."

"You don't know what I've seen." Eric's voice had gone
cold and dead. He got up, whacking snow from his jeans.
"It's none of your business what I've seen."

Edie jerked the trigger, missing the target, missing the
tree, and Eric immediately cheered up. He'd been in a good
mood all morning; he always was when they had a guest.
Having a guest set something free in him. He'd woken her
up first thing this morning and proposed this jaunt in the

woods, a shooting lesson, and she knew they would have a good day. He grabbed her from behind, now, steadying her grip. "Never mind. If it was too easy, it wouldn't be any fun."

"Why don't you show me? Let me watch you. That'll help me get the hang of it." The submissive act worked like a charm, it usually did.

"You want to watch the master at work? Okay, baby. Pay attention."

Edie listened like a puppy with cocked head, while Eric explained again the importance of the proper stance, demonstrating the grip, the crouch, the proper way to sight along the barrel. He was at his best when telling her things: lore he had picked up in Toronto or Kingston or Montreal. Except for a class trip to Toronto when she was in high school, Edie had never set foot outside Algonquin Bay. Twenty-seven years old, she had never lived on her own, and she had never met anyone like Eric. So totally self-sufficient. And so beautiful.

Edie's diary, June 7, the previous year: *I don't know why he has anything to do with a hideous thing like me. Me with my horrible face and flat as a board. He has no idea how gorgeous he is. So lean, with ropy muscles, and the way he walks—that slight crouch—just makes me weak in the knees.* She pictured his face with its fine bones, its clean lines, on a movie screen forty feet wide. You could sell tickets to anything he was in.

Like an artist, with those rings under his eyes, haunted by genius. I can see him on a cliff by the edge of the sea, with the wind blowing through his hair and a white scarf streaming out behind him.

He had come to her counter at Pharma-City with some aftershave and some Kleenex and he'd asked her for some double-A batteries and a little bottle of PowerUp.

I'm doomed, she'd written in her diary that first day he'd shown up in the drugstore. *I've met the most powerful man in the universe. His name is Eric Fraser and he works at Troy Music Center and he has a face that looks like God to me. What eyes!* She reread her diary from time to time, to remind herself of how empty her life had been, and then how full it had become since the arrival of Eric Fraser. *Even his* name *is beautiful.*

"Ever try this stuff?" he'd said to her. The cash register acted up and they were staring at each other while the manager fiddled with it.

"It's like No-Doz, isn't it? Caffeine pills?"

"Oh, they may *say* it's just caffeine. They can *say* whatever they want, but take my word for it: You can do amazing things with PowerUp."

"Stay awake all night, huh?"

But he'd given her a sly smile and shaken his head in pity. "Amazing things can be done."

She could never have guessed how amazing.

He had been dressed all in black and skinny as a knife, and when he put his dark glasses on you could have sworn he was in some underground rock-and-roll band. It still amazed her that someone so handsome and smart and worldly-wise as Eric Fraser could be interested in her—a nothing, a no one, a loser like Edie Soames. Just three days before the first entry in her diary that mentioned Eric Fraser she had written: *I am nothing, my life is nothing, I amount to a big fat zero.*

Eric went to look at the target, his breath trailing behind him in feathery clouds. He made an incongruous figure all in black against the snow, with his spiky hair and his sunglasses. He came back clutching the paper target, holding it up like a trophy. "Excellent work. You're beginning to show some consistency. It's not just luck anymore."

They shoved the target in the back of Edie's rusted Pinto and drove downhill to the highway, Eric slouched back in the seat like royalty. He had his own vehicle, a blue Windstar at least ten years old that he kept in perfect running condition, but Eric Fraser never drove unless he had to.

Edie made a left by the old drive-in theater and drove the short distance to Trout Lake. She parked at the marina, under a sign that said, PARKING FOR MARINA CUSTOMERS ONLY.

The lake was perfectly smooth, blinding white in the sunlight, except for the ice-fishing huts. Children were skating at the public beach where a square of the lake had been cleared for a rink.

They dodged traffic on the highway and went tramping up the hill. Now and then a toboggan loaded with children shot past them. He loved his walks, Eric, loved the outdoors. Sometimes he walked for three or four hours, out to Four Mile Bay and back, or out past the airport. She would never have guessed this about him, he looked so, well, urban. But the long walks, the hills and snow and quiet, seemed to calm a restlessness in him. It was an honor to share these times with him.

They stepped over a chain-link fence that was bent practically to the ground and continued up the hill past the new pump house. Edie was huffing and puffing long before they got to the top and stood beside the frozen circle of the reservoir. A small plane with skis where its wheels should have been buzzed overhead and wafted down toward Trout Lake. They stood gripping the protective fence with its warnings against swimming in or skating on the reservoir. Edie could see the spot, two hundred yards downhill, where they had buried Billy LaBelle. She knew better than to mention it, though, unless Eric did.

"You know how to be quiet. I like that," Eric had said to her once. He'd been in a sulk the whole day, and Edie had been terrified he was going to tell her he was tired of her, that he was finished with her and her fish face, but instead he had praised her. It was the first time anyone had praised her for anything, and she treasured his words like rubies. Now she could go for hours, not saying anything. When sad thoughts came, or the bitter ache of hating her own face, she just put them aside and remembered his sweet words. Utterly silent, Edie could stand beside him staring at a circle of frozen water, and Eric seemed to like it just fine.

"I'm hungry," he said eventually. "Maybe I'll get something to eat before I drop over."

"Do you want to come for supper?"

"I'll get my own supper." He didn't like her to see him eating. It was one of his peculiarities.

"What if our guest wakes up?" Eric had taught her never to call the guest by name.

"After what you gave him? I don't think so."

Edie turned away from the reservoir and looked out over the hills, the subdivisions around Trout Lake. Smells of pine and woodsmoke hung in the air.

"I wish we didn't have to earn a living," she said. "I wish we could just spend all our time together. Walking places. Learning things."

"Waste of time, most jobs are. And the people. Jesus, I hate them. I hate the bastards."

"Alan, you mean." Alan was his boss, always on Eric's back about something, telling him to do things he'd already done, explaining things he already knew.

"Not just Alan. Carl, too. Fucking faggot. I hate them all. They think they're so fucking perfect. And what they pay me—I'm forced to live in that pigsty."

Edie was getting really cold standing there, but she didn't say anything. When he started talking about people he hated, she knew what was coming. There would be a party, that was Eric's word for it. They already had their guest of honor in safekeeping. A flutter started up in Edie's chest, and suddenly she badly needed a bathroom. She pressed her lips together, holding her breath.

"I think we should move the schedule up a bit," Eric said casually. "Have the party a little earlier than we'd planned. Don't want our guest to get bored, do we."

Edie soundlessly released her breath. Liquid spots swam in the corners of her vision. From far below on the toboggan run, the happy screams of children rose high into the air and echoed off the cold white hills.

BUMP, bump, bump. It made Edie want to scream. They'd just finished dinner half an hour ago, what could she want, now? *Bump, bump, bump.* Like she's rapping that cane on my skull. Never any peace. Work all day at a nothing job, in a nothing store, in a nothing town, and then come home to what? *Bump, bump, bump.*

"Edith! Edith, where are you? I need you!"

Edie turned from the sink with a wet plate in her hand and yelled toward the stairs, "I'm coming!" Then, in a normal voice, "You old bitch."

The tree in the backyard swayed, scraping an icy finger on the window. How green and benign that same tree had looked just months ago. Eric had come into her life, and everything had turned into the greenest summer Edie had ever seen.

Bump, bump, bump. She ignored the thump of Gram's cane on the ceiling, willing the icy branch to turn green once more. The whole summer had been rich with color, saturated with a million different shades of green and blue, drenched with the rapture of getting to know Eric. From boredom and nothingness, Eric had created passion. From emptiness, excitement. From misery, thrills.

I am a conquered country, she had written in her diary. *I am Eric's to rule as he sees fit. He has taken me by storm.* The words put her in mind of another storm, a stupendous blast of wind and rain that had come whipping across the iron gray of Lake Nipissing, last September.

They'd killed the Indian kid. Well, Eric had killed her, technically speaking, but she'd been in on it, she'd helped him pick her up, she'd kept the kid in her house, she'd watched him do it.

"Do you see that look in her eyes?" he'd said. "There's nothing like the look of fear. It's the one look you can trust."

The girl was tied to the brass bedstead, gagged with her own underpants and then a scarf tied round on top of that. All you could see was the tiny little nose, the brown almost black eyes widened to their limit. Deep pools of terror from which you could drink deep and long.

"You can do it just like that," Eric had said a few nights earlier. They had been talking by candlelight in the living room, Gram fast asleep upstairs. Eric liked to come over at night and sit with her in candlelight—not eating, not drinking, just talking or sharing long silences. He had been telling her his ideas for weeks, giving her books to read. He had leaned forward toward the coffee table, the candlelight deepening his sharp features, and snuffed the flame with thumb and forefinger.

And he did it just like that: with a little pinch of the nostrils. Snuffed her little life out with a delicate pinch of thumb and forefinger. It wasn't in the least violent, except for how the girl struggled.

Edie's knees had wobbled, and her stomach had turned over, but Eric had held her, and made her a cup of tea, and explained that it took a little getting used to but that eventually there was nothing like it.

He was right about that. Virtue was just an invention like the speed limit: a convention you could obey or not, as you saw fit. Eric had made her understand that you didn't have to be good, there was nothing *forcing* you to be good. A realization like that was pure jet fuel in your bloodstream.

That day had been weirdly hot for September, and when the girl was dead the room seemed suddenly full of birds, singing with delicious sweetness. Sunlight spilled through the window like gold.

Eric packed the body into a duffel bag that he could sling over his shoulder, and they set off in his Windstar for Shephard's Bay where he had rented a small boat. He'd even rented fishing rods, thoroughness and foresight being just two of the qualities Edie admired in him. Eric barely crossed the street without first writing out a detailed plan of action.

The boat was a twelve-foot aluminum thing with a thirty-horsepower Evinrude clamped on the stern. Once he had started the motor, Eric was content to let Edie steer. He sat in the prow by the duffel bag, the wind ruffling the soft spikes of his hair.

The wind seemed to tear right through Edie's thin nylon jacket. And it was suddenly colder when she steered out of the bay into the expanse of Lake Nipissing. The clouds fused into a somber landscape, and before long, it became dark as evening. Edie stayed near the shore, and soon they were passing Algonquin Bay, the limestone cathedral white against the charcoal sky. The city seemed tiny from out on the lake, hardly more than a village, but Edie was suddenly afraid that someone on the shore would sense something wrong about the boat—sense something odd in the couple heading into the teeth of a storm. Then a boat would approach, and police would demand that they open the duffel bag. Edie twisted the throttle, and the waves smacked louder at the hull.

Eric pointed west, and Edie turned the motor so that the town hove round behind them. Across the whole vaporous landscape, there wasn't another boat in sight. Eric grinned and gave her the thumbs-up sign, as if she were his copilot on a bombing run.

Soon, the island took shape on the horizon, the shaft-head rising into the sky like a sea monster. Edie steered toward it and lowered the throttle. Eric made a circling gesture, and Edie took them slowly round the tiny island. There was nothing else besides the mineshaft, there wasn't room. They scanned the lake for other boats, but there were none in sight.

Edie steered around a rocky point and nosed the boat in. Waves rocked them wildly, and when Eric stood up he had to clutch the gunwale, nearly pitching over the side. He jumped onto a flat rock with the rope. He pulled the boat the rest of the way onto the pebbly beach, the stones screeching against the hull.

"I don't like the look of those clouds," he said. "Let's get it done fast."

The duffel bag weighed a ton.

"God, old Katie's a dead weight, isn't she."

"Very funny," Edie said.

"You can let go, now. I've got it."

"You don't want me to help you up that slope?"

"Stay in the boat. I won't be long."

Edie watched Eric stagger up the slope with the duffel bag. Good thing no one had seen them with it: From this distance, it was obvious the bag contained a body. The girl's spine was a vivid curve inside the canvas, the bumps of her vertebrae clearly outlined. There were twin bumps where her heels strained against the fabric. There was a hard straight line where Eric had slipped the crowbar he would need to break the shafthead lock.

The first heavy raindrops falling into the boat sounded like gravel hitting a bucket. Edie huddled in her nylon jacket. Clouds flew overhead at incredible speed. The waves were frothing into whitecaps.

Eric had been gone about ten minutes when there was a loud throbbing, and a small outboard appeared at the end of the point. A boy stood up and waved at Edie. She waved back, gritting her teeth. Go away, damn you. Go *away.*

But the boat came purring closer. The boy clutched his windshield and shouted, "Are you all right?"

"Yes, just had a little engine trouble." The worst possible thing to say, and Edie immediately regretted it.

The boy brought his boat in closer, dead slow among the rocks. "Let me take a look for you."

"No, it's nothing. I just flooded it, that's all. And now I'm waiting for it to clear. It'll be fine. It's just flooded."

"I'll stick around, just in case."

"No, don't. You'll get soaked."

"That's all right. I'm already wet."

What if Eric came back out of the trees with the duffel bag still slung over his shoulder?

"How long ago did you try to start her up?"

"I don't know," Edie answered miserably. "Ten minutes maybe. Fifteen. It's all right. *Really.*"

"Let me give her a pull for you." He drew alongside and gripped the aluminum gunwales, grinning. "Can't leave a damsel in distress."

"No, please. I want to give it a bit longer. It floods easily, this motor."

From beyond the boy's shoulder, Eric appeared. Seeing their visitor, he drew back among the trees.

The boy was smiling at Edie. He was a gawky adolescent, all pimples and Adam's apple. "You from in town?"

Edie nodded. "Maybe I'll try it now," she said, lurching around. She yanked at the cord, and the motor coughed blue smoke.

From the corner of her eye, she could see Eric threading his way through the trees and down to the point. Another minute and he would be directly behind the boy. Something long and black gleamed in his hand. The crowbar, slick with rain.

"Is the pressure good? Better pump up the tank there."

"What?" Edie yanked the cord. And again.

"The rod on top of the gas tank. You probably have to pump it up. Want me to do it?"

Edie grasped the pump and worked it up and down. She felt the resistance stiffen, and it began to hurt her thumb. She pulled the cord again, and this time the motor caught with a roar. She gave the boy a big grin. Eric was maybe twenty yards behind him, half-hidden among the pines. He raised the crowbar over his shoulder.

"If you want, I can ride alongside. Make sure you get home okay."

"No, thanks. I'd rather do it alone."

The boy revved his own engine a couple of times. "Don't hang around too long. Storm could get a lot worse." There was a clunk as he slipped into reverse, the waves exploding into spray over the stern. When he was pointed away from the island, he gave her a solemn wave and went throbbing off into the storm.

Edie looked over at Eric, standing like a woodsman among the trees with his crowbar on his shoulder. "Jesus Christ," she said. "I thought he'd never get out of here."

Eric waited until the boy was a white speck in the distance before jumping into the boat.

"Jesus Christ," Edie said again. "I thought I'd wet my pants."

"Would have been simple enough to bust his head open." Eric dropped the crowbar, and it hit the floor of the boat with a bang. "Lucky for him I didn't happen to be in the mood."

Thunder cracked, and spears of lightning flung themselves at the horizon.

BUMP, bump, bump.

"All right, for God's sake!"

She went upstairs.

The old woman lay festering among the pillows. The air in the room was stale and hot. The television was on, but there was no picture.

"What do you want?"

"The thingamajig's gone. It's nothing but snow."

"You called me up just for that? You know it's always in your bed."

"It isn't in the bed. I've looked all over."

Edie flounced into the room and plucked the errant remote from the floor. She aimed it at the television and pushed the button till there was a picture.

Gram snatched the remote from her. "That's French! I don't want French!"

"What do you care? You don't have the sound on anyway."

"What?"

"I said, you don't have the sound on anyway!"

"I want company, that's all. People I could talk to if I met them." As if Alex Trebek's going to stop in for tea on his way to the studio.

Edie opened the window. She refilled the water glass, plumped the pillows, brought up a *Woman's Day* and a *Chatelaine* she'd swiped from the drugstore. Oh, Eric, save me from this.

"Edie, honey?" The wheedling tone was nauseating.

"I don't have time. Eric's coming over."

"Please, sweetie-peetie-pie? For your old Gram-Gram?"

"We just *did* your hair three days ago. I can't be drop-

ping everything just to do your hair. It's not like you're going out dancing."

"What? What's that?"

"I said, it's not as if you ever go anywhere!"

"Please, honey. Everyone wants to look nice."

"For God's sake."

"Come on, honey. We'll watch *Jeopardy* together." She
fiddled with the remote until the sound from the TV was
earsplitting. A newscaster was going on about Todd Curry,
promising an in-depth report at six. Yesterday's *Lode* had
carried a high-school picture of him, looking a hell of a lot
more innocent than he really was. Was it a drug deal gone
bad or is there a serial killer at large? *Pulse News at Six.*

Edie fetched the basin and washed Gram's hair. It was
so thin it took only a few minutes, but she hated the
soaked-dog smell. She put the rollers in, while Gram
shouted wrong answers at the television.

Edie emptied the basin of dirty water, and when she was
on the landing the doorbell rang, making her jump so hard
she dropped the basin. She was sure it would be the police.
But when she peered through the curtain, her blood leaped.
*Whenever Eric appears at my door, the chasm I dwell in
seems suddenly a shallow, bearable place and not the
black pit I imagine when he's gone. All the darkness seems
a figment of my imagination. Then there is air, and hope
once again. Suddenly, it becomes a livable place, my bot-
tomless pit. What light breaks over the rim!*

19

"I must say, it's all very fascinating," the librarian said. She was plump and pale, with bright blue eyes that shone behind a pair of glasses that were unflattering in the extreme. "Not to be ghoulish or anything, but there's nothing quite like a good murder to prick the intellect, get the brain humming, don't you find?"

"Did somebody mention a homicide?" Delorme said quietly. "I didn't say I was investigating a homicide."

"Oh, come now. You and that other detective were on Channel Four the night they found the Pine girl. Dreadful business. And when the boy was found in that house. No, no, Detective, you don't forget a thing like that. This isn't Toronto, you know. Have you definitely connected the two? It just gives one the *shivers*."

"Ma'am, I can't talk about an investigation in progress."

"No, no, of course you can't. You police have to keep certain details to yourself—otherwise any old nut could confess and who would ever know the truth? But what could possibly be the motive in such a case? I mean, the boy was sixteen—approximately sixteen I believe they said in the *Lode*—but that's still a child, and what kind of monster kills a child? *Two* children. The Windigo Killer, the *National Post* calls him. Ugh, it makes your blood run cold. You must have some theory you're working on?"

The librarian, surrounded by stacks of Agatha Christie and Dick Francis, living out her days among towers of Erle Stanley Gardner and P. D. James, seemed to imagine that Delorme had stepped out of a mystery novel for the sole purpose of enlivening her day. A fine sweat beaded on her upper lip.

"Ma'am, I can't discuss that case with you. Are you coming up with anything?"

The librarian's attack on her keyboard was like a murder lifted from one of her authors—a multiple stabbing. "This computer system," she said with a frustrated hiss, "is less than state of the art. Quite wretched, in fact. Oh, damn this thing."

Delorme left the librarian inflicting futile injuries on her keyboard and found the bins of CDs. Around her, readers drifted in and out of the stacks. Delorme had spent a lot of time here as a teenager, even though the library was notoriously short on French books. She had preferred to do her homework here, among the smells of print and paper, the quiet rustle of pages, rather than at home with the hockey game blaring on television and her father yelling at his beloved Canadiens. Of course, Delorme had done a lot of daydreaming here, too. She couldn't wait to go away to college, and then she had surprised herself in her final year at Ottawa U. by realizing she was homesick. It was sometimes weird to be a cop in your hometown—she had arrested more than one former classmate—but the big city was not for her. She had found the people in Ottawa far colder than anything Algonquin Bay could throw at her.

The library's CD collection yielded no Pearl Jam, no Rolling Stones, but yes, she did come up with the Anne Murray. The plastic cover was smudged and smeared with a thousand fingerprints. She slipped it into an envelope and went back to the counter.

"My goodness, you're impounding something? You've found actual evidence?"

"The Anne Murray album. I didn't see any of the others."

"It seems we don't carry the other two. We never had the Pearl Jam, no surprise there, and the Rolling Stones we *used* to have but it was so popular it got damaged or worn out or something and it was removed from circulation"— she prodded her keyboard mercilessly—"two years ago. Now, tell me, Detective. Can it really be true you police don't know how that little girl died?"

"Ma'am . . ."

"I know, I know. Just too curious for my own good. But I did dig up those names for you." She adjusted her glasses and peered at a piece of paper on which she had noted the information. "The album you have there was borrowed by Leonard Neff, Edith Soames, and Colin McGrath. As it happens, I remember Mr. McGrath. His behavior was unruly. We had to ask him to exit the premises." She pronounced it premi-*sees*.

"Unruly in what way? Had he been drinking?"

"Oh, no doubt Mr. McGrath was intoxicated. But there's no excuse for obscenities of that kind. I nearly summoned some of your colleagues—my hand was positively trembling over that dial."

"And the others—Miss Soames and Mr. Neff. Do you remember anything about them?"

The librarian closed her eyes as if in prayer, then said with conviction, "Not a thing."

Delorme pulled out her notebook. "I'm going to need addresses on all three."

DELORME had ignored Algonquin Bay's retail music outlets. None of the albums was new, all three were extremely popular, and there was no reason to believe they were even purchased in town. Cardinal—except for the possible radio angle—had finally discounted the music altogether. If Delorme had found that all three CDs were held by the library, and all three had been checked out around September 12 to the same person, *that* might have meant something. But tracking a single piece of music to the library carried no weight at all. After six years in Special Investigations, Lise Delorme knew a dead end when she saw one.

And yet, following up on the library CD made her heart beat a little faster. The library CD was something she could hold in her hand; it gave the illusion of direction because it led somewhere right now, not a week from now—and besides, the library CD was her *only* lead.

Mr. Leonard Neff's address was a modern brick bungalow in Cedarvale, an affluent subdivision of mewses, courts, and places laid out with sterile precision at the top of Rayne Street. There was a hockey net set up in the driveway, where a couple of boys in Montreal Canadiens jerseys were firing slapshots at each other. The Taurus parked out front had ski equipment strapped to the roof rack. Apparently a sporting family, the Neffs. The windows of the house were modern and triple-glazed, not likely to rattle with every passing truck. In any case, Cedar Crescent, Cedar Mews, and Cedar Place (the town council apparently did not waste its creative energy on the naming of streets) attracted little traffic of any sort, certainly not trucks.

Delorme's second stop was the home of the unruly Mr. McGrath. This turned out to be a small apartment house at the turnoff to Airport Road. Delorme got out of the car and listened a moment. The drone of an Air Ontario plane coming in for a landing. Highway 17 was less than fifty yards away; the traffic was a constant hiss. A woman heavily burdened with groceries tottered up the front steps and struggled with her keys. Delorme rushed to hold the front door open for her and entered the building enveloped in the woman's gratitude. Mr. McGrath's apartment was on the first floor at the far end of the building. Delorme stood in the hallway, listening. No traffic, just sounds from other apartments: a vacuum cleaner, the cry of a parakeet, the metallic chatter of a TV game show.

The last name on the list sounded like a little old lady: Edith Soames. All right, I *know* it's a dead end, Delorme told herself. There isn't a chance in hell that Todd Curry or Katie Pine was killed by some little old lady, but sometimes you just go with what you have, you take a flier, you see what happens.

The Soames address was just two blocks east of the house Delorme had grown up in, and she was sidetracked for a few moments by nostalgia. She drove past the rock cut where at the age of six Larry Laframboise had given her a split lip. On the corner was the North Star Coffee Shop where she had overheard Thérèse Lortie—formerly a friend—saying Lise Delorme could be a real slut sometimes. Half a block farther: the park bench where Geoff Girard had told her he didn't want to marry her. She recalled the sudden heat of tears streaming down her face.

She drove by her old house and tried not to look, but at the last minute she slowed the car and stared. The place looked more rundown than ever. She and Geoff used to sit on that dilapidated front porch for hours, feeling each other up under a blanket. One night her father had come out and chased him halfway down to Algonquin Avenue, sixteen-year-old Lise screaming at him the whole time. It was on that porch that she had first had sex—with another boy, not with Geoff. Maybe Thérèse Lortie had been right.

Well, her father was long gone—vanished out west to Moose Jaw or somewhere, and her mother was dead. Geoff Girard was married and father to about fourteen bright blond children out in Shephard's Bay. The house had long ago been divided into apartments, as had most of the old houses in the neighborhood.

The Soames house was as rundown as the rest of the block. The facade of fake red brick had blackened with age and was peeling around the windows, which were the heavy ancient storm variety. Delorme had a sudden memory of her father teetering on a ladder with one of those huge windows clutched in his hands. When traffic went by, they rattled.

The door opened, and a little old lady was helped onto the porch by a woman in her twenties, perhaps a grand-daughter or a visiting nurse. Their progress was hampered by heavy winter coats and the old woman's terror of slipping on the icy steps. The young woman steadied her elbow and frowned impatiently at the faltering steps.

Delorme got out of the car and waited for them on the sidewalk. "Excuse me," she said, flashing her badge. "I'm working on a string of burglaries in this neighborhood." It was true that Arthur Wood had looted several apartments in the area, but Delorme didn't mention that the burglaries had occurred three years previously.

"What's that?" the old woman yelled. "What's she saying?"

"Burglaries!" the younger one shouted back. She made a face of helplessness at Delorme, a face that said, Old people—what can you do with them? "We haven't had any break-ins," she said.

"Have you seen anything unusual? Vans hanging around? Strangers watching the street?"

"No. I haven't noticed anything strange."

"What's that! What's she saying! Tell me what she's saying!"

"It's okay, Gram! It's nothing!"

Delorme gave them the ritual warning to keep their doors and windows locked. The young woman promised they would. Delorme felt a twinge of pity: a bad case of eczema or some other disease had damaged her face. Her skin looked as rough as elephant hide, and there were raw patches, as if it had been scrubbed brutally with wire wool. The woman was not ugly, but the hangdog look and the averted eyes spoke of an inner conviction that she was. The world was unlikely to offer her anything other than this crabbed existence with her aged grandmother, and the young woman knew it.

"What's she saying? Tell me what she's saying!"

"Come on, Gram! The store'll be closed by the time we get there!"

"Tell me what's going on! I like to know what's going on, Edie!"

So, the younger one was Edith Soames. Well, as grandmother and granddaughter they might both have that name; it made no difference. A lonely young woman had once borrowed from the library one of the most popular records in the country, a record thousands of people had bought or borrowed or taped; it meant nothing.

Delorme left them to their slow struggle toward MacPherson Street. It would have been so nice to report to her suspicious partner that she had made some headway. But Delorme turned the corner, swerving a little on the icy road, certain that the morning's progress amounted to exactly zero.

20

ERIC Fraser opened the side of his brand-new hot-off-the-truck Sony video camera. He put in a tape, fresh from a shrink-wrapped pack of three—courtesy of the Future Shop's five-finger discount—and slapped the side of the camera closed. He told Edie to just act natural, to pretend he wasn't there, but it seemed to make her all the more nervous.

"Why do you want a tape of me doing dishes?" she whined. "Can't you wait till I'm doing something more interesting?" She was scrubbing vigorously at the bottom of a saucepan. "I haven't even brushed my hair."

As if brushing her hair would make some incredible difference. He wanted to test the camera before putting it to use in the field. On location, so to speak. The last tape had been very poor quality—the lousy camera he'd used had pretty much ruined it.

He opened the lens to its widest angle, taking in Edie, the cupboards, even the back door with its cracked window, its view of the scraggly, snowy tree. Can't beat the Japanese when it comes to cameras; the lens was first-class. Sound was supposed to be good, too. Eric had read up on the specs.

Edie was plunging the dishmop in and out of a glass so that it made exaggerated sucking noises. It made Eric want to hit her. Sometimes I don't know why I bother, he said to himself. I swear I don't. This was the running commentary Eric Fraser carried on with himself all the time. Yet it was hard to resist Edie's sheer worship of him; he had never experienced anything like it. And if she didn't look the way he wanted her to look, well, he told himself, maybe I shouldn't even think of her as a woman. I should think of her as a pet, some kind of reptile.

"Eric, we already talked about this when we taped . . . you know. When we taped—"

"Todd Curry getting his brains beat out. It's just words, Edie. You can say them." He hated it when she went all mealymouthed.

"We can't be making movies of this stuff."

"*Stuff*. What *stuff*? Say the words, Edie. Say the words."

"I thought we agreed it's a surefire way to get caught. We talked about it. I thought we agreed."

"What *stuff*, Edie? If you can do it, you can say it. What *stuff*? Say the words. I'll quit talking altogether, if you're going to get all mealymouthed."

"Stuff like Todd Curry getting his brains bashed out. Stuff like Katie Pine getting suffocated. Like Billy La-Belle. There. Are you satisfied?"

"We didn't tape Billy LaBelle. Thanks to you letting him choke on his fucking gag."

"I don't see why that's my fault. You're the one who tied him up."

Eric didn't push it; Edie's face, that patchy hide, had gone tomato red. Such a turn-on to hear her say the words. *Suffocated. Bashed.* Eric basked in the sounds for a few moments before speaking again. "People want to see violence, Edie. They have a *need* to see violence. They've always had a need to see violence. Just like they've always had a need to inflict it." *Inflict.* He turned the lovely liquid sound over in his mind. *Inflict.*

"We can't keep going on camera, Eric. And you certainly can't show the film to anyone. It's insane."

Inflict. Inflict. So lovely and liquid on the tongue, Eric couldn't stop repeating it to himself.

"How long can we keep films of this stuff—these parties. It's just so risky."

Eric was opening the camera, now, extracting the videotape. There was an input for a stereo microphone, and his thoughts turned toward music. What would be the proper accompaniment? Heavy metal? Something electronic?

Edie's voice yanked him out of reverie. "There was a cop outside, today. A female cop."

Eric looked up. He told himself there was no need for panic, it was probably nothing.

"She was parked across the street. Said there'd been a bunch of burglaries."

Probabilities flickered through Eric's mind: Had they made any terrible errors? Could the cops know anything about them? No. There was no reason for the cops to suspect them of anything. He relayed this to Edie, in his calmest, most rational voice. Algonquin Bay. How smart can the cops be in a snowbound dump like Algonquin Bay?

"It scared me, Eric. I don't want to go to prison."

"You won't."

Eric was not in the mood to talk, but he didn't want Edie backing out on him, and he could see she needed reassurance. That was easy enough. Edie was like a telephone menu: you just had to push the right button. *For soothed nerves, push 1.* "If the cops were really watching us," he said reasonably, "there's no way she would have spoken to you. Obviously, Edie, if the woman suspected you of anything, the last thing she's going to do is let you know it. The most logical explanation is she was checking out burglaries, just like she said. Nothing to worry about." It was the most Eric had said to Edie in three weeks.

She was already responding. She was still standing at the sink, and her back was to him, but he could see her shoulders relaxing. "Really, Eric?" she said. "Do you really think that?"

"I don't think it, I *know* it." He could see her muscles loosen at the sound of his confidence. He *was* confident, wasn't he? The appearance of a cop in the neighborhood was—well, all right, maybe it was a little unnerving, but it would serve to make him more careful, more alert. Until the discovery of Katie Pine's body, the police had remained abstract figures, the black shapes of nightmare. Then they had appeared on television; they had taken on human form. And with the finding of Todd Curry, they had even become familiar, at least that one detective—the tall one with the sad face.

Television had made the Windigo Killer familiar, too. Eric had almost come to believe in the mythical murderer. He had a vague idea of him as some middle-aged nonentity, a janitor, say, or a middle manager, who stalked the playgrounds and swept children away to their doom. He certainly didn't think of himself as the Windigo Killer. That was just television chatter. News nerds telling ghost stories.

But the police had taken on flesh and bone. Flesh and bone waiting outside in the falling snow. Waiting for him. Let them. It would make him all the stronger.

"I'd rather die than go to prison," Edie was saying. "I wouldn't last a day in there."

"No one's going to prison," Eric told her. This cop had no connection to them. He aimed the camera at Edie, sending the zoom out to its full length so that her nose and cheekbone filled his entire field of vision. Christ, what a beauty queen. But that's my Edie's hidden strength: She's so disgusted by what she sees in the mirror that it makes her loyal. The complete control of another human being was not to be sneezed at, even if it was only Edie. *For cowed acquiescence, push 2.* "You're not going to turn into a weakling," he asked casually. "Like all the nobodies out there? I thought you were different, Edie, but maybe I was wrong."

"Oh, don't say that, Eric. You know I'll stick with you. I'll stick with you, no matter what."

"I thought you had guts. Backbone. But I'm beginning to have doubts."

"Please, Eric. Don't lose faith in me. I'm *not* as strong as you."

"You don't act like you think I'm strong. You think just because I'm forced to live in a dump I'm not different? I am different. I am fucking extraordinary. And you'd better be fucking extraordinary, too, frankly, because I don't have time for nobodies."

"I'll be strong, I promise. It's just sometimes, I forget how—"

They both went still, listening. There was a thudding noise. The old biddy banging her cane.

Edie had gone pale. "I thought it was Keith," she said. "Maybe it's not such a good idea to keep him here. It's dangerous, don't you think?"

"Don't call him by name. How many times do I have to tell you?"

"Our guest, then. Don't you think it's dangerous?"

Eric was tired of reassuring her. He took his camera and went down the basement steps to a door beside the furnace. Taking a key out of his pocket, he snapped open the padlock and went into a small dank bedroom where Keith London lay sleeping.

The room was perfectly square, built by a previous owner of the house who had rented it out to students at the Teachers College nearby. Keith London was sprawled on his back, mouth open, one hand clutching a blanket to his chest, the other hanging over the edge of the bed, like someone dead in a bathtub. A tiny window high in the wall that Eric had boarded over admitted flat blades of light. The walls were cheap pine paneling.

Eric turned on the lights.

The figure in the bed did not stir. Eric checked the edges of the window, the doorjamb, the possible routes of escape, even though it was evident his guest had never left the bed. Even without the party, this one had proved quite a haul. His wallet had contained over three hundred bucks, and they had helped him retrieve a very nice Ovation guitar from the train station.

Eric looked through the camera without running any tape. He slid the zoom out to full length, focusing on the adolescent face. The beginnings of a wispy beard bristled on the chin. A filling gleamed in the back of the open mouth, and under the eyelids the hidden eyes jerked back and forth in a dream.

Humming to himself, Eric reached down and tugged at

the corner of blanket clutched in Keith's hand. He pulled the blankets down to the knees and looked through the lens at the hairless chest, the pale smooth belly, zooming in on the small, slack penis. When he heard Edie coming down the steps, he pulled the blankets back up to Keith's chin.

"Still out cold," Edie said. "That stuff is really strong." She leaned over the bed. "Hey, genius! Up and at 'em! Rise and shine!"

Eric handed her the camera. Edie fiddled with the lens, focusing. "He looks so funny," she said. "He looks so stupid."

Later, Edie wrote in her diary: *I bet that's how we look to angels and devils. They see everything bad we do, they see all our weaknesses. We lie there totally oblivious, dreaming our sweet dreams, and all the time these supernatural beings are hovering over the bed, laughing at us, waiting for just the right moment to prick our balloons. He doesn't know it yet, but I'm going to see that boy bleed.*

21

PERHAPS because he had been raised a Catholic, the idea of having an address on Madonna Road had always appealed to Cardinal; the word held rich associations of mercy, purity, and love. The Madonna was the mother who had survived the sorrow of her Son's murder, the woman who had been received physically into heaven, the saint who interceded for sinners with a God who could be, let's face it, something of a hard-ass.

The associations were muddied now—a pop star had come along and replaced mercy with commerce, purity with camp, and love with lust—but Madonna Road was still a peaceful address, a curved narrow lane along the western edge of Trout Lake, where the birches creaked in the cold, and the snow slipped from their branches in silent clumps.

Cardinal had long ago stopped going to Mass, but the habit of continual self-examination and self-blame stayed with him. He was also honest enough to admit that most days these habits only served to make him neurotic, not good. He had reason to be thinking this way at the moment: His tiny house on Madonna Road, far from being a comfort, was freezing. "Winterized lakefront cottage," the ad had said. But when the temperature dropped out of sight, the only way to keep the place warm enough was to get both the fireplace and the woodstove going full blast. Cardinal was wearing lined corduroys and a flannel work-shirt over long underwear. Still cold, he had wrapped himself in a terrycloth bathrobe. He was sipping from a steaming cup of coffee, but his hands were frigid. It had taken ten minutes to fill the kettle from his frozen pipes. On this less-than-merciful stretch of Madonna Road, the wind whipped off the lake and pressed right through his windows with their very expensive and completely futile triple glazing.

The surface of the lake was so white it made Cardinal's eyes water to look at it. He drew the curtains closed in an attempt at insulation. Somewhere out there across the frozen lake, somewhere in the middle of town perhaps, the killer was going about his normal day. He, too, might be enjoying a cup of coffee while Katie Pine lay dead and her mother sat grieving, while Billy LaBelle lay buried god-knows-where, and Todd Curry was on a coroner's slab in Toronto. The killer might be listening to records—Anne Murray, anyone?—or hiking through the dazzling snow with his camera slung over his shoulder. Cardinal made a mental note to check the local camera club, if there was one. If the killer took pictures of Katie Pine, he could hardly risk taking them to the drugstore; he would have to develop them himself. Such a person might belong to a camera club.

Thinking of cameras made him think of Catherine. One of the worst things about her illness was how it robbed her of all creative energy. When she was well, the house was always full of photographs in various stages of completion. She would be in and out, cameras hanging from both shoulders, excited about some project or other. Then the illness came and the cameras were the first thing to go, jettisoned like dead weight from a sinking ship. He had called her before breakfast, and she had sounded pretty good; he even allowed himself to think she might be home some-time soon.

BUT now the telephone waited for him with the implacable silence of an executioner. Cardinal had resolved after a long sleepless night that he would call Kelly this morning and tell her she would have to find another, cheaper grad school next term; her Yale days were over. She'd done her BFA at York, no reason why she couldn't go back. From the moment he first took that money, guilt had begun to drip inside him. It was not just the prospect of being exposed by Delorme; there was not much chance of that. But month by month, year by year, the acid of guilt had eaten through the layers of denial, and he couldn't stand it anymore.

The worst thing was knowing that he was not the husband that Catherine loved, the father that Kelly loved. They both had this misconception about him: They thought he was good. Although his crime might be victimless—who was going to care in the long scheme of things whether Cardinal in a moment of weakness had relieved a criminal of a large sum of money?—for years, now, he had been an unknown quantity to the people he loved, an utter stranger. Kelly respected the father and cop he *used* to be. The loneliness of being unknowable was becoming unbearable.

And so he had resolved to call her and explain what he had done and that he could not afford to keep her at Yale. Christ, the girl has an IQ of 140, can't she figure it out? How does a small-town Canadian cop send his kid to Yale? Did she really buy the story about the money coming from the long-ago sale of his grandparents' house? Did Catherine? Self-delusion must run in the family. All right, he would tell her, let her complete the semester, and then, having wrapped up the little matter of nailing the killer of Katie Pine and Billy LaBelle and Todd Curry, he would confess to Dyson and the chief. He would lose his job, but jail time would be unlikely.

He picked up the phone and dialed Kelly's number in the States. One of her roommates answered—Cleo? Barbara? he couldn't tell them apart—and shouted for Kelly to pick up.

"Hi, Daddy." When did she start calling me that again? Cardinal wondered. They had gone through a brief "Pop" phase, which Cardinal had barely tolerated, then back to the usual "Dad," but lately it was "Daddy." It must be an American thing, he decided, like saying "real good" for "really good" and pronouncing "probably" with the accent on the last syllable, but this was one American mannerism he enjoyed.

"Hi, Kelly. How's school going?" So plain, so flat. Why

can't I call her princess or sweetheart, the way fathers do on TV? Why can't I say the place is colder without you? Without Catherine? Why not tell her this tiny house is suddenly the size of an airport?

"I'm working on a humongous project for my painting class, Daddy. Dale's taught me that I work best on a monumental scale, not on the crabbed little canvases I always stuck with before. It's like being set free. I can't tell you how good it feels. My work is a hundred times better."

"Sounds good, Kelly. Sounds like you're enjoying it." That's what he said. What he thought was: God, it moves me so to hear you're happy, to hear that you're growing, that your life is full and good.

Kelly chattered on about learning at last how to wield paint, and normally Cardinal would have basked in her enthusiasm. In the course of his sleepless night he had stood in the doorway of her bedroom and stared at the narrow bed she had slept in for a week, picked up the paperback she had been reading, just to touch something his daughter had touched.

He stood in the doorway now, the cordless phone tucked under his chin. The room was a pretty pale yellow, with a wide window looking out on birch trees, but it had never really been Kelly's room. Cardinal and Catherine had moved to Madonna Road after Kelly had gone to university, and the room was just a place she inhabited when she visited.

A TV father would tell her how he had touched her book just to touch something she had touched, but Cardinal could never say such a thing.

"One thing, though, Daddy. A bunch of us are planning a trip to New York next week. It's the last week of the Francis Bacon exhibition and it's really something I should see. But you know I didn't budget for any trips, and this would cost about two hundred dollars by the time you factor in meals and gas and everything."

"Two hundred American?"

"Um, yeah. Two hundred American. It's too much, isn't it?"

"Well, I don't know. How important is this, Kelly?"

"I won't do it if you think it's too much. I'm sorry. I shouldn't have mentioned it."

"No, no. That's okay. If it's important."

"I know I'm costing you a fortune. I do try to save money wherever I can, Daddy. I mean, you wouldn't believe all the things I *don't* do."

"I know. It's okay. I'll wire the money to your account this afternoon."

"You sure it's okay?"

"It's fine. But next year will have to be different, Kelly."

"Oh, next year will be real different. I mean, I'll be done with all my classes—I'll just have my final project: two or three canvases for the group show, depending how much Dale thinks I should do. I'll be able to take a part-time job next year. I'm sorry everything's so expensive, Daddy. Sometimes I wonder how you manage. I hope you know how grateful I am."

"Don't you worry about it."

"I hope one day I make a ton of money off my painting so I can pay some of it back."

"Really, Kelly, don't you even think about that." The phone was slick with sweat in Cardinal's hand, and his heart flapped at his rib cage. Kelly's gratitude had unmanned him. In the core of his being, a door clicked shut, a bolt shot home, and a sign long out of use was hung over the window: CLOSED UNTIL FURTHER NOTICE.

"You sound a little tense, Daddy. Work driving you crazy?"

"Well, the press is yelling at us. I get the feeling they won't be happy till we bring in the Air Force. I'm not making the progress I should."

"You will."

They closed with an exchange on their separate weathers: hers sunny and warm and measured in Fahrenheit; his bright and cold and measured in centigrade degrees below zero. Cardinal tossed the phone onto the sofa. He stood dead still in the center of the living room like a man who has just received terrible news. There was a noise from outside, and it took him a few moments to realize what it was. Then he rushed through the kitchen and threw open the side door, yelling, "Go on, beat it, you little rodent!"

He saw the raccoon's fat hindquarters wriggle under the house. Normally a raccoon would be hibernating this time of year, but the floor of Cardinal's house was leaking heat—enough heat to confuse this raccoon into thinking there was no winter. The first time Cardinal had caught sight of the masked face, the raccoon had been examining half an apple in its precise black paws. Now, it emerged two or three times a week to topple the garbage cans in his garage and root through the mess for edible scraps.

Shivering furiously, Cardinal scrambled after the bits of plastic wrap, the empty doughnut container, the gnawed chicken bone strewn across the garage floor. He went back inside just in time to hear the phone ringing.

It took him three rings to remember where he had tossed the handset. He snatched it up from among the sofa cushions just as Delorme was about to ring off.

"Oh," she said, "I thought you must be already on your way in."

"I was just leaving. What's up?"

"We got the tape back from the CBC guy. Also of course he sent the digital version? The enhanced version?" Delorme's French Canadian interrogatives had never sounded so welcome.

"Did you listen to it yet? Did you play it?"

"No. It just arrived this second."

"I'll be right there."

22

KEITH London sat up groggily in bed. The room he was in looked unfamiliar, and he wondered if this was partly because it seemed to be turning, ever so slowly, like a carousel running down. When it came to a stop and his eyes managed to focus, he saw four walls covered with cheap wooden paneling, warped and stained by water damage. An armchair tilted on three legs, its arms scarred with cigarette burns. On the floor, a short flat space heater buzzed intermittently as if a bug were trapped inside. Overhead a dim bulb throbbed behind a cheap fixture, and a Via Rail poster of Vancouver curled on one wall. The tiny window was boarded up from the outside. The air was clogged with smells of heating oil, mold, and wet concrete.

Then he remembered: He'd picked up his stuff from the bus station while Eric and Edie waited for him outside. He remembered getting into a small car with Eric and Edie and having a beer in their kitchen. But he didn't remember going to bed or taking his clothes off. After the beer, nothing. His limbs felt gross and exhausted as if he had slept too long. He rubbed his face, and the flesh felt rubbery and strangely hot. His watch—evidently he had forgotten to take it off in his hurry to undress—said three o'clock. The need to urinate was pressing.

Although the room could not have been more than nine feet square, it had two doors. Keith set his feet on the cold floor, sitting on the edge of the bed. He remained like this for some time, and would have fallen asleep again, if the need for a bathroom had not been urgent. He forced himself up onto his feet and leaned against the wall for balance. The first door he tried was locked—stuck, anyway—but the second, luckily, proved to be a bathroom, the fittings almost miniaturized to fit the tiny cubicle.

Tottering back toward the bed, he caught sight of his guitar case propped in a corner. He had just enough time to register that his duffel bag and his clothes were nowhere in sight, before he slid headlong into a dark pit of unconsciousness.

When he woke—hours later? days?—Eric Fraser was sitting on the bed, big grin on his face. "Lazarus awakes," he said quietly.

Keith, with a great effort, propped himself up against the headboard. He could feel his body listing to one side but hadn't the strength to right himself. His mouth and throat were terribly dry; when he tried to speak his voice was a feeble croak. "How long have I been asleep?"

Eric held two fingers so close to Keith's face that he couldn't focus. It looked like three fingers.

"Two whole days?" Was that possible? Keith could not remember ever having slept that long in his life. A couple of times in early adolescence he'd slept for sixteen hours, and once, when very ill with a fever, he'd conked out for twenty. But two days?

If I've really been asleep for two days, I must be very, very sick. Healthy people don't sleep for two days. That's called coma. Keith was about to express some of this when Eric preempted him by pressing a cold hand against his forehead and holding it there with a thoughtful expression. "Yesterday you had a fever of a hundred and three. Edie took your temperature. She used your armpit."

"Where are my clothes? I think I better see a doctor."

"Edie's washing your clothes. You threw up."

"Did I? That's awful." Keith rubbed his throat; it was burning. "Is there any water?"

"Bathroom." Eric pointed to a small door. "But you'd better drink some of this." He presented a steaming mug. "Edie's concoction. She brought it home from the drugstore. Don't worry. Edie's a pharmacist."

Steamy aromas of honey and lemon were flowing from the cup. Keith took a sip, scorching his tongue. It was a flu remedy or something, probably nothing more than Tylenol and antihistamine, but it felt good going down. After a few sips Keith began to feel better. The fog lifted a little. He pointed to the Polaroid hanging from Eric's neck. "What's that for?"

"Test shots. Edie and I are deeply involved in filmmaking. It's one of the reasons we noticed you. We were hoping you'd be in our film."

"What kind of film is it?"

"Low budget. Experimental. Poetic. I wanted to ask you the other night, but I was afraid it would be . . . inappropriate."

"That's okay. I'd be glad to help." Keith slid back down in the bed and curled up. Sleep seemed once again like an excellent idea.

Eric held up a newspaper. *"The Algonquin Lode,"* he said. "We call it *The Load of Bull*." He rattled noisily through the pages. He cleared his throat and began to read in a slow, deliberate voice. *"Algonquin Bay police were out in force at the corner of Timothy and Main streets earlier today where the body of an unidentified male, apparently murdered, was discovered in the coal cellar of a vacant house. Investigators have not ruled out the possibility that the murder was committed by the same person who killed Katie Pine last September.*

"According to Detective John Cardinal, the victim had been savagely beaten, suffering multiple facial injuries, and the genitals had been kicked until they were almost completely separated from the body."

"Jesus," Keith said. "That happened here?"

"It took place right here in Algonquin Bay. Not far from this room."

"Jesus," Keith said again. "Imagine being beaten like that. It doesn't sound like your normal bar fight."

"Well, let's not rush to judgment. They don't say what the victim was like. Maybe he started it. Maybe the world is a better place without him. I don't miss him. Do you?"

"Nobody deserves to die that way. I don't care what he did."

"You're soft-hearted. Edie always goes for the gentle ones. Your girlfriend must love that about you. What did you say her name was?"

"Karen. Yeah, I don't know. Karen'd be happier if I were a little more future-oriented. She's pissed off right now."

"Tell me about the sexual customs in Toronto. I hear oral sex is all the rage. Is Karen a devotee?"

"Jesus, Eric." Keith had been slipping into the blood-warm waters of sleep. I'll just sleep a little more, he assured himself, then I'll get the hell out of here.

"I couldn't help noticing your penis, Keith, when we undressed you. Big pair of balls, too. Karen's a lucky girl."

Keith wanted to tell him to lay off, but he couldn't transmit the message from his brain to his tongue. That honey and lemon had really knocked him for a loop.

Eric placed a hand on Keith's knee, gripping it. "People don't understand the terrible things I've seen—the rape, the sexual abuse. I've had a rough time, Keith, and sometimes it makes me a little . . . uneasy. Would you like me to stroke your genitals?"

Keith tried to focus. God, what was in that drink?

Time passed. Five minutes, possibly twenty. Eric drew the covers up to Keith's chin. "I'm excited about this film, Keith. So is Edie. You're just right for the part. You said you like experiences. This film will be a new experience."

Keith finally managed to work his tongue. "What's wrong with me? I can hardly move." He was sinking down, down into oblivion, so he couldn't be sure if he just imagined this, but Eric Fraser leaned over and kissed his forehead. Then whispered, "I know."

23

"Tell me how good I am, Cardinal. We have this tape sitting here, I don't even touch it. You wouldn't have waited. You'd have listened to it five times by now."

"It's a character flaw of mine," Cardinal said, still stamping snow from his boots. "Did Len Weisman call yet?"

"No. I got the feeling you didn't want me to bug him too much."

"Two days, though. How long can it take to match dental records?"

Delorme just shrugged. Cardinal was suddenly aware of her breasts and felt his face color. For God's sake, he scolded himself, Catherine's sick in the O.H. Besides which, Detective Lise Delorme may have a cute shape and a good face, but she's also trying to nail me to the wall and I will not allow myself to be attracted to her. If I were a stronger person, it wouldn't happen.

Delorme handed Cardinal a postal carton the size of a shoe box. Inside, swaddled in bubble wrap, lay a brand-new cassette tape. Someone had written across the CBC label in blue Magic Marker: "Digitally Enhanced."

"I borrowed Flower's Walkman," Delorme said. "It takes two sets of headphones." Delorme handed him a pair and they both plugged in.

Cardinal cleared a patch of her desk and sat down, holding the wire that connected them like Siamese twins joined at the ear. He switched on the tape and stared out the window at a grader shooting up a tidal wave of snow. Immediately, he hit the pause button. "It's a lot clearer, now. You couldn't hear that jet before."

"You think it's up Airport Drive, maybe?" Delorme's face when she was excited became wonderfully animated; Cardinal could see the girl she had been. For a fleeting moment he thought he might be wrong: She really had left

Special, she really wasn't investigating him. Then back to the horror on tape.

All hiss was gone. When the windows rattled, it was as though you could reach into that faraway room and shut them. The killer's footsteps rang out like rifle shots. And the child's fear, well, that had come through loud and clear on the first version. They listened through the last tears Katie Pine had shed. The killer's footsteps receded from the microphone. Then there was a new sound.

Delorme snatched off her headphones. "Cardinal! Did you hear that?"

"Play it again."

Delorme rewound. They listened again to the girl's last sobs, then the footsteps, and then, unmistakably, just a split second before the machine was switched off, the solemn chiming of a clock. Halfway through the third chime, the recorder had been switched off, and silence followed.

"It's fantastic," Delorme said. "You couldn't hear it at all on the original."

"It's great, Lise. All we have to do is match it to our suspect's clock. The one minor problem, of course, being that we don't have a suspect." Cardinal used Delorme's phone to dial the CBC.

"You got the tape, I take it." Fortier's radio-announcer voice came over the line deep and clear, as if he, too, had been digitally enhanced.

"You did a great job, Mr. Fortier. I'm worried you did a little too well."

"There's nothing added that wasn't on the original, if that's what you mean. With an analogue equalizer you're limited to boosting or suppressing frequencies. With digital, you can play around with individual sources. I split each source into an individual track—one for the windows, one for the clock, one for his voice, one for hers. What you have in your hand is the final mix, not intended for court-room evidence, obviously, but possibly useful in other ways."

"Can you do anything about the man's voice? It still sounds like he's down a well."

"Hopeless case, I'm afraid. He's just too far from the mike."

"Well, you've done a terrific piece of work."

"Any engineer could have done it—assuming he heard that clock in the first place. I have the advantage of being blind, of course. Even so, I didn't hear the clock till the fourth or fifth pass."

"Sounds like a grandfather clock to me."

"Not at all. Listen to it. It's not nearly resonant enough for a grandfather clock. It's a shelftop—and fairly old, I'd say. What you want now is a clock expert—some gnarled old Swiss guy. You play it back for him, he tells you the make, model, and serial number."

Cardinal laughed. "If I can ever do anything for the CBC, give me a call."

"A budget increase would be nice. And say hi to Officer Delorme. She has a very attractive voice."

"Actually, Brian, you're on the speakerphone here."

"No, I'm not, Detective. Nice try, though."

"You like him," Delorme observed, when he hung up. "You don't like a lot of people, but you like him."

"He said you have a nice voice."

"Really? And about the clock?"

"Shelf-size, probably old. Said we should play it for an expert."

"In Algonquin Bay? What expert? Zellers? Wal-Mart?"

"Must be some place that repairs clocks. If not here, certainly in Toronto."

The phone rang and Delorme picked it up. After a moment, she held it out to Cardinal and said, "Weisman."

"Len, what the hell happened? Where's our dental report?"

"Fucking dentist, I can't believe this guy. Keeps putting us off, screens his calls, doesn't show up, etcetera. Finally, I get ahold of the creep personally and we go in. Know why he's putting us off? Turns out he's been overbilling like crazy."

"What do you mean, Len? What's on the chart?"

"It's full of fillings the guy never did. Makes it look like the kid had enough fillings to pave Lake Ontario. Patient in the morgue, on the other hand, shows only five small fillings."

"But those five, Len, those five. Do they match?"

"Luckily, the work this crooked bastard really did was marked in a different color. Five little fillings marked in red pen: perfect match. Our patient is Todd William Curry."

24

TODD Curry's parents lived in a two-bedroom apartment in Mississauga, a vast sprawl on the western edge of Toronto that ranges from charmless malls and high-rises to a leafy wood shot through with rivers and streams. They did not live in the leafy part. The Currys had been told to expect the two detectives from Algonquin Bay and consequently had gone to a lot of trouble to prepare; smells of Windex and Mr. Clean hung heavy in the air. There was not a cushion out of place.

"They told us you'd be coming." Mrs. Curry greeted them at the door. "My husband stayed home from work."

"Hope that won't upset your boss too much," Cardinal said to the man who rose energetically out of a well-padded armchair.

"I'm not worried about it. Place owes me about a year's worth of vacation days." He shook hands forcefully, as if to prove that grief could not dent his manly vigor. He even managed a broad smile, but it lasted no longer than a camera flash, and then he sank back into his chair.

Cardinal turned to the mother. "Mrs. Curry, did Todd have any relatives in or around Algonquin Bay?"

"Well, there's his uncle Clark in Thunder. But that's hundreds of miles away."

"What about friends. Maybe someone he met at school?"

"Well, I wouldn't know about that. But there were certainly no friends that we knew of from Algonquin Bay."

The father roused himself out of reverie. "What about that young man who came to stay last summer? The one with the mismatched sneakers."

"You mean Steve? Steve was from Stratford, dear."

"No, no. I'm talking about someone else altogether. I'm talking about a different boy."

"Well, the one with the mismatched sneakers was Steve,

and he was from Stratford. You know my memory's better than yours. It always has been."

"I guess that's true. I guess your memory was always better than mine."

Once in Algonquin Bay, Cardinal had been at the scene where a gas line had exploded, removing the whole front of an apartment building and collapsing three floors. Husbands and wives had drifted through the smoke and ashes like souls in purgatory. Now, their family having been exploded by grief, Mr. and Mrs. Curry were trying to recognize each other through the smoke and ashes.

"Did Todd have any other reason to stop at Algonquin Bay that you know of?"

"No. None. Boyish curiosity. Maybe someone he met on the train. Todd's an impulsive boy. Was." Mrs. Curry's hand drifted up to her mouth as if it would push the past tense back. Her face was a picture of confusion.

Then Mr. Curry was at her side, his arm around her shoulder. "There, there, girl," he said in a low voice. "Why don't you come sit down on the couch?"

"I can't sit down. I haven't even offered them any tea. Would you like some tea?"

"No, thanks," Delorme said gently. "Mrs. Curry, we know Todd got into trouble with drugs at least once. Do you remember anything to do with drugs—maybe a name that came out in his court hearing—that might have led him to Algonquin Bay?"

"Todd was over his drug problem. He didn't use drugs anymore. There, I said it: was, didn't—they're just words, aren't they." She managed a ghastly smile. "Are you sure you won't have some tea? It's no trouble."

It was a new art form for Delorme, picking shards of fact from the exposed hearts of the bereaved. She looked to Cardinal for help, but he said nothing. He thought, Get used to it.

"I didn't know Todd at all, Mrs. Curry, but—well, let me put it another way, I mean—the thing is . . ." Delorme bit her lip, then said, "You know. A cup of tea would be very nice. Can I help you make it?"

Cardinal said to the father, "You mind if I look at Todd's room, meanwhile?"

"What? Todd's room?" Mr. Curry scratched the top of his head. In another context, the cartoonlike gesture would have been comical. He gave a nervous laugh. "I'm sorry. I just don't know how to act. Todd's room, yes, that makes sense I guess. You need to know more about him, yes, I can see how you do. All right, you go ahead, Detective, you do your work and don't let me get in your way."

"It's this way?"

"Oh. Yes. Sorry. Second on the right. Well, I'll show you." He led Cardinal down a short hall. There were two bedrooms on the left, closets on the right, bathroom at the end; that was the whole apartment. Mr. Curry opened the door and gestured for Cardinal to enter, then stood leaning against the door frame, as if his son's bedroom were located on an exalted plane he was not worthy to enter. His eyes flicked nervously back and forth, death having infused the most mundane objects—the half-deflated basketball in the corner, a broken skateboard on a shelf—with the power to utterly undo him in front of this intruder.

"Mr. Curry, you don't have to watch, if you don't want."

"I'm all right, Detective. You just go ahead and do what you have to do."

Cardinal stood in the middle of the room and said nothing, just absorbed the relationships of various objects. There was an elaborate boom box on top of the dresser and small towers of tapes. Posters of pop stars were tacked to the wall: Backstreet Boys, Tupac Shakur, Puff Daddy. There was a small desk, the surface of which was a map of the world. A small Macintosh computer sat on top of Africa. Bookshelves were neatly fitted into either end of the desk. Cardinal was certain Mr. Curry had built them. He ran his hand along the edge of Antarctica. "Nice desk," he said, and knelt to examine Todd's books.

"Yes, I built that. It was easy really. Still, you know, a project like that takes more than a few hours. Todd hated it, of course."

"Oh, they're hard to please, teenagers."

"Todd and I didn't get along very well, that's the truth of it. I didn't know how to handle him, I guess. Tried being lenient, tried being tough. Nothing seemed to work. Now, I just wish he was here."

"I'm sure the two of you would have made it up," Cardinal said. "Most families do." The titles on the shelves: *Treasure Island, Catcher in the Rye,* several Hardy Boys installments, all dusty. The rest of Todd's library consisted of science fiction paperbacks with garish covers. He was tempted to tell Mr. Curry about his own daughter, how in her teens she used to tell him regularly she hated him and now they got along just great. Wrong tack to take, though.

"Todd and I won't ever get the chance to make it up, now. That's the terrible thing." Mr. Curry took a sudden step into the room, pushed by the urgency of his thought. His grip on Cardinal's forearm felt like a claw. "Detective, whatever you do in this world, don't postpone your life. Anything important that you keep putting off? Anything you keep telling yourself you'll just wait for the right moment? I mean, anything important you've been meaning to tell some loved one, or anyone—don't put it off, you hear me? Don't postpone your life. Say the words, whatever they are. Do the thing, whatever it is. All that stuff you hear on the news—I don't care if it's tornadoes or the so-called Windigo Killer—any kind of disaster, you never think it applies. But the fact of the matter is, you never know. You never know when people are just going to get up and go out that door and never come back. You just don't know. I'm sorry. This is terrible. I'm babbling."

"You're just fine, Mr. Curry."

"I'm not. I don't have much experience with this kind of thing," he said, then added as if pleading a handicap, "I'm in reinsurance."

"Tell me, Mr. Curry, did Todd use that machine a lot?"

Cardinal pointed at the Macintosh. There were software manuals and video games piled under the desk, and he had noticed the line connecting the computer to a phone jack in the wall.

"Todd wasn't a hacker, if that's what you mean. He used it for homework, mostly. When he did his homework. Thing's a mystery to me. We use IBMs where I work."

Cardinal opened the closet and looked at the clothes. There was one suit, one blazer, two pairs of dress pants, not the things a boy like Todd would wear often. On the shelf above, there were stacks of board games: Monopoly, Scrabble, Trivial Pursuit.

In the dresser, Cardinal found—besides the usual torn jeans and ripped T-shirts—a tangle of copper and tin bracelets, bits of chain, studded leather collars and cuffs. It didn't mean anything; a lot of kids wore them now.

"My wife's in pieces," Mr. Curry said. He had retreated to the doorway again. "That's the worst thing. It's hard to see someone you love in so much pain and not be able to—" He had spoken of grief, and now, like a demon hearing its name, it burst its bonds and pounced, possessing him utterly. Mr. Curry was transformed from robust father into a pale, crooked figure shrinking in a doorway, crying.

Cardinal didn't ignore him, exactly, but he didn't say anything, either. He looked at him briefly, then looked away out the window at the high-rise next door. From the parking lot between them came the mechanical hysteria of a car alarm. In the distance, Toronto's CN Tower glittered in the morning sun.

After a few minutes, the sobbing behind him eased, and he handed Mr. Curry a twenty-cent pack of Kleenex he had bought at the Pharma-City on Queensway. He opened Todd's dresser drawers one by one, feeling the undersides.

"Sorry about the wailing. Must feel like you've walked into a soap opera."

"No, Mr. Curry. It doesn't feel like that at all."

Cardinal could feel the magazine behind the bottom drawer. He pulled it out, mentally apologizing to the boy as he did so, knowing it was probably more secret and personal than glue sniffing or marijuana. He remembered his own stack of *Playboy*s from youth, but the magazine now in his hand showed a naked man.

Mr. Curry stopped breathing for several seconds, Cardinal heard it. He reached in and pulled out three more magazines.

"Shows how well I know my own son, I guess. I would have never guessed. Not in a million years."

"I wouldn't put too much stress on a few pictures. Looks like curiosity to me. He's got *Playboy* and *Penthouse* here, too."

"I would never, never have guessed."

"Nobody's an open book, Mr. Curry. Not you, not me . . ."

"I'd like to keep this from his mother."

"Certainly. There's no need to tell her, at least not now. Why don't you take a break, Mr. Curry? There's no need for you to watch."

"She's a very strong woman, Edna, but this—"

"Maybe you better go see how she's doing."

"Thank you, yes, I'll do that. I'll just go see how Edna's doing." It struck Cardinal that, to a teenager, Todd's father must have seemed a mother hen.

From the desk, the Macintosh was staring at him with its cool blind eye. Cardinal knew enough about Macs to boot it up and find the list of programs; it only took him two minutes, but he didn't recognize anything. He went out into the living room and signaled to Delorme, who was next to Mrs. Curry on the couch, going over a family album.

Delorme was no computer specialist, either, but just that morning Cardinal had watched her put Flower's Mac through its paces. It made him feel old. It seemed like anybody under thirty-five was comfortable with computers, which frustrated Cardinal at every turn. Delorme whipped that mouse around like a slot car.

"Can we see what he's been tapping into?"

"That's what I'm doing right now. Threader, here, is a

useful program. You set it up to stop in at your favorite ports of call. It visits them all at top speed then clicks back off, so it saves connect charges. Only someone who goes on-line a lot would have it."

The screen changed, showing a list of newsgroups. Cardinal read them aloud: "Email, HouseofRock, House-ofRap—rap music? That's gotta be unusual for a white kid."

"Boy, are you out of date."

"Okay, what's this Connections thing?" He tapped an icon of a kissing couple on the screen. "That a talk-dirty outfit?"

"Not necessarily. Let's log on and see what we get."

Delorme moved the mouse and clicked. There was a dialing sound, then the raspberry noise of modems shaking hands. The screen flashed, scrolled at blinding speed, and clicked off.

"It's like trolling in your favorite bays," Delorme said. "Now let's see what we hauled in."

She clicked through the messages. There was a lot of computer chat about new games for Mac users, none addressed specifically to Todd. Then there was a discussion about buying tickets for an Aerosmith concert at the Sky-Dome.

"Ah," Delorme said. "Here's his mail basket. Oh boy, he liked his e-mail hot."

"Jesus," Cardinal said. He was glad he was standing behind Delorme, because he wouldn't have been able to look her in the eye.

"See, it's all anonymous," Delorme said, pointing. "He called himself Galahad in this newsgroup."

"Well, it certainly goes with the *Blueboy* magazines. Looks like he's got ten different correspondents, there."

"Oop, look here. This guy knows his real name."

Todd, Cardinal read. *I'm sorry things didn't work out between us. You seem like a good kid and I wish you well, but I don't think we should meet again. Probably not even talk again, but I'm open on that point. —Jacob*

"John, look at the date."

"December twentieth. The night Todd Curry showed up at the Crisis Center. Hey, we could be getting warm, here."

Delorme flipped through several screens, flashing through previous "letters" from the same Jacob. The sex was explicitly detailed. There were repeated invitations to come and visit, to stay the night.

"What a perfect setup," Cardinal said. "Size up your victims over the computer lines. Reel them in, long-distance."

They read more. Not all the messages were explicit sexual fantasies. Some were more thoughtful discussions about the problems of accepting oneself as gay. Well, that's right, Cardinal thought, put the kid at ease. Next to alcohol, sympathy was probably the most potent weapon in the seducer's arsenal.

"Is there any way we can get this guy's real name and address off this?"

"Address, I doubt. Name, maybe. I'm a little rusty, though. It could take a while." Delorme set the mouse moving in circles again, while Cardinal knelt on the floor, going through the boy's collection of video games. After about ten minutes, Delorme touched his shoulder. "Look at this."

Cardinal stood up and looked over her shoulder.

"This is his sex group listing, the Jacob guy. And his e-mail address." She read out: " 'Top, body-building, oral, hot E-mail . . .' So far, so good. In one of his discussions he mentions Louis Riel—you remember your history?"

"Small rebellion out west, right?"

"Not that small. Anyway, I figure maybe he's into history, so I click on the history newsgroup, right?" Delorme clicked the mouse, and the screen changed. "Next stop: history newsgroup, membership directory. Put in a search for Jacob's e-mail address . . ." She typed in as she talked. "And look what comes up! Same address."

"That's Jacob?"

"That's Jacob. Only in this group, he's using his real name." She tapped the screen with her index finger. Cardinal read, *Jack Fehrenbach, 47: e-mail (French or English). Algonquin Bay.*

"Fehrenbach's a teacher at Algonquin High. We sure that's his real name?"

"Not a hundred percent, no. But it's probably the name the account is under."

"Kelly had that guy one year. It could be someone just using his name, right? A pissed-off student, maybe."

"Could be. But the Internet service bills your credit card, so it would have to be a pretty big scam."

"This is first-class work, Lise. First-class."

Delorme grinned. "It's not too bad, I have to admit."

25

THE nausea had finally lifted. For days it had hung over the bed like smog, so that the slightest movement made his head whirl and the bile climb in his throat. A few bites of food, and the bed had begun to feel like a boat pitching headlong from crest to trough.

At other times—usually just before Eric or Edie brought in his tray—the nausea would recede a little, and he began to think he would soon be out in the sunlight and fresh air. Then strange fancies would take hold of him: The bedposts dissolved into minarets, his feet beneath the covers formed distant dunes, a dripping tap became a tambourine. He would imagine he was in some exotic locale—Bahrain, Tangiers—where he had been laid low with exotic fevers. His eyes felt webbed; his muscles were dead as meat.

The figure on the edge of the bed blurred and shifted. Keith tried to focus. The smell of toast and jam was overwhelming. When was the last time he'd kept anything down? "God, I'm so hungry." He spoke to where the figure had been, but it had shifted again.

"Take it." Eric was holding the plate under Keith's nose. The smell nearly made him faint.

Keith ate four pieces of toast. He began to feel solid again, as if he could get up and do things. "Eric. I need to use the phone. I need a phone."

"Sorry. Edie doesn't have a phone. I have one, but I live across town."

"She doesn't have a phone?"

"No. I just told you."

"Karen will be worried. We arranged to call regularly. I've been sick for, what—three days?"

"Four."

Keith started to sit up. His muscles were achy from being in bed so long.

"You're too sick to go out, Keith. Why don't you write her a letter?"

"She lives in Guelph. It would take days to reach her. She'd be so pissed off by then she probably wouldn't read it. Do you guys have e-mail?"

"No," Eric said. "Why don't you give me her number? I'll call for you."

"Thanks, Eric. But I think I'd better get to a doctor anyway. I shouldn't be sleeping like this. I'll call Karen from the hospital."

"All right. Why don't you stand up and give it a try?" Eric got off the bed and sat in the broken chair. Keith made a great effort to lower his feet to the floor. Slowly, fixing his gaze now on the radiator, now on Eric, he straightened. He swallowed hard and forced his right foot toward the door. He gave up and fell back down on the bed with a groan. "Why am I so exhausted?"

"All your traveling. No doubt you picked up some exotic bug somewhere."

"Please, Eric. Take me to the hospital."

"Sorry. Can't. I don't drive."

"Oh, come on." He tried to sound stern, but it was hard when he could barely keep his eyes open. "You told me you had a van. The other night. You said you'd bring the tape stuff over in your van."

"My license has expired. I just discovered it this morning. It expired six months ago."

"Edie, then. Let Edie drive me. God, I'm so sleepy."

Darkness closed around him. Once more he was drifting down a web-filled corridor, pulled as if on skates toward a receding tower of light. Or was it the CN Tower? Insects the size of cats hung from a low ceiling; their mandibles worked up a foul white foam that dripped on him and scalded his flesh.

He slept and woke, slept and woke.

Then finally he woke with a new clarity. Whatever succubus had been draining his energy seemed to have relaxed its grip, and except for the aching muscles, he felt almost normal. He discovered pen and paper beside the bed, even a stamped envelope. He wrote a letter to Karen, a letter filled with love and longing. He remembered her face with tenderness, her body. Details of the physical joys he and Karen had shared came back to him, and he wrote of them in vivid images. He had to stop for a moment; he was trying to think of another word for *rapture; enthrallment* wasn't right, and he'd already used *pleasure* twice. *Bliss,* he was thinking. He was about to write the word, when a noise from upstairs made him stop with pen poised over the paper: the muffled but unmistakable sound of a ringing phone.

26

EDIE'S stomach hurt, she was laughing so hard.

"I've been very sick for a week," Eric was reading. *"I'm not exactly sure how long, but you wouldn't believe how boring throwing up can get after the tenth time."*

"See, Eric. Keith liked my ipecac cocktails. My magic barf potions. It's mixing it with the Valium does the trick. Gives it that extra something special." Oh, she loved it when Eric laughed. Why couldn't he be like this all the time? So funny, so easy. At times like this, she could almost believe they were a normal couple, just your normal basic couple enjoying a good laugh together. You could forget the dreary winter and the endless cold. At times like this she could almost forget what she looked like: Oh yes, she had seen Keith London's eyes do that male survey of her face and figure, summing her up and spitting her out, despite his friendly manner. He'd just as soon run her over. But it didn't matter when Eric was with her, when Eric was happy.

"Better ease up on the ipecac and stick with the Valium," Eric was saying. "Can't have him throwing it up as soon as we give it to him. Listen to this."

There was a *thump, thump, thump* from upstairs. God, Gram, give it a rest. I'm with the man I love and I'm having fun for once in my life. Why can't you let us be?

Eric's response to the summons was just to read all the louder. *"I'm staying with a young couple. They're very strange, Karen, but the fact is without them I'd probably be dead."*

"Hear that, Eric? Without us, Keith would probably be dead."

"The woman, Edie, works in a drugstore and gets all sorts of medicine free. At least she says she gets it free. I have a feeling she's just stealing it."

"That rotten little prick," Edie said. "He's going to wish

he never wrote that letter, Eric. You watch. I'm going to make him scream."

Another *thump, thump, thump* from upstairs.

"Listen to this." Eric read, *"I think of you, I dream of you, I miss you. I miss making love with you—you make me feel so good!"* There were some very explicit passages after that, and Eric read them in a funny, high-pitched voice that had them both doubled over with laughter, tears rolling down their faces.

"Eric told me they don't have a phone here, but I heard one ringing just now. It's a little disturbing."

"A little disturbing, is it, Keith? You find the phone ringing a little disturbing?"

"We'll show you disturbing, Keith. We'll disturb your balls right off your bloody carcass."

"We'll disturb your brains right out of your bloody head, you little shit. What's wrong?"

Eric had suddenly gone quiet.

"What is it, Eric?"

He showed her the letter, pointing to a line scrawled across the bottom. It was Edie's address. "How did he remember the address, for God's sake? He was drunk as a skunk."

Eric folded the letter and slipped it back into the envelope they had steamed open. "I'll throw it away. In fact, I'll flush it down the—"

"What's going on in here? Why didn't you come when I called you?" Edie's grandmother tottered in the doorway, leaning on her walker. Her red-rimmed eyes were pits of accusation.

"Sorry, Gram. We were just listening to some music."

"I don't hear any music. I've been banging and banging, Edie, and you didn't come. Banging and banging. Why is Eric still here?"

"Hello, Gram," Eric said with a sweet smile. "Want me to bash your skull in for you?"

"What's he say?"

"Nothing, Gram. Come on, I'll take you upstairs."

But Gram wasn't finished. You could never shake her off an indictment when she got going. "I don't see why you can't come when I call, Edie. I don't ask you to do much for me. A lot of people would ask a lot more of the person they raised up as if they were their own."

"It's because she hates you, Grammy. Nothing to worry about. She just hates your stinking guts."

"Leave her alone, Eric. I'll take her." Edie helped her grandmother get turned around, glaring at Eric over the old woman's shoulder.

When they were gone, Eric went into the tiny bathroom under the stairs.

There, he stared at the letter for a long time. He had intended to tear it into tiny pieces, but the erotic sections had captured his interest. He closed the lid of the toilet and sat down to read them again. This Karen must be quite an interesting number. It would be a shame not to send her a little something.

27

YOU could have cast Jack Fehrenbach in a magazine ad for hiking boots, all six-foot-eight of him. He looked the perfect outdoorsman—right down to the five o'clock shadow. You would photograph him pitching a tent or frying a freshly caught trout on a Coleman stove. His shoulders were a wide solid shelf, and the rest of him looked to be cut from the same oak. The outdoors effect was softened somewhat by a conservative tie and a pair of bifocals that Fehrenbach snatched from his face to get a better look at Cardinal and Delorme, who had arrived on his doorstep unannounced.

"I hope this isn't about parking tickets," he said, when Cardinal showed his ID. "I've told them five times—I've told them till I'm blue in the face—I've *paid* the damn things. I have the canceled check, for God's sake, I sent them a photocopy. Why can't they keep track of these things? We have the technology. Do they not have a computer at City Hall? Where exactly is the difficulty?"

"This isn't about parking tickets, Mr. Fehrenbach."

Fehrenbach scanned Cardinal's face for defects and found plenty. "Then what can you possibly want?"

"May we come in, please?"

The man allowed them to penetrate no more than four feet into his home. The three of them were stuffed into a small foyer full of coats. "Is it about one of my students? Is someone in trouble?"

Cardinal pulled out a photograph of Todd Curry. It was a good snapshot that Delorme had sweet-talked out of the boy's mother. His smile was wide, but the dark eyes looked preoccupied, as if the eyes did not trust the mouth. "Do you know this boy?" Cardinal asked.

Fehrenbach peered at it closely. "He looks like someone I met exactly once. Why do you want to know?"

"Mr. Fehrenbach, do we have to stand in the vestibule? It's a little crowded, don't you think?"

"All right, you can come in, but you have to take your shoes off because I've just polished the floor. I don't want you tracking snow in here."

Cardinal left his galoshes behind and joined Fehrenbach in the dining room. Delorme followed a moment later in her socks. The room was light and airy, with plants everywhere. The hardwood floors gleamed, and there was a pleasant smell of wax. Along one wall four massive shelves sagged under their burden of history: Fat tomes were crammed together in rows and stacked at odd angles. Beneath them, a computer was all but buried.

"I won't beat around the bush, Mr. Fehrenbach." Cardinal pulled a piece of paper from his pocket and read the words he had copied there. *"Five-four? Hundred and twenty pounds? Good things come in small packages, Galahad, and you certainly sound like the kind of package I'd love to receive."*

Fehrenbach's response was surprising. Instead of shock, a look of disappointment crossed his face. Almost sadness. Cardinal read a little more: *"In fact, I'll even pay the postage, if you'd care to mail yourself to me . . ."*

"Where did you get it?" Fehrenbach took the paper from Cardinal's hand and scrutinized it through his bifocals. The corners of his mouth had gone white. The bifocals came off again, the eyebrows drew together over the hawkish nose. He would be stern in the classroom. "Officer, this is private correspondence, and you have no right to it. Have you heard of improper search and seizure? We happen to have a constitution in this country."

"Galahad is dead, Mr. Fehrenbach."

"Dead," he repeated, as if Cardinal were a student who had volunteered a wrong answer. "How can he possibly be dead?" A fine sweat had broken out on his upper lip.

"Just tell us about your meeting with him."

Fehrenbach folded his arms across his chest, a movement that threw muscles into sharp definition. You wouldn't want to piss him off, Cardinal thought, the man could do damage. "Look, I didn't know he was a kid—he told *me* he was twenty-one. Come in and I'll show you—it's still on disk. I can't believe he's dead. Oh, my God!" A hand flew to his mouth—a gesture egregiously feminine in a figure of such heroic proportions. "He's not the one that was found in that house, is he? The one who was . . . ?"

"What makes you think that, Mr. Fehrenbach?"

"Well, the newspaper said that boy was from out of town. And he'd been dead a couple of—I don't know. Your manner suggested it."

Nothing about him betrayed guilt, but Cardinal understood that the person who had killed Katie Pine and Todd Curry could be *anyone*. He had planned his killings and he had tape-recorded at least one of them. That spoke of control. The profile had said the killer would be able to hold down a job, and he might well prefer employment that kept him near kids.

"Look, Officer Cardinal. I'm a high-school teacher, and Algonquin Bay is a small place. If this gets out, I'm finished."

"If what gets out?" Delorme put in. "If what gets out, Mr. Fehrenbach?"

"That I'm gay. I mean, this is not just a local case anymore—even the *Toronto Star*'s going on about the Windigo, now. And the e-mail—how's that going to look on Channel Four? You have to understand something: From the gay perspective, e-mail is safe sex. It's infinitely preferable to cruising bars or—"

"But you weren't going to leave it at e-mail," Delorme insisted. "You arranged for Todd to come up here. To stay with you."

"You know what my first words were to that boy when he showed up on my doorstep? *Oh, no.* God's truth. I looked at him standing there—a little runt of a thing, and I said to him, *Oh, no—this will never do. Not a chance. You're far too young. You can't stay here.*"

Cardinal had telephoned Kelly the previous night, sending roommates scurrying in search of her, finally dragging her out of the studio where she had been working late. Her take on Fehrenbach: "Jack Fehrenbach is a world-class teacher, Daddy. He gets you involved in the material, gets you thinking about history. Yes, he makes you learn your dates and numbers, but he also forces you to think about causes and effects. He's enthusiastic as hell, but he doesn't try to be your buddy, know what I mean? He was kind of aloof, when you get right down to it." In response to Cardinal's observation that the man was gay: "Every student in Algonquin High knows Mr. Fehrenbach is gay—and not one of them cares. That should tell you something. You know they'd be merciless, if he gave them any reason. He never did. He's just not the kind of guy students give a hard time to." In short, Jack Fehrenbach was one of the three best teachers Kelly'd ever had—and she didn't even like history.

Cardinal wasn't about to let his only suspect know any of this. "You'll appreciate, Mr. Fehrenbach—having read what we've read—that it's a little hard to believe you decided to turn this kid away. Suddenly you were so concerned about correct behavior."

"I don't care what you believe! Who do you think you are!" The hand shot up again and clamped itself over his mouth for a second. Then he said, "I don't mean that. I'm just upset. Obviously, I care very much what you think. I'd invited Todd to come up here. I felt bad. I made him some dinner, and let me tell you, the conversation was tough going. I don't know about you, but my knowledge of the complete works of Puff Daddy is sketchy at best. I mean, I think this kid's highest ambition was to be a DJ—the kind that scratches records for a living. In any case, he was none too friendly, after I told him he couldn't stay the night. I'm sorry—a sixteen-year-old stranger? In a gay man's apartment? A high-school teacher?—I'm not *crazy*. I dropped him off at the Bayshore with enough money for one night, his return bus fare, and breakfast. Why are you looking like that? I'll show you his e-mail."

It took a couple of minutes for Fehrenbach to boot up his computer and call up his correspondence. "Here. Look. Very early on—this is our second private exchange. I say, *Tell me about yourself. What do you do? How old are you?*" He scrolled up the screen. "There's his reply."

Delorme leaned beside him and read, *"I'm twenty-one and I'm hung like a bull—what more do you need to know, Jacob?"*

"It never occurred to me that he'd be younger than he said. See, most people on-line lie about themselves in the other direction. I've been known to shave a few years off *my* age. Anyway, it was all explicitly sexual at first, but then when he got iffy about meeting, I realized he wasn't secure with his sexuality. It became more of a friendship then—I didn't want to rush anything, and I suppose I became a bit of a mentor."

Delorme said, "Excuse me, but your correspondence did not look that intellectual."

"Intellectual, no. That doesn't mean it was unintelligent. Look, things may be more liberal than they were when I was growing up, but the fact remains that coming to terms with yourself—accepting that your sexuality is going to be regarded by the majority of people as deviant—is the most difficult piece of self-analysis most people are ever called upon to make. If you're fair, you'll see that our chat becomes much less explicit after the first five or six notes."

He scrolled down a couple of notes. What he said was true: Gradually, the content changed from lingering, almost painterly, fantasies to focused discussions of sexuality in general. Fehrenbach's e-mails were as he claimed—those of a mentor addressing someone facing an enemy he had long ago engaged and overcome.

Toward the end, there was a specific exchange about the logistics of getting "Galahad" from Toronto to Algonquin Bay—should he take bus or train, and how to get the money to him.

"I'm catching the eleven forty-five tomorrow morning.

Supposed to be in Algonquin Bay by four. See you soon!"
Dated December 19. After that, nothing.

"You didn't meet him at the train station?"

"No, I'd already mailed him the money for the train and
a cab. By then, I was worried he was not as old as he
claimed. I certainly didn't want to be seen in the company
of a minor."

"You're awfully careful, Mr. Fehrenbach," Delorme observed. "Some people, they say you were suspiciously careful."

"I have a friend in Toronto—he used to live in Toronto—
who liked to have long friendly chats with his students in
his office. Private chats, with the door closed. Based on that,
and based on the testimony of a boy he had failed, my friend
got sent to prison for four years. Four years, Officer. No, no.
I'm prudent, that's all. My door stays open—*wide* open—
and I never see students *anywhere* outside of school."

"According to that note," Cardinal said, "and according
to what you're telling us, Todd would have been at the
Bayshore on December twentieth."

"That's right. I drove him there. I watched him go in. I
stayed in the car, but I watched him go in."

"Must have been hard to do. You'd had all this hot talk,
you were expecting a hot weekend, and then you cut it off
right at the threshold. Must have been difficult."

"It wasn't. You say he was sixteen; he looked fourteen.
That's still a child in my book. I sleep with men, Officer
Cardinal, not children."

"We need to know where you were the rest of that
weekend."

"Well, that's easy. I was at loose ends because I had set
aside the weekend, and now it was going to be empty. So
I took up an earlier offer from a friend in Powassan and
spent the weekend with him. On the Monday I went
straight down to Toronto to spend Christmas with my parents. My friend will remember. I told him exactly what I
just told you, and he had a good laugh at my expense."

"We'll need a name. And keep in mind that if you call

this person to rehearse your stories we'll know it from phone records."

"I don't need to rehearse the truth. Neither will he." Fehrenbach fetched his address book and gave the details to Delorme, who wrote them all down. He kept leaning over her shoulder, making sure she got it right, as if he were checking her homework.

Cardinal remembered the respect in Kelly's voice: "How many teachers do you know who get kids arguing, *arguing* about Henry Hudson and Samuel de Champlain? The man is Mister Correct Procedure, Mister Memorize Your Dates and Gather Your Thoughts and Review Your Notes Because You'll Be Tested On This."

Cardinal held out a hand. "Mr. Fehrenbach, you've been very helpful."

The teacher hesitated, then took his hand.

Delorme was sullen in the car. Cardinal knew she had a temper, and he could sense her attempts to control it. As they turned onto Main, the car suddenly fishtailed on a patch of ice, and Cardinal took the opportunity to pull over.

"Look, Lise—the guy has a sterling reputation, all right? First-rate teacher, nothing against. His manner was open and honest and straightforward—a lot more honest than I would have been in his situation."

"This is a mistake we're making. Right now, Fehrenbach is sitting at his computer erasing every trace of his mail with that kid."

"We don't need it. We have it all from Todd's computer. We'll check his alibi, and we'll post some guys to keep an eye on him. And none of it will lead anywhere."

THE desk clerk at the Bayshore didn't remember Todd Curry from the photograph. And the kid had never signed the register.

"See," Delorme said. "Fehrenbach was lying."

"I didn't expect to see the kid's signature here. Fellowes at the Crisis Center already told me Todd Curry checked in there on December twentieth. He hung out somewhere, heard about the Crisis Center, and decided to save the money Fehrenbach had given him by staying there for the night. And at some point between the Crisis Center and the house on Main West, he met the killer."

DELORME didn't have a lot of close friends on the force. Working in Special Investigations didn't exactly encourage camaraderie, and Delorme had never been the sort to put herself forward, insert herself into a group. For friendship, she relied on old high-school friends, and a lot of the time it was tough going. There were those who had gone away to college and come back changed or married, usually both. There were those who had not gone on to college, whose horizons lay no farther away than their high-school boyfriend and a baby at the age of eighteen.

Most of them had kids now, meaning Delorme did not share the central concern in their lives. Even when she did see old friends, she sensed in their eyes that they saw a change in her. Working around men all the time, around cops, had hardened her, made her more guarded and, in some way she could not quite fathom, made her less patient with women.

It all added up to a lot of time alone, which was why, unlike practically everyone else on the force, she had a quiet dread of the end of shift. So when Cardinal suddenly suggested—in the middle of a sup-writing marathon—that they go out to his place to brainstorm that evening, a flock of confused feelings took wing in Delorme's heart like swallows around a barn. "Don't worry," Cardinal had said before she could reply. "I won't inflict my cooking on you. We can order in a pizza."

Delorme, stalling, had said she didn't know. By the end of the day she'd be pretty tired; she wouldn't bring much brain to the storm.

"Fehrenbach checked out, right? There's nowhere else to go with that."

"I know. It's just . . ."

Cardinal had looked at her, frowning a little. "If I was

going to make a move on you, Lise, I wouldn't do it at home."

SO they had driven their separate cars out to Cardinal's freezing little cottage on Madonna Road, and Cardinal had built a fire in the woodstove. Delorme was touched by how friendly he was. He showed her some carpentry work he'd done in the kitchen. Then he showed her a huge landscape painted by his daughter—a view of Trout Lake with the NORAD base in the background—when she was twelve years old. "She gets the artistic genes from her mother. Catherine's a photographer," he said, pointing to a sepia-tinged photograph of a lonely rowboat on an anonymous shore.

"You must miss them," Delorme said, and immediately regretted it. But Cardinal had just shrugged and picked up the phone to order the pizza.

By the time it arrived, they had begun tossing out ideas. The ground rules of brainstorming were that you couldn't laugh at anything the other person suggested, you couldn't say anything inhibiting. Which was why it was a good idea to do it away from headquarters; they could zing out some really wild ideas and not feel too foolish.

They were just getting warmed up when the telephone rang. Cardinal's first words into the receiver: "Oh, shit. I'll be there in ten minutes." He tossed the phone onto the couch and started putting on his coat, patting his pockets for keys.

"What? What's going on?"

"I forgot, we have a press thing at six. R. J. arranged it, so Grace Legault doesn't get her knickers in a knot. Sorry. You know, it's one of those deals where we tell them things we don't really want them to know, so that they don't say things we don't want them to say. That's the idea, anyway."

"Whose idea?"

"Dyson's. I went along with it, though."

"Well, I guess I should go, then."

"No, no. Please. Don't let the pizza get cold. Shouldn't take more than an hour."

Delorme had protested, Cardinal had insisted, and in the end she stayed, nibbling halfheartedly at the pizza in the sudden silence of his departure. It seemed so—what was the word?—orchestrated. Inviting her all the way out here. "Forgetting" his press meeting. The pizza arriving just so. It was as if he wanted her, for the space of an hour at least, to have his house to herself: Go ahead. Look. I've got nothing to hide.

Was this Cardinal's way of saving her (or Dyson, or the department) the embarrassment of a search warrant? Or was it a preemptive strike, designed to take the wind out of her sails? A guilty man would never give her free access to his home. But then again, it was the same as with his desk: A guilty man might well leave it wide open precisely so you would think him not guilty.

Delorme wiped pizza grease from her fingers and telephoned Dyson. This press thing Cardinal was going to, was it for real? It was most certainly real, Dyson assured her; R. J. was very high on it, and Cardinal had better get his ass in there *toot sweet* (his French sent a shudder down Delorme's spine) or Dyson would personally see him writing traffic tickets before the week was out.

"He's on his way."

"How do you know that? Are you at his place? What are you doing at his place?"

"I'm having his baby. But don't worry, I can still look at things objectively."

"Ha ha. The fact is you have an opportunity here, just like we discussed."

"What I can't figure out is why he's giving it to us—unless he's innocent."

"Wouldn't that be nice."

Delorme stood up, brushing crumbs from her lap. Above the fireplace there was a black-and-white photograph of Cardinal, dressed in an old workshirt and jeans, planing a piece of wood, leaning over it like a pool player. He had a three-day stubble and sawdust in his hair, and he looked kind of sexy for a cop. Well, sexy or not, first he leaves his desk drawer open, and now he was giving her the run of his house. As far as Delorme was concerned, that was asking for it.

The Algonquin Bay police department does not have rules for surreptitious searches for the very good reason that its officers are not supposed to conduct them. Delorme had never relied on clandestine methods to collect evidence, nor would she now. Any clandestine search was of necessity in the nature of a reconnoiter, a preview of what might be available to those (armed with a warrant) who might come after. The only thing the Ontario Police College at Aylmer teaches about such searches is that they are illegal and their fruits inadmissible. What Delorme knew of this unsavory art, she had taught herself.

She had an hour, say forty minutes to be on the safe side. It was essential to be highly selective. She ruled out all the places she'd seen cops search in the movies: the hard-to-get-at places like tops of cupboards, the attic space—anything requiring something to stand on. Also off the list: any spaces that required moving furniture. There was no way she could lift up rugs or check under couch and chairs without Cardinal's seeing the disruption, and in any case she did not believe that if Cardinal had anything to hide he would hide it in such places. She would not be lifting the lid of the cistern, either.

No, within minutes of Cardinal's departure, Lise Delorme had decided she would search only the most obvious place for incriminating material: Cardinal's personal files. These he kept conveniently labeled (and unlocked) in a two-drawer metal cabinet, much dented. In no time at all she learned exactly what he earned from the department (with all the overtime, it came to a lot more than she had expected) and that his charming but subzero lakeside house was not paid off. The monthly payments were high but manageable on Cardinal's income, unless he had other major expenses—such as a daughter attending an Ivy League university.

Delorme was more interested in Catherine Cardinal's income. If she had some private source, Cardinal might be off the hook.

She pulled out tax returns.

Last year's filing, a joint one, was in Cardinal's handwriting and showed that he told Revenue Canada exactly what he earned. It also indicated that Catherine Cardinal made little more than pocket money as a part-time photography instructor up at Algonquin College. But there was a second file that was of considerably more interest, a return for the U.S. Internal Revenue Service. It was for Catherine Cardinal but filled out in Cardinal's messy but intense hand. You'd never hire an accountant, would you? Far too vain about your mental faculties. The form showed that Catherine Cardinal had earned eleven thousand U.S. dollars in rental income from a Miami condominium. Apparently it was vacant for most of the year.

"Date of purchase," Delorme whispered aloud, flipping through the unfamiliar form. "Come on, now. Date of purchase. You claim depreciation, somewhere you've got to say when you bought the damn—" She sat back on her haunches, gripping the blue-and-white form. Catherine Cardinal had bought the condo in Florida three years ago, with a down payment of forty-six thousand dollars U.S., just six weeks after the first Corbett fiasco.

Careful, now, Delorme's inner voice said. You don't *know* anything. You keep looking and you keep your mind open. We are in collecting mode here, not judging.

Cardinal had claimed a portion of his homeowners insurance policy as a deduction. Delorme found the file marked *Insurance.* The amount of the policy seemed low at first glance, but then she remembered that it was the property, not the house, that was expensive. The file contained receipts for large purchases—Cardinal's Camry, a new refrigerator, a table saw—but then Delorme came upon a receipt that made her catch her breath. It was from the Calloway Marina in Hollywood Beach, Florida, in the sum of fifty-thousand dollars for a Chris-Craft cabin cruiser. Dated October, two years ago. That would put it just two months after the second Corbett raid went bad.

Again, Delorme made an effort to calm her beating heart, told herself not to jump to conclusions. Jumping to conclusions turned you into a danger to everyone who got near you. But that amount, and on that date—well, it was damaging, no question.

At the rear of Cardinal's bottom drawer, she pulled out a file marked *Yale.* She scanned the contents swiftly, correspondence from Yale on expensive letterhead that confirmed what she already knew: that John Cardinal was paying a damn fortune to send his daughter to a famous school. Over twenty-five thousand a year in Canadian dollars, not including living expenses, and then there were travel costs and art supplies on top of that. Cardinal had said Kelly was in her second year of grad school, so he was looking at close to seventy-five thousand dollars and she was not even done yet.

Delorme put the papers back and closed the drawer. Stop while you're ahead, she told herself: the boat, the condo, they're more than enough to follow up.

She put Cardinal's half of the pizza in the fridge, washed her plate, and put on her coat. She switched off the light, wondering why on earth her partner would allow her to search his place when there was so much incriminating evidence around. It didn't make sense.

Driving into town, she called Malcolm Musgrave on her cell phone. "I've been looking at some very interesting receipts—large purchases right after your Corbett raids. But I can't tell you where I found them just yet."

"He's your partner, I understand that, but you're not running this investigation on your own."

"Ninety-six thousand dollars U.S. That's in addition to a kid at Yale."

"Probably our exalted commissioner makes that much, but I don't and you don't and neither does your partner."

"It looks bad, I know. But he doesn't live high. He doesn't spend a lot of cash."

"You're forgetting there's a considerable stick here as well as the carrot. Once someone like Kyle Corbett gets his pincers into you, you don't just decide you're tired of the game. You do what he wants, or he'll get you where you live. You might want to interview Nicky Bell on that subject. Oh, that's right, he's dead. Silly me." Musgrave told her to hang on a minute.

While she was waiting, she saw John Cardinal driving back out to his place. She raised her fingers off the wheel to wave, but he didn't see her. Suddenly Delorme regretted making the call. Then Musgrave came back.

"Look, I'm gonna need to know more about these receipts. We don't have time for prima donnas here, sister."

"Sorry. I don't think I can do that. Not yet, anyway."

Musgrave pressed her. Gave her his You're-playing-with-the-big-boys-now basso aria.

"Look, I'm doing my job, all right? I'm investigating the guy. That's all you have to know right now." Musgrave started in on her again, but Delorme clicked off the phone.

When she got home, she remained in her car with the motor running, leaning her head on the steering wheel. She tried not to identify the feelings that flowed inside her. Delorme had come across a lot of larcenous men in her six years with Special. And in that time she had come across motivations that rivaled the northern woods in their richness and variety. Some men steal for greed. Those are simple, and easy to nail. Then there are other men, more complex, who steal out of compulsion. Still others steal out of fear: Delorme thought those were by far the most common: the middle-aged manager who sees the specter of a penny-pinching retirement. Delorme didn't think Cardinal could be any of these. And so she wasn't dwelling on that fancy cabin cruiser, or even that Florida condo. The objects that shone clearest in her mind were the letters from Yale. She could feel the expensive weave of the stationery in her hand, the embossed seal, the enormous cost of an Ivy

League education. Some men, she was realizing, might steal for love.

"John Cardinal," she said aloud. "You are such a stupid fool."

29

ERIC had brought him the soup—it was all they'd been feeding him for the past two days, despite his protests—and sat at the end of the bed to make sure he finished it. He didn't say a word, just sat and stared at Keith like a crow. Then he'd smiled that ferrety smile of his, as if they shared some secret, and left the room.

Keith went straight to the bathroom and made himself throw up. He was not bothered by nausea anymore, but he was sure they were drugging him with something that made him sleep all the time. He wanted his wits about him, now; he wanted to know what was going on.

Afterward, exhausted and hollow, he sat on the edge of the bed, listening to their voices upstairs, droning on and on. They were directly overhead, but he couldn't make out any distinct words, just the voices.

Throwing up had made his eyes water. He wiped them on the corner of the sheet, and now with his cleared vision, he saw that there was a new addition to the furniture in the room. In the corner, where the camera and tripod had once stood, was a small TV and a VCR. Christ, how long were they expecting him to stay down here? It was clothes he wanted, not a bloody television.

But his clothes were not on the back of the chair. Not under the bed. Not hanging in the bathroom. And his duffel bag was missing, too.

He tried the door, but it was locked from the other side. For the first time, a thread of fear flowed into his bloodstream. He wrapped himself in a blanket and sat for a long time, thinking. At some point, he wasn't sure when, he heard Eric and Edie go out, heard the car starting up in the drive.

His head was still not clear, but he tried to assess how much trouble he was in. The door was locked, his clothes were gone—definitely bad signs, but he simply could not assess how bad. Eric and Edie just didn't seem all that scary. Worst case, he thought, what's my worst case: They think I'm rich and they're going to hold me for ransom.

He came to a decision. Next time they opened that door he'd be out in a flash, no hesitation. I may be wrong, they may be harmless, but it doesn't matter. I'm out of here.

There was a buzzing sound from overhead. He looked up just as the single bulb flickered and burned out. The room went dark. Slats of daylight, thin and pale, framed the boarded-up window.

Darkness had never frightened Keith London before, but it did now. He switched on the television. In such utter gloom, even this cold harsh glow was welcome. There was no aerial, no cable; the reception was hopeless. On one channel the ghost of a newscaster stared earnestly out at him, but no voice penetrated the static.

Keith pushed the eject button on the VCR, and a tape popped out. Handwritten on the label were the words, *Life of the Party*. Eric's film, he remembered, either that or home movies. He pushed the tape back in and pressed play.

The scene was badly lit, atrociously lit, in fact. There was a hard circle of light in the center of the screen, and around this, blackness. A boy was sitting in the patch of light, a skinny kid with long hair. He didn't look any too swift, sipping from a beer and grinning a stupid grin. He belched a couple of times, goofing off for the camera.

Then a woman entered the scene—Edie—and sat beside him. Here we go, Keith said to himself. Amateur porn time. God, they grow them kinky up here in the North.

The lighting did nothing to flatter Edie's complexion. Her skin gave off a dull glare as she reached over, felt between the boy's legs, and rubbed at him. The boy laughed, looking nervous and embarrassed. "You guys are too much," he said.

Music was switched on in the background, a boom box, it sounded like, Pearl Jam distorted by cheap speakers. Edie kept rubbing the boy's crotch mechanically. He opened his fly and she reached inside.

Then another figure entered the scene. It was Eric, pretending to be the outraged husband, shouting the most ridiculous phrases. "You do this to me? After the way I've treated you?" It was even worse than he had imagined.

Eric pulled the woman away, still shouting inanely.

The kid, for his part, did a terrible job of acting—holding up his hands in the hammiest way. He looked ridiculous with his pants half-down.

Then Eric struck a theatrical pose in the foreground, raising a hammer. "You try to screw my wife behind my back! I'm going to kill you!"

"No, please," the kid pleaded, laughing of course. "Please don't kill me! I didn't mean it! I'll make it up to you!" Then, hopelessly out of character: "Sorry. I can't help it. It just feels so stupid, you know?"

"You think it feels stupid?" Eric stepped forward, the hammer high. "I'll show you what feels stupid."

The hammer came down on the boy's head, changing everything. Even with the bad quality of the sound, Keith knew instantly that the crunch of bone was real. Also real was the sudden emptiness in the boy's face—the open mouth, the vacant, astonished eyes.

Eric swung again. "You bastard, you scum, who do you think you are?"

There was another minute and a half of video. As it played on the screen before him, Keith remained utterly still in the flickering pool of light. Then he raised his head and howled like a dog.

30

OUTSIDE, someone was stuck in the snow. The futile whine of tires could be heard even in the interview room, where Cardinal was listening to a sad young woman named Karen Steen. It had been an unhappy morning altogether. First, he had stopped off at the O.H., only to find Catherine sullen and uncommunicative. He had cut the visit short when he felt himself getting angry with her. His first phone call of the morning had come from Billy LaBelle's mother—crying, her speech slurred under the influence of too much of whatever her doctor had prescribed to dull her pain. Then Mr. Curry had called (only out of concern for his wife, of course), and Cardinal had had to tell him he was still no closer to catching whoever had beaten his only child to death. Then Roger Gwynn had called from the *Lode,* asking in his halfhearted way if there was any progress. When Cardinal responded in the negative, Gwynn had lapsed into an ode to their days at Algonquin High, as if nostalgia would make Cardinal more forthcoming. This was followed in short order by calls from *The Globe and Mail, The Toronto Star,* and Grace Legault from Channel Four. The newspapers were no problem, but Grace Legault had somehow got ahold of the tidbit about Margaret Fogle. Was it true they had thought she was also a Windigo victim? And she had turned up alive and well and living in B.C.?

Cardinal summed it up for her: Margaret Fogle had been a missing person. She had in some ways fit the killer's profile. However, now she was found and no longer of interest to the Algonquin Bay police. The call rattled him because it meant someone was talking to Legault without keeping him informed. The thought of having this out with Dyson made him very, very tired.

Cardinal wanted to devote his time to footwork. He and Delorme had split the camera and clock leads. They had re-

recorded the sounds from the tape, making multiple copies that they would send to camera and clock repair experts in Toronto and Montreal. Delorme would have run through twenty camera repair shops by now, while Cardinal had got nowhere. Instead, he had got caught up first on the phone and now in person with this sincere young woman who was telling him about her missing boyfriend.

Cardinal was angry at Sergeant Flower for telling Miss Steen he would see her. Especially when it turned out she was from Guelph, a largely agrarian community some sixty miles west of Toronto. "If your boyfriend's from Toronto," he told her, "you should be talking to the Toronto police."

Karen Steen was a shy woman—girl, really, not more than nineteen or so—who tended to stare at the floor between sentences. "I decided not to waste a lot of time on the telephone, Officer Cardinal. I thought you'd be more likely to pay attention to me if I came in person. I believe Keith is here in Algonquin Bay."

All young women made Cardinal think of his daughter, but—except for her age—Ms. Steen had nothing in common with Kelly. Kelly was the epitome of the hip and casual—in Cardinal's eyes at least—whereas the young woman seated across from him in the interview room had a kind of girl-next-door look. She was wearing a business suit that was too old for her, and silver wire-frames that gave her the air of a scholar. A very serious girl next door.

Miss Steen looked at the floor again—at the little puddle of melted snow at her feet. Cardinal thought for a moment she was going to cry, but when she looked up her eyes were clear. "Keith's parents are away on a dig in Turkey—they're archaeologists—and it's going to be impossible to reach them. I didn't want to wait for them to tell me what to do. I've read about the murders you've had up here. They weren't just murders—the people were missing for some time before they were killed, I think."

"That doesn't mean everyone who disappears has been abducted by this lunatic. Besides, your boyfriend's hitch-hiking across Canada—it's a big piece of real estate to be missing in. You say he was expected in the Soo on Tuesday."

"Yes. And it isn't like him to just not show up somewhere. One of the things I love about Keith is he's very considerate of other people. Very reliable. He hates to cause trouble."

"It's out of character, you're saying."

"Way out of character. I'm not hysterical, Mr. Cardinal. I didn't come here lightly. I have reasons."

"Go on, Miss Steen. I didn't mean to imply anything, except—Well, go on."

The young woman drew a deep breath and held it a minute, staring into the distance. Cardinal suspected this was a habitual gesture of hers, and it was an attractive one. There was a pleasing gravity to Miss Steen. He had no trouble imagining a young man in love with her.

"Keith and I are opposites in many ways, but we're very close," she said finally. "We were going to get married after high school, but then we decided to put it off for a year. I wanted to go straight on to university, and Keith wanted to see the world, so to speak, before settling down to study again. Anyway, we thought it wouldn't hurt us to wait another year. I'm only telling you this so you'll understand that when Keith said he would write to me, and e-mail me when he got the chance, he meant it—it wasn't casual. We even arranged the timing of our letters to make sure they wouldn't cross."

"And has he written? The way he said he would?"

"His letters haven't exactly come like clockwork, but yes—one letter a week, and one phone call and sometimes, if he was near a computer, I'd get an e-mail. Every week. Until now."

Cardinal nodded. Miss Steen was not just a serious young woman, she was also—and this was not a judgment Cardinal made very often—a good person. She had been well brought up, probably strictly, to respect other people and the truth. She looked Dutch, with her wheat-blond hair cut short as a boy's, and her eyes the deep blue of new denim.

"Keith's last phone call was Sunday the fifteenth—a week and a half ago. He sounded fine. He was in Gravenhurst, staying at a hideous little hotel and not having a particularly good time, but he's basically a cheerful person, Keith—the kind who makes friends easily. He's a pretty good musician—lugs his guitar everywhere. People tend to take him in. That's partly what worries me."

Lucky Keith, Cardinal thought, to have someone like Miss Steen worrying about him. She pulled a photograph out of her purse and handed it to Cardinal. It showed a boy with long curly brown hair, sitting on a park bench. He was playing an acoustic guitar, frowning with concentration.

"He just hasn't got a suspicious bone in his body," she continued. "He's always getting cornered by pamphleteers and people like that because he always believes their opening pitch, you know what I'm saying?" Her denim-blue eyes—dark, and slightly turned up at the corners—implored him to understand. "Which is not to say he's stupid. Far from it. But the others who disappeared, they weren't stupid, either, were they?"

"Well, two of them were very young, but no—none of them were stupid."

"Keith was planning to head for the Soo on Monday, but he wasn't really looking forward to it. He's not really big on seeing relatives, but . . ." She looked away, took a deep breath again, and held it.

Keith, my man, Cardinal thought, if you let this young woman get away, you are truly an idiot. "What is it?" he asked gently. "You're hedging, now."

The breath was let go in a long sigh. The serious blue eyes held him once more. "Detective, it's only honest to tell you that Keith and I had a—a bit of a quarrel, as well. A couple of weeks ago when he called. I guess I was feeling kind of lonely and vulnerable. Anyway, we went over a lot of old ground about how we're spending our respective years. He's lugging his guitar cross-country—I mean, really, if I have a rival for his affections it's that Ovation of his—but I'm not as spontaneous as he is. I just want to get on with my education. It wasn't a serious fight—please believe that. We didn't hang up angry or anything. But it was a quarrel, and I wouldn't feel right not telling you."

"But you don't think this quarrel is the reason for Keith's . . . sudden silence."

"I'm sure it isn't."

"I appreciate your telling me. How were things left, exactly?"

"Keith said he would probably stop off in Algonquin Bay—he'd call me when he got here."

"Miss Steen, Keith didn't want to go to the Soo, didn't want to see his relatives. Now, you say he wasn't angry with you, and I accept that, but why should we assume he's in trouble when he doesn't show up at a place he said quite clearly he didn't want to go to?"

"On its own, I agree, it wouldn't be alarming. But no letter? No phone call? No e-mail? After being so reliable about it? And you have these unsolved abductions here, these murders, right?"

Cardinal nodded. Miss Steen was holding her breath again, working her way to another thought. Cardinal waited for her to reach it. Lise Delorme leaned in the doorway, but Cardinal shook his head, warning her off. Miss Steen resolved whatever hesitations she had; when she spoke, her voice was louder. "I told you there was no letter this past week, Detective."

"Yes. You made quite a point of it."

"Well, that isn't quite true. And that's really why I'm here." Miss Steen reached into her purse and pulled out a manila envelope. "The letter's in here—the envelope, I mean; it isn't a letter. It's Keith's handwriting on the address, but there wasn't any letter inside."

"It arrived empty?" Cardinal took the manila envelope from her.

"Not empty." This time she didn't look at the floor. Her serious blue eyes looked directly into his.

Cardinal tore off the top sheet of his desk blotter pad and emptied the contents of the manila envelope onto a fresh sheet. The smaller, enclosed envelope was postmarked three days ago, Algonquin Bay. Using tweezers, Cardinal opened the flap, saw the yellowish, dried contents, and closed it again. He folded it into the clean blotter sheet and put both back inside the manila envelope.

In the brief silence that followed, Cardinal was certain of two things: Every word this young woman had told him was true, and—if he were not already dead—Keith London had very little time left to live.

He dialed Jerry Commanda's number, then put his hand over the mouthpiece. "When did this arrive?"

"This morning."

"And you came straight here?"

"Yes. It didn't occur to me for one moment that Keith did it. But he did address the envelope. I know his handwriting. I'm right to be frightened, don't you think?"

Jerry Commanda was on the line, now. "Jerry, this is important. I need to helicopter something down to Forensic. What are my chances?"

"Zero. If it's desperate, I might be able to weasel something out of the flight school. How urgent are we talking?"

"Very. I think our boy just mailed us a sample of his semen."

31

ALGONQUIN Bay's government dock is a quiet place on a winter evening. The only sounds are likely to be the sawtooth buzz of a passing snowmobile, or a sudden quake in the ice as massive plates shift against each other, emitting an otherworldly sigh, a slow-motion squeal, sometimes a horrendous gasp.

Eric Fraser and Edie Soames huddled side by side in a corner of the wharf out of the wind. Lake Nipissing stretched out into the gray like some bleak Nordic vision. Eric wasn't saying anything, but Edie was luxuriating in the thrill of knowing another mind so well that no words were necessary. In fact, she knew what Eric was going to say—he would say it any minute now. He'd been restless and irritable all morning and into the afternoon. And now, although taking the photographs was calming him a little, Edie knew where things were headed, even if Eric didn't. Any minute now, he would say it.

But Eric moved away to stand below the *Chippewa Princess,* a tour boat that had been turned into a restaurant—at least, during summer it was a restaurant; in winter, it hung clear of the ice like a white whale on a hoist. Eric adjusted a lens, cursing the cold. Edie fussed with her hair, trying to get it to hang across one eye like Drew Barrymore's in a movie she'd seen. Some hope, she thought bitterly. But at least it would hide some of her face.

Watching Eric in his long black coat, she wished they could sleep together. The problem was Eric didn't like it. His entire body would go stiff as a board when she touched him—not with desire, but with revulsion. At first she had thought the revulsion was directed just at her, no surprise there. But Eric seemed revolted by sex in general. Sex is for weaklings, he always said. Well, she could live without it, especially now that they shared this other, deeper excitement. He would say the word within the hour, she was sure.

"Move over." Eric motioned her to her left. "I want to get the islands in."

Edie turned to look. Out there, where the sky and the lake met in mutual shades of ash gray, lay the islands. *That* island. Windigo. Who would have thought such a tiny island could have a name? Edie remembered the dead girl, the curve of her spine against Eric's duffel bag. So momentous it had seemed at the time, the *murder,* such a grim weight to that word. But it was amazing how little it mattered, the actual event, when you got right down to it. A human life had been extinguished, but no pillar of flame had descended from the sky, no maw of hell had opened. The cops and the newspapers got a little excited, but essentially the world went on exactly as before, minus Katie Pine. I wouldn't even remember her name, Edie thought, if they hadn't yammered about it day in and day out on the news.

She moved a little to the left, just as the ice shifted with a squeal like tearing metal. Edie let out a cry. "Eric, did you hear that?"

"The ice moved. Give me a smile, now."

"I don't want to smile." Cameras were no friend to Edie, and the ice had rattled her—as if the island had spoken her name.

"Look grumpy, then, Edie. I don't care."

She gave him her biggest grin, just to spite him, and he clicked the shutter. Another one for the record.

They'd started their photographic expedition out at Trout Lake, up near the reservoir. Eric had snapped one of Edie making an angel in the snow right over the spot where they'd buried Billy LaBelle. With all the snow, there wasn't the slightest trace of anything untoward. The hill with its view of the lake, the deep blue sky, would have looked good on a postcard.

Then they'd driven down to Main Street and taken a few shots in front of the house where they'd killed Todd Curry. One of Edie, one of Eric, and then one of the two of them

(Eric had used the timer for that one). A man had seen them—a man walking his big woolly dog, and Edie had imagined for a moment that he had glared at them. But Eric had reassured her: just a young couple playing with a camera, what's the old fart going to care?

They moved to the lee of the bait shop so Eric could light a cigarette, cupping his hands around the match. He leaned against the wooden wall and looked at Edie through narrowed eyes. She could hear the words he was going to say before he said them, as if she had already dreamed the scene, as if she had created Eric, constructed the dock and the cold and the smoke all in her own mind. She sensed the same dark thrill running in his blood as was running in hers, now. She could smell it, like the metallic smell of ice that quivered on the frigid wind. Seeing the house again had set her nerves humming. Seeing the island. She was shivering with cold but said nothing. She didn't want to spoil this moment.

They got back in the van and turned the heat up full blast. It felt so good that Edie laughed out loud. Eric dug a book out of the glove compartment and handed it to her. It was a large paperback, very grimy, with a *used* sticker on it.

She read the title. "*Dungeon.* Where'd you get this?"

He told her he'd picked it up last time he was in Toronto. It was a historical document he'd been looking for. A catalog of torture devices used in the Middle Ages. "Read it to me," he said. "Read page thirty-seven."

Edie flipped through the glossy pages of photographs and drawings. The photographs showed the chair, whip, or restraint; the drawings illustrated the device's use: hooks to yank out guts, iron claws to tear the flesh, saws for splitting a human in two. The illustration for that one showed a man hanging upside down, while two others sawed him from crotch to navel.

"Read page thirty-seven," Eric said again. "Read it to me. I love it when you read to me. You read so well."

Oh, he knew how good his praise felt. Like coming home to a roaring fire after freezing half to death. Edie found the page. It showed a sort of helmet that was fixed over a wooden bar. Above the helmet was a huge screw.

"*Skull crushers,*" she read. "*The accused's chin is braced against the lower rod. As the screw is turned, the iron cap is forced downward, smashing the teeth together and gradually into the upper and lower jawbones. As more and more pressure is exerted, the eyes are pushed from their sockets. Eventually the brain itself is forced through the splintered cranium.*"

"Yes. The brain squirts through," Eric breathed. "Read another one. Read about the wheel."

Eric had his hands deep in his pockets. Edie was sure he was touching himself, but she knew better than to mention it. She flipped through the pages, the pictures of old iron instruments, the funny little woodcuts with their cartoon-like expressions of horror.

"Come on, Edie. Read about the wheel. It's near the end."

"You seem to know this book very well. Must be a favorite of yours."

"Maybe it is. Maybe that's why I want to share it with you."

Oh, I know what's coming, Eric. I know what you're going to say. Finding the page, she felt a throbbing in her belly like a second heart. "*The wheel. Stretched out, naked, on his or her back, the victim's arms and legs were fixed to the outer rim of the wheel. Blocks of wood were placed beneath all the important bones and joints. Wielding an iron bar, the torturer smashed arms and legs into pulp, using all his skill to avoid actually killing his victim.*"

"They just smashed people to bits," Eric said. "But keeping them alive the whole time. What a thrill it must have been. Can you imagine? Read the rest."

"*The report of one eyewitness described how the victim was turned into 'a sort of huge screaming puppet writhing in rivulets of blood, a puppet with four tentacles, like a sea monster, of raw, slimy, and shapeless flesh mixed up with splinters of smashed bones.' When there was nothing left to break, the limbs were woven among the spokes of the wheel. The wheel was then raised horizontally on a pole. Birds of prey pecked at the eyes and tore off bits of flesh. Wheeling was probably the slowest and most agonizing death the human mind has ever conceived."*

"Read what comes after. Bottom of the page."

"Wheelings were extremely common and considered good fun. Woodcuts, drawings, and paintings through four centuries depict crowds of people laughing and chatting, clearly enjoying the hideous pain of a fellow human being."

"People used to love it, Edie. People still love it. They just won't admit it."

Edie knew. Even Gram loved watching wrestling or a boxing match. Well, it was better than staring at this god-forsaken sea of ice. You bet Gram loved it. Watching some guy get beaten half to death.

Perfectly normal, according to Eric. It just didn't happen to be perfectly legal at the moment, that was all. It had fallen out of fashion. But it might come back—look at the United States. Look at the gas chamber, the electric chair. "You can't tell me people don't love it, Edie. It would have died out centuries ago if people didn't get a big bang out of inflicting death. It's just the biggest thrill known to man."

It's coming, now, Edie thought. I can see the words forming in the air before he even says them. "I agree," she said quietly.

"Good."

"No, no. I mean I agree with what you're *going* to say. Not just what you said."

"Oh you do, do you?" Eric smiled slyly. "What was I going to say? Come on, Madame Rosa. Tell me my thoughts. Read my mind."

"I can, Eric. I know exactly what you were going to say."

"So go ahead. Tell me my thoughts."

"You were going to say, 'Let's do him tonight.'"

Eric gave her his profile. Blew smoke in a thin stream

into the gathering darkness. "Not bad," he said quietly. "Not bad at all."

"I don't know about you, Eric, but I'd say it's party time."

Eric rolled down the window and flicked his cigarette into the snow. "Party time."

32

THE house was much smaller than it had looked from the outside. The upstairs had only two bedrooms—Woody could have sworn there would be three—and a tiny bathroom.

As he had so carefully explained to that foxy Officer Delorme, Arthur "Woody" Wood was not in the burglary business to enhance his social life. Like all professional burglars, he went to great lengths to avoid meeting people on the job. At other times, well, Woody was as sociable as the next fellow.

He had seen the weaselly-looking guy from the music store coming by here all the time. In fact, he had followed him home from the mall one day, after watching him load a tasty-looking Sony box into his van. He knew the couple was out, now, because he had sat outside in the van for the past hour and a half. It was perfectly safe to watch a place that way; nobody worries about a beat-up old ChevyVan labeled COMSTOCK ELECTRICAL INSTALLATIONS AND REPAIRS, nobody pays the slightest attention. Even so, Woody changed the lettering every three months, just to be on the safe side.

So he had sat out there listening to the Pretenders on his tape machine (a Blaupunkt he'd happened across while doing a little inventory enhancement up in Cedarvale last winter. Man, those Germans knew their engineering) and reading the sports pages of the *Lode*. In between worrying about the Maple Leafs, he was thinking about his shopping. Woody, besides being an industrious thief, was also a conscientious father and husband, and it was time to pick up a little something for the son and heir, whom he referred to affectionately as Dumptruck.

The kid needed a nifty toy—a set of blocks would be nice; he'd see what was around. Of course, this couple didn't have any children, he'd watched long enough to know that, but you never know what people will have cluttering up their closets. He'd picked up a little plastic Yogi Bear a couple of weeks ago that Truckie carried with him everywhere.

The side-door lock had presented no problem: twenty-seven seconds—not a record, but not bad, either. Woody had proceeded directly to the top floor, his usual practice; he had a superstition that you were working with nature, then, letting gravity assist you on the way down. He moved now in his quietest Reeboks toward the back bedroom; reason and observation had told him this had to be where the happy couple slept.

It was not what he expected. This was a single girl's room, not a couple's. The walls were pink, the bed was white wood, and the dresser was littered with pots of cream, mostly medicinal. The wallpaper—ancient and peeling in more than one corner—had at one time been pale yellow with a motif of little parasols. A stuffed tiger on top of the dresser caught his eye—Dumptruck might like that—but on closer inspection it proved to be a mangy, dog-eared tiger, clearly clutched and drooled on through many an illness. He could hardly take that home. "What were you thinking of?" Martha would say. "It's completely unhygienic."

He paused for a moment, alert for any sounds. No, the old lady wasn't stirring. Probably deaf, too. Poor old girl hadn't been trundled out for at least three days.

The headboard of the bed had an interesting feature: built-in bookshelves with little sliding panels—exactly the sort of cubbyhole people like to stash their jewelry in. Woody, an inveterate optimist as all of his trade must be, slid back the little panel full of expectation.

And met up with his second surprise. He had expected a couple of Danielle Steel novels, Martha read them all the time, or maybe a Barbara Taylor Whatshername. But this was a grim little library, indeed: *History of Torture, Japanese Atrocities of World War II, Justine,* and *Juliette*—both by the Marquis de Sade. He'd heard of that guy.

Woody always allowed himself one lingering moment on a job, a moment when, holding some treasured or peculiar object, he would indulge his imagination and picture the life he was invading. This was that moment. He pulled out *Juliette*. Wasn't the marquis that guy who liked to prance around in whips and chains and things? Woody flipped through to a page that had the corner turned down and read a passage that had been marked in the margin: *I grasp those breasts, lift them, and cut them off close to the chest; then stringing those hunks of flesh upon a cord . . .*

Woody flipped through a few more pages and saw that things only got worse. The flyleaf bore an inscription in cheap ballpoint: *to Edie from Eric.* "Jesus, Eric," he said under his breath. "This is not a book you give a woman. This is one sick book, and you are one sick puppy." Woody vowed strict professional deportment for the rest of the job.

Martha would have shivered with revulsion at the bathroom: the sink was rust-stained, the tiles scummy. You could smell the towels from the hallway. The cabinet was chock-full of Pharma-City sleeping pills and tranquilizers, just the sort of happy accident that could make a man's day. Unfortunately, Woody was not into drugs. Didn't use 'em, didn't sell 'em, thanks to Martha. But oh, he thought wistfully, there was a time . . .

A noise from somewhere. Voices. He froze in front of the cracked mirror, head cocked to one side. Just the old lady's TV. Lonely damn business watching soap operas all day. She had the front bedroom, he knew from his vigil, and there wouldn't be anything worth taking in there, some horrible old black-and-white TV with a terrible picture.

He went downstairs and took a quick, disappointing inventory of the kitchen. The handful of old appliances would net him nothing. Even the dark little living room was a bust. Just a lot of overstuffed furniture that looked like one too many dogs had died on it. Woody ignored the funny old clock on the mantel, not into antiques. To his disgust, there wasn't even a VCR: Now, that was truly an anomaly in this day and age.

He was batting zero, and the place was nearly done. He'd totally misread the situation. The music-store guy didn't even live here. Guy worked at the fucking music store, for Christ's sake, he had to have some great equipment stashed away somewhere—Woody had seen him with that Sony carton, just the other day, pulled it out of the back of that spiffy old Windstar he drove.

"Truly fucked up," Woody murmured. "A TV table and no TV." The dust pattern showed that there had been a TV in the spot until a day or two ago. And the small stack of videotapes beside the table sang to him of a VCR. Either both items were in for repair—big coincidence there—or they'd been shifted to another part of the house, maybe Granny Goodwitch's room.

Well, he couldn't disturb Granny, so he was stuck with the basement. Woody's optimism hadn't deserted him, not yet—basements sometimes yielded unexpected dividends: a case of tools, an outboard motor, sets of golf clubs, you just never knew—but basements were cold and dank, and the shivers they gave you felt a lot like fear. You couldn't hear as well in a basement, either, which is why a lot of his colleagues got caught in basements: It was a vulnerable position. They were the anal sex of burglary, basements: not without interest, but not his first choice, either. Not on a bright sunny day.

At the bottom of the steps, Woody paused amid the Wellington boots and battered skates and rusting snow shovels, waiting for his eyes to adjust. The basement smelled of laundry and old cat piss. Outside, it was dark; a light would be seen. The windows, he noticed with a flutter of nerves, were high and tiny and probably not big enough to climb through should a sudden exit prove desirable.

Gradually, various objects took on form: an old washer with a wringer attachment, a filthy furnace, a pair of broken skis, a battered aluminum toboggan, and a woman's bike with the front wheel missing. He considered the bike for a minute: Just that fall, Martha's ten-speed had been stolen. Martha had gone into her hell's-own-fury mode, especially when Woody had taken the detached view of a professional. This wreck of a bike was out of the question, though; it would take more work to fix than it was worth. He turned and saw across the gloom a door, a solid slab of oak leading to—well, here Woody allowed his optimism free rein: It would lead to—yes, that's it, his studio. The weaselly-looking guy with the cameras and tape recorders kept a studio in his girlfriend's basement. This room with its Medeco lock and its three solid bolts would contain cameras, tripods, recording gear, TVs, and VCRs. Woody, my man, you're on the threshold of paradise.

Of course, if there was equipment in there, the bolts were on the wrong side of the door—you wanted to keep people like Woody *out* of your treasure trove, not invite them *in*—but even while Woody was aware of this, it didn't slow him down. The bolts took no time at all and the Medeco, well, you could grow old trying to pick a Medeco, so Woody used a locksmith's tool to yank out the whole thing. He pushed the door open and saw instead of treasure trove a naked boy sitting on a heavy wooden chair.

Woody's first thought was, Oh, fuck, I'm in for it now. But then, by the light of a pictureless TV, he saw that the boy was actually tied to the chair: mouth taped shut, wrists taped to the chair, and naked as a goddam jay. He was struggling at the tape and groaning; his eyes were wild.

This sort of thing will throw a burglar, even a seasoned professional. Not thinking clearly, Woody went straight to the TV and disconnected the VCR. Okay, the kid's caught up in some heavy-duty sexual escapade, it's none of my business. But as he was wrapping the cord around the VCR (Mitsubishi, four-head stereo, only a year old) several aspects of the situation pressed themselves on Woody's attention: The kid was naked. There were no clothes in this room. There was piss and also from the smell that was shit in the basin under his chair. Not a game, not a practical joke. Woody paused at the door, VCR tucked under one arm. "I get it," he said to the kid. "Drug deal went bad, right?"

The boy struggled furiously at his bonds. Woody leaned forward and yanked the tape from his mouth. Instantly the kid was screaming. It was mostly incoherent but certain phrases were repeated: maniacs, perverts, they're going to kill him.

"Hold on, now. Hold on. You're going to have to put a lid on the screaming. Going to have to shut that up right now. You can't be screaming." This last Woody screamed himself.

"Get me out of here, you fucking bastard!" Tears poured down the kid's face. He was squealing about a videotape, a murder. The details were crazy, but the terror was real. Woody had seen some sick-making things in his stints in the Kingston pen, but he had never, not in the weakest, most victimized inmate, seen such abject terror.

Woody's reaction was not complex: You see a man tied up, you untie him. He looked into a tiny bathroom for clothes and found none. "Where the fuck's your clothes, man? It's twenty below out there. And that's not counting no wind-chill factor." He was already opening the Swiss Army knife, when he heard the car pull up outside. The kid was screaming like a rock star: set me free, set me free, set me free.

"Shut up, man. They're right outside."

"I don't give a fuck, get me out of here!"

Woody slapped the tape back over the kid's mouth and made sure it stuck. The side door of the house was already opening, and he could hear the couple talking. He shut the door and snarled in his meanest voice, "You make the slightest fucking noise, I mean it, I'll stick you myself. You got that?"

The kid nodded furiously: he's got it, he's clear.

"Make one fucking sound and we're both up shit creek. There's only one door out of here and if we lose the element of surprise, you can kiss that exit goodbye, I mean it. Make a noise, I'll poke a hole in your liver."

The kid was nodding like a maniac. Shit, Woody could

dash up the basement steps and be out the side door in a flash and—Oh Christ, we got footsteps right overhead.

"Here's what we do," he said, slitting the tape around the kid's ankle. "I cut you free, you put on my coat, and we're out the side door. I got a ChevyVan waiting across the street." He wouldn't have to tell the kid to run.

He set the other foot free. Already the kid was trying to stand up, still attached to the chair. "Hold on. Hold on, for Chrissake!" Were those voices closer? One wrist was free, and before he could finish with the other the kid ripped the tape from his mouth and was out of control again, setting up a holler. Woody slammed a hand over the kid's mouth and brandished the knife, but it was too late: The voices upstairs were suddenly charged, the footsteps fast and heavy.

Woody started on the last of the tape—fuck the kid's noise—but the kid didn't wait for him to finish. He was on his feet, still attached to the chair by one wrist and he was pushing past Woody taking the chair with him. He flung open the door, and there was the weaselly-looking guy with a gun.

The kid shoved past, the chair clattering with him up the stairs.

"You can't get out," the man said over his shoulder, but staring at Woody. The kid was already at the top of the stairs, bare-assed, banging his shoulder into the door, but Woody knew there wasn't a door on earth that broke like they did in the movies.

"Be cool," Woody said to the weasel guy. "No need for violence."

Weasel looked him up and down, no rush about it. "Maybe I like violence."

"Here's the deal: I leave your VCR and shit, and you let the kid go. I don't know what he did—probably you have every right to kick his ass—but you can't keep a kid tied up in a basement. It ain't right."

The kid was still slamming away at the door, still doing the banshee thing.

"Shut up," the man said toward the stairs. "Guy's fucking hysterical."

"Yeah, he's definitely upset. Look, man, I gotta go."

The weasel left the doorway and went to the bottom of the stairs. "Keith," he said sharply. "Get downstairs right now."

"No way, man! I'm out of here!"

The man went to the bottom step, held the gun a foot away from the boy's leg, and pulled the trigger.

The kid shrieked and fell down the stairs, clutching his thigh. He was rolling on the concrete floor, when the man kicked his chin like he was trying for a field goal and the kid went still.

"Jesus Christ, man." It was all Woody could manage and he repeated it a couple of times. "You didn't have to do that."

"Sit down in that chair."

"No, sir. Negative. Obviously you're pissed off, but let's be realistic here." There was no way in hell he was going to let himself be tied up. This was one sick weasel.

"Sit down in that chair or I'll shoot you, too."

"He woke Gram up"—this surreal offering from the top of the stairs, where the woman now stood gripping the rail. "All his damn screaming." She came down a couple of steps and stood over the kid. "I ought to pee all over your face."

"He broke into your house, Edie. He was stealing your VCR."

The woman looked at Woody. "It so happens that VCR means a lot to me. It has sentimental value."

"Okay. I hear you. I'm just in it for the cash, know what I mean?"

"Fuck, Eric. Let's kill him."

"Videos, hey, I love 'em, too, you know? Me and the wife'll rent a Clint Eastwood now and again—well, I like Clint. She likes the stuff about sisters and girlfriends and that. But, hey—a good movie, some popcorn, we love it!"

Make a little conversation, get on their good side, works wonders with the cops sometimes.

"Shoot him, Eric," the woman said with feeling. "Shoot him in the belly."

"Listen, you guys—Edie, Eric. Obviously, I'm not welcome here, so I'll just go, okay? I'll just hit the road. Sorry for the inconvenience and shit. I apologize."

"That van outside, the blue one, is that yours?"

"The Chevy Van, yeah. And the fact is, Eric, I parked in a bad spot. Snow removal. She's gonna get towed if I don't move her."

The man didn't react to this at all. He was sighting down the barrel at Woody's belly.

"Eric?" The woman came down another couple of steps and watched them intently, her mouth open a little. There was something wrong with her face. "Why don't you break his nose?"

Woody was gauging the distance to the gun, still in the man's hand, still pointed at his stomach.

"It's something I'd like to see," the woman went on. "Hear the bone break and everything."

The kid stirred, and the man turned and kicked his head. It was now or never. Woody shoved him hard, straight-armed the woman, and he was up the stairs, hand on the doorknob. The door was swinging open when the bullet tore into his back, somewhere near the love handles. He toppled over backward, landed on top of the kid, and hit his head a hell of a bang on the concrete floor.

A guy he'd shared a cell with once had told Woody what it was like to be shot: like a hot iron pressing through your body, man, those little fuckers are hot. And Woody discovered now that this was true.

The man was standing over him, big as King Kong. That's how I must look to Dumptruck, Woody thought, and wondered how long before Martha started to worry.

The man's hands were around his neck. Strong thumbs closing his windpipe.

"Break his nose," the woman said again. "Why do you want to choke him, when you can break his nose?"

And carefully, using the butt of his pistol, the man did exactly that.

33

DELORME sat in the half-dark of her kitchen, finishing her third cup of Nescafé. Before her was a stack of files Dyson had sent over. She liked to work in her kitchen at anything except cooking. The remains of a frozen dinner lay forgotten on her plate.

The files were also mostly forgotten; Delorme was thinking about the three Fs. If she was going to do anything with the boat receipt she had seen in Cardinal's files, it would be through them. The three Fs stood for February, French Canadians, and Florida. As anyone who has been to that particular state in that particular month can testify, the Florida gulf in February becomes the Gulf of Quebec. Miami becomes Montreal-On-Sea. Suddenly, Cuban becomes a minority accent, and every other license plate proclaims *Je me souviens.* Come February, Florida's waiters and bellboys polish off their seasonal stable of Canadian jokes: What's the difference between a Canadian and a canoe? Answer: Canoes tip.

Forty-five minutes and half a dozen phone calls later, Delorme had talked to two French Canadian cops who were about to visit Florida on vacation. Neither of them, unfortunately, was going to be anywhere near the Calloway Marina. So Delorme made a few more calls and got the number of Dollard Langois, who had been in her class at Police College. They had even dated a couple of times, and Delorme was at this moment very grateful to her younger self that she had not slept with him. He had been an awkward, gangly young man, with big gentle hands and hound-dog eyes, and one night after a movie in Aylmer he had confessed that he was absolutely crazy in love with her. Delorme had been all set to sleep with him until he said that. Dollard Langois had been one attractive guy, but she had not been about to mess up her budding career with romance. She had often wondered since, on lonely nights, how he was doing, and what would have happened if—Well, Dollard Langois was a road not taken, put it that way.

They spent a few minutes catching up—speaking English, perhaps because that had been the language at Aylmer. Yes, she told him, she was pretty happy with her career as a cop. No, she was not married.

"That's too bad, Lise. It's so nice to be married. Doesn't surprise me, though—and I don't mean that in a negative way."

"Go ahead, Dollard. Tell me what a failure I am as a human being."

"No, no. I just meant you were hell-bent on a career is all. Single-minded. It's a good thing."

"I can't take any more. Tell me about you."

He was *Sergeant* Langois, now, assigned to a Quebec Provincial Police detachment twenty miles outside Montreal. Two kids, lovely wife—a nurse, not a cop—and every February they spent a week down in Florida at a place where they had a time-share arrangement. "Why'd you ask?" he wanted to know. "Awful late in the season to be looking for a share."

"It's for work. Something I need to trace."

A heavy sigh traveled down the line from Montreal. "Why am I not surprised?"

"I wouldn't ask unless it was really serious, Dollard."

"It's my vacation, Lise. I'm going to be with my family."

"I wouldn't ask unless it was serious. Do you remember me well enough to know that? We've got a child killer here, Dollard. I can't leave, even for a day."

They went back and forth for a bit. Then, as much to distract him as anything else, Delorme asked where exactly he was going to be staying. It turned out—unhappily for Sergeant Langois—that he would be staying in Hollywood Beach at a condo in the same block as the Calloway Marina. His fate was sealed, and Delorme hung up exceedingly pleased with herself.

* * *

SHE spent another hour with the files—early cases of Cardinal's—and found nothing of interest. According to the files, John Cardinal was exactly what he appeared to be—a hardworking cop who got the job done efficiently and thoroughly, without bending the rules. Nearly all his arrests resulted in convictions, although not in the case she was reading now, involving a ne'er-do-well called Raymond Colacott who had since killed himself. The suspect had been brought into custody along with four kilos of cocaine that Cardinal had every reason to believe Colacott was selling. But when the matter was brought to trial, the evidence had gone missing, stolen from the evidence locker. Case dismissed.

The Crown had put its own investigator on the case (file handily included, courtesy of Dyson) and drawn a resounding blank. Cardinal had not been a particular suspect; too many people had had access to the evidence locker. A report was issued, procedures were changed.

Yes, it could have been Cardinal, but for a cop in Algonquin Bay to start selling coke would be far too risky. And Raymond Colacott was not Kyle Corbett, not someone capable of putting a cop on his payroll. If the investigation at the time had got nowhere, Delorme was certainly going to get nowhere nine years later when half the personnel involved had transferred to Winnipeg, Moose Jaw, or God knows where else.

Delorme scraped off her plate and put it in the sink. She had always intended to develop an interest in cooking, maybe even take a course up at the college one day, but lack of time and enthusiasm always seemed to weigh against it. Her mother, were she still alive, would have been horrified.

She went into the living room and pulled aside the curtain. Snowbanks glittered under the streetlights. She remained at the window for some time, staring through her ghostlike reflection, coffee cup in hand. Ten minutes later, she was in her car, driving with no clear intention up Algonquin toward the bypass. She made a right onto the highway, keeping the speedometer well below the speed limit.

It was a peculiarity of hers, this aimless driving, and she would have been embarrassed if any of her colleagues had discovered her nocturnal habit. She wasn't sure if it was restlessness or if it was just a way of making daydreaming a physical, as well as a mental, process.

The bypass had a pleasant sweep to it, a graceful curve that held the higher end of town in a gentle embrace. It was a great pleasure to feel the slight but steady centrifugal pull as one drove the length of the city. Sometimes Delorme just drove the bypass out to the intersection with Lakeshore and then back into town along the bay. Other times, only when she was agitated, she did something rather more idiosyncratic: She drove out to the neighborhoods of friends and colleagues, not stopping to visit, just driving by seeing their lights on, their cars in the driveway. She knew it was neurotic, but it gave her a soothing sense of peace all the same.

She made a left on Trout Lake Road and drove all the way out to where it turned into Highway 63. In winter you could see right through the trees down to the houses on Madonna Road. She glanced over and saw the lights on in Cardinal's place, even saw a dark shape at the rear window. Probably that's the kitchen, she figured; he'd be doing dishes or having a late supper.

At the Chinook Tavern, she turned around and headed back into town by way of the college. Traffic was sparse now, and the city below her was all lit up. Thoughts of the Pine–Curry case were turning in her head, and she tried not to force them in any direction. She would just have her little drive and let things fall into place. A few minutes later she was cruising by a handsome, two-story stucco house in a not-quite-posh enclave all but hidden in the shadow of St. Francis Hospital. Dyson's car was parked in the driveway.

Delorme stopped at the side of the street, debating whether to pull in or not.

A pretty little girl, perhaps twelve years old, came walking uphill toward the house, accompanied by a boy of the same age or not much older. She clutched a collection of books to her chest the way girls do, and walked with head down, staring intently at the sidewalk. The boy must have said something funny because she looked up suddenly, laughing, showing a mouthful of braces. Then her mother, a bony, wraithlike figure, appeared in a side doorway and called her daughter away in a voice utterly devoid of affection.

The image stayed with Delorme all the way out to Edgewater Road. But somewhere between Rayne Street and the bypass, a plan of action had dropped into her head. She pulled into the driveway of the Swiss-style A-frame and rang the side doorbell. She had time to prepare her little speech, then forgot it all when the door was opened by Police Chief R. J. Kendall himself. "This had better be good," was all he said.

She followed him down to the basement, the same clubby room where it had all begun. The cover had been removed from what she had taken to be a billiard table. On it tiny soldiers in uniforms of red and blue did battle along the steep bank of a papier-mâché river. Delorme had interrupted the chief in the pursuit of his passion, building recreations of famous battles in fanatical detail, and he was not about to abandon it for the sake of an unmannerly visit.

"Plains of Abraham?" Delorme asked, trying to ease her way in.

"Just get to it, Detective. General Montcalme is beyond your help."

"Sir, I've been combing the files for anything about Cardinal. Going over old cases of his, notes and everything."

"I assume you've discovered something sensational in those files or you wouldn't be breaking every rule of protocol, not to mention common courtesy, by showing up at my home unannounced."

"No, sir. The thing is, the files aren't going to lead anywhere. I'm just running in circles, and it's getting in the way of Pine–Curry."

"Look at this." The chief held out a smooth hand, palm up. A tiny cannon nestled in his palm. "Exactly to scale.

There are twelve of them I have to fix into fittings that are barely visible to the naked eye."

"Incredible." Delorme responded with all the energy she could muster, but she could hear it wasn't enough.

"The files are important. A jury will expect a pattern of behavior."

"Sir, that will take forever, and it will all be old stuff impossible to prove."

"You have the Florida condo. You have the boat receipt."

"Dyson told you about those already?"

"He did. I asked to be kept closely informed."

"The receipt doesn't have Cardinal's name on it, sir." She had been about to tell him about Sergeant Langois, but no, better to wait and see what he might turn up down in Florida. "I've already contacted his American bank, but they're not exactly rushing to cooperate. What we need is something totally convincing. Something from right now. Something plain and simple."

"Naturally. If you want to ask your partner for a signed confession, go ahead. I don't expect you'll see a lot of success." He turned to her, a miniature tube of glue in his hand. "Or were you intending to interview Kyle Corbett on the subject? Excuse me, Mr. Corbett, is one of our detectives supplying you with confidential information? Gee, no, Officer, I have far too much respect for the law."

The chief was not by nature a sarcastic man. Delorme braced herself for one of his famous explosions, then plunged on. "Sir, I have an idea."

"Please. Enlighten me."

"What we do is we plant some information with Cardinal that he's sure to pass along—if he's really working for Corbett, that is. Something he'll have to let him know. Musgrave's crew will tap his phone and keep him under surveillance."

Kendall regarded her coolly, then turned back to his model, a tiny soldier pinched between thumb and forefinger. "I'll say one thing, Detective. You've got nerve."

"Sir, I think this could clear the air relatively—"

The chief cut her off with a wave of the hand. "I'm rather surprised that you're seriously—you are serious, aren't you? Yes, I can see you are—proposing to wiretap your own partner."

"With respect, sir. You're the one who assigned me to investigate him. Well, you and Dyson. If you want me to stop, I'd be happy to stop anytime."

"You see this?" Kendall pointed to a frigate parked in the midnight-blue St. Lawrence. "This assembly here, with the mainmast and stays? Just that part of this project took a week to put together."

"Incredible."

"Sometimes making a thing convincing takes a little time, Sergeant Delorme. A little patience. I hope you're not entirely lacking in that quality."

"My plan is better than thumbing through those endless files. If you look at it objectively, sir, I think you'll agree."

"I am. Hand me the little silver tube, would you? Thank you." Using the point of a pin, the chief dabbed a trace of glue onto a cannonball the size of a bug's eye, and set it onto a tiny stack. "You're still intent on leaving Special Investigations, I suppose. Hate to lose someone with a record like yours."

"Well, Chief, you're not losing me. I'm just moving over into CID."

"I know, I know. But Special Investigations—one could make the case that it's the most important part of the department. Take away Special Investigations, you've got a brain, certainly—all the motor functions are intact—but without Special Investigations, you've got a brain without a conscience. And that, my young friend, is a dangerous thing."

Delorme tucked away that *young* somewhere warm for later examination. "Sir, if we give him something no one else knows—even if we don't get him on the tap—we'll know he's the guy."

"I have one question." The chief was bending the limbs of a soldier into a climbing position. He dabbed glue onto each miniature hand and knee and pressed the figure into position against the face of a cliff. Then he turned to face Delorme, and his gaze was suddenly almost sexual in its intensity. "Why are you bringing this to me? Why aren't you bringing it to Dyson?"

"I'm working closely with Dyson, sir. But for this plan to stand up in court, there has to be no chance of anyone else having the same tainted information as Cardinal. You and I will be the only ones who know."

"Of course you must do it, there's no question. The sooner the better. Is Corporal Musgrave on board?"

"More than on board, sir. He can't wait."

"Good. Talk to a JP and get your approval."

"We've got it, sir. Musgrave got it."

Kendall cut loose with that big laugh of his, Hah! Hah! Hah! Delorme felt the variation in pressure on her eardrums along with considerable relief. Then the chief held her once more with that prehensile gaze. "Listen to me, young Delorme. I'm older than you and wiser— they're possibly the only reasons I'm your boss, but they're good reasons, so hear me: I have read up on Corporal Musgrave, and Corporal Musgrave is hot to trot, Corporal Musgrave is a barn-burner, Corporal Musgrave does not like our inscrutable Mr. Cardinal. If said Musgrave were under my command, which he is not, he would not be on this case. So you be careful. I'm not saying he's the type to manufacture evidence, but he *is* the type to blow a case with an excess of zeal. So you be sure and keep your head—which is where, at the moment?"

"Sir?"

"Where is your head on this case, Delorme? How do you see your Cardinal at this point?"

"Do I have to answer that, Chief?"

"Certainly."

Delorme looked up at the ceiling, staring at the exposed beams.

"I'm waiting."

"To be perfectly honest, sir, I don't know. I *do* know

there's no hard evidence against him. Nothing that would stand up to a good defense lawyer. So me, I consider him innocent until proven guilty."

"You're being legalistic. Is that out of loyalty? Are you too close to Cardinal to be objective? You can speak honestly."

"I don't know, Chief. I'm not a very introspective person."

Kendall laughed again, hard and loud, as if Delorme had told a fabulous joke, then he stopped as suddenly as he had started, and the quiet that followed was deep, like the quiet that follows the silencing of a car alarm. "You bring this guy in, you understand me? If he has been selling out to some godless thug, I want him off the force and I mean now. If he hasn't, the sooner you're off his case the better. I'm not a very introspective person, either, Sergeant Delorme. Which means without facts I tend to become bored and upset. You don't want to see me bored and upset."

"No, sir."

"So, run your little experiment. And Godspeed."

34

AN Ontario Hydro lineman named Howard Bass was repairing a transformer out on Highway 63, about five posts north of the Trout Lake marina. The job required a whole new crossbar, and Howard had been up in the cherry picker most of the morning, freezing his ass off. And, twenty feet up like that, he was catching a bad ricochet of sunlight off the snow that practically blinded him, RayBans and all. A couple of hours into the job, though, and the sun had shifted around, casting a sharp shadow of Howard and the arm of the cherry picker across the snow.

Stanley Betts, who was driving today, had strolled back to the marina to buy them both a couple of doughnuts and Cokes. He came back whistling a risqué little tune called "Good Morning, Little Schoolgirl," the cat-eyed Lolita behind the counter having put him in that frame of mind.

This stretch of 63 was always busy. You had the traffic coming down from the NORAD installation, you had the people coming in from Temiskaming, and you had the residential traffic for Four Mile Bay and Peninsula Road. Stan was stranded across the highway for a good few minutes, waiting for the traffic to clear. "I'm turning into a dirty old man!" he called to Howie. "You shoulda seen the little babe at the store!"

Howie didn't turn, didn't hear him over the roar of a speeding eighteen-wheeler.

"I swear, Howie," Stan said again, when he was across the road and clear. "I'm turning into a dirty old man!"

Although cold as hell, the day was perfectly clear. The yellow arm of the cherry picker seemed to flash against the blue of the sky. Howie looked strange up there, his breath making tiny white clouds. He was gripping the edge of the box in a weird way, looking down at something.

"What the hell you staring at?" Stan followed his gaze, but he couldn't see over the six-foot ridge of roadside sludge. He clambered to the top of this and shaded his eyes. When Stan saw what Howie saw, one of the Cokes fell and burst open on his steel-toed boot, shooting a miniature brown geyser over the snow.

35

"YOU can't possibly say it's the same killer." Dyson spread his spatulate fingers fanlike and counted off his reasons. "One: the victim is in his thirties; the others were teenage or younger. Two: totally different MO. The others were beaten or strangled. Three: he was dumped where he'd be easy to find."

"Not that easy. If the Hydro guys hadn't been working on that particular transformer, it could have been months before he was found. Next time they plowed 63, the body would have been totally covered up."

"Arthur Wood was a well-known criminal. Had to have a lot of enemies."

"Woody didn't have an enemy in the world. You couldn't hope to meet a nicer guy—long as you kept your eyes on the silverware."

"Bad blood from prison, maybe. Talk to his old cellmates, talk to the guards in his wing. We don't know everything about our clientele."

"Woody was a hardworking thief. This time, he broke into the wrong house. When we find that house, we find our killer." He's going to assign it to McLeod, Cardinal could see the decision forming in Dyson's all-but-transparent dome. The letter opener stirred a furrow through the dish of paper clips. "Look," Dyson said, "you've already got enough to do."

"Yeah, but if this is the same guy, we're just going to be—"

"Let me finish, please." The voice was soft, still thoughtful. "You've got more than enough to do, as I say. But why don't we do this: You take the Woody case for the time being. It's your case so long as nothing comes up that definitely *dis*connects it from Our Local Maniac. Moment that happens, and I mean *instantly,* it's McLeod's case. Understood?"

"Understood. Thanks, Don," Cardinal said, and flushed a little. He never used the detective sergeant's first name, it was just the excitement of the moment. Before he opened the door, he turned back and said, "Sudbury TV got ahold of the thing on Margaret Fogle."

"I know. That was my fault. I apologize."

Dyson apologizing. One for the record books. "Didn't exactly help. I don't even see why it would come up."

"Grace Legault is not Roger Gwynn. That woman is not going to linger long on Sudbury's esteemed Channel Four. That's a Toronto-bound bitch if ever I saw one. Knows what she's doing. Somehow, she got ahold of a bunch of Missing Persons and—well, it doesn't matter—she caught me off guard. Obviously, I should have kept you informed. My mistake. Now I think we're done here, aren't we?"

As he came out of Dyson's office, Cardinal bumped smack into Lise Delorme. "I've been looking all over for you," she said. "Woody's wife is out front. She wants to report him missing. We'll have to take her up to the O.H. to identify the body."

"Don't jump the gun here, Lise. I don't want to tell her right away."

Delorme looked shocked. "You have to tell her. Her husband is dead, for God's sake. You can't keep that from her."

"The moment we tell her, you can forget about getting any information out of her. She'll be too upset. I'm just saying we don't tell her right away."

MARTHA Wood hung her coat on a rack in the hall and beside it her son's tiny down parka. She was wearing a T-shirt and jeans—an outfit that on her tall, lean figure looked like something out of Vogue. She sat in the interview room where both cops had interviewed her husband numerous times over the years. Her toddler, like his mother, dark-haired and dark-eyed, sat quietly on the chair beside her, squeezing a plastic Yogi Bear that from time to time emitted a nasal moan.

Martha Wood twisted her wedding ring as she spoke.

"When Woody left the house, he was wearing a blue V-neck sweater, Levi's 505s, and cowboy boots. They're black. Lizard skin."

"Okay. It was cold on Saturday. What kind of coat did he have on?" The body with its nine bullet wounds had been found naked. Woody's clothes might turn up somewhere else.

"A blue down parka. Shouldn't I be filling out a form or something? A Missing Persons form?"

"We're taking it all down," Cardinal assured her.

"You need his height and weight, right?"

"We have that," Delorme said.

"Oh, right. I forgot about his arrest records. It's weird, all this time I go around thinking of cops as the enemy. Now Woody's disappeared, I feel different."

"We do, too," Cardinal said. "Was Woody driving that old ChevyVan of his?" They had already put out an all-points for the van, license plates and all.

"Yes. I should give you the license plate number." She reached into her purse for keys.

"I have the plate numbers from before," Delorme said. "His van, it's still blue?"

"Still blue, right." Mrs. Wood paused with her hand in her purse. "But he liked to change the license plates sometimes when he went on a job. I don't know if he did that or not this time. The sign is new: It says COMSTOCK ELECTRICAL REPAIRS on the side."

"You knew he was going out on a job?"

"Look. Woody's an electronics repairman. That's what he tells me, okay? I long ago learned to stop asking questions. He's a loving father and a dependable husband but he's never going to change his line of work—not for you, not for me, not for anyone."

"Okay. Do you know what area of town he was going to . . . work in?"

"He never tells me things like that. Look, the operative word here is 'dependable.' Woody said he'd be back by six o'clock. That's a day and a half ago, and I'm fucking scared."

"It may help us find him," Cardinal said gently, "if you have any information about the likely area of town to look in." He ignored Delorme's hard stare.

"I don't know. He did mention the old CN station the other day. He'd only just noticed they'd boarded it up. Maybe he was in that neighborhood, but I don't know." Suddenly she stood up, her purse spilling open on the floor. "He's in some kind of trouble, I'm telling you. Just because he steals things doesn't make him evil, you know. This is the first time he's ever not come home without phoning. Ever. The only time that happens is when he's under arrest—and if you're holding him, you'd better tell me, or so help me, I'm going to have Bob Brackett on your case until you're bounced off the goddam force." Bob Brackett was Algonquin Bay's best defense attorney. There wasn't a cop on the force he hadn't humiliated.

"Mrs. Wood, would you sit down, please?"

"No. If you haven't arrested my husband, I want to know why you aren't doing anything to find him!"

Her little boy stopped squeezing Yogi Bear and looked up at his mother with a worried expression.

"John, would you give me a minute alone with Mrs. Wood?"

Delorme took him by surprise—this wasn't in the script, and he didn't like it.

"Why?" Martha Wood wanted to know. "Why does she want to talk to me alone?"

"John. Please."

Cardinal went down the hall and into the monitor room. He put some coins in the Coke machine before he realized it was sold out of diet. He bought a Classic and sat down at the table, watching the video monitor, which was turned on but without sound.

From its high, corner angle, the video camera looked down pitilessly on Martha Wood. Both she and Delorme were absolutely motionless. Mrs. Wood was still standing, hands slightly away from her body, absorbing the blow, not yet feeling the pain, her face a picture of pure inquiry. The full lips came together as if to speak, but she said nothing.

Delorme reached out and touched her arm, but the woman still stood, swaying slightly. One hand came down slowly to touch the table, steadying her. Slowly, she lowered herself to the chair, covered her face with her hands, and folded forward.

The little boy started poking at her shoulder with Yogi Bear.

36

"WHY haven't we seen the goddam truck?" McLeod was unloading his Beretta as he spoke, neatly setting nine rounds nose up on the conference table. It looked like an exaggeration to Cardinal; he was so used to six rounds. "I've searched that ChevyVan myself—probably we all have at one time or another. It just boggles my mind that it hasn't been spotted yet."

"If we're right that Woody made the mistake of burgling the maniac's place, then the killer's probably stowed the thing somewhere. All he's gotta do is park it indoors and how're we gonna find it?"

Dyson put in, "Narrows the field a little, if we can assume the guy has a garage."

"I don't think we can assume that just yet. Woody's only been dead twenty-four hours. We've got an all-points out with the OPP. We'll find the truck."

The phone rang and Cardinal by prearrangement picked it up. "Okay, Len—I'm going to put you on the speaker. There's me and Delorme, Detective Sergeant Dyson's sitting in with us, and also Ian McLeod."

They were assembled in the conference room—a first, as far as Cardinal could remember. The conference room was usually reserved for commission meetings, state visits from the mayor—in short, for very special occasions only.

But this was the biggest investigation the Algonquin Bay police department had ever handled, and now all eight detectives on the force were assigned bits and pieces to follow up.

"Okay, here's the deal," Len Weisman said. "There are nine bullet wounds on the body. Clearly, they were not fired in a frenzy, they were too carefully placed. He was shot in both shins, both thighs, both forearms, and both upper arms. That gives you all the major bones of the human body—and I believe the killer was trying to break them all.

He succeeded with both tibias. These were contact wounds, by the way—muzzle against flesh—inflicted at leisure, when the victim was totally helpless."

"I make that eight bullets, Len. Not nine."

"Aren't you sharp. He was shot in the back first—it's the only one that wasn't a contact wound. It was from maybe ten feet away, with an upward trajectory—Dr. Gant's note: She says a stairway would be consistent with the damage, killer shooting from below. Oh, and there's residue from duct tape around the mouth."

"Jesus."

"There's blood on him other than his own but I can't match the type to the semen that was in the envelope—whoever that belongs to, he isn't a secretor. We won't know if it's the same guy until the DNA test comes back—that's gonna take another week."

"A week! We've got kids being murdered up here, Len."

"It takes ten days, that's just the reality. Now, the facial injury: At first, we thought the facial injury was the result of a fall—you know, the guy gets shot, falls facedown and breaks his nose. But we found traces of gun oil in the wound."

"He was hit with a pistol?"

"Exactly. What's amazing is, this victim has nine bullet wounds in him, but he was killed by a broken nose. With the tape over his mouth, he couldn't breathe—aspirated a ton of blood trying."

"What have you got from Ballistics—Beretta? Glock? Gotta be something that shoots nine rounds, right?"

"The microprint is in my fax. He used a regular Colt thirty-eight."

"Can't be, Len. Colt only holds six rounds."

"Like I say, we're not dealing with a man in a frenzy. Bastard takes his time to reload so he can have a little more fun."

"Guy's an animal," McLeod muttered.

"Genital mutilation was postmortem. Dr. Gant thinks the guy tried to literally kick his balls off."

"That links it to Todd Curry, boss."

Dyson nodded sagely, as if he had thought so all along.

Weisman said, "I've told Ballistics to call you direct, soon as they have more on the slugs."

"All right. Thanks, Len."

"I'm not done yet."

"Sorry. Go ahead."

"Fingerprint section picked up partials. Both thumbs."

"You couldn't have. Our body was found nude—not even a belt to lift a print from."

"They lifted them from the body itself."

"You're kidding me. Our guys didn't get anything."

"Little something we picked up at the Tokyo forensics conference last year: soft-tissue X ray. We X-rayed the subcutaneous tissue of the neck—if you get it within twelve hours you can do that and get a decent print. Looks like he tried to choke the guy—maybe before he decided to aerate him. It's on the fax, too."

"Jesus, that's great, Len. Tell 'em we said, 'Thanks, guys.'"

"Better not. Those *guys* happen to be women."

Delorme dipped her head, smiling slightly.

"You know what stinks?" McLeod said to the whole table. "What stinks is we're buried in leads here. We're practically drowning in evidence. The guy hands us a tape of his *voice*, for Chrissake, and we can't do anything. He shoots his wad into an *envelope* for us, and we can't do anything. Now he leaves us thumbprints. It's like we're holding out for his business card or something. Guy's playing with us, and we're not getting anywhere."

"No, we're making progress," Cardinal said, wanting to believe it. "We're doing classic footwork. We just haven't found the connecting link yet, that's all. Something that's gonna whack all these little bits of info together."

"It better happen soon," Dyson said. "If I get one more call telling me to call in the OPP or the Mounties . . ."

"The Horsemen?" McLeod seemed to take it personally. "The Horsemen don't have any fucking jurisdiction."

"You know that and I know that. Would you care to educate the public on that point?"

"Anyways, the first thing the fucking Horsemen'd do, they'd blow something up, or steal some fucking evidence, or sell some dope to the wrong fucking judge. Besides which, you never know if what they *say* they're doing is what they're *really* doing. I'll tell you the problem with the Horsemen." McLeod was warming up now. Cardinal usually enjoyed a good McLeod rant, but not today, please. "The problem with the Horsemen is they're broke. Fucking five-year pay freeze killed 'em. They're all fucking broke, and they're looking for creative ways to make up the difference. I liked it better when they made more money. You can *trust* a rich Mountie. Now that they're practically fucking homeless, all they're good for—"

The intercom crackled and Mary Flower's voice came over. "Cardinal, OPP's on the line. Patrol unit on Highway 11's got a make on Woody's truck. What do you want to do?"

"Where exactly are they?"

"Out near Chippewa Falls, heading back to town."

"Patch it through, Mary. I'll speak to them from here."

Every cop at the conference table had shifted position; the air in the room was charged.

"Don, we need the war room. Shotguns, body armor, the works."

"It's yours. Fuck the Mounties."

The phone rang, and Cardinal snatched it up. "Detective Cardinal, CID. Who am I talking to?"

"OPP patrol unit fourteen—George Boissenault, here, and my partner, Carol Wilde."

"Are you sure it's our man?"

"We have a blue '89 ChevyVan in view, Ontario plate number 7698128, stolen. Sign says COMSTOCK ELECTRICAL something."

"My show, partners. Your driver is primo suspect number one in the Pine–Curry case. My show, understand?"

"Roger. They gave us the lowdown in muster."

"Good. I want you to follow him, but don't stop him."

"We may have to stop him. He's really hoofing it."

"*Do not stop him.* He has a hostage and we do not want this kid to end up dead. Radio home and have them close the road, but they stay out of sight, follow? Have them close the on ramps."

"Will do."

"You're in a regular patrol unit, I take it."

"Regular patrol, that's right. He's got to see us pretty soon."

"Keep a low profile but don't lose him. Do you have kids, Wilde?"

"Yes, sir. One's eight, and one's three."

"Our hostage is just out of high school. I want you to think of him as if he's your own, understand? We can save this kid if we play this right."

"Looks like he's going to turn down Algonquin. Nope, I'm wrong. He's sticking with the bypass."

"Stay on him. Detective Sergeant Dyson is here with me, and in five minutes you're gonna have more backup than you've ever seen. If he breaks for it, stay on his tail. I don't have to tell you this guy is armed and dangerous."

"We'll stay on him. We can match frequency, if you want to coordinate from a command post."

"You read my mind. Work it out with Flower. We're on our way."

37

THE "war room" was a large closet big enough to hold maybe four cops at once. Delorme and McLeod came out first wearing full Kevlar and carrying twin shotguns. As Cardinal emerged, Szelagy called out across the squad room: "I've got that teacher Fehrenbach on the line. Says the Curry kid may have stolen his credit card."

"We'll get back to him," Cardinal said, cinching his vest. "Stick a note in the file."

The phone in the hallway rang, and it was Flower with Jerry Commanda on the line. He was already airborne.

"Jerry, where can you set that thing down and pick me up?"

Jerry Commanda's voice came over with the shake and thrum of the rotor. "Government dock's closest, but you'll have to clear off any bystanders."

"Where's our boy?"

"Just past Shephard's Bay."

"Good. He's taking it easy. Government dock in five."

As they tore out of the lot, Cardinal reached for the mike. "We should've radio'd St. Francis for an ambulance."

"I already did. They're southbound on 11 by now."

"Delorme, I'm going to give you a great big kiss."

"Not on duty, you're not. Not off duty, either."

"Big smacker, Delorme, soon as we take this guy down."

Delorme hit the siren and scared the hell out of the Toyota blocking their way. Cardinal swerved around it and onto Sumner. Four minutes and three red lights later, the two of them were out of the car and running down government dock, where the copter sat perched like a dragonfly, the rotor blasting a miniature snowstorm every which way. Behind it, the lake and sky were a pale gray canvas.

Cardinal didn't fly a lot. His stomach was still on the dock when they crossed over Shephard's Bay, with its stubble of ice-fishing huts. The scene was as still as a

Christmas card, except for a dog cavorting on the ice and his master, who trudged on snowshoes toward his hut, a case of beer under one arm.

"Look at 'em backed up on Water Road. Means they've closed the on ramps." Jerry spoke into the mike: "Boissenault. Command Post is airborne. What's your position?"

"Half-mile north of Powassan turnoff. Guy's none too steady with a steering wheel, I'll tell you that."

Delorme pointed. "There they are."

The ChevyVan was a blue lozenge traveling round a curve of scrubby pine. The OPP car trailed two hundred yards behind. Jerry shouted to the pilot, "Stay in his blind spot. We don't want to spook him."

Cardinal spoke into the mike. "Boissenault, anybody get a look at him yet?"

"Old-clothes team coming the other way says we have a single Caucasian male, early thirties, brown hair, black jacket. No visible passengers."

"We don't know what's in the back, though. He could have the kid in there."

"You think he'd drive the kid around in a stolen car?"

"He doesn't know we're looking for it. Even if he did, we can't know how much self-control he's operating under. Fourteen, let a couple of cars get between you. He's gonna spook."

"Roger."

Jerry Commanda said, "They're just a patrol unit—not a surveillance team."

"They don't have to stay on his tail with us up here. Stay back, Fourteen. Let the Camaro get in front."

A hot red Camaro with a raised back end pulled out and passed the patrol unit. "My," Cardinal said, "the citizenry is well behaved around the highway patrol."

"Oh, you'd be surprised," Jerry said.

The pilot pointed southeast. "Sun's out." A rip in the gray eiderdown of sky let the sun through, and a copter-shaped shadow flickered on the hills and rock cuts twenty yards ahead of the van. The pilot dropped back, and the shadow moved away from the van. A quarter mile behind the first patrol unit, a parade of police cars—unmarkeds, patrol units, and OPP—augmented now by a fire truck and two ambulances, snaked along the curves and hills like a traveling circus.

"Goddam," Jerry said. "I hope this bastard isn't heading to Toronto for the weekend."

"If he is, we're not going with him." The pilot tapped the fuel gauge. "We go to Orillia, max."

"What are those guys doing up there!" Cardinal pointed to an OPP unit parked at the side of the highway with lights flashing.

"Must've been off-frequency for some reason. I'll radio in to have 'em move." Jerry took the mike from him. "Central, we have a unit on Highway 11 southbound, get them the hell out of there, now. I mean now."

"Central. Roger."

"Too late, now. He's spooked."

The van had lurched and slowed. Now it was speeding up again.

"Command Post, we're losing him. You want us to pull him over?"

"Stay with him. Don't pull him over. We have to know where he's going."

"Cardinal, you can't direct a high-speed chase from the air. It's their lives, their call."

"Fourteen—you have two cars coming northbound, then you're clear." Then to Jerry, "How did they get on the road?"

"Lots of little turnoffs here. We didn't have time to shut them all down. Look at that."

The blue van went wide on a curve and was now on the wrong side of the road barreling straight for a head-on with a white Toyota.

"Move," Delorme prayed. *"Move."*

At the last second the Toyota veered onto the shoulder, fishtailed wildly, and veered back onto the lane. Cardinal was sweating heavily in his body armor. He had come within an inch of killing the occupants of that car; his hand was so wet, he could barely hold the mike. "Okay, Fourteen—cut him off, now. Let's get him off the road."

"Roger. We'll shut him down."

"All units, lights and sirens. We're going to yank him." Then to Jerry: "Do we have the K-9 guy in case he runs into the bush?"

Jerry pointed. "Greg Villeneuve. Gray pickup in front of the fire truck."

The lead patrol unit pulled forward, lights flashing. Through the *whomp* of the rotors they heard the high, thin wail of sirens. The van veered over to the right again, straddling road and shoulder, then back onto the road. When Fourteen came up on his left he veered in front of them.

"Jesus," Jerry yelled. "That was close."

Fourteen pulled even with the van.

"Fourteen, Fourteen. Back off. You got a snowplow round the next bend, repeat, snowplow southbound in *your* lane, and he's standing still."

Fourteen didn't respond. The two cars moved into the curve as if joined at the fender. A matter of seconds and the van would rear-end the plow.

"Christ, the kid could be in that van. Why don't they back off?"

"They want to pull ahead. Do a single lane that way."

Delorme sat back from the window, unable to watch.

At the last second, Fourteen pulled in front of the van, leaving the left lane clear. The van swerved to avoid the plow, hit a patch of ice, and shot across two lanes and onto the median.

For a hundred yards, the van straddled the road and the divider. Fourteen slowed to stay with it. The van went farther over the divider into heavy snow. The wheels caught in a drift, flipping it once, twice, three times. Then it slid on its side, turned elegantly at an angle and plowed along the oncoming lanes on a bed of sparks.

"Thank God we closed the road," Delorme said.

The van smashed, wheels first, into the retaining posts,

did a one-and-a-half in the air, and slammed into a rock cut, where it burst into flames.

"Take us down. All units: I want this section sealed off. Let the hook-and-ladder put out the fire and get the hostage out. Repeat. There could be a hostage in the back. Get him out first."

The pilot set them down in a lumberyard after scattering workers with a bullhorn. As the cops scrambled into a waiting patrol unit, workers yelled epithets at them from behind stacks of plywood and two-by-fours.

When Cardinal reached the wreck, the fire was already out, and the blackened truck was covered with foam. A firefighter jumped down from the opened side door, shaking his head.

"No passengers?"

"No driver, neither. Nobody a-tall."

"There he is. They got him." Jerry Commanda was pointing to the divider strip. A quarter mile back, a cruiser was parked on the median, lights flashing. Two constables had weapons trained on a motionless dark figure in the snow. Twenty seconds later, that figure was the still point of a semicircle of shotguns, all cocked and ready.

The figure lay, hands outflung like a drowning victim's around a jagged block of shale. Suddenly it emitted a groan, and the head lifted slightly. Larry Burke slid down the embankment and clipped cuffs on him, then turned him over, patting him down. "No weapon, Sarge."

"Identification?"

Burke flipped through a wallet, pulled out the driver's license. "Frederick Paul Lefebvre, 234 Wassi Road. Photo's a match."

"It's Fast Freddie!" Delorme exclaimed. "He's been out of jail for, what—two weeks?"

Two medics hurried down the embankment. They started pushing and probing, firing questions at the confused heap of humanity in the ditch.

"Oh, my," Fast Freddie repeated several times. "Oh,

my." One of the medics wiped the blood off his forehead with snow. Then for the first time he looked up at the shotguns and hiccuped. "Oh, shit," he said, stifling a belch. "Ever drunk, eh?"

38

FOR Cardinal, the aftermath of chasing down Woody's vehicle was mostly paperwork. His sup alone was developing the heft of *Moby Dick,* and on any operation involving another force, such as the OPP, the reports just multiplied. Even using the war room required a detailed accounting of equipment requisitioned, personnel involved, rounds fired, etcetera.

He wanted to question Freddie Lefebvre, but Fast Freddie, having lapsed into unconsciousness moments after his confession of intoxication, was sobering up in a well-guarded hospital bed.

The message light was flashing on Cardinal's phone. It was Karen Steen asking if there was any progress, to please call her when he had the chance. He remembered the denim-blue eyes, the absolute candor of her features. He wished he had something to tell her, some words of encouragement, but there was nothing. The ident boys, Arsenault and Collingwood, were locked up in the garage with Woody's van. There would be no point pressing them for prints for several hours.

Cardinal pulled a stack of paper from his In box. There were several fat envelopes from the Crown, the usual notices, forms, and requests for information. Then there was an interoffice envelope containing a memo from Dyson telling everyone for the hundredth time not to make idiots of themselves in court. The word *contemporaneous* appeared several times, underlined.

There was another piece of paper attached to the memo apparently by accident, held there by traces of something that looked a lot like honey glazing. It was a note labeled *From the Desk of Det. Sgt. A. Dyson,* addressed to Paul Arsenault. Arsenault was to make himself available to the Mounties' document people on an upcoming weekend. The combination of the RCMP and document experts could only be the Kyle Corbett case. And a weekend—that would mean a big production, something serious in the offing.

"Jesus Christ. Why should I testify again? I'm starting to feel like a voodoo doll. Everybody wants to stick pins in me!" McLeod was shouting into his phone and searching for something buried under the junkyard on his desk. He hung up, cursing. "Fucking Crown. It's like he *wants* me to have a heart attack."

"Maybe he does," Cardinal said mildly.

"It's my kid's piano recital on Thursday. I missed his birthday, courtesy of the Corriveau Brothers. If I miss this, my wife—pardon me, my *former* wife, Lady Macbeth with a court order—will cut me out of the picture altogether. She's already got the Family Court in the palm of her hand, I swear. Far as that place is concerned, I'm somewhere between Attila the Hun and Charles Manson. And Corriveau—what's the point of dismissing a witness if you're just gonna call him back every five minutes?"

Without warning, Cardinal was suddenly thinking of Catherine. McLeod's paranoid yowling faded into the background, and he remembered Catherine's hollow face, and the way she would look over at him from her book, peering over the tops of her reading glasses. Her gaze was so intent at such moments, as if she feared some alien had stolen into bed beside her in her husband's shape. "Are you all right?" she would ask, and the memory of those four simple words was unbearably sweet.

"Hey, where you going?" McLeod called after him. "I'm not finished whining yet. I haven't even *started*."

CATHERINE Cardinal came down the hall toward her husband, arms stretched out before her. Her hair was still wet from the shower. She held him tightly, and Cardinal breathed in the smell of his wife's shampoo. "How's my girl?" Cardinal said softly. "How's my girl?"

They sat on the couch in the sunroom again. Catherine was so much better, Cardinal felt a flutter of hope. She looked him in the eye, and her hand made only intermittent nervous movements—not the obsessive circles of before. She opened her mouth to say something, but no sound came out. Then she turned away, and Cardinal waited while his wife wept, his hand resting gently on her knee. Finally, Catherine caught her breath and said, "I thought you'd be down at the divorce court by now."

Cardinal shook his head and smiled. "You won't get rid of me that easy."

"Oh, I will. If not this time, then next time or the time after. The worst thing is, there's not a soul in the world who would blame you."

"I'm not going anywhere, Catherine. Don't worry yourself with that."

"Kelly can look after herself now, and she wouldn't blame you one bit for leaving me. You know she wouldn't. Even *I* wouldn't blame you."

"Will you stop? I said I'm not leaving."

"Well, maybe you should have an affair with someone. I'm sure you come across lots of willing young women in your job. Have an affair, but just don't tell me about it, all right? I don't want to know. One of your female colleagues, maybe. Just don't fall in love with her."

Cardinal thought of Lise Delorme. No-nonsense, down-to-earth Delorme. Delorme who might or might not be investigating him. Delorme, as Jerry Commanda had noted, of the nice shape. "I don't want an affair," Cardinal said to his wife. "It's you I want."

"God—you never do anything wrong, do you? You never lose your temper, never lose patience. How can you hope to understand someone as fucked up as me? I don't see why you bother trying. I mean, you're practically a saint."

"Come on, honey. That's the first time you've accused me of sainthood."

Catherine, of course, didn't know about the money. Cardinal had taken it during her first bout with clinical depression, years earlier. She had been hospitalized, adrift among a sargasso of lost souls, for eighteen months. Then her parents had weighed in, phoning him every other day from the States, making him feel like a rotten husband, and he had cracked. For a time Cardinal had told himself that's why he had done it, that his wife's insanity had broken him. But the Catholic in him, not to mention the cop, could never accept that. He gave himself no excuse.

"Husbands leave their wives all the time," Catherine was saying. "No one else would put up with what you put up with."

"People live with lots worse things." I should tell her about the money, prove to her that she's better than me: She loses her mind once in a while, but she's the one who never does anything wrong. But the thought of how she would look at him stopped Cardinal cold. "Look, I brought you a present. You can wear it on your first day out."

Catherine opened the tissue paper with terrible gentleness, as if cleaning a wound. The beret was light burgundy, a color Catherine liked to wear. She tried it on, fitting it over one ear at a rakish angle. "How do I look? Like a Girl Guide?"

"You look like someone I'd like to marry."

That made her cry again.

"I'll go get us a Coke," Cardinal said, and went down the hall to the machine. It was the old kind that poured syrup and seltzer water into a paper cup—no loose metal objects here. He stood for a few moments in the corridor looking out at the white slopes of the grounds, the surrounding pines with boughs bent low under their weight of snow. Near the coroner's office a couple of orderlies taking a cigarette break hunched in a doorway, stamping their feet to keep warm.

When he came back to the sunroom, Catherine had curled up tightly at the end of the couch, her expression a fixed scowl. She wouldn't drink the Coke; the paper cup sat untouched on the table. Cardinal stayed with her another fifteen minutes, but she remained as numb as wood. Nothing he said would evoke a response. When finally he left, she was still in the same clenched position, glaring with ferocious concentration at the floor.

* * *

DYSON motioned Delorme into his office, and once she was in, he proceeded to ignore her—taking a phone call, looking for a file, badgering Mary Flower on the intercom. Finally, he faced forward, plucked up his letter opener and braced it between his palms. Delorme thought for a moment he was going to take it between his teeth. "An update. How are we doing on Cardinal, Lise?"

She hated it when he used her first name; he sounded like a low-rent movie producer. "The files aren't giving me much so far. Nothing the Crown would be interested in."

Dyson held the letter opener at an angle, making it glitter in the afternoon sun like a tiny Excalibur. Outside his window an icicle glowed and dripped. "Well, maybe it's time we ran a tap on his phone."

"Musgrave's planning to do exactly that. But he's not going to get to it right away."

"Oh?"—lowering his sword with irritation. "And why's that?"

"They're planning to hit Corbett on the twenty-fourth."

"The twenty-fourth? Jesus, what is it with those guys? They can't bring themselves to do one thing at a time? Do they have to do everything badly all at once? I mean, why in God's name do they have to do this before you finish your investigation? Where is the sudden urgency?"

"Corbett's planning to take out some guy who runs a Black Diamond Riders chapter down south."

"So they're jeopardizing an ongoing investigation to save the life of some no doubt murderous biker. The Mounties move in mysterious ways. Who's their source on this?"

"They didn't tell me. I'm not surprised, under the circumstances."

"No." Dyson let out a big sigh. "No, indeed."

Delorme wasn't sure whether to say what was really bothering her, but seeing Dyson uncharacteristically reflective, she plunged on. "Maybe it's not a bad idea to lay off

Cardinal for the moment, D.S. Have you thought what it will do to Pine–Curry if we haul him in just now?"

"I have. And it'll be a lot worse if it comes out later."

Afterward, when Delorme was at her desk filling out sups, Cardinal came back trailing clouds of cold air, as if he were returning from the Underworld. The lines on his face looked deeper, and Delorme had a sudden intuition that he had been to see his wife.

39

MALCOLM Musgrave and his team were encamped at the Pinegrove Motel. The room was a standard-issue box, with faux colonial furniture and violent orange curtains. Maid service had apparently been suspended. Between tape recorders, video monitors, and radios, a heap of pizza boxes and Chinese food containers had grown into a precarious pyramid.

The place stank of sweat and old hamburgers.

Delorme was surprised to find Musgrave personally involved in the stakeout and said so.

"What, and miss all this?" He waved a massive arm at their surroundings, shoulder holster creaking. "I could have stayed out of it, sure. In fact, my hands-on attitude has been known to upset the more sensitive troops. But you know what? I don't give a damn. Call me vindictive, but this boy fucked up my operation royally, and I want to reel him in myself. With your help, of course," he added with feigned politeness.

Musgrave hoisted an extremely ugly chair across a bed and set it down for Delorme. He sat on the bed, crushing it almost to the floor, and shouted at a gray-faced man in headphones, who until now had paid them no attention whatever. "Play back our prize for Detective Delorme, here, Larry. It's showtime."

Larry put another tape on the reel-to-reel outfit in front of him. He set it winding forward so fast that Delorme thought she could see traces of smoke. He punched a button, twiddled a couple of dials, and yanked out the headphone jack so they could all hear.

"Came in a couple of hours ago," Musgrave said. "Don't you return your calls?"

"I was working with Cardinal and couldn't get away. We're trying to catch a killer right now, in case you haven't heard."

"Don't try and put me in my place, Ms. Delorme. It's above yours." Musgrave nodded at his associate, and the tape started at the end of a conversation.

"*—because that's the way we do business, that's why. Tell Snider to get his act together. Fucking asshole.*"

"That's Corbett," Musgrave said. "Nice bedside manner."

"*How many times we going to deal with this shit? You tell him. One more time and he's gonna be—*"

"*I got it, Kyle. I hear ya.*"

"Peter Fyfe. Longtime Corbetteer. He was actually a cop at one point, for about two weeks, down in Windsor decades ago. Only thing on his sheet's assault and battery, 1989. Been a choirboy ever since, just like Corbett."

"*He's gonna wish he never knew my name, you tell him.*"

"*I'll tell him, Kyle.*"

"*I mean it this time. Only reason I tolerated him this long is Sheila. And that is not going to cover his sorry ass anymore.*"

"*I'll give him the word.*"

"*Do that.*"

There was a click as Corbett and Fyfe hung up. The tape recorder being voice-activated, the next conversation started exactly ten seconds later.

"*Yeah.*"

"*Kyle, any way you can get out of Fat Boy?*"

"*Fat Boy's got a lot of juice, Pete. I can't just dump him.*"

"We know who Fat Boy is," Musgrave said. "Gary Grundy, runs the Lobos gang down in Aylmer, weighs three forty if he's an ounce."

"*Well, I got the word from our pet cop is all. He's got something hot he doesn't want to talk about by phone.*"

"*Fine. Tell him to come to the Crystal.*"

"*As if. He suggested the Library.*"

"*Brilliant. No one's ever gonna notice me at the public fucking library.*"

"*Not the public library, Kyle. The Library Tavern. It's*

above the Birches Motel. Most boring bar you ever saw. Listen, he don't even want me talking to you about this by phone. Says the Mounties probably got us bugged."

"They do not have us bugged. Why do you think I pay a fucking fortune to my master hacker? We are clean."

"Well, he says they got us bugged and not to say nothing on the phone. But I'm fucked if I'm driving in from fucking Sudbury to play messenger boy."

"Tell him the New York, two A.M. I'll be at the bar."

"Two A.M. I'll tell him."

"Not tonight, for Christ's sake. I told you I gotta sit down with Fat Boy."

"Okay, okay, I got that."

"We'll do it tomorrow night. Two A.M. And tell him I'm gonna want everything. I haven't heard from him in a fucking century."

"Needless to say, the 'master hacker' Corbett consults with is one of ours. Very handy with a mouse, this guy."

"Nice." It really was nice. Delorme knew the Mounties got things right most of the time. Unfortunately, that wasn't what tended to get them into the papers. "Tomorrow night, two A.M.," she said. "Can we get a tape unit in place at the restaurant that fast?"

Musgrave rose from the bed, and it was like watching a time-lapse film of the growth of a Douglas fir. "Where's your faith, Sister Delorme? Our little monks are making arrangements even as we speak."

40

EDIE Soames kept her eyes on the clock until it finally inched its way to lunchtime, then she told Quereshi she was breaking and went to the Pizza Patio at the other end of the mall. She always had lunch by herself; Eric never got lunch at the same time. The need to be with him was particularly bad right now. They'd been holding the boy for so long, Edie's anticipation was in danger of turning into fear. Eric kept putting off the party, apparently enjoying stretching this one out. He loved having a prisoner; it gave him a renewed sense of purpose. But Edie was feeling restless and jumpy, as if her skin were on too tight.

At the next table, her ex-friend Margo sat with her back to the entrance, giggling with two other Pharma-City employees. Edie never sat with Margo anymore; Margo was not a serious person. A year ago, before Eric came along, she had confided to her diary, *Margo knows how to have fun—something I've never learned. I think I may be in love with her. She came round and set my hair last night, and we had such a good time.* But then Eric had come along, and Margo and Eric disliked each other on sight. One day, before Margo realized how much Eric meant to Edie, she had commented carelessly that he looked like a ferret. Except for unavoidable interchanges at work, Edie hadn't spoken to her since.

Edie ordered a diet Coke and two slices of pizza. She was halfway through the second slice when she heard her name. Margo had shrieked it out, but Edie wasn't being called, she was being discussed. "Oh, my God," Margo was saying. "Such a sourpuss. I mean that face could stop a truck. And she must wear like a quart of Obsession. That girl needs a makeover, big time."

"Big time," Sally Royce agreed. "A personality makeover."

The voices went low for a moment, and then there was a burst of laughter.

Edie pushed aside the rest of her pizza and left. Bitches should read the papers, get acquainted with the Windigo. They wouldn't be laughing so hard if they knew what she was capable of. She could scare the shit out of them, if she felt like it. Have them begging for mercy like that stupid Indian brat. She might've done Billy LaBelle herself, if the little runt hadn't died on them. Her courage had failed only once: She'd had to cover Todd Curry's head with that seat cover before she could help Eric move the body.

But she was getting stronger all the time. Why, less than twenty-four hours ago she'd been driving a dead body out to Trout Lake. *Eric was amazing. So cool, so calm. Killed him like he was nothing, not even a bird. And then we dumped him like a bag of garbage. Garbage—that's exactly what he was—left him at the side of the road. But the really brilliant touch—totally Eric's, of course—was leaving the van out at the Chinook Tavern. "Somebody'll steal it before you can say Rumpelstiltskin," he said. Totally correct, as usual.*

The Algonquin Mall has a massive Food Town at one end, and at the other an equally gigantic Kmart. Between them the mall itself forms a wide, fluorescent L. It is meant to afford this northern city a Main Street without winter. Blizzards, ice storms, windchill factors, who cares? A shopper can stroll from store to store, window-shopping all afternoon if the mood strikes, without freezing to the marrow.

Edie thought it very tasteful the way they had set out squares of indoor trees and large plants with benches around them. You could sit on a bench and stare at a window full of running shoes at the Foot Locker, or on the other side you could look at Records on Wheels. Or she could sit on the bench near Troy Music Center until Eric got off work.

Edie walked past the Tot Shoppe where the window was crammed with tiny parkas as if an army of dwarf Eskimos was about to invade. Then in Northern Lighting they had a high-tech chandelier fashioned from copper tubing and aluminum cones. It looked like futuristic moose antlers.

She stopped into Troy Music, but Eric was in the back doing inventory. Just as well, really, because he'd told her not to visit him at work. Eric's boss, Mr. Troy, was behind the counter, tuning a guitar for some geeky-looking kid. Edie flipped through the sheet music, reading the words to a Whitney Houston song and then a Celine Dion. Of course they were famous, look at those perfect teeth, perfect tits. Give either of 'em a case of eczema and then where would they be? Fame was a genetic lottery, just like love, and Edie had inherited neither from the unknown man who'd fathered her or from her mother, who had vanished from Algonquin Bay six years later.

Raised by Gram, the old bitch, who never made her feel like anything other than ugly and stupid. For one brief fantastic moment she had imagined she was attractive: that was when Eric first started paying attention to her. She even had sexual fantasies about him for a time, but in this as in other things, she absorbed Eric's attitudes almost by osmosis. "Edie," he told her. "You are made for something more important than sex. Both of us are. You and I are meant to push the limits of what human beings are capable of."

Edie dashed across the frigid parking lot to the Tim Hortons, where she had two chocolate doughnuts and a large coffee. Algonquin Bay boasted seventeen doughnut shops—Edie knew, because on a particularly aimless, empty day she had counted them, making a circuit around the entire city. The doughnuts really hit the spot, and by the time Edie headed back to the drugstore she felt much calmer.

Margo came rushing in a few minutes later, out of breath, stashing her purse and coat under the counter between the two cash registers. Edie didn't so much as glance at her.

Sometimes at work Edie could put herself into a kind of trance that made the time go faster. She would look up and it would be seven o'clock and she'd wonder where the afternoon had gone. But today the time dragged. She kept remembering what Margo had said, and that nauseating laughter; she hardly thought about the boy tied up in her basement or about his wounded leg. But when Quereshi asked her to keep an eye on the pharmacy while he went to the can, Edie dumped fifty diazepam into a plastic bottle she kept in her pocket.

When Quereshi came back, she asked him, "What would you give someone if you wanted them to be awake but lie absolutely still—without moving?"

Mr. Quereshi's smooth brown face wrinkled up like a walnut. "You mean to facilitate the performance of surgery and so on?"

"Right. So they wouldn't move no matter what you did to them."

"There are such drugs, it goes without saying. But we do not stock them. Why, Miss Soames—you are planning to operate on some poor soul?"

"I like to know things, that's all. I may go to pharmacy school, one day—I'm putting money aside."

"I myself matriculated in medicine, at Calcutta. But my diploma was not being recognized in this country, so I was forced to study pharmacy. Three credits, they granted me. Seven years of studies reduced to three credits only; it is a shocking waste. I would have been making an excellent surgeon, but the world is not a fair place."

"I feel like I could do something special one day, Mr. Quereshi." *Very* special. The night before, she had written in her diary: *Soon I'll be ready to kill on my own. The runt in the basement would be no problem, but maybe I'll let Eric do this one. I think I'd prefer to start with a female. I can even think of a candidate.*

"You would be well advised to settle on a course of study, Miss Soames. There will not be so many opportunities coming your way. The world discriminates not just against brown people, but also against women such as yourself."

Women such as yourself, well, she knew what he meant by that, bloody Paki. *Plain* women such as yourself. Women with fucked-up faces. He didn't have to say the words, it was in his superior tone. I wouldn't let the bastard operate on a dog, Edie thought, let alone on a human being. Quereshi handed her a bottle of pills, which Edie placed into a bag for the frail old woman across the counter. "Twenty-nine fifty."

"Twenty-nine fifty! It was only twenty-five dollars last month." The woman tottered a little, as if the price had infected her inner ear. "I can't afford twenty-nine fifty. I'm on a pension. I won't have enough for cat food."

"Well, maybe you shouldn't buy them." Or maybe you should strangle the fucking cat, I don't care.

"I need them. They're for my heart. I can't just leave them. I don't have a choice, do I?"

"I don't know. It's up to you."

"It isn't up to me. That's what I'm saying. How much did you say?"

"Twenty-nine fifty."

"That's a twenty-percent increase. More. How can a few pills suddenly go up twenty percent in the course of a month, that's what I'd like to know."

"I don't know, lady. They went up."

The woman came up with three tens that stank of talcum powder, and Edie handed back the change. "Thank you for saving at Pharma-City. Don't you get hit by any cars, now."

"What did you say?"

"I said be careful in the parking lot. There's a lot of cars out there today."

Quereshi was going to say something, she could feel it. He was sidling over to her, warming up for a sermon. Not that it was any of his business; he was just there to count pills. Store policy was none of his business.

"Miss Soames, tell me something."

Here we go. Edie started straightening the cash in her drawer, putting all the bills faceup.

"Miss Soames, I just want to ask you something. I just

want to ask you if you are having a hobby, or some other line of endeavor you are pursuing. Music, perhaps. Philately or some such."

"Yeah, I have a hobby." Killing people, she was tempted to say, just to see the expression on his silly brown face. "Special things I like to do."

"I am glad, Miss Soames. Because you will never be a success in dealing with the public. You are lacking the required sympathy."

"Who cares? Sympathy is for weaklings."

"For weaklings? You have been reading some terrible philosopher, I take it. That poor lady has no money. It hurts her when prices go up. Can you not spare a kind word for her?"

"I don't want to talk about it."

"What does it hurt you to say, 'Yes it's a shame,' or some such? You are not losing anything by it."

They were interrupted by a dark-haired lady who bought six boxes of henna. It was the beginning of the late rush. Someone else purchased damn near a year's supply of Mylanta Gas. One day they stock up on Kaopectate, next day it's Ex-Lax, Edie thought. We get 'em coming and going. A young woman bought three different cold remedies and shampoo and nail polish and conditioner. A curly-haired woman bought stuff to straighten her hair, and a girl with perfectly straight hair that Edie envied bought stuff to make hair curl. Edie herself had tried every remedy under the sun—as a Pharma-City employee, she got a ten-percent discount—but none of the ointments, creams, and steroids made the slightest difference to the dead glare of her skin. "Hey, Edie," she remembered one of her high-school contemporaries shouting at her. "You been sticking your head in the oven again? Next time don't use a microwave!" She carried the memory like an old bullet lodged in her rib cage.

A boy bought a dozen Sheiks from her. Condoms were kept behind the counter, and the boys never bought them from Margo; they felt safer with an ugly woman. Margo was working away at her cash register, happy as a lark. Margo was such a birdbrain that she actually enjoyed the stupid job. Since Edie had stopped speaking to her, Margo was at a loss during slow times; she would pull out her *People* magazine and flip through the same old tired stories, month after month, cracking her gum.

Edie was slipping on her parka when a man in a dark-blue blazer said, "Miss Soames, would you come with me, please?"

He was with the security company. He would catch shoplifters and yell at them in front of the whole store to humiliate them. Struk, his name was. Edie followed him into the little office upstairs, where a fat female security guard sat in front of a surveillance monitor. Struk pointed at her purse. "Miss Soames, would you open that, please?"

"Why? I haven't taken anything."

"Pharma-City reserves the right to spot-check its employees. You signed a release when you were hired."

Edie opened her purse. Struk carefully fingered his way through her Kleenex, her address book, her chewing gum. He even went through her wallet. Did he suppose she was hiding condoms in it?

"Would you turn out your pockets, please?"

"Why?"

"Just do it. Otherwise, I'll have Franny here pat you down. Let's get it over with."

Two minutes later she was back outside the office, straightening her purse. Margo was joking with Struk as he led her into the office. They left the door open, and Edie heard Struk go through the drill once more.

"Help yourself," Margo said. "Nothing in there but makeup and chewing gum."

"Uh-huh." There was a pause. "And I bet you're gonna tell me you have a prescription for these."

"Are those pills? I didn't put those in there. They're not mine, I swear. I don't know how they got in there."

"Don't lie to me. This is grounds for dismissal. There

must be fifty diazepam here. How did they get into your purse?"

"I don't know! I swear I don't! I didn't take them, you have to believe me! Someone must've put them in my purse!"

"And why would anyone do a thing like that?"

Margo had broken down in tears by then, and Edie didn't hang around to hear the rest. She hurried downstairs and out into the shopping mall. Suddenly, she was in such a good mood that she went straight into Kmart and bought herself a new pair of shoes.

41

WHEN she got home from the mall Edie kicked off her snowboots, which were soaked through with slush, and went upstairs in damp socks to check on Gram. The old biddy was snoring away, mouth hanging open like a garage door. She hadn't even asked about the gunshots the other day, more concerned about the shouting. Time to check on the prisoner.

The three bolts were still in place. Edie put her ear to the door and listened for a full minute before opening it. Eric had told her not to speak to the prisoner unless he was there, too, but they'd been holding him so long, Edie could no longer resist. What was the point of having a prisoner, if you couldn't show him who was boss?

He was seated upright in the chair, his wrists and ankles still securely fastened. The blanket had fallen off, leaving him completely naked. His entire body was pimpled with goose bumps.

He raised his head when Edie came in. Above the taped mouth, the eyes were red and pleading.

Edie sniffed. "Couldn't wait, could you. Pig." They hadn't fed him for at least twenty-four hours, or given him anything to drink, so using the basin they had set under the hole in his chair seemed a deliberate provocation.

She checked his leg wound. It was just a little hole with a bit of a burn around it, nothing serious.

The prisoner was trying to say something, grunting and groaning under the tape. Edie sat on the bed and observed him. "Pardon me, prisoner? Can't hear you." The red eyes bulged wider, the groans were louder. "What's that, prisoner? Speak up."

Whatever it was he was trying to communicate, he must have been shouting it. It filtered through the tape as a kind of subterranean roar.

"Stop that racket. I'll get a screwdriver and stick it in your bullet hole. Want me to do that?"

The prisoner shook his head in a comic, exaggerated way.

She squatted down in front of him. "You know the only reason you're still alive?" she said softly. "I'll tell you. The only reason you're still alive, prisoner, is because we're trying to find a place where no one will hear you scream."

Suddenly a hot tear fell on Edie's wrist, and she jumped back, staring at it. "Bastard," she said, and spit, catching him square in the face.

The prisoner bent his head down to evade her.

Edie had to squat down again to get him. She spat at him again and again—calmly, there was no passion in it—and after a while her prisoner stopped even trying to avoid it. Edie kept spitting until his face was glistening all over. She didn't stop until she was completely out of spit.

42

CARDINAL led Fast Freddie back to his cell and ushered him inside. "I had nothing to do with no killings, and you know it. You ain't got a shred of evidence."

For the tenth time, Cardinal told Fast Freddie that no one suspected him of any killings, but Fast Freddie was a small-town drunk and druggie—he lived out beyond Corbeil when he was not in jail—and being charged with murder would be the only interesting thing that ever happened to him.

"I have an alibi, you son of a bitch. I can prove where I was, and you know it. I'm gonna have Bob Brackett on your case, man. Fix your ass good."

Of course Freddie could prove where he was: Approximately twenty-seven inmates at the district jail—not to mention the guards—could testify that Fast Freddie had been securely locked in that institution for the past two years less a day. Cardinal had confirmed this within ten minutes of Fast Freddie's crack-up on Highway 11. He closed the cell door.

"You can charge me with murder, manslaughter, homicide, or whatever the hell you please, you ain't taking me down, Cardinal. I did not kill no one."

"Freddie, I know you find this hard to accept, but the fact is you're only charged with theft auto, driving under, and liquor forty-two."

Despite his useless clarity on his innocence, Fast Freddie was hazy on the one thing of any interest to Cardinal: Had he seen anyone parking the van at the parking lot of the Chinook Tavern? Cardinal had people out there now, tracking down tavern patrons and staff, anyone who might have seen the van drive into the parking lot. Fast Freddie's memory was unreliable on anything that happened after his second pitcher of Labatt's Ice.

Five minutes later, Cardinal relayed this to Delorme as they headed down the corridor to the garage. "That's it?" she said sharply. "That's all you got out of him?"

"Guy gets drunk, suddenly he has an urge to go to Toronto. Nothing else to get."

Delorme had been uptight the last couple of days, and Cardinal wanted to ask what was up. She may already have proof of his own crime; she could be waiting to spring the trap shut at any moment.

"Ready?" Delorme paused with her hand on the doorknob.

"Ready for what?"

The smell hit Cardinal like a ball-peen hammer. "My God. Don't you guys believe in oxygen?"

Arsenault and Collingwood were poring over Woody's van. Nobody loves their work like ident guys, Cardinal thought. The two of them had been in this stinking garage for going on ten hours, fuming the scorched wreck with superglue.

Arsenault waved a gloved hand like a white paw. "Just about done, here. You ever see so many prints? Must be like four billion or so." He giggled.

"All Woody's, right?"

"Also Woody's left." Arsenault looked at young Collingwood, and the two of them fell into gales of helpless laughter.

"You guys are high," Cardinal said mildly. "You better take a break." Woody's van—the entire vehicle—had been encased in Plexiglas for the fuming, but now that the Plexiglas had been removed, the glue vapors were overpowering. "Come on," Cardinal said. "Outside."

The four of them stood outside in the blinding sun, all heaving in deep breaths. It was warmer than it had been since December. You got strange periods of warmth like this sometimes in February, just long enough to fool you into thinking spring was near. The snow at the edges of the parking lot was the color of cinders. Patches where it had melted steamed in the sun.

"Sorry," Arsenault said weakly. "Sorry about that."

"You ever hear of ventilation? You guys are lucky to be alive."

"I think we've built up a tolerance for it, right, Bob?"

Collingwood, hugging himself against the cold, nodded solemnly.

"Almost all the prints are Woody's—those that aren't smudged. The ones on the wheel that are liftable all belong to Fast Freddie. Dashboard and driver door are just smudges. Somebody wiped that sucker down—interior, anyways."

"Christ, Arsenault. You didn't get anything?"

Arsenault looked offended. "We got tons of stuff. Picked up two completes right off the rearview. Lifted those even before we started fuming. Idiots always forget to wipe there."

"And?" Cardinal looked from Arsenault to Collingwood and back.

"We're running it now for national," Arsenault said. "If there's a record, we should know soon. Couple of hours, max."

"I don't believe you guys. You didn't compare the prints on the van with the prints Forensics lifted off Woody's neck? You got a fax pinned up in your office. Are you out of your minds?"

"Oh, those. Yeah, we got a thumbprint matches right up."

"Right. But you weren't going to mention it."

"We were waiting for the computer matchup. We wanted to surprise you, eh?"

Delorme shook her head in wonder. "You guys are completely stoned."

Collingwood and Arsenault shuffled a little, looking sheepish. Cardinal stood at the garage door, looking at the dissected van. Fumes from the glue had formed white deposits wherever a human hand had touched the surface, giving a polka-dot effect.

"One time we did a whole Cessna," Arsenault volunteered. "Wasn't much bigger than this, though."

"Get outa here, Paul. The Cessna was way bigger than this thing. Specially if you count the wings."

Cardinal, Delorme, and Arsenault turned to stare at Collingwood. It was the first time any of them could remember him speaking without being spoken to. He stood there facing the van, a lopsided grin on his face and the sunlight shining through his ears.

AFTER lunch, Cardinal and Delorme drove to Woody's place, a tiny whitewashed bungalow out in Ferris. They sat in the kitchen, where Martha Wood focused intently, almost desperately, on feeding her toddler, as if even a glance at anything else, while she spoke of her dead husband, might blast her into smithereens.

"Woody liked stereos, boom boxes, tape recorders—stuff that was easy to carry, easy to sell. Laptops, when he could get his hands on them. He'd wait until he had enough to fill up the van, then he'd drive down to Toronto with it. He'd usually be back the same day. Come on, Truckie, eat some more." She spooned a little more poached egg into the toddler's mouth. The boy swallowed it, blinked, and reached for the spoon for more. "You like that, don't you. Yes, I know."

Sorrow takes people in different ways. From the far end of the kitchen table, Cardinal watched the way Martha Wood turned gingerly, the delicate way she scooped the egg. She was struggling mightily to deal with the routine of feeding, to deal with the cops. All her movements were slow, careful, as if she had suffered burns. Cardinal sensed an edge of anger under her obvious pain, but it was hard to read; her answers were all aimed at Delorme.

"He's so cute," Delorme said. She reached out and touched the thin soft film of dark hair on the baby's head. "You call him Chuckie?"

"Truckie. His real name's Dennis, after Woody's father, but Woody always called him Dumptruck." She wiped some egg from her child's face, scooped up another microscopic portion on the end of the spoon. Small fat fingers clutched at the spoon and misguided it toward an eager mouth. "When I was pregnant, Woody used to say, 'But we don't *need* a baby! We need a *radio,* we need a *reading lamp,* we need a *dumptruck!* Why can't we call him one of those?' So we used to joke and refer to him as Reading Lamp and Dumptruck, and unfortunately . . ."

The kitchen was full of baby smells—powder, wet sheets, bleach. Cardinal thought he had never seen anything sadder than this pretty woman with her baby and her perfect features.

"Hi, Truckie," Delorme said and stroked the soft hair. "How you doing?"

For the first time, Mrs. Wood looked directly at Cardinal. "Would you leave, please?"

"Me? You want me to leave?" Cardinal was caught off guard. He'd assumed he was the last thing on her mind at this moment.

"You knew my husband was dead, yesterday, the whole time. And you just kept asking me questions like it didn't matter. Like it was just nothing. How do you think that made me feel?" She was a strong woman, but her voice was trembling now.

"I'm sorry, Mrs. Wood. I wanted to get the information as fast as possible."

"You made me feel horrible. You made me feel like shit. And I don't want you in my house."

Cardinal stood. "I made a mistake," he said. "The pressure was on and it threw my judgment off. I'm sorry."

He left by the side door and sat in the car making notes. Christ, I'm a rotten cop, he thought. People have no idea how rotten. A stupid piece of misjudgment had cost him the opportunity to look around Woody's house. He would never even know how far back that set the investigation. Let Channel Four get ahold of that one, they'd have a field day.

Delorme came out half an hour later. "That poor woman," she said, slipping into the driver's seat.

"Did she let you look around?"

"Yeah, there wasn't much to see. But I found these." She handed him a manila envelope.

Cardinal pulled out a stack of Polaroid photographs, some of them stuck together. There were pictures of the Algonquin Mall, the Airport Hill Shopping Center, and Gateway Mall, all taken from the back.

"I just glanced at them," Delorme said, "but it looks like he was casing the malls."

"Seems out of character for Woody."

"He only hit houses, far as I knew. We never nailed him for anything else."

"There's just the one of Gateway. There's more of the other two places."

"Lot of parking lot in there. Maybe he was following a particular car?"

"He wouldn't need to take pictures of that. But he might take pictures of stores he wanted to break into. Someone may have seen him. Might've seen somebody *with* him."

43

ERIC Fraser finished polishing the D-35 and hung it up on the rack behind the counter. It was one of his tasks to polish the guitars once a week, and he preferred it to working the cash or uncrating amplifiers; he liked cleaning things—it was pleasantly mindless, allowing his thoughts to drift wherever he cared to let them: to the island, to the abandoned house, to the boy in Edie's basement.

"How much is the Martin?" a fat kid with a mustache of sweat wanted to know.

"Three thousand six."

"And what about the Gibson you got there?"

"This one's twelve hundred."

Eric could tell the kid wanted to try it out, but he didn't suggest it. Alan didn't like people trying out the expensive guitars unless they were serious.

The kid shuffled over to the music books, and Eric started polishing the Gibson. He never played the guitars himself. Carl and Alan were real musicians, and Eric hated to display his lack of talent in front of them. Keith London's guitar, an Ovation in excellent condition, lay at home beneath his bed. He'd tried it out, but he was so out of practice that the strings hurt his fingers.

A young girl came in and started studying some sheet music, trying to memorize a Whitney Houston song. She was about twelve, with long straight hair. It was wonderful to be able to look at her without desire; having a prisoner made him impervious. Katie Pine had not been so lucky. Eric had actually been thinking about Billy LaBelle when Katie Pine happened along, looking at the band instruments but not buying. But the moment she had come in, Eric had felt the grip of destiny; she would be his, and nothing anyone could do would stop it.

The LaBelle kid was a different matter. Billy LaBelle came in regularly for his lessons, and Eric had watched him over a period of weeks. Always came in by himself, always went home alone after a lesson, lugging his guitar. He'd had big plans for Billy, and then he'd gone and died on them. Well, he and Edie had learned their lesson; it wouldn't happen again. No, no, he had big plans for this one.

He thought about his prisoner all the time, now, imagining all sorts of things to do to him. Keith London's picture was everywhere—it was up in the mall right outside Troy Music, on the streets, at the bus stops—but he'd been in town only about two hours before disappearing. No one was ever going to find him, certainly not the cops he'd seen on TV.

If only he could find exactly the right place—somewhere secluded but easy to equip, somewhere he could really be free in. Somewhere he could set up camera and lights. It wasn't easy. Abandoned houses don't come along all that often.

"Finish that tomorrow, Eric. Look after the cash for a while, will you?"

"Okay, Alan. You said there was some inventory stuff, too."

"You can take care of that tomorrow. Look after the register now."

The reason I have to look after the register, he thought, is because you have to play the old expert, don't you. Have to show these suckers how to play a thing or two, right? Alan was tuning up a Dobro for some guy with hair down to his knees. In some ways, with his firmness and his gentleness, Alan reminded him of his last foster father.

The girl finally gave up trying to memorize the chords right there in the store and decided to buy the Whitney Houston song after all.

"You play piano?" This bit of friendliness for Alan's benefit, of course.

"Piano, yeah. A little bit."

"That's good. These chords will sound good on piano. They're not great for guitar. Too many flats." It was easy to talk when he was feeling so free. Having a prisoner available enabled him to chat with people just like Alan and Carl did. Eric tore off the receipt and taped it to the bag. "Good luck with this now. Let us know if there's any other music you're looking for."

"Oh, thanks. That's great." Sprinkling of acne, mouthful of braces. Amazing. Just a week ago, I'd have been too upset to speak to her, too *gripped.* My heart would have been pure thunder, and terrible images would have blotted out the cash register.

Now Eric could watch her flick that long straight hair without a trace of nerves. This was control.

Jane, his foster sister, had had long straight hair like that, except Jane's was blond. It used to fascinate him. She was always playing with it, too. Twirling a strand unconsciously while she watched TV, squinting at it cross-eyed looking for split ends. Sometimes Eric would touch it and she wouldn't even know. If she was sitting in the front of the car, say, and he was sitting in the back, he could touch that golden sweet-smelling stuff and she'd be none the wiser.

He daydreamed about Jane for a while. All the things he would have done to her, if he'd had the chance. Eventually Alan Troy told him things were looking pretty slow, he could take the rest of the night off.

"You sure, Alan? I can hang around for a while, if you want."

"No, that's okay. Carl's here to close up."

Eric had his coat on and was just about out the door when on an impulse he asked, "How much you figure an Ovation's worth, secondhand?"

Alan didn't look up from the register, where he was counting money. "Why, Eric? You have one to sell?"

"Some guy tried to sell me one the other day. Wanted three hundred for it."

"Well, it depends on the model, of course. You can't get an Ovation new for under eight hundred, though, so it sounds like a good deal—depending on the action and so forth."

"Seemed pretty good. I'm not exactly an expert, though."

"Why don't you bring it in, if the guy'll let you. I'll check it out. Give you a mechanic's report, so to speak."

"Maybe I'll do that. I think the guy left town, though. 'Night, Alan."

"Goodnight, Eric."

"Be careful driving home. It's turning into slush city out there."

Alan gave him an amused, assessing look. "You're in a good mood these days."

"Am I?" Eric thought about it. "Yeah, I guess I am. Had some good news from home. My sister just got her pharmacy degree."

"Hey, that's great. Good for her."

"Yeah. Jane's a good kid."

ERIC had not in fact heard from his foster sister for over fourteen years. He had always figured he would get tossed out of the foster home because of the fire he started next door, but they never caught him for that. Never caught him for the wretched series of parties he had with the dog and cat that went missing, either. In the end they got him for something completely stupid. In the end they got him for nothing at all.

Thirteen-year-old Jane had been the cause of it. If she had not been so stuck up, things would have gone smoother, he would have settled in better, he would have been able to relax. But she was always working him up, the way she flicked her hair at him, the way she ignored him. When he had kidnapped her dog, he had found himself strangely free of yearning for Jane. He could talk to her. He could even comfort her, when she cried for her lost pet.

But less than a week after the dog was dead, Eric was tormented again with a ferocious aching in his chest. Jane had gone back to ignoring him, treating him as if he were a clod of dirt under her heel. He swallowed his pain until he could stand it no more, until finally he determined that—

for one night, at least—Jane would pay attention. Beyond this, he did not really know what he was going to do. He was going to play it by ear.

He stayed awake one night until his foster father's grizzly-sized snores shook the walls of the house. Then he put on his jeans and a shirt—even his socks—and tiptoed down the hall to Jane's door. The door had no lock, he knew, none of the bedrooms had locks.

Sometimes Jane stayed awake reading or listening to her pink plastic radio, but there was no light under her door now. Eric did not even pause. He turned the knob, stepped right into her room, and closed the door. His eyes were already adapted to the dark, and he could clearly see the outline of Jane's hip beneath the covers. She was curled up facing the wall, her features hidden behind a curtain of blond hair.

The room smelled of running shoes and baby oil. Eric stood perfectly still for a long time, watching the rise and fall of Jane's rib cage, listening to the soft swell of her breath. She's fast asleep, Eric thought. I can do anything I want.

He held his hands out just above the outline of her body as if she were a radiator and he could absorb her heat. Then he touched her hair, hooking a yellow strand over his index finger and breathing in the smell of Halo shampoo.

There was a hitch in Jane's breathing, and Eric froze. You're just having a dream, he almost said out loud, it's just a dream and there's no need to wake up. But she did wake up. Her eyes opened, and before he could stop her, Jane sat up and screamed. Eric covered her mouth, and she bit his hand and cried out, "Mom! Dad! Eric's in my room! Eric's in my room!"

A long night followed, a night fraught with tears and raised voices, and in the end, Eric's claim that he had been sleepwalking was not believed.

And so, to his astonishment, Eric Fraser was banished from his fourth and final foster home, not for the abduction and torture of their pet dog, nor for the abduction and torture of their cat, nor for burning their neighbor's field. He was exiled for the apparent felony of setting foot in their daughter's bedroom.

That was it for foster homes. Instead, Eric was shipped to one group home after another, where his behavior quickly deteriorated. More animals went missing, more fires were set. A smaller boy who made fun of Eric for wetting the bed was tied up and beaten with an electrical cord.

This last offense landed Eric in the Juvenile Court at 311 Jarvis, his third and last appearance. He was found to be a young offender under the meaning of the Act and consigned to Saint Bartholomew Training School in Deep River, where he remained under the care and guidance of the Christian Brothers until he was eighteen years old.

The only good thing that happened to him in Deep River was that a fellow inmate named Tony taught him how to play guitar. When they got out of St. Bart's, they moved down to Toronto and formed a grunge band, but the rest of the members were more talented than Eric, and it was only a matter of weeks before they got rid of him. After a succession of progressively less interesting jobs, and a succession of smaller and smaller rooms, he began to feel that he was drowning in Toronto. Oh, that suffocating sensation, as if his lungs were closing down. He made no friends. He spent his evenings alone, with magazines that arrived in plain packaging, his fantasies turning darker and darker.

Toronto was killing him, he decided. He would move to someplace with lots of fresh air, where you wouldn't feel like you were choking all the time. In his methodical way, he made lists of small cities and their various amenities, finally narrowing his choices down to Peterborough and Algonquin Bay. He decided to visit them both, but the day he arrived in Algonquin Bay he had seen the help-wanted ad for Troy Music, and that had made up his mind. When he met Edie in the drugstore a week later, some inner part of him had suddenly felt stronger. Those first flickers of utter devotion in her eyes gave him the sense that this was someone he could share his destiny with. Whatever it might be.

But Eric Fraser did not like to think of the past. Those terrible, suffocating years in Toronto, the hostility of St. Bart's. It was as if there had been a bureaucratic mix-up and he had been assigned a cramped little life that had been meant for someone else. His own life, his real life, had been stolen.

And all of it could have been prevented, he thought, as he drove past the old CN station on the way to Edie's. The whole damn mess need never have happened, if only he'd been smart enough to tape Jane's mouth shut.

44

LISE Delorme had not spent a lot of time on stakeouts. She was discovering on Wednesday night that she was not much good at standing around waiting, especially in the middle of the night in an unheated storefront next door to the New York Restaurant. Luckily, the warm snap—assisted by a space heater—made it just about bearable.

The New York Restaurant has been a favorite with Algonquin Bay's criminal element for as long as anyone can remember, certainly stretching back well before Delorme's time. No one quite knows why, but they know it isn't because of the food, which must give pause to even the most hardened ex-con. McLeod claimed the steaks were Aylmer-issue policewear. Perhaps the big-city name lends it—to the mind of a small-city thug—a certain glamour. It is doubtful in the extreme that any of Algonquin Bay's casual assortment of lawbreakers has been anywhere near New York City; they're no more keen on high-crime cities than anyone else.

Musgrave thought it was the two entrances. The New York is the only Algonquin Bay eating establishment that you can enter from the bright lights of Main Street at one end and exit into the darkness of Oak Street at the other. Delorme thought it might be the gigantic gaudy mirrors on one wall that made the place seem twice its actual size, or the red vinyl, gold-flake banquettes that must have dated from the fifties. Delorme had a theory that bad guys were in many ways like children and shared the toddler's taste for bright colors and shiny objects, in which case the New York Restaurant, from its gold-tasseled menus to its dusty chandeliers, is a felon's natural playpen.

And of course the New York is open round the clock, the only restaurant in Algonquin Bay that can make that claim, which it does boldly, in a flashing crimson neon invitation—or warning: "The New York Never Sleeps."

Whatever the reason for its popularity, the New York is as a result of great interest to the various law enforcement agencies as well. Cops are encouraged to eat there, and often do, smack in the midst of people they have put in jail. Sometimes they chat with each other, sometimes merely nod, sometimes exchange cold stares. Unquestionably, it is a place where a smart cop might overhear useful information.

"Couldn't have picked a better location," Musgrave said. "Anyone spots you, it's easy to explain how you happen to be in the company of a creep like Corbett. Not that anyone's going to see them at two A.M. on a cold Wednesday morning."

The former linen shop next to the New York Restaurant had been empty for six months, and the landlord, a bank, had happily provided the Mounties with a key. To cover their activities, they had boarded up the window with an OPENING SOON sign. The only lights in the place came from clip-ons above the electronic gear. Delorme was waiting in the shadows, along with Musgrave and two Mounties dressed in workman's coveralls who—probably on orders—said not a single word to her. The "contractors" had been in place since noon; Delorme had come at nine P.M., entering through a back hall shared with a candle shop. Pleasant smells of sawdust and bayberry hung in the air.

A black-and-white video monitor showed a wide angle that took in most of the bar. Delorme pointed to the screen: "The camera's movable?"

"Corbett said he'd be at the bar. Be very hard for Cardinal to explain how he happens to be at a table, actually sitting down with Canada's number-one counterfeiter. Being at the bar's a little different. You don't control who your neighbors are."

"Yes, but what if—"

"The camera's on a turret; we can move it with a joystick from in here. We have done this before, you know."

Touchy bastard, Delorme almost said. Instead she walked over to the boarded-up window and watched the street through a small hole carefully drilled in the dot over the I in OPENING SOON. She knew he would enter through the back, the Oak Street entrance, if he came at all, but she wanted to be looking at something other than that vacant bar or the backs of her unfriendly colleagues. The peep-hole didn't afford much of a view. The slush on Main Street was ankle-high. The sidewalks, thanks to their shopper-friendly heaters, were dry. Across the street an arts center that had once been a movie theater advertised an exhibition, called *True North,* of watercolors by new Canadian artists and an evening of Mozart courtesy of the Algonquin Bay Symphony Orchestra. The snow that had been forecast was coming down now as a light drizzle.

There were no pedestrians. A quarter to two in the morning, why would there be? Don't come, Delorme was thinking. Change your mind, stay home. Sergeant Langois had called from Florida, confirming her worst suspicions, less than three hours before. From that moment on, her feelings had been all over the place. All very well to talk about putting the cuffs on a man who sold out the department and the taxpayers to a criminal; another thing to destroy the life of someone you work with every day, the actual person, not the abstract prey. Even when she had bagged the mayor—now there was a man who had betrayed the city and had every reason to expect a stretch in jail—Delorme had gone through the same regret-in-advance process. When it came time to lock him up all she could think about were the unintended victims of her expertise, the mayor's wife and daughter. Collateral damage, she thought. I'm some true-believing pilot on a mission, following orders no matter what the cost: I should have joined the Air Force, I should have been American.

A red-and-white Eldorado came gliding into view, fishtailed a little in the slush, and stopped in front of the restaurant. Bright lights, shiny metal, like something you'd hang in miniature over an infant's crib. Here we go, Delorme thought, too late for regrets now. It's probably just stage fright, anyway. The car had pulled too far forward for her to see who got out.

A radio crackled, and a male voice said, "Elvis is here," and Musgrave tersely acknowledged. Delorme hadn't even realized they had men positioned elsewhere. She hoped they were indoors somewhere.

She joined Musgrave in front of the video monitor. On-screen, Kyle Corbett was handing his coat to someone out of view. Then he sat at the bar, well within the camera angle. Corbett looked mid-forties but styled himself like a much younger man, perhaps a rock star. He had long hair, cut all one length and swept back from a knobby brow, and an artistic goatee. His sports jacket was suede, with wide lapels, and he wore a crew-neck sweater underneath. He leaned forward to adjust his hair and mustache in the mirror, then swiveled on his stool to greet the bartender. He flashed a billboard-size smile. "Rollie, how's it going?"

"How you doing, Mr. Corbett?"

"How'm I doing?" Corbett gazed up at the ceiling for a moment as if pondering deeply. "Prospering. Yeah, I think you could say I'm prospering."

"Pilsner?"

"Too cold. Gimme an Irish coffee. Decaf. I wanna sleep sometime this century."

"Decaf Irish coffee. Coming up."

"That's my man."

Delorme was trying to place what it was about Corbett's manner that was so familiar: the big smile, the apparent thought expended on trivial questions. Then she realized what it was. Kyle Corbett, former drug runner and current counterfeiter, had adopted the kindly condescension of the very famous. Delorme had once seen Eric Clapton in the Toronto airport, cornered by fans, signing autographs. He chatted with them in the same easy yet distant manner that Corbett had appropriated for himself.

He had swiveled his back to the camera and spread his

arms along the bar as if the place were his. "He doesn't look that dangerous," Delorme observed.

"Tell that to Nicky Bell," Musgrave said. "May he rest in peace." Then he gave a thumbs-up to his men. "Crystal clear, sound and picture both. Nice piece of work."

The radio crackled again. "Taxi on Oak."

Musgrave spoke into his radio. "Tell me it's our man of the hour."

"He's getting out now." There was a pause. "Can't see his face. It's raining and he's wearing his hood. Headed your way, though."

There was a loud clink of glassware, and the two men at the video console suddenly sat back.

"Jesus Christ," Musgrave said. "The screen's blank."

"They put something in front of it. Stacks of bar glasses." Frantic hands twiddled at dials. "It's those huge dishwasher trays they have."

"Jesus. Hit the joystick. Can't you swivel around them?"

"I'm trying, I'm trying."

"Shhh!" Delorme said. "Let's at least hear what's going on."

Corbett was greeting somebody loudly, expansively, in his best "just folks" manner, and implying for the benefit of any restaurant staff that this meeting of cop and criminal was entirely accidental. "You gonna join me for a drink? Always glad to know a fellow insomniac, even if he's playing for the wrong team."

The reply was unintelligible. The other person was somewhere out of mike range, perhaps hanging up his coat.

"You guys always dress like Nanook of the North when you're off duty?"

"Larry," Musgrave said icily, "fix the fucking camera. We're losing the main event."

Christ, Delorme prayed. Let's get it over with.

"What're you drinking?" It was Dyson who spoke. "Shirley Temple or something?"

Musgrave whirled on Delorme. "Who is that? Is that Adonis Dyson? I thought you fed this pill to Cardinal."

Delorme shrugged. A mixture of relief and sorrow was flowing into her veins as if from a hypodermic. "I fed Cardinal one date. Dyson got another."

"You have something for me?" Dyson was saying on the darkened screen.

There was a crackle of paper. "Invest it wisely. Personally, I like index funds."

"I got a cab waiting. So I'll get right to the nitty-gritty."

"What are you scared of? Didn't you hear I'm immune these days? Amazing what a court order can do. I gotta say, the law's really something when it works."

"It's late, and I've got a cab waiting."

"Sit down. Don't you haul ass on me. I told you I want a full fucking rundown. I don't pay you for chicken feed."

"The Mounties are going to hit you on the twenty-fourth. No chicken feed. The twenty-fourth. That's all you need to know."

"That's the poison pill," Delorme said quietly. "The twenty-fourth. Dyson's the only one I gave that to."

"And don't clear out this time," Dyson went on. "Leave something for them to find, and a couple of guys, too. You've got nine lives, I realize, but you're running on number ten and so am I, and if they nail me we're all going down."

Musgrave spoke into his radio. "We're in play. Close the exits." Then to Delorme: "Let's get him, Sister."

MUSGRAVE went in through the front door, Delorme through the back, each accompanied by two Mounties. Musgrave took Corbett, and Delorme dealt with Dyson. "Really," Delorme told people later. "It was smooth as a business transaction. Corbett didn't put up any struggle. Just cursed a few times."

Perhaps Dyson had been expecting this ending all along. He folded his arms and put his head down on the bar in the time-honored pose of the melancholy drunk, hiding his face.

"D. S., would you put your hands behind your back, please?" Delorme had no need to draw a gun, the Mounties behind her were taking care of all that. "D. S. Dyson," she said, louder. "I need you to put your hands behind your back. I have to cuff you."

Dyson sat up, his face paper-white, and put his hands behind his back. "If it means anything, Lise, I'm sorry."

"I'm arresting you for dereliction of duty, official misconduct, obstructing justice, and accepting a bribe. I'm very sorry, too. The Crown tells me more charges are likely." She sounded very much the well-trained, don't-mess-with-me, modern policewoman. But she wasn't really thinking of the Crown, or the charges, or even Adonis Dyson. The whole time she was executing this by-the-book arrest of her boss, Lise Delorme was thinking of that gawky young daughter she had seen outside his house and of the wraithlike figure who had called her away.

45

I⊤ was three-thirty in the morning, and Cardinal had the photographs pinned up on a shelf above the stereo, where a Bach suite was playing. He was not a classical music buff, but Catherine was and Bach was her hero. Listening to his wife's favorite music made the house seem less lonely, as if he might step into the living room and find Catherine curled up on the couch, reading one of her detective novels.

Katie Pine, Billy LaBelle, and Todd Curry stared at Cardinal from across the room like a very young jury who had found him guilty. Keith London—who might yet be alive—was abstaining from the vote, but Cardinal could almost hear his cry for help, the accusation of incompetence.

There had to be some connection between all four victims; Cardinal did not believe a killer could be entirely random in singling out his prey. There must be some thread, however slender, that united the victims—something that later would turn out to be obvious and he would curse himself for not seeing sooner. It would exist somewhere: in the files, in the scene photographs, in the forensic reports, perhaps in a stray word or phrase, the import of which had been missed at the time.

A car prowled by on Madonna Road, its motor muffled by the banks of snow. A moment later, footsteps sounded on his front steps.

"What are you doing here?"

Lise Delorme was on his doorstep, rain sparkling in her hair, her cheeks pink. Her voice was full of excitement. "It's a ridiculous hour, I know, but I drove past on my way home and saw your light was on and I have to tell you what just happened."

"You drove by on your way home?" Madonna Road was three miles out of her way. Cardinal held the door open for her.

"Cardinal, you aren't going to believe this. You know the Corbett case?"

DELORME sat on the edge of the couch, hands flying every which way as she told Cardinal everything, from Musgrave's first appearance to Dyson's laying his head on the bar like a man about to be guillotined.

Cardinal leaned back in his chair by the woodstove, countercurrents of dread and relief flowing across his belly. He listened as she outlined Musgrave's suspicions, Dyson's ambivalence, her own moments of doubt when she discovered the Florida condo, the boat receipt.

"You searched my place without a warrant," Cardinal said with as little inflection as possible.

She ignored him, small hands moving in the light, her accent stronger than he'd ever heard it. "For me, the worst moment." Hand on heart, small round breast momentarily emphasized. "Worst moment absolutely was finding that boat receipt."

"Which boat receipt was that?" Cardinal placed the question between them with a coolness he did not feel. Brazen as a professional thief, Delorme went straight to his file cabinet. She half knelt to open the drawer, and then her pale fingers were riffling through his papers. Cardinal was citizen enough to feel outrage at the invasion, cop enough to feel admiration, and man enough, he noted with annoyance, to find it slightly erotic. Delorme pulled out the receipt: One Chris-Craft cabin cruiser, fifty-thousand dollars. "When I saw that date, my heart went like the *Titanic*. Boom. Straight down."

"It's right after we raided Corbett." Cardinal held the thing to the firelight, looking for—well, he wasn't sure what for. "It's not mine."

"You know what saved you? The three Fs saved you." She proceeded to explain about Florida and French Canadians and how that peculiar combination had allowed her, from her location nearly a thousand miles north, to run down the purchase of that cabin cruiser. "I fax Sergeant

Langois the receipt number, he goes over there, and this guy, he's very good-looking, okay? This poor Florida girl working in the back office she'll do anything for him. I mean, his accent, everything about the guy is charming."

The willing Florida girl, it turned out, had dug up the records of the sale. And because the boat was going to be delivered out of state (as much to avoid sales tax as anything else), they had required a photo ID. "Sergeant Langois sent me the fax this afternoon—not downtown, of course—a fax with a picture of Detective Sergeant Adonis Dyson."

"So until this afternoon you thought I was working for Kyle Corbett."

"No, John. I didn't know what to think. This setup, it was really because I wanted to rule you out as a suspect. I didn't know it would bring down Dyson. I didn't have that fax when I set it up."

"He must've known we'd be able to trace the receipt. What was he thinking?"

"There was no name on it. And he didn't know they had photocopied the ID in the back office and kept it on file. Anyway, these past couple of weeks, he's probably not been *able* to think. He's trapped between Kyle Corbett and Malcolm Musgrave, and he's scared. He probably just panicked."

"But you're saying he placed that receipt in my personal files, in my home. I can't believe he'd try to frame me. I mean, we weren't exactly friends, but . . . What about the condo? That must've looked pretty bad."

"I tried not to jump to conclusions. I know your wife is American. Her parents must be retirement age. A condo in Florida is not out of the question. I had my vacation friend check that out, too. By then, I of course have your wife's maiden name. She gets a condo from her parents, it's supposed to make you a criminal? I don't think so."

Cardinal could not begin to sort out the tangle of his emotions. "So does this mean you're finished investigating me?"

"Yes. It's over. Me, I'm out of Special, and you, you're in the clear."

Cardinal didn't feel ready to believe, either. And there were things he wanted to know: "Why'd Dyson do it? I mean, Corbett was a disaster from beginning to end. Absolute disaster. It was obvious someone was tipping the guy off, but I always assumed it was one of Musgrave's crew. When I ran that by Dyson all he said was, 'If you want to start investigating Mounties, do it on your own time.' Then Katie Pine disappeared, and Corbett was off my radar. Why'd Dyson do it? I don't love the guy, but I never pegged him for anything like this."

"Few years ago, he's feeling his retirement fund isn't everything it should be. He takes most of it and puts it into mining stocks. One of my finance teachers used to say, 'A mine is a hole in the ground owned by a liar.' In this case, he turned out to be right."

"Dyson sunk his money into Bre-X?"

"A lot of people did, John. Just not so much of it."

"Jesus." He gave it the briefest of pauses, then: "You searched my place, Lise. I wasn't sure you'd actually do that."

"Sorry, John. You have to see what position I was in: either search your place or get a warrant. When you told me to stay that night you had to go back to the office, I took it as your permission. I'm sorry if I was wrong." Those brown eyes, bright with flecks of firelight, searching his face. "Was I wrong?"

Cardinal waited a long time before answering. It was after four o'clock, and suddenly exhaustion hung about his shoulders like a leaden cape. Delorme was still wired from her triumph; she'd be running on the high octane of victory for hours to come. Finally, he said, "It may have been permission. I'm not really sure. That doesn't mean you had to take advantage of it."

"Okay, look, it wasn't nice. Every once in a while, I remember that a good cop—like a good lawyer or a good doctor—is not necessarily a nice person, or pleasant to be around. So, you and me, we don't have to work together if you don't want. You can take me off Pine–Curry and I'll understand. But me, I think we should finish out this case together." *Togedder,* she pronounced it, and Cardinal was so tired it made him smile.

"What?" she asked him. "What are you smiling about?"

Cardinal got up stiffly and handed Delorme her coat. She did up the snaps, looking at him the whole time. "You're not going to tell me, are you."

"Be careful driving home," he said softly. "That slush could freeze again anytime."

46

ERIC was getting on Edie's nerves. For several days he'd been completely serene, cheerful even. But now he was bossing her around all the time. First he wants her to make his dinner. Where the hell did that come from? Usually he couldn't stand to have her watch him eat. Suddenly he wants sausages and mashed potatoes, and she has to hustle out to the supermarket through a sea of slush to get them, soaking her feet. Then he eats in the living room by himself while she and Gram eat in the kitchen. Two days previously she had written in her diary: *I love Eric with a terrible passion, but I don't like him. He's mean and selfish and cruel and a bully. And I love him.*

Now they were in the basement with Keith tied to that chair with the hole in it and the pot underneath. First thing she'd had to do was empty his damn pot. She hated coming down here now, it was like changing a litter box. Eric would never do it, he just complained until Edie took care of it. And she was feeling horrible to begin with, hollowed out inside, the way she did when the eczema came back. It was crawling over her face up from underneath her jaw-line, her skin was cracked and red and weeping. When she had come out of the supermarket some louts driving by had rolled down their windows to make barking noises at her.

She came back from the little bathroom just as Eric was explaining his reasoning to Keith. Eric seemed to take pleasure in this talking in front of the prisoner, but it was making her edgy.

"See, prisoner, we don't want to worry about bloodstains anymore. You reach a certain point, you start to feel like you shouldn't have to clean up after yourself, know what I mean?"

The prisoner, taped into immobility and silence, did not reply; he'd even given up making pleading eyes at them.

"I've found the perfect place to kill you, prisoner. It's a

locked-up, bricked-up, fucked-up former pump house. How often do you think people go there? Once, twice every five years, maybe?" Eric put his face six inches away from the prisoner, as if he would kiss him. "I'm talking to you, honey."

The red-rimmed eyes shifted away, and Eric grabbed the prisoner's chin, forcing him to look.

Edie held up the pad of paper. "You wanted to do the list, Eric." Thinking, he'll kill him right here, if I don't get us upstairs pretty quick.

"We were considering going back to the mineshaft, weren't we, Edie. They'd never expect us to show up at the mineshaft again."

"You're not getting me on that ice," Edie said. "It's been above freezing three days in a row." She pointed to the pad. "What about a tub of some sort? Catch the blood."

"I'm not gonna lug a tub around, Edie. The whole point of going out to the fucking pump house is that we don't have to worry about the mess. A table would be nice, though. Something a comfortable height. Right, prisoner? Right. Prisoner number zero-zero-zero agrees." Eric unfolded *The Algonquin Lode* and spread it out on the bed where the prisoner couldn't help but see his own high-school graduation picture along with the subhead: SEARCH FOR TORONTO YOUTH AT A STANDSTILL.

"Maybe a bag of lime," Edie offered. "To obliterate his features after we kill him. Maybe even *before* we kill him."

"Edie, you have such an interesting take on things. Don't you just love that about her, prisoner? The youth of Toronto agrees, Edie: You have a very interesting take on things."

47

CANDLE wax, wood polish, and old incense. The smells in the cathedral never changed. Cardinal sat in a pew near the back and let the memories come: There was the altar where he had served Mass as a boy in surplice and soutane, there the confessionals where he had owned up to some but by no means all of his first sexual adventures, there the rail where his mother had lain in her coffin, there the font where Kelly had been baptized, a doll-faced banshee whose shrieks had unnerved everybody, especially the young priest who had anointed her.

Cardinal's faith had left him sometime in his early twenties and it had never come back. He had attended Mass regularly throughout Kelly's girlhood only because Catherine had wanted it and unlike, say, McLeod, who had nothing but contempt for Rome and all her works, Cardinal had no strong feelings against the Church. Or in favor of it. So he wasn't sure why he had stopped by the cathedral this Thursday afternoon. One minute he had been in D'Anunzio's eating a ham and Swiss, next minute he's in the back row of the church.

Gratitude? Certainly, he was glad Delorme's investigation was over. And, as for Dyson, he felt terribly sad, almost a kind of heartbreak. McLeod had heaped scorn on their fallen boss all morning. "Good riddance,"—barking across the squad room to anyone available. "It's not enough he's an arrogant fuck? He also has to be dirty? Some people don't know when to stop." But Cardinal felt no moral superiority; it could just as easily have been him hauled off to the district jail in cuffs.

A gigantic gold-fringed medallion of Mary being assumed into heaven hung above the altar. As a boy, Cardinal had often prayed to her to help him be a better student, a better hockey player, a better person, but he didn't pray now. Sitting in the fragrant expanse of the cathedral was enough to evoke that sense of wholeness he had known as a boy, and as a young man. He knew to the hour when he had lost that wholeness. Just because Delorme had stopped investigating him didn't mean his own conscience was going to grant him a reprieve.

"Excuse me."

A bulky man edged his way past Cardinal into the pew—pretty annoying with the place utterly empty, but people had their favorite pews, and Cardinal was, after all, an interloper, not a regular.

"Nice little church you got here."

The man was almost exactly square. He perched beside Cardinal like a perfect cube of meat, a solid mass devoid of neck or waist or hips. He pointed to the medallion of the Assumption. "Cool medal. I like churches, don't you?" He turned to Cardinal and smiled, if you could call that sort of mirthless display of teeth smiling. Two gold incisors gleaming for an instant, then gone. The man's face, flat and round as an Eskimo's, was harrowed by four symmetrical scars, vivid white grooves that ran across the forehead and chin, and vertically down each cheek. The nose had the misshapen, imploded look of a pepper. The man had to turn a full ninety degrees to face Cardinal, because his right eye was covered by a black leather patch. On this, some wit had stenciled the word *Closed*.

Was he someone Cardinal had put in jail? Surely he would have remembered this creature molded from the clay of pure thug.

"Warm for February." The man slid a black watch cap from his skull, revealing a perfectly shaved scalp. Then, with surprising delicacy, he removed first one leather glove and then the other, resting his hands on his knees. The knuckles of one hand were tattooed with the word *fuck*, the knuckles of the other said *you*.

"Kiki," Cardinal said.

The gold incisors flashed again. "I thought you'd never remember. Long time no see, huh?"

"Sorry I didn't visit you in Kingston, but you know how it is. You get busy . . ."

"Ten years busy, right. I been busy, too."

"I see that. Been doing some decorating. I love what you've done with the patch."

"No, I been working out. I can bench-press three hundred, now. What about you?"

"I don't know. Around one seventy last time I checked." It was closer to one fifty, but he was talking to a Visigoth; ruthless honesty was not called for.

"Doesn't that make you a little nervous?"

"Why should it? Unless you're threatening me. I hope you are—given that you're a paroled felon and all."

The gold incisors shone wetly. Kiki Baldassaro, better known to his circle of intimates as Kiki B., or Kiki Babe. His father was a mid-level Mafioso who had been stoutly protecting the Toronto construction industry from labor problems for decades. One of the ways he did this was to insert his rhomboidal son into a company's payroll as a "welder." And welding paid very well indeed, especially when you considered that Kiki B. was not expected to actually show up at the site. God forbid.

Despite the guaranteed income, Kiki B. was not one to sit at home idle. He liked to work with his hands, and when the indebted needed encouragement, or the forgetful needed reminding, he was happy to help out with a bit of pressure in the right place. In fact, Cardinal was recalling now, that was how Kiki B. had met his boss and spiritual adviser, Rick Bouchard. On a routine assignment for Baldassaro *père,* he had put a Bouchard henchman in traction. Bouchard showed up at Kiki's door and explained his position to him with a crowbar. They had been friends ever since.

"Musta taken a crane to get that thing up there." Kiki had returned his attention to Our Lady of the Assumption, aloft on her medallion.

"You didn't hear about that?" Cardinal unbuttoned his coat. It may have been fear or it may have been the church's heating system, but sweat was running down his rib cage in cold rivulets. "Night before they were supposed to hoist Our Lady in place, the crane operator skids off the highway down at Burke's Falls and breaks his arm. This is the day before Easter, thirty years ago or so. They're in despair because the next day's Easter and the Bishop is coming all the way from the Soo to say Mass. Big occasion, and it looks for sure like Our Lady's gonna sit it out in a crate. So they rush around calling for crane operators—they don't exactly grow on trees up here the way they do in Toronto—and finally they get one. He agrees to come in at five A.M. to hang the medallion."

"Sure he does. Five A.M., that's triple time."

"The point, Kiki, is he never got to do it."

"Okay. 'Nother accident, right?"

"No accident. Next day he comes into the church, five A.M. Rest of the crew is already here. He finds them all kneeling in the front row, and these are not Catholics, you understand, not all of them. But they're all kneeling in the front row and their mouths are hanging open. And then the new crane operator looks up and sees the reason why they're all so ga-ga." Cardinal pointed.

"She was already up there."

Cardinal nodded. "She was already up there. How? When? Nobody knows. Clearly several natural laws were broken—gravity, for a start."

"So somebody came in at night and hoisted her up there."

"Well, yeah, that's what everybody figured. But they never figured out who. Place was locked up tight. Crane's sitting outside, no keys in it. Foreman had the keys. It was spooky. They kept it really quiet and everything, but—maybe I shouldn't tell you . . ."

"Tell me what? Go on, tell me. You can't start a story and then quit halfway."

"It's a long time ago, I guess I can tell you. The Vatican sent one of their investigators over here. A priest who was also a scientist. Only reason I know, they had to tell us. It was a professional courtesy."

"The Vatican. They find anything?"

"Nope. It's a mystery. They do call her Our Lady of Mysteries."

"That's right. I forgot that. That's a good story, Cardinal. I think you made it up, though."

"Why would I do a thing like that? I'm sitting in a church, I'm not about to start blaspheming. Who knows what could happen?"

"It's a good story. You could tell it to Peter Gzowsky. He's a good listener. That's what got him on the air."

"That show's not on anymore, Kiki. You miss things like that in prison. Are you aware of the legal concept of menacing?"

"It hurts me that you could even think something like that. I'd never threaten you. I always liked you. I liked you right up till you slapped the cuffs on me. All I'm saying is I'd be nervous sitting beside a guy who could remove my arms and legs and lay them out in front of me."

"You're forgetting you're a lot stupider than me, Kiki."

Air whistled in the flattened nostrils. Over the one eye, the eyelid lowered to half-mast. "Rick Bouchard got fifteen years 'cause of you. Ten of those years are up. He could be out any day now."

"Think so? I don't see Rick racking up points for good behavior."

"He could be out any day now. But the point is, when he gets out, he's going to want his money. I mean, look at it from his point of view. Here he is doing fifteen years for a few kilos and five hundred grand. He loses the fifteen, the kilos, and the five hundred grand. He doesn't even mind that."

"Yeah, I heard that about Bouchard. Very even-tempered."

"Really, it's not about that. You were just doing your job. But here's the thing. The thing is, Rick had seven hundred thousand, not five. Seven. So all's he wants back is the two hundred thousand. That's pretty reasonable. The way Rick sees it, taking that money wasn't part of your job."

"Rick says, Rick thinks. That's what I admire about you, Kiki. Your independent spirit. You always go your own way. Real maverick."

The one good eye, red-rimmed, regarded him—sadly? It was difficult to tell, one eye being harder to read than two. Kiki rubbed his nose with the letter *F* and sniffed. "You told me a good story. Now I gotta tell you one."

"Is it about how you lost your eye?"

"No. It's about this guy. There was this guy in my block. Not Rick's block, my block, you understand? They had to move him out of Rick's block 'cause—well, I guess you could say 'cause he was an independent spirit. Real maverick.

"Anyways. He moves into my block. And I guess he figures he's home free because he like immediately starts trying to run with the big boys. Which you don't do. You work your way up. See, he could've come to me, asked my advice how to patch things up with Rick. I could've helped. There wasn't that much money involved. Not like you. But, he was like you say, an independent spirit, a real maverick, so he didn't come to me. And instead of ending up friends with Rick, instead of doing his time safe and sound, guess where he ended up?"

"I don't know, Kiki. Banff?"

"Banff? Where'd you get Banff?"

"Sorry. Just tell me. Where'd he end up?"

"I guess his own conscience got to him after a while. Because he went to bed one night and spontaneously combusted." The red-rimmed eye looked Cardinal up and down. It was like being examined by an oyster. "I'm telling you, I never heard screams like that. There's a lot of metal in prison, you know? Acoustics are not designed for comfort. But even so. It frightened me, him screaming like that. And the smell of a human being on fire, well, it's not very nice. Total mystery, too. Like your Virgin. A miracle, maybe. Guy just spontaneously combusting like that. They never did figure out how it happened."

Cardinal glanced up at the Virgin and, without thinking, said a little prayer. *Help me do the right thing.*

"So. You're just going to sit there, you're not going to say anything? What's the matter? You didn't like my story?"

"No, no, it's not that." Cardinal leaned toward the flat round face, the one stewed eye. "It's just kind of weird for me, Kiki. I've never talked to an actual cyclops before."

"Huh." Kiki shifted his weight, the pew creaking under him. Cardinal left him contemplating his knuckles. First *fuck,* then *you.* He was back at the baptismal font, when Kiki called after him, "That's funny, Cardinal. I'm going to be laughing at that for a long time. Couple of years from now? There you'll be: dead and all. And there I'll be: laughing. You're such an independent spirit."

Cardinal pushed open the massive oak door, squinting in the watery winter light.

48

DELORME placed a Baggie on top of the computer; something metallic gleamed dully through the plastic.

Cardinal glanced at it. "What's that?"

"Katie Pine's bracelet. It came with her clothing from Forensic. Negative for prints except hers. You going to join us in the Museum, or what?" The Museum of Unsolved Crime was Delorme's personal term for the boardroom, which was now fully taken over by their case materials. The bracelet would join the audiotape, the fingerprint, the hair and fiber, the Ballistics and Forensic reports—the growing catalog of leads that led nowhere.

"Give me a few minutes," Cardinal said. "I have to finish this, now."

"I thought you did all your sups at night."

"It's not a sup."

Delorme could see his computer screen from where she stood, but Cardinal was pretty sure she couldn't read it. If that was a flicker of suspicion in her eyes, fine, let her wonder. Delorme reluctantly left, and he read the last part of what he had written. *I've come to realize that, because of my past, my continuing presence on the Pine–Curry case could jeopardize the outcome of any trial. I must therefore . . .*

I must therefore get the hell out of this and all my other cases, because evidence from an admitted thief is not going to carry a lot of weight. I am the weak link in the chain; the sooner I get out, the better. For the hundredth time that day he wondered how he would tell Catherine, pictured for the hundredth time how her face would crumple in grief, not for herself, but for him.

He had outlined the facts of his guilt for the record: It had happened his last year on the Toronto force. They had raided a dealer's house, Rick Bouchard's distribution center for northern Ontario, and while the others on the squad had been reading rights to the likes of Kiki B. and Bouchard himself, Cardinal had found the cash in a hidden compartment of a bedroom closet. To his everlasting shame he had walked off with nearly two hundred grand; the other five hundred was used as evidence in court. The suspects, he added, had been convicted on all charges.

In my defense, I can only plead . . . But Cardinal had no defense, not in his own mind. He picked up the Baggie from the top of the computer. There is no defense, he said to himself, moving the little charms between thumb and forefinger like prayer beads: a miniature trumpet, a harp, a bass fiddle.

In my defense, I can only plead that my wife's illness had upset me so much that . . . No. He would not hide behind the sorrows of the person he had most wronged. He deleted the sentence and typed instead, *I have no excuse.*

Jesus Christ, he said to himself. Not a single extenuating circumstance? Nothing to soften the image of himself as a uniformed thug? *None of the money was for myself,* he typed and quickly deleted.

It had happened during Catherine's first hospitalization; Cardinal was still a junior detective on the Toronto Narcotics Squad and had been living the nightmare of watching his wife transformed by mental illness into a person he didn't recognize: dull, lifeless, depressed to the point of speechlessness. It had terrified him. Terrified him, because he knew he was not strong enough to live with this debilitated zombie who had taken the place of the bright, chipper woman he loved. Terrified him because he knew nothing at that time of mental illness, let alone the complexities of raising a ten-year-old girl by himself.

Through the Baggie, his fingers traced the form of a tiny guitar.

Catherine had spent two months in the Clarke Institute. Two months with people who were so confused they couldn't write their own names. Two months while the doctors tried various combinations of drugs that seemed only to make things worse. Two months during which she recognized her husband only intermittently. After a torment of inner debate, Cardinal took Kelly to see her mother, which was a mistake for all concerned. Catherine could not bear even to look at her daughter, and it took the little girl a long time to get over it.

Then Catherine's parents had come up from Minnesota to visit and had been horrified by the doleful, panda-eyed creature that had shuffled through the hospital corridor toward them. Although they were never less than polite to him, Cardinal could feel their stares boring into his back: Somehow *he* had caused her breakdown. They began to talk up American health care ("Finest in the world. Cutting edge. Brilliant psychiatrists. Who do you think writes all the books?"), and the message was plain. If Cardinal truly cared about their daughter, he would seek treatment for Catherine south of the border.

Cardinal had given in. What galled him even now, fifteen years later, was that he knew that treatment in the States would be no better. He knew they would have the same drugs, the same enthusiasm for shock treatment, the same lack of success. And yet he had caved in. He couldn't bear to have Catherine's parents think he was not doing his best for her. ("Don't worry. We know the fees can be pretty steep. We'll contribute.") But they could not contribute much, and the bills at the Tamarind Clinic in Chicago quickly mounted into the thousands, and over the months, into the tens of thousands.

In a matter of weeks, Cardinal had known he could never pay the bills; he and Catherine would never own a house, never get out of debt. And so, when the opportunity presented itself, Cardinal had taken the money. It had paid off the bills, with almost enough left over for Kelly's very expensive education. The trouble was, he found when he crossed that ethical line, he had left his true self stranded on the other side.

I have no excuse, he wrote. Every penny of that money was for my benefit, to keep up appearances in my in-laws' eyes, to buy the love and respect of the daughter I spoil.

*For now, the most important thing is that Pine–Curry be
pursued without the risk of the department's credibility being destroyed.*

He wrote that he was sorry, tried to improve on that
statement and found he couldn't. He printed the letter out,
read it over, and signed it. He addressed the envelope to
Chief Kendall, marked it *Personal,* and dropped it in the
interdepartmental mail.

He had planned to join Delorme in the boardroom, but,
suddenly exhausted, he sank back down in his chair with a
deep sigh. Katie Pine's bracelet glittered dully in its plastic
cocoon. Katie Pine, Katie Pine—how he would love to get
some measure of justice for her before he left the department. The tiny gold instruments seemed out of character
for her—or at least for the idea he had of her—of Katie the
little math whiz. The tiny gold bass fiddle, trombone, snare
drum, and guitar—they would be more in character with
Keith London. Miss Steen had said he had a guitar with
him. And Billy LaBelle had taken lessons at Troy Music
Center, which Cardinal might not have recalled but for the
fact that Troy Music Center was the last place Billy La-
Belle had been seen alive.

"And what about Todd Curry?" Cardinal said it aloud,
though he hadn't meant to.

"Are you talking to me?" Szelagy's head appeared over
the top of another computer, but Cardinal didn't answer.
He pulled the file across the desk; it was woefully thin.

"Billy LaBelle, Keith London, and Katie Pine were all
into music. What about Todd Curry?"

He recalled vividly the boy's suburban room in his suburban house, his devastated father hanging back in the
doorway. He recalled the games in the closet, the map on
top of his desk—but music? What sign had there been of
music? Yes, there it was in the sup on the interview with
the parents: Todd Curry had belonged to music newsgroups on-line. Alt.hardrock and Alt.rapforum. That's
right, he had thought it strange that a white kid was so into
rap music.

Then something else fell out of the file, a scrawled note that made Cardinal's heart begin to pound. Someone, he couldn't be sure who, had taken a call from the teacher, Jack Fehrenbach, who was reporting a stolen credit card. "Szelagy, is this your handwriting?" Cardinal waved the note at him. "You take a call from Jack Fehrenbach?"

Szelagy looked at the note. "Yeah. I told you about it, remember?"

"Jesus Christ, Szelagy. Don't you realize how important this is?"

"I did tell you about it. I don't know what else you want me to . . ."

But Cardinal wasn't listening; he was staring at the note in his hand. An unusual charge on Fehrenbach's statement had alerted him. On December 21, the night after Todd Curry had visited him, someone had charged two hundred and fifty dollars at Troy Music Center, apparently for an elaborate turntable.

Cardinal ran down the hall to the boardroom where Delorme was on the phone, scribbling notes onto a yellow legal pad.

"It's music." Cardinal snapped his fingers at her. "Todd Curry was into rap music, remember? Wanted to be a DJ, Fehrenbach said."

"What's going on, Cardinal? You have a funny look on your face."

Cardinal held up the Baggie in which Katie Pine's bracelet floated like an embryo. "This little item is going to break our case."

49

"MCLEOD, where's your sup on the Troy Music Center? Didn't you interview them when you were working LaBelle?"

"Why you asking? It's in the file somewheres."

"It's not in the file. I'm looking at the file. You remember who works there?"

"Two guys. Alan Troy—he's the main guy—and some other guy, some guitar geek been there forever. He's the one taught Billy LaBelle."

"You remember his name?"

"Fuck, no."

"McLeod, we're trying to nail a killer here."

"I wasn't. I was just tracing Billy LaBelle's steps, for Christ's sake. We weren't working a homicide back then. We were working a routine missing kid, so don't come on like I'm Mr. Dereliction-of-Duty, all right? I think our late lamented leader Detective Sergeant Dickhead Dyson takes that title. Carl Sutherland, that's the guy's name. Carl Sutherland."

"You have a middle initial?"

"F for Fucking. Try the file, Cardinal." McLeod left the boardroom, muttering to himself.

Cardinal wasted another ten minutes riffling through folders from the previous fall. "Delorme, why don't you feed Troy's ID into the computer and see what it spits out."

"I did. We're waiting."

McLeod came back in. "Carl A. Sutherland," he said, shoving a report into Cardinal's hand. "Some asshole stuck it in the Corriveau file by mistake. If people would stop second-guessing my work for a change—and maybe stop fucking with my stuff for five minutes—maybe I could get some work done around here."

Delorme took the report over to the computer and typed

the information into it. She tore a sheet from the printer. "Negative on Alan Troy. No record in local or national."

Cardinal was reading McLeod's report on his interview at the music store four months previously; it was one page, single-spaced. The first paragraph stated the positions of the two men—Troy the owner, and Sutherland the assistant manager—and how long they'd been working there. Troy had been running the place, at various locations in the city, for the past twenty-five years. Sutherland had been with him for ten, joining just before the store moved into the mall.

The second paragraph discussed Billy LaBelle. Both men knew him and were concerned (*where* concerned, McLeod had written) about the boy's disappearance. Sutherland was the one who actually taught him guitar. The boy had come in for his usual Wednesday evening lesson and left without incident. The next night, Billy LaBelle disappeared from the Algonquin Mall parking lot.

Cardinal stared out the boardroom window at the filthy meringue of slush in the parking lot. The snowbanks looked like slag heaps, and black puddles glittered in the sunlight. What about Katie Pine? Troy and Sutherland hadn't been asked about Katie Pine; the cases hadn't been connected then.

Delorme stepped in front of him with a sheet of computer paper. "I don't know about you, but Carl Sutherland just jumped to number one on *my* hit parade."

Cardinal took the printout from her. Carl Sutherland had been arrested in Toronto two years previously for public indecency.

Seeing this, Cardinal suddenly felt that he was moving through the slow, inevitable motions of a dream. Seeing this, he knew, even though no one had told him and he could not prove it, he *knew* that Katie Pine had been in the Troy Music Center and had met Carl Sutherland. Then the ground had opened.

Reading his thoughts, Delorme said, "We have to close the circle. We have to put her in Troy Music."

Still moving in the dream, Cardinal reached for the

phone. Delorme watched him as if she, too, were caught in the dream, biting her lip.

"Mrs. Pine, it's John Cardinal." He had always hoped his next conversation with Dorothy Pine would be to tell her that her daughter's murderer was in jail. "You remember telling me Katie wanted to be in the school band?"

The dull affectless voice was barely audible. "Yeah. Don't know why she wanted to so bad."

Then Dorothy Pine went so silent, Cardinal thought the line had gone dead. "Are you still there?"

"Yeah."

"Mrs. Pine, did Katie ever take any music lessons of any kind?"

"No." She'd already told him this. She'd told McLeod, too; but Dorothy Pine was not the type to complain.

"Never took piano or guitar? No lessons at all?"

"No."

"But she wanted to be in the band, you said. She had a picture of the school band on her closet door even though she wasn't a member."

"Right."

"Mrs. Pine, I don't understand how Katie got so excited about music if she hadn't studied it. She was obsessed with the band, and she had a charm bracelet with musical instruments on it."

"I know. Found it at some music store somewheres."

There it was, the dream was in control again. It was dreaming Cardinal, and Mrs. Pine, and it was dreaming the words she was about to say. He could feel them traveling down the telephone line before he even asked the question. "Which music store did she get it from, Mrs. Pine? Can you remember the name? It's very important."

"No."

The words would come. Dorothy Pine would say them. She was going to tell him the name of the store, and it would be Troy Music Center, and they would have their man. Cardinal could feel a breeze from the phone, like the wind that arrives before the train pulls into the station.

"I don't know the name," Dorothy Pine said. "The store out in the mall there."

"Which mall, Mrs. Pine?"

"It was the only place she could get the charms for it. She'd go back every month or so and buy a new charm. She got a tuba last time, just like two days before she went away. Before she, uh . . ."

"Which mall, Mrs. Pine?" Tell me, now, he thought. You're going to say the words. The same dream that's pulling me and Delorme is pulling you, too, and it's pulling the words from your throat. He wanted to scream *Which mall, Mrs. Pine? Which mall?*

"Was the big one out on Lakeshore there. The one with the Kmart and the Pharma-City."

"The Algonquin Mall, you mean?"

"Yes."

"Mrs. Pine, thank you."

Delorme tossed him his down coat. She already had hers on.

"Grab Collingwood. I want a scene man with us."

EVEN a place the size of Algonquin Bay has a rush hour, and rivers of slush made the going even more mucilaginous than usual. It was not quite six o'clock, and they had to use the siren on the bypass, and then again on Lakeshore. Collingwood sat in the back of the car, whistling under his breath.

Cardinal tried to look nonchalant as they went through the mall, but there was a rush hour here, too, and he found himself pushing people aside outside Pharma-City to get to the music store.

"Mr. Troy, is Carl Sutherland here?"

"He has a pupil at the moment. Can I help you with something?"

Cardinal headed to a series of doors past the counter and beyond the shelves of guitars. "Which room?"

"Wait a minute, now. What on earth is this about?"

"Collingwood, stay here with Mr. Troy."

The first door was a supply closet. In the second, a startled woman looked up from the piano where she was counting aloud to a metronome. In the third room, Carl Sutherland was shaping the little fingers of a ten-year-old boy around a guitar chord. He looked up sharply.

"Are you Carl Sutherland?"

"Yes?"

"Police. Would you come with us, please?"

"What do you mean? I'm in the middle of a lesson."

"Would you excuse us?" Delorme said to the boy. "We have something to discuss with Mr. Sutherland."

When the boy was gone, Cardinal shut the door. "You gave Billy LaBelle guitar lessons, didn't you?"

"Yes. I already talked to the police about—"

"And you also knew Katie Pine, didn't you?"

"Katie Pine? The girl who was murdered? Absolutely not. I saw her picture in the paper, but other than that I never saw her in my life."

"Our information is different," Delorme put in. "Our information says Katie Pine was in here two days before she disappeared."

"If she was, I didn't see her. Why are you coming to me? It's a big mall out there. Everybody in town goes through."

"Everybody in town doesn't get picked up for public indecency, Mr. Sutherland."

"Oh, God."

"Everybody in the mall doesn't get arrested for exposing himself in the back seat of a porno theater."

"Oh, God." Sutherland swayed slightly in his seat, his face utterly white. "I thought that was over and done with."

"You want to come down to the station and tell us about it? Or maybe we should ask your wife."

"You can't bully me like this. I was acquitted on that charge." Sutherland's voice was now harsh, indignant, but his face was still white. "I'm not proud of what happened. But I don't see why I have to be humiliated over it, either. A pitch-dark theater is not public. It's not public, and the judge agreed. Besides which, what went on was entirely between consenting adults and it's none of your business."

"Billy LaBelle is our business. You were one of the last people to see him alive."

"Well, what does this have to do with Billy LaBelle?"

"Why don't you tell us?" Delorme said. "You were his teacher."

"Yes, I was Billy's guitar teacher. I've already discussed all this. Billy left the store one Wednesday night—the same as every other Wednesday night—and I never saw him again. It's very sad. Billy was a really nice kid. But I didn't do anything to him. I swear I didn't."

"Are you telling us you don't know this boy?" Cardinal produced the photo of Keith London playing guitar.

"I don't. I don't know every kid that happens to play guitar."

Sutherland hadn't been phased at all by the picture. He was scared, yes, he was shaken, but the picture of Keith London did not seem any particular threat. Cardinal's certainty began to slip. He pulled out the picture of Katie Pine.

"That's the girl who was killed. I recognize her from the papers. Other than that I don't think I've ever seen her."

"She was in here two days before she disappeared. She bought a musical charm for her bracelet. You sell them out front."

"She could have got it somewhere else."

"She bought it here."

"I never saw the girl, I'm telling you. Look in the inventory, and you'll see."

"Inventory?"

"We've had computerized inventory for years, now. It'll tell you who sold the thing to her. It's not like we sell a million of them. Three or four a month, I'd say."

As they came out of the practice room, Alan Troy called, "What is it, Carl? What's going on?" But Sutherland ignored him, leading Cardinal and Delorme to a cramped office in the back. Almost buried among stacks of invoices, a computer screen glowed with columns of numbers. Sutherland sat down and typed in a couple of commands. The screen went dark, except for the cursor pulsing in the top left corner.

"You have the date?" he asked without looking at them. "The date the girl disappeared?"

"September twelfth, last year. She bought the charm two days before."

"Fine. Now, I need the item number." He consulted a printout the size of a telephone book, flipping through the double-sized pages until he found what he wanted. He typed in the number. "This should tell us how many we sold in the past year." He drummed his fingers on the desk as he waited. "Seven. Okaaay . . ." He typed in another command, the monthly breakdown.

"September tenth." Delorme pointed at the screen. "Two days before."

Sutherland moved the mouse and clicked. The screen filled up with a copy of the register receipt. He tapped the long fingernail of his right hand on the upper right corner. "You see that number three? That's the salesperson. One is Alan, two is me, three is Eric."

"Eric who?"

"Eric our part-timer. Eric Fraser. Mostly he helps with the stock, but busy times—lunch hours, after-school rush—he helps with the cash, too. If you look at the top left there you can see the time of the transaction: four-thirty P.M. If you look at our calendar, it's going to show you I was teaching a lesson at that time. I think you want to talk to Eric Fraser."

"Mr. Sutherland, is there anything around here that Mr. Fraser touched recently? Something nobody else touched?"

Sutherland thought for a minute. "Follow me."

Alan Troy dodged around Collingwood, finger jabbing the air, demanding to know what was going on. Sutherland cut him off. "Alan, did Eric polish the Martins yesterday?"

"I'm calling the chief of police on this. My employees do not get treated in this way. These people have to—"

"Alan, for Chrissake, just tell them. Did Eric polish the Martins yesterday?"

"The Martins?" Troy squinted first at Sutherland, then at Delorme, then at Cardinal, and back to Sutherland. "You want to know if Eric polished the Martins. Suddenly the urgent question of the moment is, did Eric Fraser polish the Martins? All right, then, yes. Eric did polish the Martins."

Cardinal asked if anyone else had touched the guitars. No. Business had been slow, Martins are expensive, no one had touched them.

Cardinal, still wearing his gloves, reached up for the guitar hanging against the wall. "He'd have to hold it at the bottom to put it back up there, right?"

Mr. Troy, his anger giving way to fascination, nodded. Cardinal held the guitar out toward Collingwood.

Collingwood, silent as ever, dusted a small amount of powder along the top of the soundboard, then blew it off. Two perfect thumbprints took shape. He pulled the Forensic card from his pocket, the thumbprints lifted from Arthur Wood's throat.

"Perfect match," Collingwood said. "Perfect match, plain as day."

50

ERIC and Edie had been right about duct tape. It was even more effective—and less trouble for them—than the drugs. Strain as he might, Keith London could not get the tape to give even a sixteenth of an inch. Each wrist, each ankle was securely fastened. The only tape he had managed to loosen at all was the tape on his mouth. By wetting it, he had gradually loosened it so he could actually make audible sounds now.

But there was some give in the wooden chair to which he was fastened. Rocking from side to side, he could feel the joints loosening.

Whenever Eric and Edie were out of the house, as they were now, Keith rocked from side to side, feeling the joints widening, the screws chewing their way through the wood. They hadn't fed him for a couple of days now, and his efforts were exhausting. He had to stop every few minutes to catch his breath.

Eric and Edie would be moving him soon. They would inject him with a sedative and haul him to some isolated place and—He tried to banish from his mind the memory of the videotape.

He had been rocking for over an hour this morning, ever since he had woken up; his wrists and ankles were chafed raw; his wounded leg was pure agony. But there was some progress, he could feel some give in the chair. It leaned about twenty degrees to either side when he shifted his weight.

He paused, listening. Footsteps crossed the ceiling, and then there was the sound of chairs scraping. Eric and Edie were directly overhead. Keith started rocking again, despite his terror that they would hear him. No, he told himself, the chair is on concrete, the noise won't travel, they won't be able to hear.

He leaned again, side to side, side to side, rocking the

chair and straining at the tape. Once. Twice. Three times. Yes, the chair back was definitely looser. He could twist it a little now. If he could just put strain in the right place, shift his weight over just the right spot, put stress where the chair back joined the seat, it could be broken.

UPSTAIRS, Eric opened the duffel bag—Keith's duffel bag—and emptied it onto the floor. He felt no sense of trespass, exposing another's personal belongings: the pairs of socks, neatly folded, the long underwear slightly stained. There were sunglasses and suntan lotion—Christ, was he planning to take up skiing?—a Frommer's guide to Ontario and a dog-eared paperback of *The Glass Bead Game*.

Eric stood up and brushed off his jeans. "I'll read from the list. You put the stuff in the bag." He took the list from his back pocket and unfolded it. "Duct tape."

Edie pulled it from the drawer beside the fridge and put it in the duffel. "Duct tape."

"Rope."

Edie picked up the tight coil of clothesline, purchased in Toronto, and put it into the bag.

"Screwdriver, flat head . . ."

"Screwdriver, flat head."

"Screwdriver, Phillips head . . ."

"God, Eric. Who else would make a list of screwdrivers? Whole *categories* of screwdrivers."

Eric looked at her coolly. "Someone else would get caught. Pliers . . ."

"Pliers."

"Blowtorch . . ."

"We'd better test it, first. Make sure it works." Edie pulled a box of kitchen matches from the drawer. Eric opened a brass collar on the blowtorch, and the nozzle started to hiss. Edie struck the match and held it out; the torch lit with a *pok*. She turned the collar and the blue bullet-shaped flame nearly caught Eric's sleeve. "Oo," she said. "This'll be incredible." She turned the collar, and the flame slipped back into the bottle like a tongue.

"Crowbar . . ."

"We don't have a crowbar."

"I left it here after the island. It's down in the basement, beside the stairs."

Edie left the table and headed for the basement.

"Check on the prisoner while you're at it."

Eric took a filleting knife out of his knapsack. He unsheathed it and tested it with his thumb. He turned toward the basement and called, "Bring a whetstone, too, if you have one!"

He pulled the shrink wrap off a package of PowerUp and laid out six pills along the edge of the table. He found a glass in the cupboard and ran the water until it was cold and clear. Then he sat at the table and took the tablets one by one, shaking his head each time to help them go down. A shiver ran up his spine.

"Edie!" He yelled again at the doorway. "Bring a whetstone!" He listened for a moment, one ear cocked toward the basement. Then he set down his glass of water, very deliberately, not making a sound. He sheathed the filleting knife and stuck it in his front pocket. He moved to the top of the stairs. This time, he spoke quietly, "Edie?"

"Come and get her, you pathetic prick."

Eric stepped softly down the stairs. He could get around this, he could handle it. Everything depended on conquering emotion. At the bottom of the stairs he picked up the crowbar and hooked it on his belt behind his back. It felt heavy and it dangled precariously, but it would not be visible from the front—unless it fell from his belt.

Eric took a deep breath and stepped into the tiny room. It stank of shit and fear. The chair was a tangle of tape and broken wood. The prisoner had Edie from behind, a wooden bar—a piece of the chair—pressed against her throat.

"Lie down on the floor."

"No. Let her go."

"Lie down on the floor, or I'll break her neck."

He won't kill anyone, Eric thought. If he was strong

enough to kill, he would have forced Edie to the top of the stairs. Edie was looking frightened and ugly, her skin glistening where the eczema cracked and wept, her whimpering muffled by duct tape. The wooden bar pressed tighter against her throat, and her face purpled.

"Lie down on the fucking floor! I'll kill her, you creep, I don't give a fuck."

Remain calm, Eric told himself. The prisoner is half-starved, he's terrified, and he's still wounded—how strong can he be? If we fight, I will win. Remain calm. *Think.* "The problem, Keith, is that once I lie down, there's nothing to stop you killing us."

"I'll kill her right now, if you don't."

"Calm down, Keith. You're choking her."

"Damn right I am." His words were tough, but tears were streaming down the prisoner's face; he was sobbing so hard he could hardly speak. A weird reaction, Eric thought. Was it nerves? Was it self-pity? Whatever the prisoner's emotional state, the wooden bar was biting cruelly into Edie's throat. Oh, prisoner, you are making such a mistake, you will die so badly for this.

"You've got a knife in your front pocket. I can see the handle. Take it out slowly and toss it over here."

Eric did as he was told, bringing the knife out, sheath and all, and tossing it past the prisoner where he could not reach it.

"Now get the fuck down on the floor." Eric hesitated, and the prisoner started shrieking, "Do it now!" over and over again until Eric started to lower himself toward the floor.

Behind him, the crowbar hung heavily from his belt. The problem was, he couldn't swing it at the prisoner without bashing Edie. "I'm getting down, Keith. Just don't hurt anyone, all right? I'm getting down." He sank slowly toward his knees.

What happened next took only a moment to unfold. Eric reached behind for the crowbar. Keith screamed something at the top of his lungs and pulled back on Edie's throat, trying to shield himself with her. But Eric didn't swing for the prisoner, he swung for Edie.

The iron bar caught her a solid blow to the side of the head. Her knees buckled, and she sank toward the floor. The prisoner staggered and lost his grip. He launched himself toward the door, but by then Eric had flipped the crowbar so that he was holding it by the straight end. The prisoner was not even halfway out when the crowbar hit him—a terrible blow to the back of his neck just below the skull—and he crumpled like a poleaxed cow.

51

THE address, according to Troy's records, was 675 Pratt Street East; they were heading there now, without sirens. The radio had been predicting a snowstorm, but the warm patch had held and rain hammered on the roof of the car. The wipers squawked on the windshield. Cardinal had already called for backup, plain dress, but there were no cars in sight when they got to the corner of Pratt and MacPherson.

"I didn't know there was anything after the five hundred block," said Delorme. At the end of the five hundred block, the ONR tracks crossed Pratt Street, and after that the road wasn't even paved, and the small ratty houses on the far side were hidden behind a rock cut.

The radio sprayed static, and Mary Flower's voice filled the car. "Could be a wait for backup. Jackknifed tractor-trailer on the overpass's got traffic backed up for two miles."

"Acknowledged," Cardinal said into the mike. "What's the computer say about Eric Fraser?"

"Nada. Zero locally on Eric Fraser. Nada."

"Doesn't surprise me," Cardinal said. "Troy says he can't be more than twenty-seven, twenty-eight."

"Also zero for nationwide," Flower said. "Clean as a whistle."

"What about Juvie? That's where we'll find him, if he has a record."

"Hold on. Juvie's coming." They heard Flower scream to someone to bring her the printout sometime before next Christmas. "Bingo on Juvie. You ready?"

"Cruelty to animals," Cardinal said to Delorme. "Bet you anything. Go ahead, Mary."

"Age of thirteen, break and enter. Age of fourteen, break and enter. Age of fifteen, cruelty to animals."

"That's our boy," Delorme said.

A faint electrical charge tingled along Cardinal's fingertips. If he had to resign, this was the way to go: stop a serial killer in mid-career—you couldn't ask for a better exit.

McLeod pulled up at the corner by MacPherson, wipers flapping. Cardinal had warned everyone to stay away from the house till he got there. When McLeod saw them he got out of the car and came sprinting across the intersection, holding his hood up with one hand against the rain. He climbed in the back with Collingwood, cursing. "Fucking February, I ask you. Who ever heard of a fucking monsoon in February? It's the fucking pollution from Sudbury doing it. Whole fucking town's melted."

Flower said, "Fraser also did a stint at St. Bartholomew's Training School. Two years less a day."

"Assault, I bet," Cardinal said into the mike.

From the radio, "Aggravated assault. Had a disagreement with his shop teacher concerning the whereabouts of certain equipment."

"And he did some carving on him, right?"

"Nope. Right there in class. Went after him with a blowtorch."

52

KEITH London dreamed he was swimming in a bright green pool, deep in a jungle, where monkeys sat in a row upon a low-hanging branch and drank thirstily with cupped hands. Except for the ripples that spread outward from the monkeys' hands, the surface was tranquil as jade. The smell of water was strong.

He opened his eyes. That smell of water. Was it from rain? He could hear the sound of rain pelting against wood.

His head felt as if it had been split open from crown to nape; the pain made him nauseous. He turned his head slightly and nearly vomited. Wherever he was, the place was very dark, very damp, and very cold. He was dressed, now, in clothes he did not remember putting on—a torn sweater and jeans—and they were not enough to keep out the cold. Off to one side, a space heater glowed a fierce scarlet, but its heat did not reach him. Eric Fraser was about ten feet away, setting a camera on a tripod.

I'm on a table. They have me on a table in a basement somewhere. That damp smell. I'm near a lake. The damp has a definite, full-time smell. And yes, that is rain—rain blowing against boarded-up windows. Huge pipes criss-crossed the ceiling overhead, disappearing into darkness. Of course. The pump house.

He tried to move, but his arms were strapped tightly to his sides and to the table. The only thing he could move was his head. Eric was concentrating on leveling the camera, bending down to adjust first one leg of the tripod, then another. Try to reason with him, reach him before he goes into a frenzy like he did on that videotape. "Listen, Eric," Keith said quietly. "My girlfriend will be missing me by now. I told her where I am, who I was staying with. It was in the letter I wrote."

This was ignored. Eric Fraser adjusted yet another leg of the tripod, humming to himself, and then, apparently satisfied, began pulling objects out of a duffel bag—Keith's duffel bag—and laying them out on a wooden counter.

Keith tried not to look. He concentrated on controlling his voice. "Eric, I could get you money. I'm not rich, but I could get you money from somewhere. My family is quite well off. So is my girlfriend's. They would pay you something, I'm sure they would."

It was as if Eric Fraser heard nothing of this. He pulled something from the bag—a pair of needlenose pliers, and then he stood over Keith for a moment with glistening ferret's eyes, clicking the pliers open and shut just above his nose.

"We could arrange the payments so no one finds out who you are. It should be possible. It wouldn't have to be a single payment, necessarily. There's no reason why it couldn't go on for some time. Please, Eric. Will you listen, Eric? You could make thirty or forty thousand dollars. Maybe fifty. Think what that could buy over the years. Why don't you let me call them, Eric?"

Eric Fraser pulled a paper bag from the duffel bag and unwrapped a sandwich. There was a sudden smell of tunafish. He sat in the darkness, blocking the glow from the space heater. A bone in his jaw clicked every time he chewed. After a while he said, "I wish Edie would get here with the lights." He tapped a large battery on the floor with the toe of his boot. "Lighting will be better in this one. Hate it when you can't see what's going on."

"Think about it, Eric. You could be quite well off. You wouldn't have to work. You could buy things. You could travel. You could go where you want, do what you want. What's the use in just killing me? It won't get you anywhere. You'll get caught sooner or later. Why don't you get some money out of this at least? Wouldn't that be better than just killing me?"

Eric finished his sandwich and threw the wrapping on the floor. "I wish Edie would get here with the lights," he said again.

"Eric, I'm begging you, all right? If you want me on my

knees, I'll get on my knees. Just tell me what I have to do. Eric? Eric, are you listening? I'm begging for my life. I'll do anything you want. Anything. Just let me live."

This got no response whatever.

"Eric, I'll get more. I promise. I'll steal it. I'll rob a store. I'll do anything, Eric. Just let me go."

Eric slid down off his stool and selected a pair of scissors. He stood over Keith and snicked the blades open and shut. Then, taking hold of Keith's hair just above the ear, he cut away a small lock and held it up in a dim shaft of daylight. "I wish Edie would get here with the lights."

53

BEYOND the railroad tracks, the old house leaned against the storm. A piece of the eaves trough hung slackly from the porch, weighed down by melting icicles. At one corner of the roof, a piece of tar paper flapped like a shot bird. Horns from traffic on the overpass honked in the distance.

McLeod remembered the place from his days in uniform. "Had to boom their door in practically every Saturday. Old Stanley Markham—Cardinal, you remember Stanley—old Stanley used to go on a toot and come home and tear the place to bits. Strong son of a bitch, too. Broke my arm in two places. That little maneuver cost him three years. Few years back, his liver finally killed him and, boy, do I ever not miss him. Goddam house always stank of cat piss."

Cardinal asked, "Who lives there now?" They were watching the house through flapping wipers as if it might at any moment hoist up its foundations like a tattered skirt and haul off into the freezing rain.

"Who lives there now? Sweet Celeste lives there now, Stanley's loyal widow and one of nature's true troglodytes. Three hundred pounds, voice that can peel paint, and tough as her bastard of a husband, too. If her IQ was any lower you'd have to water the bitch."

"Fraser drives a Ford Windstar," Delorme said quietly. "I don't see it in the driveway."

"Fraser also has a hostage. I'm not going to wait around to find out if he's home or not."

"Hold on, now. How about a little backup before we waltz in there?" McLeod said. "We ain't exactly a SWAT team, here." He didn't say so, but the implication was, We're lumbered with a woman and a scene guy—we're asking for it.

A brown UPS truck was lumbering to a stop behind them. Ancient brakes howled in protest.

"Give me a minute," Cardinal said. Splinters of rain

stung his face as he got out of the car. He showed the driver his badge and climbed in on the passenger side. The driver was an Indian named Clyde. Under the peaked brown cap his wide cheekbones made him look like a Mongolian soldier.

"Clyde, I need your help with a police matter. I need to borrow your uniform."

Clyde kept his gaze out the window, as if he spoke to the rain, the heaps of dissolving snow. "You going undercover?"

"Just for about ten minutes. It'll save us pulling out weapons. Don't want gunfire on a residential street in the middle of the day."

"How about a trade. You get my uniform, I get your badge." Still speaking to the rain.

"It doesn't work that way, Clyde."

The Indian turned and grinned, displaying the most perfect teeth Cardinal had ever seen. "You can borrow my uniform anytime you want. Hate wearing the thing anyways."

Cardinal took off his coat and struggled to put on Clyde's brown jacket. It was tight across the shoulders, but it would pass.

"What kind of gun is that?"

"Beretta."

"Use it much?"

"Never. Brand-new issue. How do I look?"

"Like a cop in a UPS outfit. Take a couple of parcels, there, it might get you in the door."

"Good thinking, Clyde. You should be a cop."

"I can't stand cops," Clyde said, speaking once more to the weather. "You about ready? I got deadline issues."

"I need the truck, too, Clyde. Can you wait somewhere else? Two guys in a UPS truck looks funny. You guys don't drive around in pairs."

"That's true." He grabbed a pack of cigarettes from the dashboard. "I'll be in Toby's. Store on the corner." The Indian swung down out of the truck. "Second gear's a bastard. Just rev like hell and shove her straight into third. Sure you don't want me to drive?"

"Thanks. I'll manage." Cardinal nearly stalled the truck right on the railroad tracks—oh, smart move, he thought. Get creamed by a freight train before backup even gets here—then he revved it like Clyde said and threw it into third. The truck juddered, then caught, and he drove through a swamp of slush to the unmarked. Delorme rolled down the window.

"I'm going to go straight up to the front door like this," Cardinal told them. "Give me exactly three minutes after she opens the door. Soon as I'm in, McLeod deals with her, and you follow me. We straight?"

"You're in. McLeod takes her. I follow you."

"Collingwood heads straight for the basement."

McLeod leaned forward from the backseat. "Watch out for Celeste. She's got kind of a negative take on law enforcement."

Cardinal steered the truck up to the front of the house. He selected a medium-sized parcel that would cover the Beretta in his hand. He was wishing he had his thirty-eight. I should have spent time on the range, he scolded himself. I'm not used to this weapon. It felt long and unwieldy in his hand.

Celeste Markham opened the door, and Cardinal nearly gagged at the corrosive odor of cat piss. The woman's eyes, two black buttons nearly lost in the dough of her face, emitted twin beams of boredom and hostility. A filthy flower-print robe hung half-open over massive collapsing breasts. On her upper lip, a mustache of fine blond hair glistened. "Wrong house," she said sullenly. "I didn't order nothing."

"Mrs. Markham, I'm a police officer and I have business with Eric Fraser." Stairs to the right, living room to the left. The basement door must be under the stairs.

"He ain't home. You ain't coming in here." She started to close the door. Cardinal blocked it with his foot. When Delorme and McLeod were on the porch stairs, he pushed his way past the woman, his elbow disappearing into the humid depths of her belly.

He heard her cursing McLeod as he took the stairs two at a time. He flew past a bedroom where a television was blaring with a game show. Cardinal glimpsed what looked like a dozen cats sprawled around a two-liter bottle of Dr Pepper and an immense bowl of Chee-tos.

There was a blackened bathroom and, at the end of the hall, a closed, new-looking door. "Police!"

The door was locked. Cardinal kicked at it, and Celeste Markham screamed from downstairs, "You better not break nothing!"

The door was cheap, hollow-core, and it splintered easily. Cardinal reached through and unlocked it from the inside, and stepped in with the Beretta in his hand, Delorme behind him.

After the stench and filth of the rest of the house, the room was shockingly clean. Instead of cat piss, it smelled faintly of soap. The bedcovers were drawn tight, with hospital corners. The window, although ancient, offered a pristine view of the overpass; someone had cleaned it carefully, and Cardinal did not suspect Celeste Markham. Cars rippled in the old glass. Something Cardinal had often noted in people who'd done time, even juveniles: They kept their rooms neat as Marines.

The closet contained four shirts, all pressed, all on hangers. Two pairs of pants, also ironed, also on hangers. One pair of boots with Cuban heels, well worn, spit-shined.

The desktop was empty. The small drawer contained a ballpoint pen and a yellow notepad, with no writing on it. Underneath the desk, they found a box of maybe thirty books, neatly stacked.

"So empty," Delorme said, voicing Cardinal's thought. "It's like no one lives here at all."

Collingwood filled up the doorway behind them. "Nothing in the basement. Big Mama says he just uses this room. Doesn't have the run of the house."

"Where's he eat, even?" Cardinal asked of the room at large. "It's like the guy's not human."

"Something under here." Delorme's voice was muffled;

she was down on her knees, checking under the bed. She dragged out a guitar case. Careful not to smudge fingerprints, she pressed open the latches. It was an Ovation guitar, in good condition.

"Keith London plays guitar. I'm pretty sure Miss Steen said an Ovation. We'll seal this room and let Arsenault at it later."

The search proceeded in silence for the next few minutes. The guitar was solid; it might link Fraser conclusively to Keith London, but it didn't lead anywhere *now*. Cardinal was getting increasingly frustrated with the neatness of the place. He pulled a file box out of the closet. Nothing but neatly filed receipts. He twisted the lid from an old candy tin. Nothing but paper clips and rubber bands. Then he opened a shoe box—it was bound with a piece of blue velvet ribbon as if it might contain precious mementos. Cardinal was expecting photographs, perhaps a diary. But what he found there was worse than coming upon Todd Curry's body.

"Place is like a hospital," Delorme was saying. "I should get this guy to clean my place."

"Oh, no. I don't think you want to do that." Cardinal found it an effort to speak. He was staring at three items laid out neatly in the shoe box, three items that made him feel suddenly very weak. Delorme peered into the box, and her sharp intake of breath was an echo of his own feelings.

The shoe box contained three locks of hair, each a different shade and texture, each neatly taped at one end. One lock of hair was straight and black as sable, that would be Katie Pine's; another—almost certainly Todd Curry's—was dark brown and curly, finer. The blond, that would be Billy LaBelle's. There was none for Woody—that killing had been unplanned, almost incidental—nor was there any for Keith London, whose hair was long, straight, light brown.

Downstairs, Celeste Markham and McLeod were hurling threats at each other. If he didn't get out of her way, she had every intent of breaking his other arm. McLeod suggested she might want to repeat that to a judge.

"Collingwood," Cardinal said at last, "tell McLeod to keep it down so we can think. Have them argue in the car."

Cardinal opened dresser drawers one after another: socks stacked like missiles, T-shirts folded into crisp squares, sweaters that looked as if they'd never been worn. Just their luck the guy had to be a neat freak. Even the wastebasket was empty. Cardinal picked up the yellow legal pad again and riffled the pages. Nothing fell out. He held up the top page like a screen against the window. Faint impressions took on shape, a list of some sort.

"What do you suppose 'P.H.' stands for?" he asked in the blessed quiet that filled the place, now. Somewhere a cat was meowing.

"P. H. Maybe some victim we don't know about?"

"No, it says Trout Lake P.H. We know this guy likes to move around: the mineshaft, the empty house. And we know he's familiar with the Trout Lake area because Woody was found near the marina. And look what he's planning to take with him: duct tape, pliers . . ."

"I think the next one is 'crowbar.' What else does it say?" Delorme was practically climbing over his shoulder. He felt her moist breath on his neck. "Then it's 'battery' lower down."

"What's P.H. on Trout Lake, though? What's on Trout Lake that begins with P.H.?"

"Public housing! There's that housing development past St. Alexander's. That's it, John. Another empty house—a house that isn't finished!"

"Except that's not public housing out there. Port Huron? No, there's no Port Huron around there, either."

"P.H. on Trout Lake . . ." Delorme touched his sleeve. "We can check the city directory, find who's got those initials on the roads out there."

"That'll take too long. It's got to be something simple. I keep thinking 'public beach,' but that's P.B. What else is out there? There's the reservoir and the marina and what else?"

"Well, there's the reservoir itself. I mean, that's pretty big. Pretty isolated."

In following days, there would be a lot of discussion around the department about who said it first. Some said Delorme, some Cardinal. Collingwood changed his mind about it several times and he was *there*. But Cardinal would always remember Delorme's wide brown eyes looking at him, how beautiful they were with the beauty of sure knowledge. In the end it didn't matter who first uttered the words "pump house." Cardinal, to his later shame, immediately dismissed the idea. "Can't be the pump house. It's not on Trout Lake."

"No," Delorme said. "But it used to be."

54

CARDINAL had two calls to make before they could move. He called headquarters and had a patrol unit dispatched to cruise by the old pump house. Normally, his next call would have been to Dyson, but with Dyson out of the picture, he called the chief at home.

"We know where he's planning to kill the London kid. He could be there already."

"He has the boy with him?"

"We think so. We believe he's still alive. I need eight men, shotguns, and body armor."

"You want OPP on this?"

"Chief, there isn't time."

"Go, then. Take what you need."

Delorme came back from the unmarked, beads of rain glistening in her hair. "Flower says the patrol unit went by the pump house. Fraser's Windstar is parked outside."

"They got close enough to see. Let's hope they didn't get close enough to tip him off."

"Flower says no. They're sticking nearby in case he comes out of there, though."

"We've got him, Lise. We've got the bastard cold."

In the car, Delorme said, "I ordered up the truck—hope that's okay."

"It's okay. It's good. But next time, ask."

"You were on the phone."

"You should have asked. I might have wanted cars only. I might have wanted OPP. You ready for this?"

"I'm ready."

With sirens, it took less than seven minutes to reach their agreed assembly point, the marina at Trout Lake. Other cars arrived moments later. There was McLeod, Collingwood, Burke and Szelagy, other uniforms. The rain had stopped, but the heavy clouds were a deep gray, almost purple at the edges. It was three o'clock; the gloom made it look like seven.

"All right, Trout Lake Road and Mathiesson provide the only access to Pump House Drive. You and you." Cardinal pointed to two of the uniformed men. "I want those points blocked. He isn't getting out of there. And no one's going in."

"What about the lake?"

"No one's going on the lake, not on that ice. Burke and Szelagy, you stay at the top of the drive to keep away neighborhood onlookers, and pen the guy in if he busts out of the pump house. McLeod, Collingwood, and Delorme will come with me. Everyone clear?"

Everyone was clear.

"Eric Fraser is armed. Eric Fraser is dangerous. And Eric Fraser deserves to be dead."

"You're not kidding," someone—probably Szelagy— muttered.

"But Eric Fraser also has a hostage—an eighteen-year-old boy—and we don't want to get that boy killed. If anyone's life comes under immediate threat, you take Fraser down. But only then. Are we clear?"

They were clear.

"All right, then." Cardinal opened the car door. "Let's get it done."

Cardinal raised the unit already staked out at the top of Pump House Drive. Nothing was happening. No movement of any kind. Gripping the wheel, he realized he was shaking. It felt like fear, but it was pure adrenaline. He breathed deeply to steady himself. He didn't want to be shaking when he pulled out the Beretta, wishing yet again that he'd put in those hours on the range.

The two lead cars plowed through the slush at the turnoff and jounced along the road toward the pump house. As planned, Larry Burke and Ken Szelagy stayed to guard the entrance.

Burke and Szelagy had been the first cops to see Katie Pine's body in the shafthead on Windigo Island, and, ever since, Burke had found it frustrating to watch Delorme and Cardinal from a distance and not be part of the action. He wanted to be a detective himself someday.

A car slowed, and a man in his fifties—an executive, Burke guessed—leaned out the window. "What's going on? What's with all the cops out here?"

Larry Burke waved him on. "Keep moving, sir. We need this area clear."

"But what's going on?"

"Just keep moving, please, sir." He gave the man a first-class, Aylmer-regulation dose of cold-cop authority, and it worked; it usually did. The man drove on.

Cardinal had asked for him and Szelagy to be in on this final stage of the case, and Burke appreciated it. Pine–Curry was the case of the century as far as Algonquin Bay was concerned. Cardinal had the pick of the force, but he asked for Burke and Szelagy, and Larry Burke cheered himself with this thought.

Another car rolled up. A woman driver, not attractive, Burke decided.

"You'll have to move along, ma'am."

The woman didn't even glance at him. Kept her eyes fixed on that downhill grade toward the pump house. "What's going on? What're all these cars doing here?"

"Police business, ma'am. Just move along, please."

To Burke's considerable irritation, the woman did not drive away. She just pulled to the side of the road and continued staring down the hill as if Christ himself were about to rise from the icy depths of Trout Lake. Burke sauntered over, rapped on her window, and pointed a gloved finger up the road. According to the Aylmer training manual, a silent gesture, if authoritative enough, will be just as effective as your voice. It wasn't.

"Move it out," Burke said, louder this time. "We need this road clear."

Although the rain had long stopped, the woman's wipers were still flapping; or rather, one of them was still flapping, there was no wiper on the passenger side. She had some kind of scaly thing happening with her face. Hell of a bandage over one ear, too. Intolerable, the way she stared beyond PC Larry Burke and down the hill, totally ignoring him. No way Larry Burke was going to let her get away with that. Larry Burke was not about to screw up now, no matter how tiny his role in this production might be. "Hey, lady!" Yelling now. "Are you deaf?"

He slammed the flat of his hand on the car roof. The woman jerked her head up, and he caught a glimpse of terrified eyes. Then she shoved it in gear, and the car lurched away. "Jesus," he said to Szelagy. "I hope they've got the highway blocked off by now. Did you see that?"

"Some people," Szelagy said. "Got a big nose for other people's business, you know? Have to stick it into everything."

Burke watched the car rattle up the road, belching clouds of black exhaust. Trout Lake and its surrounding suburbs were an affluent area. Very upscale. You'd think the dumb bitch could afford a better vehicle than a half-wrecked Pinto.

55

THE pump house had been out of use for five years and looked it. It was a low, squat, ugly building of gray stone, its windows boarded up, and its roof piled high with an entire winter's accumulation of snow—three feet deep despite the recent meltage. Icicles the size of organ pipes dripped from the corners. Its virtue—from a murderer's point of view—was isolation. There was not another house for half a mile on either side, and this distance was thick with uncut brush.

Cardinal did a fast reconnoiter and established that there was no door on the lake side, just a single set of stone steps that rose from the lake to the side door, forming a perfectly smooth diagonal under the snow and ice. Fraser's Windstar was parked near the lake. Footprints and drag marks led up to the pump house. A rusty outline showed where a padlock had hung.

Soundlessly, Cardinal moved to the door and grasped the handle. He turned it as gently as possible. It didn't budge. He shook his head to signal the others.

McLeod opened his trunk and pulled out the "boomer," sixty pounds of solid, door-smashing iron. Delorme and he each took a handle and prepared to ram the door. Cardinal would be first in with gun drawn. All this they agreed on without speaking.

What happened next became a featured point in department war stories as they were told for years to come. Delorme and McLeod had backed away for their run at the door. Cardinal had his hand up to make the one-two-three signals. He had just finished "one" and was raising his hand for "two," when Eric Fraser stepped out of the building.

He stood there, blinking in the light.

Later, there would be many theories about what made him step out just then. Going for supplies, was one theory, the call of nature was another. It didn't matter, the effect was the same.

Fraser stepped out of the building in his shirtsleeves—black hair whipping in the breeze, black jeans and black shirt vivid against the snow—stood there like an innocent man, blinking for what seemed like ten seconds but was probably less than one.

As Delorme put it later, "This pale skinny guy with little skinny arms. I would never have called him a killer, not in a million years. That guy, he looked like a *boy*."

Eric Fraser, killer of four people that they knew of, stood utterly still, his hands a little away from his sides.

Cardinal's voice sounded tinny to his own ears. "Are you Eric Fraser?"

Fraser spun. The Beretta was in Cardinal's hand, but Fraser was through the door before he could raise it.

Ian McLeod was first through the door after him—a bit of bravery that would put him on crutches for the next three months. The side door opened on a steep set of steel steps that led down to the pump systems. McLeod slid down it with all his weight on his ankles.

Keith London screamed from the darkness, "In here! In here! He's got a—" His shouts were cut short. Cardinal and Delorme stood at the top of the stairs, listening to McLeod's groans. Below them, the pump was a collection of deep red pipes and valves, like a colossal heart. There was a catwalk off to the right. Delorme moved along this, and Cardinal went down the steps.

"I'll be all right," McLeod said. "Get the bastard."

The gray light from the half-open door barely penetrated the dark. Cardinal could see a catwalk above the pump and, below that, another set of steel steps zigzagged like steps in a dream. Cardinal was about to make a run for these stairs when the catwalk door opened and a muzzle flash spat white and blue flame, bright as a flashbulb. Delorme was hit. She staggered back, making no sound other than the clang of her Beretta hitting the catwalk. She got as far as the outside doorway and even managed to open it a little wider. Then she sank slowly to her knees, clinging to the door on the way down, her face utterly white.

Cardinal tore up the steps three at a time, expecting at any moment another muzzle flash and a nine-millimeter hole in his skull.

He kicked open the door.

Pressed flat against the wall, Cardinal held his Beretta chest high with barrel up, as in prayer. Then he spun, crouched, and sighted along the barrel. Nothing moved. There was a door on the far side of the room. Cardinal was in what appeared to be a disused kitchen, the London kid strapped to a table, blood dripping from his head. He reached out and felt the boy's neck; the pulse was slow, and he was breathing in ragged gasps.

A rush of footsteps on metal. Cardinal crossed the room to the other door. He stepped out just in time to see Fraser—little more than a black shape—running for the door they had come in. Cardinal aimed and fired. The bullet went wide, ricocheting off the pipes with an earsplitting whine.

Cardinal ran the length of the catwalk, hopping over the motionless Delorme, and out the door. He reached Fraser's van just as the engine caught. Cardinal threw open the passenger door just as the van started to roll downhill toward the lake. Fraser swung his pistol toward Cardinal's face.

The van hit a rock, sending Fraser's shot into the roof. Cardinal fell into the passenger seat and grappled with Fraser's gun arm as the van lumbered onto the ice.

Cardinal had Fraser's gun arm forced nearly to the floor of the van. Fraser squeezed the trigger, and the muzzle flash burned Cardinal's leg. Fraser continued to squeeze off wild shots, so that events seemed to unfold in lightning flashes.

Cardinal got his right hand round Fraser's throat, his left still clutching the killer's gun hand. Fraser's foot crushed the gas pedal. The sensation of being yanked backward as the wheels caught. Cardinal managed to kneel on Fraser's gun hand, pressing all his weight onto the wrist. His right fist smashed into the killer's cheekbone, pain shooting up his arm.

And then a horrible stillness. The van had lurched to a halt. Suddenly, it pitched forward, spilling the two men against the dash. One fact registered in Cardinal's brain like a news bulletin: The right front wheel had broken through the ice.

"The ice is cracking!" Cardinal yelled. "We're going through the ice."

Fraser's struggles, already frantic, became even wilder as the van canted forward, entering black water up to its wide flat windshield.

A brief rocking. Then the front end slid downward, and black water spilled through the vents, like daggers where it touched the skin.

Another cant forward. Darkness swallowed them.

Cardinal let go of Fraser and hauled himself over the back of the seat. The van was still slipping downward as he scrabbled for the handle.

Black water. Icy white froth.

Cardinal wrenched the door up and back and clambered out on the side of the van. The whole vehicle tipped almost gracefully over on its left. Fraser was screaming.

Cardinal balanced on the edge of the sinking vehicle. Shouts assailed him from the shore.

He jumped free, keeping arms outflung even as his legs plunged through the ice. Cold sucked the breath out of his lungs.

Then Fraser's face at the van's door. His mouth a black O, as the ice gave way under the last wheel, the water crashed in on him, and the rest of the van slipped into the black hole.

56

THE Algonquin Bay Police Department had never had so much publicity. The arrest of Dyson was still on the front page of the *Lode,* and now it was side by side with the death of the Windigo Killer and a photo of the jagged hole where the van had plunged through the ice.

Cardinal and Delorme and McLeod had all been treated in Emergency the night before. McLeod was in the worst shape. He was on the third floor of City Hospital with both feet up in the air, one ankle broken, the other badly sprained. The Kevlar body armor had saved both Delorme and Cardinal. "Those kinds of temperatures," the physician had told Cardinal, "you'd normally be dead. That vest conserved body heat, and you're damn lucky it did." Delorme got off with a nasty crease in her left arm. Blood loss left her feeling dizzy and weak, but a transfusion had been deemed unnecessary and she was sent home.

Cardinal had been given a couple of Valium and kept overnight for observation. He had wanted to call Catherine and tell her all the news, but the Valium had taken hold and he'd slept for sixteen hours straight, waking up with a raging thirst but otherwise fine. Now he was in the waiting room outside the ICU waiting for the okay to visit Keith London. Visitors in winter coats walked up and down the halls with forlorn-looking patients in pajamas and gowns.

Outside, the rooftops were bleached white in the blinding sunshine. But Cardinal could tell from the way the white smoke shot up from the chimneys that the temperature had dropped deep into the minus zone again.

The news came on, and Cardinal learned that Grace Legault had moved to a Toronto station, no doubt thanks to her sterling coverage of the Windigo case. The show led with the story (more shots of the pump house, the black hole in the ice). Then Cardinal was astonished to see some new reporter doing a stand-up in front of his house on

Madonna Road. "Detective John Cardinal isn't home to-day," she began. "He's in City Hospital recovering from his near-drowning in the van that took down Windigo murderer Eric Fraser . . ."

Brilliant. Every creep I ever put in the slammer's going to show up at my door, including Kiki B. Don't they teach them that in journalism school or wherever the hell they get these people?

There was a quick cut to Chief Kendall in front of City Hall, R. J. telling her all the detectives involved in the Windigo case were tops in his book.

You may change your mind when you read my letter, thought Cardinal, but he was saved from further reflection on this point when the door to the ICU opened and the doc-tor, a red-haired woman in a rush, swiftly summed things up for Cardinal: Yes, Keith London was still unconscious; no, he was no longer in critical condition. Yes, he had sus-tained a significant head trauma; no, it was not possible to say if there was permanent damage. Yes, speech might be permanently impaired; no, it was too early to be any more conclusive. And yes, Cardinal could go in for a few mo-ments and speak to the girlfriend.

Light was dim in the ICU. The half-dozen beds with their motionless patients and attendant machines seemed trapped in permanent twilight. Keith London lay at the far end of the room, under the watchful eyes of Karen Steen.

"Detective Cardinal," she said. "It's good of you to visit."

"Well, actually, I was hoping to ask Keith a few ques-tions. Don't worry—the doctor warned me off."

"Keith hasn't said a word yet, I'm afraid. But I'm sure he will. I want him up and chatting away before his parents get here. I finally managed to reach them in Turkey. They should be here day after tomorrow."

"He looks a lot better than last time I saw him." Keith London's head was bandaged, and an oxygen tube was taped to his nostrils, yet despite this, his color looked good, his breathing strong. One slim hand lay outside the covers, and Karen Steen held it while they spoke. "The doctor seems to think he'll pull through okay," Cardinal said.

"Yes, he will, thanks to you. He wouldn't be alive if you hadn't found him. I wish I could find the words to thank you, Detective Cardinal. But there aren't words enough in the language."

"I just wish we could have found him sooner."

The ardent blue eyes searched his face. Catherine's eyes had been like that when they were courting—passionate, earnest. They still were, when she spoke of things that mattered. When she was fully herself.

"You're a very good person, aren't you," Miss Steen added. "Yes, I think you are."

Cardinal felt his face redden. He wasn't skilled at taking compliments. "It's insulting the way you duck them," Catherine had told him more than once. "It's like saying to people that if only they were more intelligent, they'd see things differently. It's rude, John. And quite juvenile."

Ms. Steen looked down at her boyfriend's slim hand and raised it impulsively to her lips, careful not to disturb the tube attached to the pale forearm. "I'm not religious anymore, Detective, but if I were, I'd be remembering you in my prayers."

"You know what I think, Miss Steen?"

Once more the frank blue eyes held him.

"I think Keith London is a very lucky young man."

THE temperature had plunged into unfathomable depths. All the way home, Cardinal had to keep scraping his windshield and the side window. He was looking forward to the outsize glass of Black Velvet whiskey he would pour himself before bed. Having been baptized beneath the ice had made him, at least in his head, a poet of warmth. Stopped for a light at the bypass, he reveled in an extremely detailed vision of the fire that would soon be blazing in his woodstove, of the steak and fries he would cook for himself, and most particularly of that double shot of Black Velvet he planned to take to bed.

57

EXTRACTING a large heavy object from three hundred feet of water is difficult at the best of times. When the temperature is twenty below zero and the surface has been frozen, thawed, and refrozen, it doesn't get any easier. When the ice was strong enough, Natural Resources had set up a towing rig at the edge of the lake—a twelve-ton truck with several miles of steel cable spooled on its back. They paid out the cable hundreds of feet across the ice, where it was then slung over a block-and-tackle affair that had been rigged over a hole in the ice about fifteen feet wide. Above the far hills, the sun looked as pale and cold as the moon.

Twenty degrees centigrade below zero is not unusually cold for Algonquin Bay, but Cardinal's recent exposure to freezing water had sensitized him to low temperatures. He stood on a small dock below the pump house, shivering from head to foot. Delorme, with her arm in a sling, and Jerry Commanda, hands jammed in pockets, stood in front of him, breath feathering out in the stiff little breeze that kicked off the lake. Even though Cardinal was wearing long johns underneath his regular clothes and a down coat on top, he felt utterly exposed.

The Natural Resources team was gathered around the hole in the ice. In their pressurized suits, the divers looked like something out of Jules Verne, Victorian astronauts. Their helmet lamps glowed dully in the wash of late afternoon light. They tested their tethers with a couple of sharp yanks and then they stepped through the hole. Black water closed over their heads like ink.

"Better them than me," Cardinal muttered.

"It was really nice of you to test the water first, though," said Jerry Commanda. "Lot of guys wouldn't have done that."

An aroma of coffee and doughnuts strayed down the

hill, and all three cops turned like dogs hearing the rattle of the food dish. A Natural Resources guy yelled at them to come and get some, and they didn't have to be told twice. Cardinal wolfed down a chocolate doughnut and burned his tongue on the coffee, but he didn't care. The heat coursed through him like a thrill.

Forty-five minutes later, the sky was darkening, the hills becoming indistinct. A shout went up, and the back end of Fraser's van emerged from the lake. Slowly, the rest of the vehicle appeared, mud and water streaming from the joins of doors and windows. The team steadied it, tugging on other cables the divers had attached. The spool on the back of the twelve-ton started to turn.

The divers' helmet lamps looked bright as headlights now, and someone told them to switch them off. The team labored under floodlights that swayed on small tripods. Suddenly the van pitched to one side, and the body of Eric Fraser slid half out of the open side door, water streaming from one black sleeve.

"Shit," said Jerry Commanda. "Nearly dropped him in the drink again."

Slowly, the spool creaking with every turn, the van was winched backward across the ice. Cardinal was remembering that first night when Delorme had called for him and they had traveled like explorers to view the frozen remains of what had once been a little girl. It began on ice, Cardinal thought, and it's ending on ice.

The body was pulled from the van and laid out on the dock like a fish. The skin was gray except over the prominent bones—forehead, jaw, nose—where it was stretched to an impossible white. A coroner examined him, not Dr. Barnhouse this time, but a young man Cardinal had never worked with before. He went about his business in a calm, thorough way, without Barnhouse's bluster.

Cardinal had always thought he would have some telling remark to make over the dead body of Eric Fraser— because, yes, it was a sight he had imagined more than once. But looking down at the frail, vanquished body, Cardinal found he had nothing at all to say. He knew what he was supposed to feel. He was supposed to feel that the monster had gotten off easy. He was supposed to wish the monster was still alive, so he could not escape earthly punishment. But everything about the body—the pale skin, the narrow wrists—said that this had been a human being, not a monster. So Cardinal's feelings were a confusion of horror and pity.

No one spoke for a long time, and then it was Lise Delorme who summed the moment up. "My God," she said in a voice barely audible. "My God, he's so small."

Finally, the coroner said to cover him up.

As Cardinal turned, he caught a glimpse of the first headlights rounding the bay. Soon it would be rush hour. Thank God they had managed to pull this off without too many onlookers. You always get one or two, no matter what, so as he turned from the body of Eric Fraser and headed back up the hill toward his car, Cardinal was not surprised to see a lonely figure—a short, plain woman—standing at the roadside, staring down at the activity below, clutching a handkerchief in one mittened hand as though she were grieving.

58

CARDINAL'S mind had been possessed by the Pine–Curry case for so long that he could not get used to thinking of other things. The hours weighed heavily. Thinking of the future made him depressed and anxious. Part of him wanted to talk to Catherine, part of him was afraid to—at least until she was home from the hospital.

In one afternoon he had replaced a cracked pane of glass, defrosted the fridge, done his laundry, and fixed the hot-water pipe. Now he was in the garage, fixing the hole that gave the raccoons access to his garbage. He had cut a piece of plywood to size, and now he set about removing the old one that had rotted away.

Anxiety gnawed at him. The chief was in Toronto for a meeting, but no doubt he would be calling soon enough. Cardinal realized he was working at trivial chores mostly to keep panic at bay. He felt on the verge of becoming altogether lost, his future a trail that suddenly vanishes in the deep woods.

And what about the rest of the money, down to just enough for Kelly's final semester? What to do with it now, give it back to Rick Bouchard? Bouchard had been convicted only of trafficking, but his list of achievements was long, including assaults sexual and otherwise, robbery with violence, and at least one attempted murder. "Rick Bouchard," his Toronto lieutenant had been fond of saying, "is a subliterate ratfucker. They'll have to add a special extension onto hell just to house that creep."

In the middle of installing the plywood panel, Cardinal discovered that he hadn't the heart to shut out the raccoons. If this was their only source of warmth and food, then fixing the hole might kill them. Instead, he trimmed a smaller square out of the panel he was inserting and put hinges on it, making a door for the raccoons. Brilliant idea, Cardinal. Really thinking now. If he was still here in summer, he would close the hole then.

If he was still here. It seemed increasingly unlikely. He'd been with the Algonquin Bay police department for ten years; any job he could get—assuming he could get one, and assuming he was free to do so—would be unlikely to pay the mortgage. Let alone the heating bills.

He went inside and brewed himself a fresh pot of decaf. It was time to distract himself from his own problems and address himself to the anguish of Billy LaBelle's parents. With Fraser dead, the chances of finding their son's remains seemed remote. The LaBelles had written a letter to the *Lode* complaining about the police having killed the perpetrator instead of capturing him. How were they supposed to ever find peace?

Delorme and Cardinal had divided the box of books and papers they had retrieved from Fraser's room. Notes, maps—they were on the lookout for anything that might give them a clue to the whereabouts of Billy LaBelle's body. There were paperback porn books with sado-masochistic themes and lurid covers. There were several works of the Marquis de Sade, heavily underlined. Cardinal flipped through an encyclopedia of torture devices. Then there was a book of martyrs and their torments. The contents made him queasy, and he found nothing useful.

He examined the stack of books remaining. Wedged among the paperbacks was a fat college edition of Chaucer's *Canterbury Tales*. Cardinal seemed to remember that some of the stories were a little raunchy, but still—Chaucer seemed worlds away from Eric Fraser's interests.

The phone rang and after the usual search for the handset Cardinal picked it up and heard Lise Delorme shouting at Arsenault to be quiet. "Sounds like chaos over there," he said.

"Some people, when there's no one in charge, you know. I can't wait till R. J. gets back and things get a little more organized."

"I'm trying to figure out where he buried Billy LaBelle. Why don't you come out here and we'll go through this stuff together, toss some ideas around."

"Sounds good to me. Anything to get away from Arse-nault. I swear, that guy, he's high on his own work."

"Why? What's up?"

"John, you aren't going to believe this. Are you sitting down?"

"What's going on, Lise?"

"John, they found another set of prints in Fraser's van. All *over* Fraser's van. Passenger side, steering wheel, all over the rear. It's someone who was in that van *a lot*. And get this, John. They've got the murder weapon. We're ninety percent sure it's the hammer that killed Todd Curry, and those second set of prints are all over it, too."

"Oh, my God. The son of a bitch had help."

"There were two of them, John. Two of them."

There was silence over the line as Cardinal took in this information. He could hear Delorme breathing. Finally he asked, "What have we got back from records?"

"Nothing. So far we don't have a clue who this new guy is. He could be anybody. I already called Troy and Suther-land. They never saw Fraser with anyone."

"Well, why don't you come out here and go through this stuff with me. Maybe we'll find something."

Delorme promised to leave in a few minutes and hung up.

Two of them, Cardinal thought. Why hadn't he thought of it sooner? But then, why would you? Why would you expect two minds equally sick? What were the chances of there being two murderers on the loose in Algonquin Bay at the same time? That's why the Mountie profile was so confused: It was describing the working of two minds, not one. He pulled the Chaucer from the stack of Fraser's books. Two of them. He mentally scanned the entire case archive in his head, trying to remember if there had been any sign. There had been no other fingerprints at the crime scenes, no other hairs.

The Chaucer felt oddly light in his hands. He riffled the pages. Someone—not very skillfully—had taken a razor and cut a hollow rectangle out of the book. A rectangle about seven inches by four. And inside this rectangle—

wadded with tissue paper to make it fit more securely—
someone had hidden a plain, unlabeled videocassette.
Holding it carefully by the corners, Cardinal pushed the
cassette into his VCR. The screen lit up with electronic
snow.

It might be nothing, he told himself. It might just be
blank. Or it could be just mail-order porn. In that case, of
course, why hide it so thoroughly? Cardinal clutched the
remote and stood in the middle of his living room, arms
folded across his chest, waiting for the screen to clear. It
flickered and went dark.

For a moment he thought the tape had switched itself
off, but then a murky image took shape: a couch, and behind it, a dark painting on a wall. Cardinal recognized the
painting. He was looking at the Cowart house, where Todd
Curry had been murdered.

As if hearing his cue, Todd Curry appeared on the
screen. He came loping into view and sat down on the
couch. "Am I on yet?" he asked someone offscreen.

The sound was even worse than the lighting. A voice answered him, but the words were inaudible. Lights came up,
and Todd Curry squinted in the glare. He sipped nervously
from a bottle of Heineken.

"Todd Curry," Cardinal said aloud. He froze the image
with the remote control just as the kid hoisted his Heineken
in a toast. The kid was caught in the harsh light like a rab-
bit in headlights, surrounded by darkness.

"Todd Curry," Cardinal said again. "You poor little bastard." He remembered the remains curled up in the coal
cellar, the jeans around his knees. If only he could hit the
stop button and prevent this kid's future. But he released
the pause, and the kid guzzled his beer.

The voice came out of the background again, tinny with
distance. "Say something," it said.

The kid belched, goofing off. "How's that?"

Cardinal tried to raise the volume, hitting the mute button by mistake. Then there was a tremendous crash from
outside, the shriek of crumpling metal, and then a car horn

blaring as someone's head hit the wheel. Through the front window he could see a small car had piled into the birches just past his driveway. The damage didn't look nearly as bad as it had sounded.

He didn't bother to put on his coat. He dashed down the front steps, and by the time he reached the car, a woman had staggered out of the driver's seat and was raving incoherently. "Some men. Help me. Please. Help me."

"Are you all right? Are you sure you can walk?"

The woman put a hand to her head, and turned this way and that, utterly confused. "Some men. There were three of them. They raped me. They said they'd kill me."

Cardinal put an arm around her shoulder and helped her toward the house. "Let's get you inside." The freezing air was slamming through his sweater like steel. The woman stumbled along beside him, head down, crying now. "They forced me, they forced me. Oh, God. Please. You have to call the cops."

"That's all right, I am a cop." He got her inside and seated her gently in an armchair by the woodstove. He picked up the phone and dialed 911. It took them an appallingly long time to answer. As he waited, Cardinal took in more details of the woman, the green down coat, the nasty crease on the side of her head, the truly awful case of eczema. The crease in her head looked bad; the bruise had come up terribly fast, and he wondered if she was bleeding under the skin.

Finally, 911 answered. "Yes, this is Detective John Cardinal, Algonquin Bay Police. I need an ambulance out here at 425 Madonna Road. Woman, late twenties—rape, head trauma, I'm not sure what else."

The dispatcher told him to hang on.

"You're the hero, aren't you? The Windigo case? I saw you on TV." The woman was hunched forward as if over a stomach wound, peering up at him strangely. Beyond her, the television had come back to life, without sound. A dark figure moved in the foreground.

"Gimme that address again?"

"Four twenty-five Madonna Road. Take Trout Lake past

Pinehaven, it's the second right after Four Mile Road. They can't miss it, there's a car half off the road out front." Cardinal covered the mouthpiece and spoke to the woman. "That's a Pinto you're driving, isn't it? Your car?"

"What? Yeah. Pinto."

"A gray Pinto," Cardinal said into the phone. "You can't miss it."

"I saw you on TV," the woman repeated, swaying slightly in her seat as if she were drunk, though Cardinal had not smelled alcohol on her. Behind her, the figure on the television screen had sat down beside Todd Curry, a woman. The hard light glittered on her damaged skin.

Now the woman before him reached up and touched her face gently, fingers fluttering over the cracked, pebbly surface of her cheek.

Cardinal tried to keep his face neutral. *She doesn't know I know*, he told himself. *She's got herself drunk so she can come out here and threaten me. But at this point she doesn't know I know.*

"Who are you calling now?" the woman said sharply.

"Headquarters. I want to get some people over here to take your statement. Don't worry, we have a rape specialist. A woman." *Can she hear it in my voice? Can she hear that I know?*

Cardinal started to dial, but the woman pulled a gun from the folds of her coat, aimed it at his face, and said, "I don't think you want to do that."

Cardinal put the phone down, holding his hands up. "Okay, look. I'm not armed, all right? Just take it easy, now."

On the TV, Fraser entered the scene and yanked the woman away. Todd Curry raised his hands in pretended surprise.

"Did you follow a script?" Cardinal asked her. "Work out the moves ahead of time?"

The woman turned to follow his gaze. "That's Eric," she said in a small voice. "That's my Eric."

Cardinal inched ever so slightly toward the closet, the

half-open door where the Beretta hung in its holster.

"Don't move."

"Just relax. I'm not moving. I'm not going anywhere." Cardinal used the gentlest, least threatening voice he could summon. On the TV, Fraser gripped a hammer. It must have been resting on the back of the couch, ready for use. He raised the hammer and was shouting something at Todd Curry.

He brought the hammer down. The boy's mouth gaped, all the facial muscles went slack. Fraser hit him again and again. The woman had moved behind the couch, behind the boy, and was pulling back on his bloodied hair. She pulled back on his hair the better to expose him, while Fraser kicked the life out of him.

"He was nothing," the woman told Cardinal. "He was just some scum off the street." She pulled the remote out from under her and pressed the rewind button.

On the screen the action reversed. Fraser pulled his boot repeatedly from Todd Curry's ribs, and the boy slid back up onto the couch. Strength flowed back into the slack, battered limbs. The woman let go of his hair and backed around the end of the couch to sit once more beside him.

Now the hammer was taking back its blows, sucking murder back into itself. Blood flowed upward into the boy's nose; scarlet tears shot backward into his eyes. He lowered his arms, and they healed. Terror gave way to astonishment, and with one last comical jerk, the hammer yanked all pain and shock from Todd Curry's face. The boy sat back and laughed.

Cardinal was backing closer to the closet. "Why don't you tell me how it happened? Did Eric force you to help? Was that it?"

The woman stood up. "Eric never made me do anything I didn't want to do. Eric happened to love me. Can you understand that? Eric loved me. We had a special love. Better than anything you read about in books. And it was real. It transcended space and time, if you can understand that. No, I don't think you can."

"Tell me about it, then. Help me understand."

She was in the proper stance, slightly crouched, left hand cradling the right. She sighted down the barrel at him.

Cardinal was moving ever so slightly back toward the closet. He began to raise his hands, to show her they were still empty.

The woman pointed the gun lower. Her expression was distracted, as if she were seeing not Cardinal, not the scene before her eyes, but some distant, remembered scene. Then her eyes cleared, and she shot him.

The bullet entered Cardinal's abdomen just below the navel. He fell to one knee as if genuflecting. A moment's grace, and then it was as if his entrails had burst into flame. He curled over and fell on his side.

The woman took two quick steps and stood over him. She neither grimaced nor smiled. "How does it feel?" she asked quietly.

The closet door was maybe three feet away. It might as well have been twenty. The woman stood over Cardinal, still gripping her revolver, keeping out of range of his hands and feet. Cardinal's only thought was for the closet, but he could not get back on his knees.

"How does it feel?" she asked again. "Does it feel good? Tell me how you like it."

Cardinal heard himself crying. You didn't often hear a grown man cry like that. He remembered a car wreck on the overpass, a man with a piece of aluminum trim clean through his belly, impaling him to the seat. He had wept like this.

Blood spilled hotly over his hand. He was trying to hold his stomach together as he struggled to his knees. The woman backed away.

Two steps to the closet. Two steps, then a long reach and he would have the Beretta. Cardinal tried to crawl, but his arm crumpled under him.

The woman came closer. She looked upside down—a trick of perspective that his brain, half-blind with pain, could not sort out. "It's a belly shot," she said. "It takes forever to die with a belly shot," she said. "What do you think about that?"

She was aiming again, pointing at his belly again.

Cardinal said, "Oh, fuck," or something like it, and raised a pathetic hand to stop her.

He didn't hear the shot this time. The bullet burst through his hand and tore into his belly. The room went white, then gradually returned like an image in a developing tank. Cardinal could not remember where the thing was that he had been trying to reach. What had he been looking for? What had been so important?

That woman was speaking, but he could not distinguish the words over his pain. Four more? Was that what she said? I have four more for you? The words lined up in his head but would not make sense. Four more where those came from, that was it. She says she has four more bullets where those came from.

The gun wavered over him. Cardinal curled up on his side, as if he could deflect the next bullet with a rib. Then there was a roar and something heavy hit Cardinal's leg. The gun had tumbled from the woman's hands.

Cardinal opened his eyes. The woman's chest was covered with blood. She had jerked up and back, as if hearing her name called from a distance. A hand drifted up to her chest wound, dabbed at it, and the woman's face creased into an expression of irritation, as if she were anticipating a nasty cleaning bill.

She's dead, Cardinal thought. She's dead and she doesn't know it yet. The woman collapsed on top of him, her breasts pressing into his hip.

Then Delorme was kneeling over him. Lise Delorme was kneeling over him and talking in the soothing tones he had heard himself use with victims of terrible accidents. You'll be all right, hang in there, don't disappear on me now. Futile in the extreme. But Delorme had something white in her hands—a pillowcase, or was it the sling from her injured arm?—and she was tearing it very efficiently into strips.

THE Intensive Care Unit at St. Francis Hospital is much stricter than the one at City Hospital where Keith London was confined. St. Francis has a firm rule: No visitors except close relatives.

How then, Cardinal wondered—even stupefied by painkillers, he turned this over in his mind—how then did it happen that Arsenault and Collingwood had been standing in this room? Arsenault and Collingwood, yes, and then Delorme had shown up, arm once again in a sling. Cardinal would have to upbraid her for not using the proper stance, for not cradling the revolver properly. That should get a rise.

Delorme had shown him—with earnestness and a great show of secrecy—a sealed envelope. He knew this was full of meaning, but treading his anodyne ebb and swell, he could not piece it together. It was his handwriting on the envelope. Why had he been writing to the chief?

And how on earth had McLeod come to be here? Wasn't McLeod laid up in traction? He had come hopping in, loomed beside the bed with crutches jammed in either armpit, displaying the filthy sock over his cast, or whatever they called those plastic things they used instead of casts. McLeod had upset some other visitors with his language. Head nurse had been summoned. Head nurse not pleased.

Karen Steen had come. Lovely, gentle Karen Steen, bearing thanks and solicitude like balm. She had brought Cardinal a teddy bear dressed in a cop's hat, he could smell her perfume on it still. From Miss Steen's visit he retained this much: Keith London was out of intensive care. The doctors at City Hospital proclaimed Keith London was on the mend. He was conscious now, and speaking slowly, Miss Steen had said, but Keith remembered nothing of the events surrounding his injury and she hoped he never would.

Or was it Delorme who'd brought the bear? Sometimes when the Demerol kicked in, he fancied the bear was speaking to him, but he knew that wasn't real. No, no, Miss Steen had brought the bear. Delorme was analytical, no friend to sentimentality.

"You come from a big family, Mr. Cardinal." This from the young nurse who came in to give him a shot. She was a stolid thing, with a gap tooth and a storm of freckles.

"My family? My family's not that—Ow!"

"Sorry. All done. If you just stay turned a minute, I'll straighten up a little." She was doing things to the bed, snapping sheets like flags. "Boy, that red-haired fellow sure has a mouth on him," she chattered on. "It's a good thing he sent the head nurse some flowers. He may even be allowed back." She flipped Cardinal the other way, then hoisted him up, then sat him back, all with the careless force of a professional. It hurt like hell. "He doesn't look much like you, though, with that red hair. I would never have thought you were brothers."

The drugs blotted up his pain like ink. He fell into a sleep that was soupy with dreams and awoke feeling cheerful. Beneath this, he was aware of a lurking anxiety, a shadow taking shape in a fog. He slipped back into sleep. He dreamed that Catherine was out of her own hospital and visiting him in his. She was watching over him like a guardian angel, but when he woke in the middle of the night there was no one, just the beep of the machines and the throbbing in his guts, and from down the hall, someone giggling.

"I just never expected it to be a woman," Delorme kept saying. "Okay, everybody knows someday you might have to shoot someone. Everybody knows you might have to shoot to save a life. Everybody knows that. But how many cops kill a woman, John? I keep telling myself she was a killer, but I still feel sick. I can't sleep, I can't eat."

Delorme rambled for a while, and he let her. He was glad she was there. She told him who the woman was and where she lived. Told him how they found the grandmother half-starved in the upstairs bedroom. Told him how she then realized where she had seen Edie Soames before, when she'd followed up on the library CD lead. Near tears, then, she had lamented how if she'd only been a little smarter, she would have hauled Edie Soames in for questioning.

Even drugged, Cardinal recalled that that lead had been wafer-thin. But Delorme would not be consoled; they might have saved Woody's life, that baby's father.

Cardinal asked about the search of the Soames house. "They killed Katie Pine with Granny sitting right upstairs. It's the house on the audiotape. First thing I heard when we went in? A clock on a mantel just like the one on the tape."

"No kidding. I wish I could have been there for that."

She told him what they'd found—a gun, a list, and Edie Soames's diary.

"A diary. I'll have to take a look at that."

"It's strange," Delorme said. "I mean, what's strange is how *normal* it is. It could be any girl, this diary—full of makeup and haircuts and how crazy she is about her boyfriend. But she talks about Billy LaBelle in it, too. They killed him, too."

"Does it say what they did with the body?"

"No, but we found something else. A camera—along with some pictures they took in front of the house where Todd Curry was killed. And another with Windigo Island in the background. And this one, near the reservoir." She pulled it out to show him: a shot of Edie Soames making an angel in the snow.

Cardinal had a little trouble focusing.

"It's near where they found Woody's body. Half a mile or so. Close to the pump house, too."

"How can you tell? It could be anywhere."

"I thought so, too, but look at the hydro pole in the corner."

"Is that a number on it? It's hardly visible."

"It's a number. Hydro gave us the exact location." She

gripped his shoulder. "I think it's where they buried Billy LaBelle."

"We should get a digging team up there right away."

"They're already up there. It's my next stop."

"That's right," Cardinal said, fighting sleep. "I forgot how good you are." He turned on his side and saw the teddy bear with the cop's hat. "Thanks for the bear, Lise."

"I didn't give you the bear."

DELORME came back later. It might have been the same day, it might have been the next, he wasn't sure. She looked tired and pale, having just come from telling Billy LaBelle's parents that their son's body had been found. "It was awful," she said. "I don't know if I'm cut out for homicide after all."

"Yes, you are. Another cop might not have found the body. Then the LaBelles would be wondering the rest of their lives what happened to their boy. Horrible as it is, at least now they can put it to rest."

Delorme went silent for a few seconds. Then she got up and went to the door, checked the corridor, and came back. She pulled an envelope from her purse. "Before, you didn't understand. You were too stoned."

"My letter to R. J. Jesus, Delorme. How'd you know about that?"

"I searched your computer. Sorry, but that day you figured out about Katie Pine's bracelet I got a look at what you were typing on your computer. I mean, I saw it was addressed to the chief. He never saw it, John. He's moving into Dyson's office temporarily, and his mail—well, I got to his mail first. He'll be in to see you later. He's worried about you."

"You shouldn't have done it, Lise. If any of it comes out at trial—"

"There isn't any trial. They're both dead, remember?"

"Lise, you're risking your career."

"I don't want a good cop to lose his job. It was a one-time thing. You were under incredible pressure. It's not like you were part of some corrupt squad. I've thought about it, John. Bringing you down would do more harm than good, that's the simple truth. Besides, Toronto's not my jurisdiction, remember? Nobody asked me to investigate Toronto."

"But now I have to go through it all again."

"You don't have to. You don't ever have to think about it again."

But he knew he would—when the drugs wore off, when he was back at home, when he woke in the middle of the night. When he could think about something other than the hole in his hand and the holes in his guts, he would have to think about his own distant crime. It would never go away. That was the shape looming in the fog. And besides, R. J. was not the only one he had written to.

NEXT morning Cardinal woke in a different room on a different ward. Sunlight poured in the windows; he could feel it before he even opened his eyes. Magnified by panes of glass, the light felt hot on his arm. It felt good; it felt like health. He would lie there like a cat and soak it up. He started to stretch, but the stitches in his stomach changed his mind. Sometime later he became aware that someone was holding his hand. A small hand, smooth and warm.

"How's my sleepyhead?"

"Catherine?"

"I'm afraid so, darling. They let me out."

Catherine sat on the edge of his bed, not at all like a guardian angel. Her eyes were not serene pools of certainty; they were shy and worried. He could see the slight droop of her left eyelid where the medication refused to loosen its grip. But her agitation had subsided—there were no restless movements; the hands that held his own remained still.

"No, I'm not deranged anymore. I'm running on lithium, like the Starship Enterprise. Sorry. That has intergalactic overtones, doesn't it."

She was wearing the beret he had given her. Such a small gesture, and yet he couldn't find the words to say how much it moved him. "You look great" was all he could manage.

"You don't look bad, either. Especially for someone who near drowned and was shot twice."

There was a silence while they held hands and tried to think of words that would help start them on the road to knowing each other again.

"There've been a lot of flowers sent to the house. Cards, too."

"Yeah. People have been great."

"There was one delivery, the fellow had a patch over one eye. Big. He seemed quite concerned about you. I brought the card along." She pulled a large, floral Hallmark from her shoulder bag. Inscribed beneath the sentimental verse: *Be seeing you. Rick.*

"Very thoughtful guy, Rick." After a pause, Cardinal said, "I guess you didn't get my letter."

"I got your letter. So did Kelly. We don't have to talk about it now."

"How'd Kelly take it?"

"Ask her yourself. She's on her way home."

"She's angry, right?"

"She's more worried about you right now. But I expect she'll be angry, yes."

"I've really done it, Catherine. I'm so sorry."

"I am, too. Yes, of course I am." She looked away from him, thinking how to phrase it. Outside, sparrows scattered like thrown seed across a blazing blue sky. "I'm sad that you did something wrong, John. It's not how I think of you, of course. And I'm sad for the pain it must cause you. But part of me—I know it sounds strange, John—John! It's so wonderful to say your name again and have it not just be in my head. To be beside you! . . . But even aside from *that* happiness, part of me is happy about the other, too. Happy that you did something wrong."

"Catherine, you don't mean that. What are you talking about?"

"You've never understood, have you? What you don't

understand—how could you?—what you *can't* understand is that no matter how hard it is for you to be encumbered with me, to have to watch over me like a child, to have to worry about hospitals and accidents and where is she this time, no matter how hard all of that is—I think it's far harder to be the one who is always looked after. To be the one who is the burden. To feel like a net drain on the economy, so to speak."

"Oh, Catherine . . ."

"So, you see, to have you do something wrong—something very wrong—to have you actually wreak potential havoc on our lives is . . . Well, I'm taking a very long time just to say it's nice to be needed. To get a chance to be the strong one, for a change."

Cardinal's doctor came in noisily, blaring greetings and questions. "No, no, you can stay," he said when Catherine started to leave. He shone a light in Cardinal's pupils. Asked him to sit up. Even had him walk a few steps, holding onto the bedrail like a little old man, his gut in agony.

"Fuck you, Doc. I'm going back to bed."

The doctor was scribbling on the chart. "I didn't really need you to walk. Just wanted to see if it hurt as much as I thought it would. You're doing great. Going to take four to six weeks for your innards to heal, though. Bullets really whizzed around in there."

"Six weeks!"

"Do you good." For Catherine's benefit the doctor jerked a thumb and said, "Big dumb hero, eh?" Then he let the chart drop with a clatter against the bed and left as noisily as he had come in.

"Christ. He could be a cop with that sense of humor," Cardinal said. Sweat was cooling on his brow.

"I better go," Catherine said. "You're whiter than the sheet."

"Don't go, Catherine. Please stay."

So Catherine Cardinal stayed. Stayed and watched over him as she had in his dream.

Cardinal closed his eyes. He wanted to ask if she would

stay with him, despite what he had done, if she could still live with him, be happy with him. But the painkillers were a soft plump pillow in his skull, and Cardinal felt sleep settle softly on his arms and legs and brow. He opened his eyes and saw Catherine beside him, wearing glasses now, reading a book she had brought to pass the time. Fringed by the flutter of his eyelids, the pale green walls turned into pale green trees. The voices in the hall became the sounds of hidden animals, and the door swung open wider on a swiftly flowing stream.

Cardinal dreamed that they were traveling. He dreamed that he and Catherine were traveling on a river—a leafy, southern river he had never seen before. Catherine paddled in the front of the canoe, and Cardinal steered badly in the back. The sun was the bright yellow of children's drawings. The canoe was bottle-green, and they were laughing.

New York Times **bestselling author**
LEE CHILD

KILLING FLOOR   0-515-12344-7

Ex-military policeman Jack Reacher is in Margrave, Georgia,
for less than a half hour when the cops come, shotguns in hand,
to arrest him for murder.

All Jack knows is he didn't kill anybody.

Not for a long time...

DIE TRYING   0-515-12502-4

When a mysterious woman is kidnapped by a politically moti-
vated fringe group and taken to their compound, Jack Reacher
must help her escape with her life—

from the inside out...

TRIPWIRE   0-515-12863-5

"A stylistic thriller as complex and disturbing as its hero."
—Stephen White, author of *Manner of Death*

TO ORDER CALL:

1-800-788-6262

(Ad # B109)

PENGUIN PUTNAM INC.
Online

Your Internet gateway to a virtual environment with
hundreds of entertaining and enlightening books
from Penguin Putnam Inc.

*While you're there, get the latest buzz on
the best authors and books around—*

Tom Clancy, Patricia Cornwell, W.E.B. Griffin,
Nora Roberts, William Gibson, Robin Cook,
Brian Jacques, Catherine Coulter, Stephen King,
Ken Follett, Terry McMillan, and many more!

**Visit our website at
www.penguinputnam.com**

PENGUIN PUTNAM NEWS

Every month you'll get an inside look at our upcoming books and new features on our site. This is an
ongoing effort to provide you with the most
up-to-date information about
our books and authors.

Subscribe to Penguin Putnam News at
www.penguinputnam.com/newsletters